THE FIRE ROSE

Is the Fire Rose the long-sought artifact that could transform the ogre race, bringing it back to the power and glory of ancient times?

The half-breed, Golgren, is now Grand Khan of the united ogre realms, called Golthuu—"the Dream of Golgren." But the fearsome Golgren is beset by traitors and villains and worse.

Golgren's beloved capital is threatened by a vast army of the undead and by the treachery of the Ogre Titans, the secretive, fanatical cult of magic-users, led by their new chieftain, the cunning Safrag.

Golgren and Safrag are both obsessed with finding the legendary Fire Rose. Little do they know that another shadowy figure, one who commands legions of gargoyles and the tools of sinister sorcery, has ambitions to eliminate both of them.

Will the Fire Rose save the Grand Khan? Or will its strange magic destroy his fledgling empire?

OGRE TITANS

The Black Talon

The Fire Rose

The Gargoyle King
October 2009

THE FIRE ROSE

OGRE TITANS VOLUME TWO

RICHARD A. KNAAK

The Ogre Titans, Volume Two

THE FIRE ROSE

©2008 Wizards of the Coast, Inc.

Published by Wizards of the Coast, Inc. DRAGONLANCE, WIZARDS OF THE COAST, and their respective logos are trademarks of Wizards of the Coast, Inc., in the U.S.A. and other countries.

Printed in the U.S.A.

Cover art by Duane O. Myers
First Printing: December 2008

9 8 7 6 5 4 3 2

ISBN: 978-0-7869-4968-7
620-21773740-001-EN

U.S., CANADA,
ASIA, PACIFIC, & LATIN AMERICA
Wizards of the Coast, Inc.
P.O. Box 707
Renton, WA 98057-0707
+1-800-324-6496

EUROPEAN HEADQUARTERS
Hasbro UK Ltd
Caswell Way
Newport, Gwent NP9 0YH
GREAT BRITAIN
Save this address for your records.

Visit our web site at www.wizards.com

To all the dedicated readers of Dragonlance throughout the years, I thank you.

Prologue

THE WATCHER

The leathery gargoyle fluttered unnoticed onto the top of the high, dusty ridge. It folded its wings tight behind it and, thrusting its beaklike snout just over the rocks, peered down at the sweeping tableau far beneath it.

Armored minotaurs ascended the ridge below in perfect martial order, their shields creating a wall before them that few weapons could readily penetrate. The seven-foot-tall, horned soldiers were clad in shining breastplates, sleek kilts and helmets designed to fit around their two-foot-long horns and their twitching, alert ears. On their silver breastplates and shields blazed the symbol of Sargonnas—the dominant god of their race—a stylized crimson condor with its wings spread as though in flight.

The gargoyle quietly hissed. Its blunt ears flattened. Even though it served a far greater power than the soldiers did, it was impossible not to be impressed by an army of thousands of such fearsome fighters.

Indeed, the land below was swarming with minotaurs, for at least three legions marched under the scorching sun. They had muzzles like those of bovines, but there was nothing comical about the Uruv Suurt, as they were called by their neighbors to the north, the ogres.

Neighbors whose land the legions were encroaching upon.

Despite the rocky terrain of the region that was once called Blöde, the legionaries kept their ranks tight and even. Hekturions—officers commanding a hundred warriors each—rode back and forth among the lines. Subofficers among the ranks—called dekarians and commanding ten soldiers—helped keep order. Farther back, the captains and other higher-ranked legionaries passed on the overall commands of each legion's master general.

And each of those generals, in turn, sought to prove themselves the best at fulfilling the edicts of their emperor.

A condor fluttered high on many of the triangular standards carried alongside each legion's own symbol. The head of a snarling brown bear marked the legion on the right flank, a flying green serpent the one on the left, and in the middle was the black silhouetted steed of the Warhorses. Once the command of the Emperor Faros Es-Kalin's predecessor—also father of his empress—the Warhorses had been rebuilt into a force fanatically loyal to the holder of the throne.

The Grand Khan of both the former Blöde and its one-time rival to the north, Kern, was a cunning half-breed called Golgren. Old enmities lay between the minotaurs and the ogres: years of slavery for Faros, a severed hand for the Grand Khan.

And evidently the emperor had set in motion the first step toward laying those enmities to rest, along with Golgren.

The gray-scaled gargoyle pulled back several yards before daring to leap into the sky. It purposely flew so that any who looked up in its direction would be staring straight into the sun. Unlike minotaurs, humans, or ogres, gargoyles had two lids over their eyes, one normal and the other a shaded, translucent pair that instinctively lowered whenever necessary—as when the creature flew into the sun.

With great, steady beats of its wide wings, the gargoyle

quickly put distance between it and the oncoming armies. No longer in their sight, it flew more out in the open, soaring above the inhospitable land. Below, the parched hills and bleak valleys—only two days' ride from the more green reaches of Ambeon—hinted at no life, although a startling variety did exist in the shadows. The gargoyle would have liked to have paused to hunt, especially for one of the horned runners called amaloks, but it was not permitted. Its lord demanded immediate knowledge of all matters in the area. To be slow in bringing that intelligence was to invite painful punishment.

And so, despite gnawing hunger, the gargoyle flew as fast as its wings could take it. It began to veer to the north—and suddenly pulled up short. Its wings keeping it hovering, the gargoyle hissed at a sight it had not been warned to expect.

Another army marched toward the location of the minotaur legions, hundreds of ogres in armor almost as immaculate as that of the Uruv Suurt. They marched in good order, their weapons well honed and held proudly. Commanders astride huge horses rode on the flanks and in the center of the ogres, keeping their warriors under control with the brutish barks that marked the ogre tongue.

The gargoyle hesitated, torn. Its primitive mind struggled to decide what would be most appreciated by its powerful master: continued flight or further investigation.

With another hiss, the gargoyle veered around so as to pace the ogres without them noticing it flying high above.

The nearly nine-feet-high warriors were in many ways a contrast to the minotaurs. They had more of a flat-faced appearance, looking like the bastard children of humans and bears—or maybe boars, since most had two long tusks jutting up at the edges of their mouths. Under heavy brow ridges, long, bestial eyes—generally bloodshot—focused ahead. A thin layer of what was more fur than hair covered most of their visible bodies, and under the open helmets shaggy mops of hair showed through.

To most outsiders, the ogres' martial order and cleanliness would have been a shock. They were supposed to be little more than flea-bitten monsters who preyed upon the unwary and who, if they joined in numbers against a foe, tended to be an unruly horde, with each warrior fighting more or less on his own with no collective strategy.

But that era seemed to be at an end, for the ogres were marching as one. A new order had spread through the ogre lands, a new order of such magnitude that even the lands of Kern and Blöde were no longer called that by their people. By decree of the Grand Khan, both realms—though separated by geography—were one. They were united as Golthuu.

Golthuu, *the Dream of Golgren*.

A familiar emblem adorned the square standard flying over the ogre force: a severed hand wielding a bloody dagger. Yet another symbol of Golgren's power.

Unaware of the gargoyle, the ogres pushed toward the ridge. From their pace and grim aspects, they expected something ahead.

The growling in its stomach no longer mattered to the gargoyle, nor, in some ways, did the mission. Like all its kind, it enjoyed a good fight, and clearly one was brewing. That it would also be serving its lord in observing and reporting was an added reward. Only the minotaurs had been expected to be in the region; how the ogres had gotten wind of their enemies so quickly, especially considering the remoteness of the area, was a question to which the winged servant needed to learn an answer. For that, the master would certainly reward it.

It flitted from ridge to hilltop to ridge, pacing the ogres until they were nearly at the ridge where it had last seen the legions. The ogres began to advance more cautiously.

Leaving the ogres for a moment, the gargoyle flew ahead, searching for the other army. It did not take long to spot what it sought. Two minotaur scouts had worked their way up and over the ridge, enabling them to obtain a view of far ahead. They spotted the advancing ogres.

THE FIRE ROSE

One scout turned in the direction of the legions. Although the scout's comrades could not be visible to him from where he stood, he nevertheless raised a hand as if to signal them.

A glitter of light flashed in the legionary's hand, the sun's reflection on a small piece of glass, or even a mirror. The first flash was followed by a second, longer one, and two shorter.

From another part of the ridge just overlooking the main force, another flash responded. The scout busied himself sending an identical series of signals to the legions, where other glints of sunlight revealed receipt of the messages.

The imperial ranks suddenly spread out in perfect coordination. As the gargoyle studied the coming clash, it noted that the scouts were not alone among the ridges. Bands of legionaries had settled into various concealed locations.

The winged spy returned its attention to the ogres, seeing that they had advance forces infiltrating the jagged rocks too. In one almost laughable sight, a band of ogres lay in hiding only a short distance from where a group of legionaries was doing the same.

The ogre ranks began to spread out as they approached, almost as if they had some warning concerning the opposing forces. The gargoyle landed atop a high peak, from where, folding its wings, it watched.

In their new formation, the minotaurs continued to spread over the first ridge. As they did, the ogres advanced toward them.

Scouts on both sides eagerly sent signals to their respective commands.

A massive ogre near the rear of the lines raised his hand. A trumpeter with a curled goat horn sounded a blaring note that echoed through the area.

The legions did not halt upon hearing the trumpet blast, but an officer in a plumed helm and purple cloak gestured to one of his own trumpeters. The legionary sent out a shrill reply.

Barely had both horns sounded than the front lines of both forces edged within sight of one another.

The minotaurs restrengthened their line of shields and held their swords, axes, and pikes ready. Opposite them, the ogres did likewise.

The gargoyle hissed in amusement. It was almost like watching one army fighting its own distorted, grotesque image. The blood would surely flow strong, the gargoyle thought.

Goatskin-covered copper drums beat among the ogres. They were met by the thumping of the iron drums of the minotaurs. For several seconds, the two different drummings vied.

The cloaked commander of the legions rode through the ranks until he and his sleek, black steed stood at the forefront. At the same time, the ogre warlord rode to the head of his forces.

The two leaders eyed one another. The minotaur raised his sword up. The ogre brandished his axe.

Both saluted one another.

The winged watcher blinked in astonishment. Its claws scraped at the rock as it tried to puzzle out the odd battle etiquette. Minotaurs could be very formal, but ogres—even the half-breed's polished warriors—did not politely acknowledge the foe they were about to attack.

Their weapons still raised, the two riders charged one another. The gargoyle understood. The two leaders would fight for dominance first. It is what gargoyles would have done too.

The ogre and the minotaur met. Their weapons clashed once. And both riders reined their mounts to a halt and bowed their heads to one another.

The other ogres barked in approval. The legionaries banged their weapons against their shields and stood down. The ogres did the same.

Sheathing their weapons, the imperial officer and the ogre warlord *clasped* hands in greeting.

The gargoyle leapt back from the scene, its suddenly outstretched wings mirroring the amazement on its monstrous staring visage. It felt certain that it must have seen wrong.

Both riders had dismounted. They spoke in low tones. Still more unbelievable, elements of each group were moving toward one another, but with their weapons sheathed and their shields down.

The gargoyle had seen enough. It leaped into the sky, heading north. It flew well above the sight of the minotaurs and ogres. The huge wings beat faster than ever. Hunger was forgotten. Fear that it would fail its dread lord was forgotten. Its master would surely be eager to be told of the intriguing, inexplicable scene.

And the Grand Lord Golgren would surely have been interested too . . . If only he had been fortunate enough to know, or to have had his own spy.

I

Lord Of Golthuu

His wounds still pained him, but Golgren didn't let it show. Several months had passed since he had led his warriors against the unthinkable: an army of the undead—or, as the ogres called them, *f'hanos*—bent on the destruction of Garantha, the great capital of his precious Golthuu. Many warriors had perished, and Golgren had nearly died himself. But the threat had been overcome, with the Grand Khan—the Grand Lord at that point—being hailed by his people as *Kala i iF'hanosi il aF'hanari Faluum iGolgreni*, or the "Final Death of the Undead That is Golgren."

But the half-breed master of the ogre race had not been entirely responsible for that victory, just as the danger that day had not come from a single source. Much magic had been involved. A great part of the magic, originated from the Ogre Titans. Indeed the damage to Garantha could be traced—at least by Golgren—to the spell the Titans had cast creating a massive quake beyond the capital.

Golgren rose from the wide, lush bed in his personal chambers. Countless silken pillows of many colors filled the bed, and elegant draperies flanked the structure. All were spoils of the conquest of Silvanesti far to the south—a conquest made in conjunction with his current bitter enemies, the Uruv Suurt. Those horned warriors had taken the bulk of Silvanesti as their prize, turning it into the imperial colony of Ambeon.

Golgren was an unlikely looking ruler of the ogre race. He was no taller than a minotaur and more sleek of form than most of his kind. His features could have been called brutally handsome, for there was much in them that spoke of his mother's people: the very elves he had helped enslave and scatter. From his mother he had inherited his almond-shaped, emerald eyes and his more pronounced—yet narrow—nose. His jaw was strong, but less so than with most ogres. The tusks that he had grown up with had long been filed to mere nubs, adding to his more elf look.

His dark mane of hair was always kept groomed, and he wore garments befitting a noble of the elf or human races. The Grand Khan did not believe it was any insult to his people, but rather an attempt to resurrect the ancient golden era when his kind had been the most beautiful of creatures. The era when elves, dwarves, and humans had all but looked to the ogres as gods.

Golgren was dressed for war. Each day new reports confirmed that his great kingdom was under threat. As Golgren forced his weary body to move, he confronted in a nearby long, crystalline mirror—yet again, a treasure from what was Uruv Suurt-held Ambeon—a figure already clad in a shining breastplate and a kilt, with sandaled feet. A green and brown cloak lay loosely spread over one side of the bed. On a moon-shaped marble table sat a helmet whose crest was shaped like a griffon, the patron beast of Garantha.

Each night, Golgren slept ready to be summoned to battle. He had no choice. With the culmination of his dreams had also come the advent of his eternal nightmares.

"My lord," came a musical, feminine voice speaking in the Common tongue. "I did not hear you rise. Please forgive me."

"Ah, my Idaria," he responded without even glancing in her direction. "Do I not always?"

Golgren had also spoken in Common for, as part of the transformation and uplifting of his realm, the Grand Khan insisted on all his subjects knowing and speaking Common. It was the accepted tongue of commerce and negotiation among the humans, elves, and other so-called *civilized* peoples. And Golgren was determined to prove his people were every bit as civilized, even if most of the other races were enemies.

A slim, but still well-shaped form clad in the tatters of a green elven gown slipped up behind the Grand Khan. The elf maiden looked years younger than Golgren—who himself was in the prime of ogre life—but she was, by his estimate, at least twice his age, if not much older. Though a slave, the silver-tressed elf looked well— Golgren desired his personal servant to always look beautiful and fit. Her gown, fashioned according to his orders to make her all the more appealing, revealed the beauty of her skin and body. Her ivory color was a sign of health among the elves, and her eyes were a bright, crystalline blue. She wore sandals that would have fit an ogre child of perhaps four years of age, and moved with an astonishing grace he could never match, even though she wore severed bracelets of chains on both her ankles and wrists.

That chains were no longer attached to those bracelets was a sign of the level of trust that had grown between the Grand Khan and his personal servant. The elf woman—already freed of her bonds by another—had, of her own volition, rejected freedom in order to help her wounded and battered master from the battlefield, and had cared for him loyally since. She had been given ample opportunity to flee or escape, but had never done so.

Golgren boasted to his followers that she adored him even more than they did. But there were other reasons he knew for her dedication that he admitted only to himself. After all, he still held in his hand the future of many of her people, kept secure—if captive—in a special pen at one end of the capital.

He had once promised to release them after his ascension to Grand Khan, but circumstances had forced him to delay their release. He might yet keep that promise, if it suited him.

Also—though he preferred not to think of the disturbing possibility—he suspected Idaria of ties to the world beyond Golthuu. He believed she might be a spy.

As to whom she spied for, that was another question. The Knights of Solamnia, the regal knighthood that ruled the realm to the west named for them, were one possibility. Once, Golgren had hoped to make peace overtures to the Solamnians, using the liberation of the elf slaves as a goodwill offering. He still hoped to join with the Solamnians, for they presented the best hope for an ally he might play off against the Uruv Suurt.

However, Idaria had shown no interest in the lone knight of the sword who had come to Golgren as an emissary. She could have fled with the knight, rather than stay with her enslaver. Yet she lingered. That made Golgren wonder whether she was working for the bands of elves who had the desperate dream of recovering Ambeon for their own occupation. Or perhaps she followed the orders of another human faction bordering his domain: the black-armored knights of Neraka—once fanatic allies of the goddess Takhisis, and a political power in their own right.

Or perhaps she served someone whose identity he did not yet know.

"It is not yet morn," the elf whispered behind him. Elves were tall, but still she had to reach up to touch his shoulders. "Why do you not sleep a little longer? You are in great need of it, my lord. There has been so much burden on you."

"I sleep enough. Bring me wine."

As Idaria moved to obey, Golgren took the moment to stretch his stiff bones. Even the elf's knowledgeable nurturing of his injuries had only been able to do so much to help him recover. And he was not about to turn to the Titans for some potion.

The blue-tinted sorcerers had been very quiet of late, far too submissive for the Grand Khan's taste. Their new leader, Safrag, had come to Golgren early on after the devastation. He had thrown the blame on whatever mysterious force had resurrected the dead, and the inadequacies—not exactly the way Safrag had phrased it, but the tone was there—of the Titans' late creator, Dauroth. Dauroth, to hear his successor describe things, had struggled hard with his followers to stave off the mysterious earthquake. The first and eldest of the Titans had perished when consumed by the very spell that had *saved* the Grand Khan and Garantha. That was good, at least.

Safrag, ever bowing, had sworn that the Titans would work hard to discover who was behind the sinister plot against their race. He had since only appeared before Golgren twice. Both of those brief appearances had been at Golgren's command and were more for him to keep his eye on what the sorcerers themselves were up to, rather than for any important business.

In both cases the ogre leader had learned very little about the mysterious activities of the Titans.

But from other sources . . .

Idaria brought him a silver goblet filled with sweet red wine—some of the last of his rare elf reserves. Soon, Golgren would have to resort to the brackish, thick brews of his own kind, or find a way to steal or trade for some of the better Solamnic fare, the most reasonable substitute.

The Grand Khan downed a good portion of the wine before stiffening.

"Tyranos," he half growled.

A shadow detached itself from one corner, coalescing into a mountain of a man, a lion-faced human nearly as tall as the ogre was and far broader of shoulder. His golden brown hair hung like a mane around his broad face. He wore a sardonic grin.

One of the human's hands turned downward. From it grew

a short staff that barely touched the ancient marble floor. Out of the top of the staff sprouted a five-sided crystal the size of a fist, which radiated a silver glow.

Although clearly a wizard, the leonine Tyranos did not wear the white, red, or black robes of the three established orders. Rather, his voluminous robe was a deep, rich brown color. Some might have taken him for a sorcerer, for sorcerers utilized a different magic. But all that Golgren had witnessed thus far indicated otherwise. Still, a wizard who did not belong to one of the three orders was a renegade, someone feared and despised by the others.

That fate did not seem to bother the powerfully built human, who looked more like a fighter than a spellcaster. The wizard bowed his head to Golgren and flashed a grin at the female slave.

"Have I intruded?" he asked teasingly.

The Grand Khan ignored the remark. "I have no patience. What is it you interrupt me with, human?"

Tyranos's grin faded. "Oh, merely the impending destruction of all you hold dear. The usual thing."

They were an uneasy alliance, the wizard and the ogre leader. Golgren relied on Tyranos to help him monitor the Titans and other problems. As for Tyranos, his motives were murky. But he did share the same obsession with the Grand Khan and the Titans.

The legacy of the High Ogres.

The lord of Golthuu purposely turned from the wizard, his eyes sweeping across his personal chambers. Although they had been repaired as best as possible, there were visible fault lines in the sealed stone walls and the marble floor. The fluted columns were likewise adorned with sealed cracks; some of them had needed rebuilding after falling into crumbling ruin. Great, colorful tapestries of elven tree homes and mythic beasts covered other damaged parts of the walls.

The chamber—the entire palace of the Grand Khan, in fact—had once been the residence of the great High Ogre leaders. Indeed, in the halls and corridors beyond could be seen extravagantly carved reliefs of the ancestors of those who populated the land. More fair of face than elves, the High Ogres had also been far more powerful. Their influence had spread throughout the continent of Ansalon to other parts of Krynn. They had wielded magic in a manner unseen in the modern age, and all other races had bowed to their superiority.

But the grandeur they had created eventually dissipated. Ogres believed that their ancestors had been betrayed by the lesser races and somehow had degenerated over the generations until they arrived at their present form. The legend as the outside world saw it—as even Golgren believed—was that the High Ogres had become so arrogant the gods had punished them.

But the Grand Khan believed that a rebirth of that golden age was destined, and he shared his belief with the Titans. However, Golgren and the mysterious sorcerers very much disagreed about the means of reaching that new golden age.

"It is the Titans?" he asked Tyranos.

"I'd venture to say that a breath is not drawn in Kern and Blöde—pardon, in all *Golthuu*—that they don't try to influence. As to actual evidence, that's always another story, eh?"

The half-breed turned to the wizard. "So? If it's the usual story, why is the news of such import that you must disturb me?"

The leonine human glanced pointedly at Idaria. Golgren generally did not dismiss his favored slave, even when talking with Tyranos. She already knew many secrets that existed only between them. The wizard had never protested before, though his reasons for trusting her were certainly not those of his partner.

"The Knights of Neraka have sent scouts over the border. And when I say scouts, I mean more than a dozen hardy warriors."

"Hmmm." Golgren understood the significance of Tyranos's visit. "Soon they will move in force."

"Yes. And as chance would certainly not have it, the empire appears to have crossed your southern border almost at the same time. Your good friend Faros yearns for your other hand, I suppose."

Golgren winced, and his good hand attempted to reach for his shadow limb. But the Grand Khan showed no other emotions. Indeed, all that he had suspected was beginning to come to pass. He looked at the elf. "What say you, my Idaria?"

She bowed low, her movements as graceful as the wind. "My lord, I am concerned only about your well-being."

"You hear that, Tyranos? She speaks the truth. Part of the truth, at least." Before Idaria could protest, Golgren waved her silent. "So . . . The Black Shells to one side, the Uruv Suurt to another. It comes as no surprise, wizard."

Tyranos's heavy brow arched. "How about the fact that some of your own armies have gone missing?"

Golgren couldn't disguise his astonishment. "Speak clearly!"

The wizard chuckled. "As to that, it would be best if you spoke with Khleeg," he answered, referring to the Grand Khan's trusted second in command. "He should be getting the information that I already know very soon."

How the human knew such things before anyone else irritated Golgren, but he let the wizard's arrogance pass. Yes, he'd speak to Khleeg. Striding to the great brass door, he swung it open fast enough to send the guards outside jumping to attention.

"Khleeg! Send Khleeg to me!"

One of the ogre warriors rushed off. Golgren shut the door again and returned to his magical visitor. The guards would not have heard the wizard's deep voice. Not only were the walls and the door intentionally thick, but Tyranos usually masked the area with magic when speaking with the Grand Khan.

"There is more?" Golgren asked.

Tyranos's eyes flickered ever so briefly over to Idaria and back to Golgren "Only . . . Have you seen any more winged *spies* of late?"

"Other than your pet?"

"Chasm only watches on those occasions when I am not available. But speaking of gargoyles, yes. Let's refer to those in particular. Any of the winged spies?"

Golgren growled, but more at himself than at the human. "No. Not since . . ."

"Not since the battle. Not since you proclaimed yourself Grand Khan." Tyranos nodded to himself. "As I thought."

"That means something to you?"

The wizard suddenly swept up the hand that held the short staff. "I'll let you know."

And with that, Tyranos turned to shadow and vanished.

Unimpressed by the grand exit but annoyed by its suddenness, Golgren faced his slave. "My Idaria, have *you* seen any gargoyles? Seen them, and failed to mention their presence?"

"No, my lord." Her expression was all innocence.

The Grand Khan turned from her. He fought off his swelling impatience for Khleeg's arrival by striding to the chamber's balcony. The first hint of daylight had just begun to spread over the capital. As Golgren stepped out onto the balcony, his sandaled feet trod upon a huge, stylized griffon crafted in mosaic on the floor. The vertical columns of the stone rail were carved to resemble the same beast.

Well familiar with his moods, Idaria did not follow her master out onto the balcony. She hung back, watching and waiting. Her gaze was no longer that of merely a servant, but had narrowed, as though in deep speculation.

Golgren moved to the rail. His first glance at what lay beyond was cursory, for he didn't really expect to see any sign, however slight, of one of the mysterious, leathery sentinels who had in the past spied upon him from one distant rooftop or another.

THE FIRE ROSE

The sky was empty of any creature save one of the fearsome, dark red predators of the type that Golgren's predecessor, Zharang, had kept as pets. The vulturelike creature was likely stalking simple fare, rather than the severed fingers of punished subjects that Zharang had liked to feed his birds. Golgren had noticed more than a few foreign birds about his city, especially since he had made Idaria his foremost slave. Birds that would have been more at home in the forests of lost Silvanost, he reflected.

Both the bird and the gargoyles were forgotten as the conqueror of Kern and Blöde drank in a full sweeping view of the capital of his new kingdom, Garantha—called Kernen by ignorant outsiders.

In the prime of its existence as one of the greatest centers of High Ogre civilization, Garantha had offered to the world tall, shining towers and obelisks, a great zoo featuring exotic animals from all over the world, and a market where one could find rare and valuable items brought from the farthest reaches. The outer walls had held gargantuan reliefs of Garantha's many treasures and triumphs. Inside those walls had been a pristine city teeming with the beautiful, blue-skinned masters of Krynn.

But centuries of neglect had left the walls crumbling, even gone, in many places. The great towers had collapsed; the zoo was but a shell of a memory. And the monstrous descendants of the High Ogres had lived like animals themselves in hovels that had once been the grand estates of their forebears. There had been attempts, especially in the past generation or two, to patch up the capital. But although the Grand Khans before Golgren had played at imitating the High Ogres, they had looked more like swine clad in fine garments. Their notions of repair and revival had been just as pathetic as their attempted playacting.

Golgren had changed all that. As he gazed over his city, he saw many at work on rebuilding the towers, clearing streets of refuse, and making the grand walls surrounding the capital whole again. Farther east, construction had nearly finished on one of the Grand Khan's personal projects: an oval tower ten stories high with twelve windows—almond-shaped like the eyes of Golgren—all covering the side facing the setting sun. The twelve windows marked even intervals once the sun began its descent. On the other side, where the sun first glimmered, there were no windows at all. In the Common tongue, the structure was called the "House of Night."

To ogres, the hot, stifling day—so savage in the height of summer—was called *iSirriti Siroth* or the "Sirrion's Burning." The ogres believed that the god of fire, Sirrion, sought to devour the land of the High Ogres and that was why few places in all of Ansalon were as desolate as Golthuu. Ogres paid great homage to no particular god—though, like the minotaurs, they honored Sargonnas the Warrior—but if there was a deity that they feared, it was Sirrion.

Golgren himself had no fear of any god. Sirrion was one of the neutral deities and, therefore, of little consequence to him. The Grand Khan naturally respected Sargonnas and Kiri-Jolith, the former's rival for the Uruv Suurt and one of the chief patrons of the Knights of Solamnia. Golgren had hoped the bison-headed Kiri-Jolith would look with favor on his plan to deal with the Solamnians, but such apparently was not the case.

And with no alliance imminent, Golgren's adversaries had apparently teamed up against him.

The Knights of Neraka and the Uruv Suurt.

He heard the door open and Idaria murmuring. Golgren started to turn, when his eye caught sight of something glittering atop the House of Night.

The ogre leader stumbled back in surprise.

A golden figure stood atop the oval tower. Tall and gleaming, the figure had no face, yet somehow Golgren knew that it stared into his eyes.

"My lord!" grunted a throaty voice.

Golgren instinctively looked to the speaker, a heavyset but muscular ogre with a face ugly even by his people's standards. The ogre's left eye appeared to be constantly squinting, and the upper half of one of his tusks was missing. His flesh was a sickly, mottled brown, and it was clear that he was not of the same hearty stock as either Golgren or the lankier guard who stood several paces behind.

Khleeg was a Blödian ogre, and in other generations his kind would have been at constant war with their cousins from Kern. But Golgren had recruited Khleeg and countless others like him to his cause, creating the first true alliance of ogrekind since the days of the ancients.

Almost as soon as he turned to greet Khleeg, Golgren cursed and glanced back at the House of Night. But he was too late. Of the golden figure, there was no sign.

"My lord!" Khleeg repeated, his expression concerned. Cradling his helmet in the crook of his arm, the ogre strode anxiously to his master. "You are—"

Golgren let out a snarl and swung at his second in command with his maimed arm. Only because there was no longer a hand attached to the limb did he keep from striking the other ogre across the jaw.

The Grand Khan immediately recovered. Khleeg, almost as well-versed in the moods of his leader as Idaria, pretended the attack had never taken place. Since the struggle against the *f'hanos*, Golgren had displayed bouts of fury that had been uncommon before.

Although Khleeg stood at attention, there was still something in the corner of his eye that made Golgren ask suspiciously, "There is something wrong with me?"

The ogre commander went down on one knee. "My head is yours, my lord," Khleeg responded, his Common much improved. Very little Ogre was spoken among those of Golgren's inner circle. Words and the occasional phrase were allowed, but no conversation or prolonged discussion was permitted. Indeed, Golgren considered the current Ogre tongue a mongrel language that needed to be put down. "I speak only as I see!"

"Khleeg's head is his still. Speak." Golgren waited for the other to tell him that he had seen the golden figure too.

But, instead, Khleeg muttered, "Your face, my lord! It is red like flame . . . *was* red like flame. No more . . ."

Frowning, Golgren looked past him to Idaria. Her eyes wide, she nodded.

"Stand aside!" The Grand Khan charged back into his chamber, heading directly for the mirror. Crystalline dryads sculpted into the ivory frame seemed to mock him as he stared at himself.

There was no sign of any redness. He spun about. Khleeg stood near the balcony, silent and loyal.

"Not any more," Golgren said.

"No, my lord. But I saw it. There was a"—Khleeg frowned and with an apologetic look, finished—"*vrakuli?*"

The word was a Blödian term for gargoyle meaning "winged vermin." Khleeg was the only one other than Idaria and Tyranos who knew—thanks to his lord—of the spying creatures. He did *not* know of the wizard's existence, though. That was something with which even Khleeg could not be trusted.

"Yes," Golgren finally answered. "A *voru tzyn,*" he added, using the more universal ogre name for the creatures. "A gargoyle."

"Gargoyle" muttered Khleeg, memorizing the Common word. The officer beat a fist on his breastplate. "I find Wargroch! Send him with warriors to search the roofs—"

"It is gone. The warriors will not search. They have other tasks, yes? And you have other reasons for coming, Khleeg."

The other ogre nodded. "My lord, Zhulom's hand cannot be found."

He did not refer to a missing appendage, as in the case of his master, but rather the formal term that Golgren had chosen to mark the ogre equivalent of an Uruv Suurt legion. Each *hand* consisted of roughly twelve hundred warriors divided into groups of five, as in five fingers. It was Golgren's latest attempt to organize the ogre might into disciplined units.

But one did not lose an entire hand, not even in the wastelands of southern Golthuu. More importantly, the fact that it was the warlord Zhulom's particular hand bothered the Grand Khan. Zhulom was an ambitious commander who had readily sided with the half-breed early on. But ambition, as Golgren well understood, did not suddenly vanish merely because one's patron had become supreme ruler. Already so close to the throne, the former warlord might be enticed by the notion of taking the final step and seizing it from his slighter, maimed lord. Golgren had already executed one warlord since the battle, a Blödian who had thought the Grand Khan's injuries a good enough reason to try a coup.

Golgren suddenly recalled something else about Zhulom's force: The commander of one of its five fingers was Atolgus, a young chieftain raised up by the Grand Khan. Commander Atolgus had brought the Solamnic knight to Golgren, stirring hopes of a pact between the knights and ogres. And although that effort had failed, Atolgus had proven very loyal. The Grand Khan had intended the chieftain for greater things.

If Zhulom had turned renegade, Atolgus and the other young leaders Golgren had been keeping a fond eye on were likely dead.

"Vaduk and Carku are very loyal," he said to Khleeg. "They are nearest. They will hunt Zhulom."

The officer grinned, revealing sharp, yellowed teeth. "Send word. *F'han* to Zhulom! Death!"

"Zhulom's head. Bring it to me."

Khleeg beat his chest again. "Aye, my lord."

As the officer rushed off to send the orders, Golgren glanced at Idaria. She said nothing, but both knew what subject crossed the Grand Khan's thoughts.

"I do not think him dead, my lord," the elf woman solemnly proclaimed, referring not to Atolgus or any of the other ogres involved in the missing hand. "I think he was called."

"Sir Stefan Rennert of the Knights of Solamnia walks into the wild as the earth quakes and *f'hanos* surround him, and yet he is not dead, you say." The Grand Khan bared his teeth, an act that made him look far more ogreish. "May whatever god has taken him return him to me. For I will have much need of him very soon." His brow suddenly furrowed as he considered another possibility. "Whatever god . . . or *Titan.*"

II

SAFRAG'S SPELL

There had been many changes in the Black Talon, the inner circle of the Titans. Their founder, Dauroth, had not been the only Titan to perish that foul day when Garantha had been assaulted by the undead and their leader had finally decided to provoke the half-breed's demise. The quake would have slain Golgren a hundred times over, save for the fact that he had carried an ancient signet once wielded by the High Ogres. There was still debate among the Titans over where the would-be Grand Khan had obtained such a valuable prize, just the sort of trinket so long sought after by the sorcerers.

The eleven members of the Black Talon sat in massive, high-backed stone chairs. They were designed not only for the Titans' great height, but also to give each the appearance of authority to any other of their number who stood before them. The most imposing of the chairs was set in the center and stood more than a head higher than the rest. All eleven were placed behind an arching wooden platform, which gave the appearance of a tribunal. Those on each end, the least in rank of the inner circle, faced one another.

The chamber in which the Black Talon gathered was itself in the center of the sprawling edifice that was the Titans' domain. The sorcerers did not dwell in Garantha, though they kept a constant watch on its happenings, especially with regard to the mongrel who sat on the throne there. Rather, their sanctum was located far south of Golgren's capital, in southern Golthuu or—as the Titans still thought it—the land of Blöde. Indeed, the magically hidden valley in which their headquarters lay was barely two dozen miles from Blöten, previously the capital of Blöde. Had anyone been unfortunate enough to stumble into the valley, it was very unlikely that the person would have survived a journey through the misty forest surrounding the sanctum. The Titans also preserved their privacy through monstrous guardians stalking the wooded land.

As the supreme voice, Dauroth had formerly held the place of honor at the center of the Black Talon. But both he and his intended successor, Hundjal, had perished that ignominious day. The apprentice had died at the whim of his master, but even so, several seats had opened up in the Black Talon, and there was a new Titan in charge—whose ascendancy to power had been a tremendous surprise to some.

No one argued that Safrag was not the true master. There had been some protest early on, but those two grumbling Titans had simply disappeared, and none of the others were at all interested in asking questions as to their fate.

For the most part, the dread sorcerers were of a kind, and the epitome of what Dauroth had dreamed was the picture of their glorious ancestors. Their skin was of an arresting blue tint, just as was said to be true of their ancestors, in the tales of the High Ogres. Dauroth's intended golden age was to have been populated by beings who were giants among giants. Thus the Titans were some fifteen feet tall, more than half again the height of their brethren. Built like graceful acrobats, they were not the brutish, muscular warriors that the rest of the race had developed into. No ordinary ogre could match a Titan in hand-to-hand combat, for the latter's sleek form hid not only tremendous strength, but swiftness and agility.

The High Ogres had been beautiful and so the Titans were also, albeit with a subtle touch of darkness. Their skin was without blemish, and their golden eyes glowed. The high, sharp point of their ears was quite visible, due to their habit of binding their long, ebony hair into tight, thick tails. Each wore an elegant, silken robe—dark blue with hints of red—that flowed down to sandaled feet. Crimson sashes stretched from the right shoulder down to the left side of their golden-belted waists. A decorative armor plate covered their left shoulders, and their arms themselves were bare, save for a gleaming silver metal band on the right wrist, a red silken one on the other.

Although they resembled each other enough to be brothers—all, that is, save for one of their number—if one looked close, one could still see distinctive features that remained as faint memories of their former lives. It was the group that was paramount, not the individual. That had been the law under Dauroth, and it was still the law under Safrag—although that law applied to everyone but the leader.

Gargoyles had been part of the discussion held by Golgren and Tyranos; not at all by chance, they were part of the current debate among the Black Talon.

The Titans despised the tongue of their base brethren and also eschewed the use of Common, save when having to deal with outsiders or those new among their ranks. Instead, they *sang* the words of a glorious language Dauroth had claimed was that of the High Ogres. Safrag, at least, knew it was simply another of his late master's creations. So much of the Titans' culture was imaginative fabrication, not true fact or history. The former apprentice had no qualms about keeping what he liked about the Titan legacy and gradually changing what he did not.

But to shape the Titans as he ultimately desired, to shape *all* ogres as he planned, Safrag needed something special. It was what he had invoked to manipulate Dauroth into slaying

Hundjal, before tricking his master into slaying himself with his own spellwork.

Legend named it the *Fire Rose*. And whoever was master of the gargoyles was interfering with his attempt to find it once and for all.

Safrag stood. He was a monumental sight even to the rest of the Black Talon, most of whom suspected him of somehow causing the deaths of Dauroth and Hundjal by his cunning. The other members of the inner circle listened breathlessly as he sang to them of the reason for their summons.

"Another!" he shouted, his song strident. Outsiders would have perhaps been captivated by the singing but would have been utterly unable to decipher the meaning of his words. "There lies another!"

He gestured to the center of the chamber, to the floor where a symbol of a great black claw had been set in stone. Directly above the claw symbol, a crackling sphere of white-blue energy was responsible for what little illumination lit the chamber.

Safrag stretched out his hand. Each nail was as dark as night, long, and tapering to a sudden, sharp curve. His nails were well matched with the shorter, but sharper, hooks at his elbows.

Black flames burst from the stone floor, the talon symbol briefly coming alive in the fire. The fire began to transform itself, taking on a constantly shifting shape that seemed to want nothing more than to leap and dance. That shape began to coalesce, and as it did, the flames started to die.

And in moments, where there had been fire, there struggled a gargoyle, gray-blue in color and with a long muzzle almost avian in its beaky shape.

"I seek for us the means to achieve our dreams," Safrag intoned. He glanced at those on his left, and those on his right. His anger was clear and righteous. "I seek that which legend says can transform our realm into the paradise it once was and was meant to be! And what do you give me, instead? *Another* winged vermin."

Unlike the members of the Black Talon, the imprisoned creature was not cowed. The gargoyle hissed and spat and tried to reach for Safrag with his claws. Its wings beat, but it did not rise so much as an inch off the floor. There was no sign of what held the beast captive, but it certainly did so thoroughly.

"It was caught observing our search near Khur," sang the Titan who had brought the creature to Safrag. Khur was a desolate land northeast of Blöde and the subject of much conjecture as to the likely hiding place of the mysterious artifact. "Better to bring it to the Black Talon and question what it knows—"

Safrag cut the other Titan off. "It knows as much as those before it, and will tell us none of it . . . will you, beast?"

The gargoyle snapped at him again. Such creatures could speak, and there were some scholars who said that they had an intelligence comparable to that of an average ogre. But the greatest tortures that Safrag had devised had proven unable to stir the creatures' tongues to wagging.

And so, to the Titan leader, one more gargoyle meant little but irritation. It was their master he desired, their chief—a master Safrag felt certain was somehow tied to Golgren.

He clenched his fist. The gargoyle howled as it suddenly twisted like a wet cloth that someone sought to tightly wring out. Bones cracked, and its scaled hide ripped open to unleash a sickening torrent of blood, other fluids, and crushed organs.

Safrag gestured. The black flames briefly burst to life again, completely devouring the gargoyle while protecting the pristine floor from its destroyed body, fluids, and organs.

The lead Titan surveyed the others with a glare. "Bring me the head of that refuse's master and nothing less! Otherwise we waste time. There must be no further interruption of our hunt."

"What hunt?" blurted Yatilun, one of the first to support Safrag's ascension and, of late, one of those most frustrated by the lack of progress in their quest. "We find one dead end after another while our cache of elixir depletes. Dauroth would have—"

A singular look from Safrag sent the other Titan withdrawing into his chair, his mouth clamped shut. The leader of the Black Talon smiled around broadly. But it was no smile of pleasure, rather a reminder that he would tolerate only so much. Like all Titans, Safrag's handsome facade crumbled when his teeth were revealed, twin rows of sharp teeth more akin to those of a shark than any other creature. Those seated on each side of Safrag surreptitiously leaned away from him.

But one Titan dared speak. A feminine hand touched Safrag's. He looked down to his right, where the lone female among the Black Talon, the only representative of her gender to be invited into the inner circle, sat as his favored apprentice.

"He is only as anxious as the rest of us, master," the female Titan whispered, her full, dark lips creased in a slight smile. Long lashes partially veiled her brilliant, golden eyes. "Yatilun merely spoke before he considered."

Her hand lingered a moment longer than necessary. While Safrag's expression did not change, he did not pull his hand away from her touch.

It was not merely because she was the only female among them that most of the other Titans were prey to her allure. The transformation from ogre to sorceress had created a seductress unparalleled in her. Her long, flowing midnight black hair—hair never bound as a male's was, beautiful hair that streamed down to her waist—framed a face that made the most glorious elf princess appear a hag by comparison.

Morgada continued displaying her half smile with hints of teeth not so grand in size as a male's, but certainly as sharp or even sharper. Safrag turned his gaze from his apprentice to Yatilun.

"We are all anxious to see the destiny of our people

fulfilled," the lead Titan sang in a conciliatory, soothing tone. "And so, I do forgive your outburst, my friend."

"Gracious is Safrag," Yatilun sang back in the Titan language.

"It is true, all trails have led to nothing thus far, and that must be remedied. That is why I have summoned all of you. I have pored over all matters arcane and have at last determined how best to pinpoint the Fire Rose."

"The small piece that Dauroth and you discovered was supposed to help us many, many months ago," pointed out another Titan. "'Like calling to like.' Is that not how it works?"

Safrag bowed his head in acknowledgment of the words he himself had uttered just after making his claim to Dauroth's position. "True, but for the first months we were too weak to undertake such an imposing spell. For the months that followed, we made the assumption that our previous conjurations would work as well for the matter in hand, as they have worked for other purposes, yes?"

"Of course," remarked Yatilun, intrigued. "Why not?"

Their leader looked to his apprentice. "Morgada?"

With a smile designed to draw every eye to her, she answered, "High Ogre magic still eludes us."

As her words registered among the inner circle, Safrag added his own satisfied smile to hers. "High Ogre magic. Though Dauroth preached to us about how ours was a power akin to that of the ancients', he failed to realize they had many, many generations of study and use that we did not."

"How can we overcome an obstacle of experience that far dwarfs ours?" asked another sorcerer. Several of the inner circle murmured their agreement with that burning question.

"Why, by using the ancients themselves, their very powers and secrets, in order to learn where the artifact is."

There was a great rumble from the rest of the Black Talon. Safrag looked again to Morgada, whose eyes flashed their approval.

"How do we do that?" Yatilun finally asked. "What do you mean by that riddle? Must we raise the dead?"

"Hardly that. We merely have to rob the dead—which we already have." He gestured at the spot where the gargoyle had stood.

Another burst of black flame erupted, but it lasted only scant seconds before retreating to the nether reaches. In its wake, the fire left a black metal chest chained by silver strands, hovering at waist level. The box was large enough to hold a small cat, and there appeared to be no separation between the lid and its main body.

Safrag suddenly stood next to the box and tapped on the top of it with one finger. With a hiss the strands became serpents that writhed and sought his hand.

Startled, the other sorcerers edged back. However, an undaunted Safrag let the serpents bite him.

The serpents stiffened as they bit. One by one, the serpent guardians turned to ash that fell to the floor and faded away.

With what seemed almost reverence, Safrag raised the lid.

A fiery light filled the chamber that nearly blinded the Titans. They were forced to shield their eyes.

His own gaze already protected by his spellwork, Safrag reached inside.

His hand thrust into a clear liquid. He removed something that was easily hidden in his returning fist yet still illuminated the chamber from between his clenched fingers.

"Behold!" he proclaimed. "Only a hint of the glory that we seek."

The lead Titan opened his hand palm up to display for the rest a tiny, tiny fragment of what appeared to be incandescent pearl. Freed of his grip, it again radiated a brilliant light.

"Behold! The slightest piece of the greatest artifact of the High Ogres."

"The Fire Rose!" more than one Titan murmured. They

had all seen the fragment once before—when they had last sought the artifact from which it had somehow broken off—but so great was its power that all marveled at it as if for the first time.

"But . . . We have used it before," the Titan on Morgada's other side finally spouted. "We came away with nothing!"

"That is true, Draug. But, as I said, we used only our own, deficient magic. It is *true* High Ogre power that we need. And a ready source for it has been awaiting us all the while."

Draug and the others held their tongues as Safrag dismissed the box almost contemptuously. Still clutching the pea-sized fragment, he spread his hands toward the other ten members of the Black Talon.

"Come to me and receive life unbound . . ."

Several of the Titans started forward warily. His words were the opening declaration to one of the supreme rituals of their kind. More than one looked to their neighbor for verification that they had heard true.

Rising smoothly, Morgada vanished from her place, only to reappear at a point close to the right of her master. The Titaness turned to him, her face expressionless.

Her bold action stirred the rest into movement. One by one, the members of the Talon took up their proper places. They glanced around at each other, wondering what their leader planned. He still held the minute piece of the legendary artifact. But surely he did not plan to use it directly on them . . .

Safrag whispered something to the fragment. Almost with reluctance, he tossed it from his palm. Yatilun gasped and nearly leaped from his place for fear that it would shatter and explode when it struck the stone floor.

Instead the artifact fragment flew up in the air, rising to a place directly above the lead Titan and just below the white-blue sphere whose light it utterly overwhelmed.

As it hovered above them, Safrag smiled at his companions.

"Do you accept what I offer?" he sang, speaking the next line of the ritual.

"I am an empty vessel," Morgada led the others in replying. "Let that vessel be filled."

"Let that vessel be filled." The rest concluded the chant.

"Magic is the blood, the blood is the magic. Take unto you that which I give, and you will live forever!"

As one, the other Titans declared, "We will live forever! Let the magic be our blood, for we would drink of eternity."

Safrag should have brought forth the dwindling supply of elixir that the Titans needed to imbibe every so often to keep their forms and power. If they did not drink it, they were doomed to a terrible fate. There was a monstrous price to pay for becoming a Titan: deprived of the elixir—which included fresh elf blood as one of its chief ingredients—a sorcerer's body would go through such withdrawals from the loss of magic that it would twist and warp and become a thing so foul even the lowest ogre would turn from it in disgust.

Donnag, once master of Blöde and believed by many at the time of his ascension to be the one who would restore the ogres to their glory, had joined the Titans at Dauroth's invitation. Yet Donnag had been far too eager to slay the upstart Golgren. When his plot had failed—risking open battle between the influential half-breed and the Titans—Dauroth had permitted Golgren to condemn the chieftain to no more elixirs.

There was question as to how Golgren had discovered the Titans' secret—and all the most likely answers pointed to the sinister Uruv Suurt priestess and empress, Nephera. But what mattered was that Donnag had become an object lesson to all, before his eventual grisly death. His body had bent, his skin had developed boils all over, and his bones had shifted to odd and unsettling positions, making it hard for him to walk or even talk. Even his own clan had finally turned on him.

There was one fate worse than to be denied the elixir, and that fate was a nightmare in itself. An end to the supply was enough to keep the Titans under Safrag's thumb. For only he had access to remaining stocks secreted by Dauroth.

In the days of plenty, each Titan would imbibe on his own. Of late, though, Safrag had insisted that the Talon always drink the elixir together. The inner circle ought to stay strong and united, so his reasoning went. If the Fire Rose was found, its wondrous power would offer the key to the golden age. But it also would free the Titans of the potion they so desperately needed to maintain their might, and the mongrel who currently kept them from its crucial ingredients. With the Fire Rose, they could rejuvenate themselves with merely a touch of its power.

That is if the tales were true.

With the fragment still hovering far above him, Safrag sang, "Let the magic come forth to quench our thirst!"

The other Titans prepared themselves to receive one of the tiny vials. But the elixir did not materialize. As the sorcerers stirred, beginning to comprehend, Safrag raised his hands upward.

Under the brilliant glow of the fragment, a long shape began to form. Some of the Titans frowned, quickly recognizing its general shape and outline—that of a body.

But it was no newly slain corpse of one of the elves used to create the elixir. Instead, the body—smaller by at least half than those of the great Titans who observed it—was no more than bones.

"The *ancient!*" Draug gasped.

They all knew the bones well, for the Titans had been the grave robbers responsible for their taking. The bones were millennia old, the remains of a once mighty High Ogre whose tomb the Black Talon had ransacked in its relentless quest for the secrets of the past. The body had been fully intact when Dauroth had led his followers to it. But despite their reverence for their ancestors, he had without hesitation, in order to better seek out any powerful secrets within, destroyed the wards that had kept it in such perfect order for so long.

After failing to unlock any secrets, Dauroth had returned the bones to the sanctum. Magic was so integral to High Ogre society that even the remains should be preserved.

And Safrag had found use for them.

The Titans stared in wonder and pleasure.

"Do you accept the power and the life?" Safrag sang.

"We accept," Morgada and the others replied.

"Let the vessels be filled, and the desire emptied from them!"

The Titans raised their upturned hands shoulder high. They bent their heads back and closed their eyes.

A faint aura surrounded each of them, a sign that the individual sorcerers had opened themselves up to receive what their leader offered. It was the only moment, waking or sleeping, that Titans left themselves unguarded, even before their own leader. Otherwise, all kept their own hidden defenses, just in case of argument or ambition. Or worse.

Seen from above, the eleven formed a five-pointed star within a five-pointed star, with Safrag occupying the center point. The skeleton hovered directly over him and just below the fragment.

Safrag stared up at the skeleton. His golden eyes flared. With one finger, he drew the star within a star pattern. The pattern blazed red and floated up to the remains of the High Ogre.

As it touched the floating skeleton, the pattern grew to envelop the bones.

Safrag muttered under his breath and his eyes closed.

The pattern became the skeleton, which burned a bright crimson. From the center of the ancient corpse, tendrils of energy shot forth to strike each Titan, hitting them full on the chest.

One last tendril rose to touch the fragment of the Fire Rose.

Some of the sorcerers gasped when struck, but for the most part they remained silent. Only Safrag could be heard, murmuring. The lead Titan opened his eyes to slits, his gaze taking in those within view. A slight smile crossed his lips as he finished the incantation.

More and more the tendrils fed the Titans, and as they did the bones began to wither. They cracked and crumbled, and even the dust that they formed burned away as the Black Talon received the inherent magic flowing from them. All semblance of a body faded away until eventually only the crimson glow remained. Even that finally faded away, and with it went the tendrils.

Yatilun was the first to find his voice. His eyes wide in awe, the Titan rasped, "Never . . . never have I felt so alive! So powerful! So—"

"So truly as one of the ancients," Safrag finished for him as the other Titan nodded. Their leader looked to the others. Each face—even Morgada's—was marked by the same rapture.

"There is nothing beyond us!" Draug managed. "We could flay the mongrel alive and take Garantha in a single minute! We could wash away Uruv Suurt Ambeon with one vast wave taken from the sea, sending all those horned devils back to Mithas to lie dead at the feet of their emperor—"

Others began to babble similar sentiments. Safrag watched them with amusement. Such euphoria was not uncommon after a Titan's imbibing of the elixir. But the power given to them by the bones had magnified that effect several times over.

"There is only one purpose for our mighty gift," he finally interjected, his brusque tone silencing all objections. "Keep to your positions."

They immediately obeyed. Safrag gazed up at the fragment, which shimmered. He raised his hand toward it. At the same time, the other members of the Black Talon pointed at him.

New tendrils of the same hue as those that had struck the Titans spread from one sorcerer to the next. The star within the star pattern was recreated; the focus of its energies was the figure at its center.

And he, in turn, focused those energies upon the fragment.

The moment the tendrils struck it, the Titans stood as if frozen. Their golden orbs turned utter white, and their skin grew so pale they looked as if death had claimed them. Only a faint rising of their chests gave any clue that life remained within them.

Safrag's mouth opened suddenly, and the voice that emerged sounded like nothing mortal.

"South . . . South to east . . . East to north and north to west and west to south . . . Under the raven's beak, and at the mark of the burning sun . . . He claims his child, and his child claims the world . . ."

Safrag jerked. His voice changed, sounding female but powerful. *"The wings stretch long and over the land. The gargoyle king seeks his hand . . . The fire calls his heart and has eaten his soul, and the king sits upon his throne, the Rose's sweet scent calling . . ."*

Again, the Titan leader jerked spasmodically. He struggled to turn his hand clockwise, but with his face contorted with the effort, his hand completed a circle.

The sorcerers shook. A vision formed before Safrag. He gritted his teeth from the effort and pain. The vision defined itself. The key to the Fire Rose revealed itself to him.

And caused him to roar in fury and disbelief.

The unexpected cry broke the spell. Some of the Titans collapsed to the floor, while the rest struggled to remain on their feet. Only Safrag retained enough strength to not only keep steady and poised, but to continue his wordless roar.

Finally able to focus, Morgada stared at him in concern. "Master! What is it? Has the spell turned on you?"

Safrag turned such a murderous gaze upon her that the Titaness crouched in fear of being reduced to a stain on the floor. Yet his anger was not aimed at her. Instead, he pointed before him. In the chaos of the spell's shattering, the vision he had summoned—and kept intact through his own magic—stood unnoticed. Morgada gazed at the revelation and was dumbfounded.

"What does that mean?" she asked, as she stalked around the image. In the center of the vision stood a figure. One by one, the inner circle of the Titans surrounded the figure, staring at it.

"What does it mean?" Morgada asked again of Safrag.

The lead Titan eyed the hated face, the mocking smile . . . the missing hand. He nodded to all the others. Their eyes did not deceive them.

"It seems that the Grand Khan Golgren is our key to the Fire Rose," Safrag finally said.

And very slowly and bitterly, he smiled.

III

SARTH

There were troubles with ruling a realm divided by broken land, mountains, and other geographic divides. Golgren borrowed his ideas in that regard from the Uruv Suurt, who claimed mastery over their mainland colony of Ambeon and many, many islands east of the Blood Sea. No realm was as splintered as the minotaur empire's, and a constant stream of ships kept communication going between the individual colonies. Under Faros Es-Kalin, the newest emperor—Golgren's archenemy—those ships had swelled in number.

The Grand Khan boasted a continuous stream of ships moving between the parts of his realm too, especially the lighter sailing craft that borrowed heavily from the empire's designs. Yet sailing around the Hollowlands, past the Misty Isle, and through the Bay of Balifor was an overly-tedious and dangerous process. Thus, while that route was necessary at times, Golgren had also opened a land crossing near Ogrebond heading south to the sea just beyond the bay, utilizing a new port town he had dubbed *Carduuch*, or "Serpent's Bite". Even that way entailed wasted time and effort, however.

And that was why Golgren had begun to study the nearby land of Khur in detail.

THE FIRE ROSE

Khur was an arid land filled mostly with human nomads. In many ways, the nomads were respected by the ogres, who acknowledged their strength, cunning, and savagery. However, being human, the nomads had made ties with the Knights of Neraka. And thus to invade them was to end the semblance of peace that existed between Golgren and the dark knighthood. Yet, if the news he had received was correct, the Black Shells had already broken that peace, and Khur was already his enemy.

Golgren studied the weathered maps on a huge wooden table in what had become his war room. The high-ceilinged chamber had likely been a grand ballroom in the days of his ancestors, for it was vast. The floor and walls still retained remnants of fanciful images, some recognizable as High Ogres in poses of merriment. The Grand Khan cared not a whit that he had turned a place of entertainment into one of planning destruction, for to ogres war was the ultimate entertainment. It gave purpose to their otherwise dismal lives and had a long ogre tradition.

Khur had been Golgren's next intended foray into conquest, one that he had felt would not be so disturbing to the Solamnians at least. Uniting the "provinces" of Kern and Blöde through Khur would prove far more vexing to the Nerakians and the Uruv Suurt. And as an ally of Neraka, Khur was an enemy of Solamnia. In Golgren's eyes, it had been the perfect next step in his master plan.

His face expressionless, the Grand Khan suddenly swept his maimed arm across the table, flinging away the maps that had been given to him long ago by the Solamnians who had come to "train" his village in warfare against the Black Shells.

Golgren strode out of the war room, with two hulking guards—one from Kern and the other from Blöde, as he always dictated—following close behind.

Signs of reconstruction and renovation were everywhere, with scaffoldings lining corridors and raw materials covering portions of the marble floors. The work had slowed over the past months, in great part because very few elf slaves were involved anymore. Having determined that they would be his bargaining chip with the Solamnians, Golgren had not wanted to let his people become too much accustomed to using the elves as slaves. Without them, ogres tried their best to imitate the meticulous skill of the elves. The results were not as pleasing.

Three ogre workers quickly scrambled to attention as he strode by. They had been seeking to patch a section of wall that had collapsed in upon itself in generations past. The work had been started by the slaves, and where elf hands had sought to ease the cracks and replace the marble, the wall looked almost as though it had never broken in the first place.

Unfortunately, where the ogres had taken over, the new marble did not match the previous stone in shade, nor were the cracks completely covered over. Instead, great splashes of plaster feebly attempted to bridge the gaps between broken pieces.

The three ogres had been chosen because of their relative skills at such craftsmanship, but so amateurish was their effort that Golgren paused to survey their handiwork. The trio dropped to their knees and cowered before their much shorter lord.

Golgren snapped his fingers. One of the Grand Khan's guards let out a grunt of warning and thrust a sword forward for emphasis. The three workers scrambled to their feet and fled down the corridor.

The Grand Khan softly placed his hand on one of the ancient reliefs. In the image, two High Ogres rode magnificent steeds in the midst of some activity, possibly a hunt. Their images had been recreated by the slaves, but whatever they were hunting for had been obscured by the pathetic efforts of the ogres.

"The elves, whatever their faults, were far more adept, weren't they?"

The two guards swung around to face the unexpected newcomer. Golgren, unfazed, slowly turned to face Safrag.

"Such a glorious piece of work," the new Titan leader murmured. Stepping past Golgren and the wary guards, the gargantuan sorcerer let out a sigh. "Please. Allow me."

Raising his palms to waist level, the Titan stood before the center of the relief. He took a deep breath.

A golden glow rose from Safrag's palms. He shivered slightly and began breathing rapidly. His eyes fluttered half closed.

Despite their responsibilities, the guards took a step back. Ogres, more than most races, feared magic.

The glow rose to envelop the image. While there was no visible change at first, where the work had either been done by ogres, or not touched at all, the energies suddenly grew bright.

And before the eyes of the onlookers, the rest of the relief took shape. The two hunters were joined by a never-before-glimpsed third figure: a female astride the back of a wingless griffon. Their prey turned out to be a huge, majestic creature that resembled a horse with lupine features and two horns. The strange creature was an amalok, one of the most dominant and useful beasts in all Golthuu. A variety of amalok breeds had once spread from the uppermost points of Kern down to the worst recesses of Blöde. They had been used for their hides, their meat, their horns, and for racing. The spotted variation pursued by the High Ogres was carved in such detail that one could distinguish the strands of hair and the split in the hooves. There could be no doubt that an animal of that kind had once lived, though no such amalok was found anymore.

With a slight gasp of effort, Safrag stepped back.

"Arresting, isn't it?" the Titan commented. "There's so much to admire of our great ancestors."

"Decorum being one of those things," the Grand Khan blandly returned. "And what does Safrag require all of a sudden, that he appears to me with such brash suddenness? Or has he a desire to offer the Titans as workers to restore the palace for me?"

Safrag chuckled. "As glorious as the palace fully restored to its former greatness would be, our gifts can be of far better service to you than that, Grand Khan," the blue-tinted sorcerer said. He gave a low bow that still did not take him down to eye level with the half-breed. "No, I come on business of importance regarding a missing portion of your armies."

With a wave of his hand, Golgren dismissed the two guards. They retreated, standing far enough away to not hear, but still close enough to be summoned back to duty, if needed.

"The Titans are slow to hear. That news is not fresh news to me, Safrag."

The Titan leader spread his hands in apology. "Naturally, we knew about it for some time. But it made no sense to alert you without first trying to find out more information. You'd certainly like to know where the missing ranks might be, after all."

Golgren did not even so much as arch an eyebrow. "And you know?"

"We have . . . evidence. Strong evidence." Safrag raised a hand toward Golgren.

A dagger suddenly appeared at the base of the Titan's stomach. The Grand Khan's face remained a mask. Behind him the guards could be heard giving a start, turning toward Golgren.

"No . . ." Golgren called to the pair. They immediately halted.

The dagger stayed pointed at Safrag's stomach.

"Your throat is a bit high for my dagger, Safrag. But a blade to the stomach can be as fatal, I think, even to a sorcerer."

The Titan was gracious even in the face of the threat. "But I mean no harm, Grand Khan! I merely have something to show you."

Over his open palm there suddenly appeared the vision of a mountainous region. Golgren did not remove the dagger while he studied the vision. He vaguely knew that particular area. It was almost directly south of Garantha, in the midst of the rugged mountain chain that extended there.

"That is near the Vale of Vipers," Golgren finally said.

"So we also found out."

"The missing hand last marched in the southern reaches of old Blöde. To be near the vale, Zhulom would have had to march his warriors far and with much good reason."

"We thought he might be seeking to build a rebellion," the Titan suggested.

The Grand Khan's green eyes narrowed almost imperceptibly. "To build a rebellion, Zhulom would need the help of the Uruv Suurt. He would be best served staying in the south of old Blöde."

Safrag bowed again. "Your wisdom is great. We considered that also, and perhaps Zhulom has done so previously. But all signs most definitely point to him being near the vale."

"The vale . . ." Golgren withdrew the dagger, which he quickly slipped back into his belt. "So very near Khur."

"Imagine the empire with Khur. And, by proxy, imagine Neraka, Grand Khan."

Golgren said nothing, showed no emotion.

Dismissing the vision, Safrag continued blithely, "Of course, I wouldn't expect you to ride there yourself. We Titans shall look into the matter there as best as possible."

"Yes. You are to be commended, Safrag."

"The Titans but live to serve you, Grand Khan."

Grinning without humor, Golgren replied, "So Dauroth also said."

With a shrug, the Titan leader vanished in a brief flash of black flame that left a slight sulfur scent in Golgren's nostrils. Slipping his hand to a pouch at his waist, Golgren withdrew a small vial. Expertly popping the bound cork off the tiny green container, the Grand Khan briefly inhaled the potion.

The elven scent managed to disperse the sulfur.

Replacing the vial, he summoned back the guards. Without a word to them, the Grand Khan glanced one more time at the wondrous relief, much improved, and continued on.

᚛᚜

Khleeg and a second officer met him outside the palace. Wargroch, also a Blödian, was in some ways uglier than Khleeg. His toadlike face was reminiscent of two other ogres who had served Golgren during his rise to power. There was good reason for that resemblance, for both Nagroch and Belgroch had been elder brothers of the warrior. They too had given their lives—in one way or another—in service to Golgren.

"Lord," the pair rumbled, striking their fists to their breastplates.

To Khleeg, Golgren asked, "Word of Zhulom?"

His second in command turned uncomfortable. "Nothing, lord."

Wargroch grunted. Khleeg glared at him.

Golgren eyed the younger warrior. "Speak, Wargroch."

The other's grasp of Common was better than Khleeg's. "Grand Khan, I hear of sightings of ogre warriors coming from the south. I understand they march through Khur—"

"All *j'nari!*" insisted Khleeg to them. "All . . . rumor!"

The Grand Khan silenced Khleeg with a look. "And the rumor? You hear it where, Wargroch?"

"Mentioned in reports, in stolen messages from Black Shell riders . . . in other places . . ."

"It is true?" Golgren demanded of Khleeg.

His second in command shrugged. "True, some word here, some there. How true that word . . ."

A brief scowl escaped the Grand Khan, a scowl he quickly smothered. "It is decided, " he murmured to himself. "Khleeg, my horse. Wargroch, you and I, we will ride!"

44

"Ride where?" asked Khleeg, clearly not pleased. His brother had been chosen over him; he would be left behind.

The Grand Khan bared his teeth—not at Khleeg, but rather thinking of the destination he had in mind. "To Sarth."

※

The ogre was a rarity among his kind, so old and wizened that he almost appeared to hail from some other race. His body was barely more than bones, and his flesh was so pale gray that he looked like a *f'hanos*. His two smallest fingers were missing from his left hand, as were the small toes of each foot. Yet the marks that were all that were left of those impairments indicated that the missing digits had been carefully *severed,* not removed by accident.

The old ogre sat in the mouth of a cave hidden in the mountains just east of Garantha. The cave was not deep, but the shape of the opening evoked the fanged mouth of a serpent. The old ogre sat under the stone fangs, drawing with a stick in the dirt.

The patterns he made were many. Some were recognizable as crude designs of local animals: the huge, elephantine mastarks, the giant reptiles called meredrakes, amaloks of varying sizes, and birds of prey were just some of the drawings. The old ogre mumbled as he drew, and whenever his mouth opened enough, it revealed that other than his two cracked bits of tusk, he had only a few fractured teeth.

His pate was bald, and what hair he bore on the rest of his gaunt body was spread in gray patches. Although the winds that howled through the mountains were harsh, they seemed not to affect the ogre, who wore only an old, torn kilt. No sandals protected his feet, whose soles were harder than leather.

In addition to the drawings in the dirt, there were other markings etched into the sides of the cave entrance.

A sun. A dragon with many heads. A huge tree. A griffon.

Beside the ogre was a tiny fire made from some of the squat brush that managed to survive in the inhospitable landscape. Tendrils of smoke wafted away from the cave and its tenant, finally drifting toward the two approaching riders.

"Gya ihul iGuyviri" rasped the elderly ogre sitting in front of the cave.

Wargroch glanced curiously at his lord. Golgren kept his expression calm, though his eyes briefly narrowed.

"And I see you too, Sarth," the Grand Khan returned, "who knows I am Golgren."

"And who speaks the tongue that is not the tongue," countered the elder, his comment followed by a grunting laugh. "As you wish to speak. Golgren you are, Guyvir. What brings you to Sarth after so many seasons? Not since *Ka i'Urkarun Dracon iZharangi*—The Dragon Who Is Zharang—brought his *f'han* to him and called him Grand Lord . . ."

The elder's ability to speak Common so well—better, in fact than any ogre other than a Titan—made Wargroch growl suspiciously. Golgren quieted him with a gesture. "A shaman, Wargroch. He is supposed to be a creature of peace."

Again came the grunting laugh. "Sarth is Sarth as he has always been. As *Golgren* has always been Golgren . . ."

The wind whipped through the Grand Khan's hair, and his cloak fluttered as if alive. Yet the air seemed still around Sarth.

"Wait," Golgren ordered Wargroch, as he dismounted.

The younger ogre grunted uneasily, but obeyed. He took the reins of Golgren's massive steed and hung back, watching warily as his lord drew closer to the shaman.

Ogres respected various gods. But more than deities—even more than Sirrion perhaps—they respected the land, which they believed was an entity everlasting. A decadent, bestial folk, ogres no longer had clerics like other races. But they did have shamans, who were revered as the watchers of the land, fulfilling its needs and guarding against its enemies.

That did not mean that, like druids—perhaps their closest equivalent—the shamans helped cultivate the flora and watch over the fauna. Rather, they were *servants* of the land, beings who listened to its silent whisperings and did what they were told, no matter the cost to them.

There had never been more than a few shamans at any one time. But those that had existed had always been treated with the greatest reverence, until what humans and elves called the Chaos War had taken place. The land had demanded that the shamans stand against the forces of Chaos, and they had done their duty and died for it. To the knowledge of most ogres, not one of their shamans had survived. With the mercurial nature of their race, most ogres had soon forgotten that shamans had ever existed.

But Golgren's mother had not been an ogre. She had been an elf. And, as an elf, she had looked to the shamans as akin to privileged beings from her own race. And so she had searched for a shaman, and somehow she had found Sarth . . . Or he had found her.

"You have grown since your mother's womb," Sarth cackled as Golgren reached him. "Not so much, but you've grown."

Only the narrowing of the Grand Khan's eyes gave hint to the emotions he smothered inside. Sarth had not been a shaman with any connection to the half-breed's village, but he had nonetheless been there the night the captive elf had given birth.

The shaman looked down at his drawings and erased all of them with one sweep of his bony hand. As Golgren seated himself cross-legged before the cadaverous but still tall figure, Sarth started making new drawings. A circle with a cross on one side. A warrior with a club. A sickle moon with a reptilian head atop it.

The drawings were immediately recognizable to the half-breed. The warrior was meant to represent his father. The circle with the cross was his pregnant mother. The sickle moon with the head of a meredrake marked the time of Golgren's birth.

"Halu i guyvari zuun delahn," said the shaman, briefly reverting to Ogre. "Such a thing cannot be born between the races. No ogre and elf may breed a child, but a child is bred," he concluded, peering up at Golgren. "A son is wealth and power. The father must have the mother. He lets live what should not exist for lust of the mother."

"I know the story," interrupted Golgren coolly. "Sarth wastes his breath telling what is already known, yes?"

But the shaman continued to draw his pictures and symbols. The head of an Uruv Suurt with a collar around his throat. An ogre standing upon a scale that was tipped to the left even though the ogre stood on the plate on the right.

A burning flower above the ogre.

"Sarth knows those things only because I have told Sarth those things." The Grand Khan deftly rose. As he did so, he saw by the cave a few small items that clearly had been brought as tokens for the shaman. An amalok horn. A necklace of meredrake teeth. A small clay figure of a female ogre. To Golgren's kind, each of the offerings suggested a specific purpose or need.

"Few believe in Sarth anymore," Golgren added. "Fewer yet come to see Sarth. Small wonder."

The shaman remained unperturbed by his visitor's insults. He studied his drawings as if seeking something.

"Dalu i surra fwaruus," Sarth muttered, sounding annoyed with himself. The bony finger thrust out and began a new drawing above the ogre on the scale.

There was a sharp, uncharacteristic intake of breath from Golgren. The shaman was busy with a simple figure that could have been an ogre, a human, or an elf. Yet where the other drawings had included details such as eyes or a nose at least, the figure had an oval head devoid of any features.

Sarth drew lines stretching forth from the body of the figure. Each line had three jagged sections to it. In such a manner did the old pictographs of ogre language indicate something that was bright or that *shone*.

A figure that shone.

Going down on one knee, Golgren leaned close to the shaman. His voice low, he murmured, "What do you know of that?"

"Kesu idwa. Sarth is told. Sarth does not question what is told. He knows that it *is."*

The Grand Khan's fingers came within inches of the old ogre's throat, itching to strangle him. Although, if standing, Sarth would have been much taller than Golgren, his body was very frail for an ogre. Golgren could have snapped his neck in two without trouble.

Sarth did not react to the potential threat, save to say, *"Yawa idwa i tuz iGolgreni.* You are not told what to do, Grand Khan. The choice was and is always yours."

Edging his hands away, Golgren leaned back. The half-breed slowly ran one foot over the drawings, eradicating them.

"That is the answer to such," he said to Sarth. "It is as you have said: I make my fate, as I have always. No drawings, no prophecies, no shamans who may speak as surrogates for the Titans . . ."

Once again ignoring Golgren, Sarth started new images. There were only two. One was a serpent coiled above a mountain; the other was a sword drawn with uncanny precision.

The Grand Khan recognized the first. Sarth had drawn an illustration representing the name of a place.

The Vale of Vipers.

But the sword, on the other hand, could suggest many meanings. A battle that would take place there, perhaps. Hardly astounding, considering recent news. Yet Golgren doubted that Sarth had drawn the sword for that purpose. It looked familiar, a specific design that did not look ogre in cast. It was more like . . .

Sarth was reconstructing the minotaur head, shaping the image differently.

It suddenly became obvious that the head was larger and rounder than an Uruv Suurt. The muzzle, meanwhile, was much shorter, almost crushed into the face.

"Yawa idwa i tuz iGolgreni," Sarth repeated, looking down with satisfaction at his latest piece of artwork. "You are not told what to do, Guyvir."

The Grand Khan said nothing. He touched neither the shaman nor the drawings, but simply turned and headed back to a perplexed Wargroch.

"My lord, did he tell you what you want?"

"No, he told me what *he* wanted. And that is how it has always been."

The toad-faced officer reached for his weapon. *"Gerad ahn if'hani—"*

Golgren stopped him with an unexpected glare. "No one shall touch Sarth, ever." Almost as an afterthought, he added, "And remember, all officers are to speak Common."

More befuddled than ever, Wargroch beat his fist against his breastplate. "I have dishonored my Grand Khan! I give my life—"

"Stop. We ride." Without another word, Golgren took the reins of his horse and mounted. Wargroch hurried to climb atop his own.

As the Grand Khan began to turn his mount around, he suddenly heard Sarth chanting in Ogre.

"Zaru iVolantori i gada tur iVolantori."

"Hear the tale of Volantor, Volantor the Mighty," was the closest translation. Like all ogres, Golgren knew the story of Volantor. It was told as a parable among his kind. Volantor had been a great warlord, with victories over the Uruv Suurt, humans, and dwarves. He had dispatched many a foe himself with his huge axe, called "Throat Eater" in legend. Volantor had become a khan in his own right and had gathered more wealth and power than most ogres could imagine.

Standing ever at Volantor's side had been his friend and comrade, Jaro. Throughout Volantor's rise to power, Jaro had guarded the warlord's back just as Volantor guarded his friend's. When Volantor became a khan, he made Jaro his second in command.

And it was as khan that Volantor achieved his greatest victory over a jealous rival. Volantor himself dispatched the other warlord, but not without receiving a wound to his chest. Fortunately, while the wound had been a large one, it had not been fatal. Volantor handed his axe to Jaro and began binding his chest.

At which point the patient Jaro took Volantor's prized axe and removed his friend's head. All that Volantor had built up became Jaro's.

Whether or not the tale was true, the moral was clear to any ogre. One's friends and allies were only such until it was no longer worth their while to be friends. It was more often those closest to power who dealt the killing blow.

Zharang had learned that lesson too late, using the ambition he saw in Golgren to further his own ambitions and thinking that he controlled the upstart. Golgren's former lord had ended up with a sword through his chest, his body sprawled across the shattered table where the Grand Khan had been supping with guests.

Golgren had played the role of Jaro, but now he wore Volantor's guise.

And if Sarth could be trusted to be right—as he generally was—one or *more* Jaros now awaited their turn, bearing some variation of Volantor's treacherous *Throat Eater*.

One of whom might even be . . . Sir Stefan Rennert?

IV

SACRIFICES

The meredrake hissed and spat, struggling to pull itself free from the heavy boulders linked to a chain around its thick neck. The dull green and sandy brown reptile was as long in body as an ogre and could easily drag the heaviest foe down if given the chance. The size of a horse, meredrakes were among the worst predators of the ogre lands. Their paws were clawed, and their teeth designed for two things: ripping flesh and crushing bone.

Slapping its heavy tail on the dusty ground, the meredrake opened its mouth and tasted the air with its long, red tongue. Its fiery eyes squinted, and the huge round nostrils at the end of its muzzle flared.

A small bit of rancid meat lay just beyond the mere-drake's reach. Driven by its basic instincts, the reptile tried again to reach the still tasty morsel. It never waited longer than several moments before attempting yet another futile lunge.

It was such determination to keep trying and fighting that was part of the reason the beast was kept prisoner.

The sun hung low on the horizon. The meredrake had been bound for some hours. The slavering beast's claws had dug deep ravines into the harsh ground, and more than once it had defecated in its frustration.

The jaws again snapped at the tantalizing meat. The meredrake hissed . . . and its entire body froze as if some spell had turned it to stone.

Its nostrils flared. The meredrake forgot the morsel for which it had struggled so hard and so long. Suddenly the reptile turned and scrambled as best it could over the boulders holding it anchored in place. However, those who had secured the beast had done their job well, and no matter where the giant lizard skittered, its tether always allowed it to go only so far.

The ground to the west suddenly rumbled, as if provoked by a minor tremor. The meredrake strained to head east or south, where the rocks rose to hills and even mountains farther on. Yet, like the meat, the higher landscape was beyond its reach.

The tremor grew closer. The earth to the west rose and buckled.

The meredrake frothed at the mouth as it twisted around in an effort to gnaw on its chain. Marks on the iron links gave ample evidence to the lack of success it had achieved thus far. Yet the savage lizard could imagine no other means of escape.

The ground continued to buckle toward the meredrake. The tremor reached the boulder to which the chain had been bolted. With little effort, the tremor tumbled the huge boulder upside down. The full weight of the rock fell upon the bolts, which snapped.

Sensing its freedom, the meredrake started to flee.

From below ground burst a massive crocodilian head at the end of a sinewy neck several times the length of the meredrake. The abomination's huge and oddly pointed jaws seized the hissing meredrake at the midsection, and raised the lizard high.

Its claws wildly scratching, the meredrake tried in vain to bite at its foe's neck. More and more of the burrowing leviathan emerged, showing two small forelegs ending in thick, webbed claws perfectly designed for ripping through dirt and rock.

The meredrake's tail wrapped around the upper neck of the other reptile. For a moment, there was a stalemate.

With the ease of biting into a piece of soft fruit, the serpentine giant bit *through* the meredrake's muscular torso.

The meredrake's hiss stopped. Parts of its tail and hind legs fell in one direction, the head and one foreleg another.

With great gusto, the burrower swallowed all that was left in its mouth. Down its great gullet went nearly a third of its prey.

Dropping its head down, the victor stuck its snout under the meredrake's tail and hind legs, seeking the best morsel. Clamping its jagged teeth around part of a haunch, it raised its snout skyward, tossed the bloody gobbet up, and let it fall into its gullet.

The burrower's head descended for more—

From behind the rocks charged a pack of stocky, muscular ogres. They were not clad so finely as those who lived in Garantha, for they were from one of the many nomadic groups that still populated much of the wilderness of old Blöde. In such harsh regions, life was spent hunting or being hunted. Or hunting the hunter.

The burrower let out a croaking roar and backed toward the hole from which it had sprung. It snapped at the first of the kilted ogres, almost biting off the eager warrior's head. Fortunately, quick reflexes sent the ogre scrambling just out of reach.

More than a dozen ogres materialized to confront the giant beast. It snapped again at one tusked attacker, tearing from his hand the spear that he was about to jab at its long neck. The weapon broke easily and, after being tasted, was spit out.

The full length of the reptile was exposed. The entire body was cylindrical, with another pair of vestigial limbs ending in digging claws at the rear of the body. The creature's form ended in a short, pointed tail perhaps three feet in length.

Another ogre threw his spear. The point went into the side of the burrower's neck. It gave another croaking roar and shook the point free. Dark blood dribbled from the wound.

As half a dozen more ogres joined those already attacking, the massive reptile chose flight over food. It twisted its body around and began digging furiously at the soil with its pointed snout. Between strength and the sharp point, the reptile dug down almost as quickly as if it were diving into water.

But as swift as the immense creature was, the ogres were even quicker. They thrust spears into its side. The reptile roared in pain as it drew back up to confront its foes.

Two ogres with smaller spears moved in close. The heads of the spears were smaller and hooked at the end, making them difficult to remove from any target. On the other end of the spears had been attached long strands of rope made from the sturdy *ki'turu* shrub, a plant known by nomadic ogres for its durability.

The first of the pair threw his spear. The small missile glanced off the upper edge of the beast's great neck and fell away. He scrambled after the spear as the second tossed.

The second's spear sank deep enough to catch in the scaled hide. Both the spear thrower and another nearby warrior immediately grabbed hold of the rope and tugged.

But as they did, the burrower's head darted down. Before the pair could pull it away, it caught the head and arm of the ogre chasing after the fallen spear.

Compared to a meredrake's tough body, the ogre's was very soft and so easy to bite through.

The bloody bits that were left afterwards twitched madly before thunking to the ground. The burrower instinctively swallowed the ogre's head and arm, its digestive system more than able to handle the bones.

But its instincts were working against it, for that move bought time for the ogres to gather nearer and bring forward more warriors with short spears. Two hurled their weapons from the opposite side. Both spears struck home. A pair of warriors grabbed each attached rope and pulled.

One spear that had barely penetrated popped out, taking a chunk of scale with it. The two ogres pulling on the line stumbled and fell, but, fortunately for them, the huge reptile was far too occupied to dip down and snack on their bodies. Another warrior threw a spear, followed by two more.

With five hooked spears sticking into the body of the monster, the ogres were able to drag its head closer to the ground. The burrower croaked its fury, and its paws scratched as wildly at the ground as those of its own victim, the mere-drake, minutes earlier.

"Ku ji f'han di ihagheed-araki ko!" roared an older hunter with a balding pate and pronounced belly.

Additional ogres advanced upon the burrower with long spears. Behind them followed ogres with axes and clubs.

But the burrower was not yet defeated. Suddenly, its body whipped back and forth in a frenzy. The rapid movements caught some ogres by surprise. Those clutching two of the ropes lost their grip, and a third rope was held desperately by only one ogre. An ogre approaching with a spear was whacked by the beast's tail and, despite it being only a yard long, its thickness and the speed with which it struck was enough to shatter the warrior's rib cage.

Other ogres rushed to seize the ropes. Another with one of the short spears tossed his weapon. As soon as the point of the spear penetrated, that rope was seized too.

With six ropes embedded, the ogres managed to keep the reptile more at bay. They pulled its head closer and closer to the ground, though its snapping jaws prevented anyone getting near.

The burrower continued to writhe in an attempt to free itself while other ogres moved in with long spears. Wherever they found an open spot on the sinewy body, they thrust hard.

The monster's roars became gasps. Its body grew sluggish.

A warrior with an axe came up next to its head—

The elder ogre grunted a warning, but it was too late. With a sudden twist, the burrower's head came around and bit through one leg and the torso of the axe-bearing ogre. The stricken warrior managed a brief cry of defeat before dying.

No longer interested in food, the trapped beast flung the bloody refuse away, the gory body parts pelting the attackers.

More spears were thrust into its body. The burrower let out one more croak, and the great head dropped with a thud.

Still wary after the beast's last trick, the hunters added a few more spears before they began hacking away at its limbs and tail. When their quarry did not even twitch, the elder ogre finally pointed to a pair of warriors with axes. They rushed up on each side of the creature, behind its huge head.

The leader pointed at the dead burrower's head. Raising their weapons, the pair hurled themselves at the spot where the skull met the neck. With great gusto, the ogres chopped away at scale, flesh, and bone.

Only when they had the head utterly severed did the hunters shout "Iskar'ai! Iskar'ai!"

Iskar'ai—victory —often meant merely surviving in the wilds. The huge burrower—called *hageed-araki* by the ogres and the "volewyrm" by the few outsiders who had survived the experience of witnessing one—had hunted and devoured more than half a dozen of the local citizens in the past two weeks. Using the same technique designed to capture meredrakes—the only difference being that they staked out goats or amaloks to lure the smaller predator—the ogres had triumphed.

But as the elder ogre shared in the victory celebration, a figure in glinting armor caught his attention. While the rest dove in to strip the *hageed-araki* of its meat and other useful parts—nothing was ever wasted in the wilds—their leader turned to the silent figure and raised his weapon in salute.

The figure, a human in Solamnic armor, saluted back with his dusty sword. The glint masked dents, dirt, and scratches all over the armor of the human. Yet, through all that, the symbol of the Order of the Sword shone clear.

The knight wore a full beard, the areas around the jaw thicker than the mustache, which had only begun growing in the past few months. The dark-haired Solamnian sheathed his weapon and turned to go. His time with Hogran and his people was over. They had done well for him as he had worked to understand his new path. Fortunately, his patron had made it clear to Hogran's clan from the start that he was a human who was a friend, not an enemy. Although he had not been permitted to be a part of the hunt—Hogran insisting that the kill must be made by ogres—the knight had contributed his share by suggesting the capturing of a meredrake for bait. The Solamnian had even stood by, ready to help if needed. But even with so many terrible deaths, Hogran had not signaled his participation.

Besides, the knight's patron had other designs for him, which required him to leave immediately.

As he walked, seemingly indifferent to both his harsh surroundings and the fact that he carried no supplies, no water, no map, Sir Stefan Rennert took heart in what dangled on his chest. He gently pulled free a leather cord hanging around his neck, drawing forth a medallion that was identical to one that he had received from the hands of his friends and comrades, Willum and Hector.

Received from their dead hands in the midst of a monstrous attack by undead on the ogre capital.

Stefan turned the triangular medallion around to study it. Its metal was steel; two long, arching horns in brass were etched in the center. His patron had given it to him. The first such pendant had been given to another who also needed guidance.

He did not recall anything of his journey so far south

from Garantha. The last thing that Stefan remembered was the ground erupting and the skeletal dead streaming everywhere. Somewhere along the way, he had lost track of the elf maiden, Idaria, who had been at his side. There had been a shower of stone, he thought, and more than one had hit him on his helmeted head.

After that, the Solamnian—minus his helmet—had awoken in a different region. Stumbling to his feet, he had walked directly into the path of Hogran and his tribe. The ogres had reacted most oddly for their kind; instead of attacking, they had raised their weapons in salute. Hogran had handed the human a water sack and let him take up a place beside him on the nomads' march to their seasonal encampment.

The ogres had helped Stefan recover. Already adept at some elements of their tongue, he managed to communicate with them enough to see to his needs. But at first, they didn't explain their hospitality.

The answer came to him barely a week after his arrival in their midst. Too weak to depart, but too frustrated to let his recuperation take the time it needed, Stefan tried his best to get Hogran to explain why the Solamnian appeared to be expected and thus was welcomed by the leader and his tribe. The elder ogre led him into the nearby wilderness. There, Hogran chose a place where the stars were brightest and sat down with legs folded. He indicated that Stefan should do the same.

The ogre pointed up at the constellations. Stefan turned his gaze to the one most prominent in that direction—

And a strong yet comforting voice had filled his head.

I've need of you, good warrior, the voice had said. *I've need of your arm, your head, and your good heart. I need you to stand before an enemy like none you have known . . . An enemy called capriciousness.*

It was a very odd request the voice had made, but Stefan knew whom the voice belonged to, and that any request by that speaker would have good cause. Entirely unaware of his surroundings, the Knight of the Sword had listened to the rest of the words.

And when the voice was done, Stefan had stirred to find not only was Hogran no longer beside him, but morning was nearly upon the human. More importantly, clasped in his right hand he had found the second triangular pendant, a token of the speaker, whose constellation was just vanishing in the light of dawn.

As he departed the ogres who had been his family for weeks, Stefan brought the medallion to his lips and kissed it lightly. "I'll make myself worthy of the honor, my lord," he whispered to his patron. "I swear by the Oath and the Measure—and you, great Kiri-Jolith—that I will."

And so, Stefan pushed on to where he knew he needed to be, to where once again he would find the half-breed ogre, Golgren.

But he did not head toward Garantha.

❧❧❧

Generation upon generation, the war machine of the ogre race had been the same: a vast horde of individual fighters relying on their brutal strength to overwhelm opponents in chaotic struggle. There was no skilled combat, no finesse with arms. Clubs, swords, and spears had been wielded with basic skills and fury. Sometimes, the swarm of ogres had brought great victory; other times, it had brought ignominious defeat.

But the age of Golgren, as some of his followers thought of it already, had begun to change all that.

The one hundred ogre warriors practicing their sword thrusts were part of the new ogre army. They wore the shining breastplates and metal-tipped kilts that were standard among all those who served the Grand Khan. Helmets had been temporarily set to the side for better hearing of the commands barked by their trainer. The swords were heavy and among most humans would have required powerful strength to hold with one hand, much less wield. The swords were well–honed, new, and of ogre make.

The warriors moved with an organized flair stunning even to those who had followed the initial transformation of Golgren's forces. The swords thrust simultaneously, and as one shifted to counter an imaginary attack.

"Feint! Thrust! Retreat! Thrust!" roared their instructor, who was not an ogre. Indeed, he was possibly the last creature one might have expected to be willingly training ogre forces.

The minotaur was nearly as broad in his chest and girth as his students. Although he was more than a foot shorter, any who watched him move agilely could not doubt that—one against one, or even two against one—the outcome of any fight would leave the minotaur the victor and his opponents dead at his feet.

The minotaur wore the armor of the imperial legions, a marred black horse on its hind legs still visible on the breastplate. His armor was polished, but clearly more well worn than that of his charges.

Dark brown of fur, the minotaur had obviously seen much action. There were scars on his arms and shoulders, and even a wicked mark across the right side of his muzzle. Part of one nostril had been severed during the making of that scar. The smallest finger on his left hand had also been lost.

But most arresting about the ogres' instructor was his singular lack of *horns*. It was not that he had not been born with any, but that those horns had, at some recent point in time, been expertly *shorn* just above the skull.

There were a handful of others like him, scattered around various parts of Golthuu. They were renegades with no life left for them in the empire. Some had served the previous emperor, Hotak, with too much fervor for his successor to accept their existence. With nowhere else to go, they had turned to the one livelihood left to their dishonored selves, while at the same time garnering a chance for vengeance against the new Uruv Suurt emperor.

And while the minotaur continued to teach and admonish, the grounds surrounding him and his students—grounds situated just to the north of Garantha—shook with activity. Hundreds more ogres were practicing, marching, and working. The latest hand took shape. Three mastarks under the guide of handlers also went through paces, learning signals that would enable them to be much more of a threat to the enemy than to their own force, as had often been the unfortunate case in the past. The handlers, seated atop the shoulders of the beasts, prodded the tusked giants left, right, forward, and even hesitantly backward.

Meredrakes went through training too, although with the huge lizards there was less that could be absorbed. Trainers used whips to teach the reptiles never to turn on them or those nearby. Meredrakes were always urged forward. To emphasize the practice, haunches of old amalok meat were hung before them; the meredrakes were only rewarded after they had learned that heading in any direction but forward was forbidden.

Another surprising activity was taking place on the training ground. For the first time, Golgren's people were producing quality weapons in mass quantity. Every sword was a replica of minotaur make, but the work was being accomplished by their own kind. A vast, round forge had been set up for the task in a mud-block structure with open slits near the curved ceiling. Burly smiths worked with molten iron brought as ore from distant mines, where slaves and ogre prisoners worked under whips both day and night. Wagons arrived each hour at the forge. Those not filled with ore carried more coal and other fuel needed to maintain the blistering heat.

The smiths wore cloths over their noses and mouths, but otherwise had no protection from the heat or the searing metal. As the newly arrived Khleeg peered inside, he saw ogres with all sorts of burns covering them. Many had patches of hair missing. Smoke rose everywhere, and the stench of sulfur was so great that the officer's eyes immediately teared and burned.

Hands protected by covers of thick meredrake skin carried orange-hot ladles of molten metal to the molds. The original molds had been stolen from the Uruv Suurt for just that purpose, stolen because even the late Emperor Hotak had not trusted his allies enough to do more than provide them with finished weapons. Of course, there were always those of any race willing to profit by theft, and so for Golgren, gaining what he needed to start the facility had not been difficult.

Khleeg surveyed the many molds, trying to make a count. Twenty were still serviceable, but two more had cracked, rendering them worthless. In another area, ogres were attempting to duplicate the consistency of the Uruv Suurt's molds, but with varying success. Still, the molds that were usable temporarily gave the Grand Khan's swelling forces what they needed.

Khleeg stepped back past workers freeing those blades cooled enough to finish upon the anvil. The clang of metal against metal was deafening, and more than a few who had labored in the forge for a few years were deaf to all but the loudest sounds.

The officer finally located the overseer. He seized the other brute by the arm and roared, "How many? Enough?"

The scarred and burned overseer—one eye had been seared shut months past after a chance encounter with a falling piece of burning metal—peered dumbly at Khleeg. Khleeg thought that the worker did not understand his Common speech, but the other ogre turned one fat ear toward him.

"Enough?" the Blödian roared at the top of his lungs. His question ended in a choking cough due to the sulfur.

The overseer waited until he had recovered before nodding vehemently. "All!" he roared back. "All!"

Stifling another cough, Khleeg finally abandoned the building. Outside, as he inhaled the relatively cleaner air, the ogre looked up at the top of the facility. Smoke did rise steadily from the vents, but not nearly as much as was needed.

A score of riders awaited his return, Golgren at the forefront. With one last cough, Khleeg reported, "All ready!"

The Grand Khan dismounted, his guards following suit. Two in the rear ushered forth a prisoner: an Uruv Suurt legionary minus his armor. The horned warrior scowled despite his dire situation.

Khleeg led his lord and the others to where several ogres were stacking new weapons in what seemed at first to be oddly arranged piles. Only as they drew closer did a pattern become visible. The stacks formed a sunburst, an homage to Sirrion, whose fire had allowed them to be cast.

A space ten feet by ten feet filled the center of the pattern. Into the area stepped Golgren. He removed all but his kilt and his sandals, handing his possessions to Khleeg for safekeeping.

The legionary was shoved into the empty space with the Grand Khan.

Khleeg stepped up. "Uruv Suurt . . . would you like freedom?"

The prisoner snorted. "I am to believe that?"

Golgren's second in command gave a warning grunt. "If the Grand Khan promises freedom, the promise is *kept*. But to win it, you must fight him . . . and slay him."

The horned soldier eyed Golgren up and down, especially the missing hand. He bared his teeth in the minotaur equivalent of a grin. "Give me but a sword!"

In response, one of the guards handed him a weapon. The legionary studied it, testing its weight. He glanced at Golgren in surprise. "It is my very weapon."

"To be fair in all ways." Golgren remarked quietly. The Grand Khan turned. However, rather than receive a blade from one of his followers, he picked out one of the newly crafted swords.

As the Grand Khan turned back to him, the captive legionary went into a battle stance. Golgren waited a breath, and nodded to the minotaur.

The two lunged at one another.

Their blades clanged sharply as they met. The legionary bared his teeth, eager for the kill. The minotaur had no doubt slain more than one ogre in the past and certainly thought that he could handle the slighter, maimed Golgren.

The legionary's blade came under Golgren's slash. Suddenly the ogre shoved the oncoming sword down with his own. The horned soldier quickly brought his weapon around in an arc, yet once again the Grand Khan's was there to block it.

Khleeg and the rest of the ogres remained oddly silent. Other warriors gathered. They watched expectantly.

The pair traded several blows. The minotaur's eyes were red with effort and fury, his nostrils constantly flaring. He had finally realized his adversary was far more skilled than most ogres.

Golgren nodded, as if he understood and pitied the minotaur's revelation. He bared his teeth, and suddenly thrust under the legionary's attack, driving his blade halfway into the other's chest without striking the ribs.

The legionary let out a choking sound. Blood erupted from his mouth. He dropped his sword and, as Golgren withdrew his own, crumpled to the ground dead.

Those surrounding the two let out low, victorious grunts. Golgren silenced them with a dark glance and stretched forth the bloody sword as far as he could. The Grand Khan held the red tip over one stack of blades.

Golgren spoke in both Common *and* Ogre. *"Tuzun i kalys i'fhani!* The weapon is the death of the enemy! *Tuzun i f'han ikalysi!* The weapon is the enemy of death!"

A drop of blood fell from the sword to the stack of new blades, staining the top of the pile. As the drop touched, Golgren let out a triumphant grunt and shouted, *"Mergos i dura tuzun holoc!* Blood has been tasted by the weapon, and it hungers for more!" He moved the red blade over the next stack. *"Holoc di sirri!* Hungers like fire ever!" Another drop fell, staining the second stack. The blade went to the third. *"Du otuzun i barikis!* Let those weapons feed!"

The Grand Khan let a drop fall on each stack. When he was done, he set the blade, still soaked, atop the body of the legionary and stepped away from the center.

Two warriors turned the corpse on its back, making certain that the blade remained on top of the body, and carried the Uruv Suurt to the building where the forge ever burned.

Golgren signaled other warriors to gather up the stacks of blades. They did so eagerly.

"The swords are blessed," Golgren explained to Khleeg. "They will find their targets well." The Grand Khan changed the subject. "The hand will be ready in three days, yes?"

"Yes, my lord. They will march well and as you command."

Golgren started to nod, but Wargroch came riding up. The younger officer wore a troubled expression.

With a nimble leap for one of his girth, the Blödian dismounted and made his way to his ruler. As was his way, Wargroch dropped down on one knee.

"Speak," Golgren quietly commanded.

"Great one!" Wargroch visibly steeled himself should he be punished for the bad news that he was bringing. "No birds bring message from the hand of Vorag. Cragur sends word that he cannot find the warriors."

Another hand was missing.

"Khleeg," Golgren began slowly, his eyes narrowed slightly, but his expression otherwise emotionless. "The hand must march tomorrow."

His second in command was too wise to argue. "My lord."

Golgren eyed the weapons being handed out to the warriors around them. "And I will lead them."

All that Khleeg did was nod.

V

WARLORD

The guards no longer actively watched Idaria. Indeed, in many respects, they treated her almost as though she were Golgren's *queen*. The elf maiden made good use of their lax attitudes toward her. All Idaria's arduous work, her suffering, seemed to have finally paid off. She could pursue her true task.

She had given up her hard-fought freedom and cast herself into slavery. Idaria had done so in the hopes that she might somehow bring the freedom she had sacrificed to those of her people who had been enslaved by the ogres. With the help of other agents, she had maneuvered herself into the position of the Grand Lord's favorite slave. It had meant dishonors that many others would have been unable to suffer and survive, but Idaria had managed to bury a part of herself deep inside, so that there was always something those shames could never reach and poison.

But she was also confident in those with whom she had made her bargain. True, they were not elves, but it behooved them to follow through on their promises. For by aiding her, they aided their own cause.

The slave moved effortlessly through Golgren's chambers,

the heavy bracelets on her wrists and ankles hindering her little. She, who knew him best, had not been entirely startled when Golgren had refused to have the links reforged. She believed his promise that he would free her people and was certain that he still would do so . . . when it served him best.

The silver-haired elf went to a window near the bed and softly sang. Yet it was no human or elf song that escaped her perfect lips, but rather the trill of a *bird*.

Mere seconds later, a small, feathered form alighted on the sill. The bird sang a few notes of the same song. It was one of her messengers, her avian friends through whom she made regular contact beyond Garantha. With Golgren away, it was the perfect time to send one of her missives.

"Thank you for taking it," she murmured to the bird as she placed a tiny note in a small container around the creature's leg. What the avians did for her was done at great risk to themselves, and she very much appreciated their bravery. Idaria had always prided herself on her rapport with birds, hints that she was perhaps favored by Astarin—or, as humans called him, Branchala—the god of song and life, and thus also the god of the woods and the songbirds who thrived in forests.

With loving care, Idaria gently raised her messenger back to the window. Setting it there, she sang a short note to bid it farewell.

The bird flew up into the sky.

A much larger, leathery, winged form suddenly burst from its hiding place atop a nearby tower. It dropped heavily upon the bird. Before Idaria's messenger could even squawk, the gargoyle had caught it and crushed it in its grip. The creature quickly spiraled back to its hiding place.

A horrified Idaria stumbled back, in part because of the death of her pet and also because that particular gargoyle was one that she had seen before.

"You're a dangerous little fish, you know that?" growled Tyranos.

She spun on the wizard, striking him across the face. Or at least she attempted to do so. The tall human snagged her wrist and held it tight.

"Why did you do that? How could you let that beast of yours kill—"

"To save us both some trouble, elf! Your friends have learned enough. Let Neraka stumble in on its own."

Idaria stiffened. "I have no tie to the dark knights! They are enemies to elves. Or have you forgotten Mina and her army?"

"Oh, I've not forgotten that fiery little madwoman. But we're long past that time, *Oakborn,* and into another far more complex era when enemies are allies, allies are enemies, and those who should have no common cause with anyone stick their tridents into the mix just to make things more interesting and frustrating!"

She pulled free, but only because he allowed her to. "And where do you fit into everything, wizard? Who—or perhaps *what*—are you really?"

His eyes narrowed appreciatively. "You are wily. I'll leave it to you to guess the answers to those questions. But let us speak of other things." As she opened her mouth to protest angrily, he added, "The bird would've died a lot harsher death if it'd made its destination, elf! Your Nerakan friends are on the move, and apparently they don't want you to know just what they've got planned. I can only hazard a guess that, for some *odd* reason, they think you might be sympathetic to the Grand Khan! I can't imagine why."

"You lie! How do you know such things?"

"Choose what you wish to believe. That is my warning to you—take it or leave it."

Idaria's eyes flashed. "Why are you really in the palace, wizard? What do you want from me?"

He laughed loudly, ever unafraid that the guards beyond would hear him. Magic cloaked his activities. "I want nothing from you, my *dear* Idaria. I want something from your loving master. If I read matters correctly, our good Golgren is about to embark on a hunt. I need you to thus relieve him of something I was foolish enough to have you give to him. You remember what I am talking about, don't you?"

"The signet."

"Clever elf!" Tyranos's leonine face broke into another grin. "And mark me, he's better off without it! In fact, keeping it is going to greatly raise the chances of him getting killed, just when we both need him the most!"

The slave eyed him closely. "You speak in too many riddles. And why do you not simply take it yourself? Golgren is no wizard."

He looked disgruntled. "I've tried, damn it. But the signet seems to like him . . . warm to him. Or at least it wants to stick around the half-breed for some reason."

"You are making no sense."

"I know. It does not make sense." The wizard turned to glare at Golgren's bed. "That's why I need your help. You can get physically closer. Maybe it won't put up a fight."

The slave stepped closer, her beautiful face a cold mask. "You forget something. Why should I believe you enough to risk being discovered stealing the signet? We have never been allies, much less friends, Tyranos."

"I told you, that signet's likely to get him killed. Isn't that enough for you?"

"Why don't you go to him and simply explain that?"

His eyes narrowed. "Do you honestly think he'd listen to me and give it back? After how it saved him during the quake?"

"And it saves him from the Titans too, as you might also recall." Idaria shook her head, sending her long tresses flying back and forth. "You will have to find another way to get it from him."

The tall human snorted. "Bah!" He raised his staff and paused. Stretching forth one clenched fist, he muttered, "I was going to give you this when you agreed to help me, but I've no use for it, anyway. So take it."

Tyranos opened his hand and revealed the songbird that Idaria had seen destroyed. It fluttered out of his hand to her.

"But I saw Chasm crush him!" she blurted out, speaking the name of the wizard's pet gargoyle.

The robed figure chuckled. "Elf, you of all people should understand that appearances are often merely illusions." He started to fade into shadow. "Just like the faint hope that your Grand Khan will still free your kind . . ."

"What—" But Idaria got no further before Tyranos vanished.

She examined the bird, looking for the message she had tried to send. Its leg was bare. Idaria started to write another message, but hesitated. After a moment, the slave brought the bird over to the window. She paused again, and murmuring sweet encouragement to the avian, set it free.

The bird soared up into the sky.

Chasm's head suddenly thrust out of his hiding place. The burly gargoyle—his muzzle thicker and more squat than those of the ones spying on Golgren—peered closely at the bird. The winged beast tensed before, with a brief glance at Idaria, settling back into his hiding place behind the stonework.

He had let the bird go because the small winged creature had not been carrying any note. Tyranos wanted no further contact between her and her conspirators. Whatever she chose to do in the future was to be her decision alone.

The elf looked over her shoulder at the bed.

⋟⋖✦⋗⋞

They had been out of communication for the past few days, but Vorag was not concerned. The Grand Khan had instituted the use of messenger birds with all his hands, but Vorag's birdcage had accidentally slipped from its secured place atop the lead mastark, and he no longer had any birds to command. However, the ogre commander expected they would be in contact with another hand before long, and they could send word to Garantha.

The terrain turned hillier in that part of southern Golthuu—the former province of Blöde—slowing the hand's advance. Soon enough they would meet up with the other force. Vorag had fresh supplies for them. With the Uruv Suurt constantly testing the borders, and the ogres doing the same, keeping warriors strong and rested in the field was a priority.

The ogre squinted as two riders came into sight—the scouts he had sent ahead almost a day ago. Another of the Grand Khan's new rules.

Saluting his commander, the first scout hesitated As best he could, he growled in Common, "Hand ahead!"

Vorag frowned. The ones they were meeting were supposed to be some days ahead, still. He started to reply, but the blare of a horn suddenly echoed from beyond the hills. The notes were exactly those he had expected to hear upon reaching the other hand.

The commander shrugged. The sooner the better. "Horn!" he shouted to his own trumpeter. The other ogre raised a goat horn and blew the replying notes. From the hills ahead came another series of notes.

Vorag urged his warriors on. Several moments passed, but at last the outriders of the other hand revealed themselves. A number rode under the banner of the Grand Khan to meet Vorag's band.

A young, tall warrior led the riders. Vorag recognized him as one of the five officers who served below Zhulom, a commander of one of the hand's fingers..

"Atolgus," Vorag rumbled, greeting the newcomer by name. "Zhulom near?"

"You will see him soon," Atolgus replied, his command of Common better than Vorag had expected. Golgren had encouraged his officers to use their extra time out in the field and learn Common. It kept the minds of the warriors active when there was nothing else with which to concern themselves.

Atolgus turned his mount around and, with the rest of his comrades, began guiding Vorag's force through the hills. The passage quickly grew narrow, but they slowly wended their way along. Atolgus set his pace to ride next to the commander.

"You bring all the supplies?" he asked Vorag.

"All."

Atolgus nodded, straightened, and looked over his shoulder at the force. Vorag responded with a questioning grunt.

"*Gar ihg,*" Atolgus said to Vorag's trumpeter. Without waiting for his commander to acknowledge Atolgus's order, the trumpeter raised his horn and repeated the signal he had been given earlier to identify Vorag's forces.

"Stop!" Vorag growled. "My command—"

Atolgus abruptly struck him along the jaw, sending Vorag tumbling from his mount.

Even as the trumpeter's call faded, another consisting of three rapid staccato bursts sounded from the hills to the column's right. No sooner had it begun, than ogres began pouring toward them from that direction.

And ranks of the Uruv Suurt flowed down from the opposite side.

Snarling, Vorag drew his shining new sword. In his excitement, he had forgotten the Common word for ambush and instead repeated, "*Bakiin! Bakiin!*"

As the ogre commander registered the scene around him, he realized that not only was his column under assault from the hills, but that it was also fighting among itself.

One of his officers had unsheathed his blade and run through another. The lead mastark handler—the very same handler from whose beast the cage with the messenger birds had slipped—urged his mount into a knot of screaming warriors. The round, flat feet of the huge tusked creature crushed a pair moving too slowly. At the same time, the huge prehensile nose seized another warrior and threw him into the rocky hillside.

The trumpeter drew his axe and tried to ride down his commander. Vorag ducked the blow and ran the edge of his blade along the rider's leg. The other ogre growled as blood poured from the long, tapering wound. He hesitated. That was all Vorag needed to finish the betrayer with a quick thrust.

Vorag tried to seize the reins of the ogre's horse, but the horse bolted. In the animal's wake, another foe pressed him. The Uruv Suurt was shorter, but skilled and wily. He traded blows with the commander, pressing Vorag back.

But the ogre, having been trained in part by one of the renegades working for the Grand Khan, anticipated many of his moves. Every time the legionary mounted an attack, the ogre countered.

His blade opened a river in the Uruv Suurt's throat. The legionary looked astounded—perhaps recognizing the training of his foe—before collapsing.

Another horn sounded. Vorag peered behind and saw a large band of riders racing toward him from the rear of his own force. A relieved grin spread across his ugly features. The traitors and their horned allies were in for a beating shellacking.

"Regroup!" Vorag roared at the top of his lungs. Several warriors loyal to him moved to obey. They gathered near the commander, awaiting the reinforcements.

The riders plowed into them, axes and swords slaughtering most of those joining Vorag.

The commander gaped in disbelief and spotted the treacherous Atolgus venturing near again. Vorag lunged at the traitor. Atolgus suddenly veered his horse around, forcing Golgren's officer to stumble back as the horse snapped and kicked at him.

As Vorag backed up, a sharp pain struck his spine. His fingers lost all sense of touch, and his weapon dropped. He felt a hot moistness cover his back.

The commander fell on his face, already dead before he hit the hard ground.

One of Vorag's own warriors grinned fiercely as he raised his bloody axe in salute to Atolgus. *"Ki e f'han firi iZhulomi!"*

"Common we speak," Atolgus corrected. "Like all good ogres." The former chieftain shrugged, "But yes, He joins Zhulom in death."

The other ogre's grin widened, and he raced off to assist his comrades. Around them, the last of Vorag's loyal followers lay either dead or dying. There was no goodwill for prisoners. Roughly half of the hand had been slaughtered quickly.

The plumed and cloaked general of the Uruv Suurt came riding up. He saluted Atolgus with his weapon, his teeth bared in the grin of his race.

"All executed as planned! I commend you, warlord!"

Atolgus grunted both in acknowledgment of the success and the title the minotaur had used. "The Uruv Suurt did their part well. Our numbers swell."

"And those of the mongrel dwindle. My emperor will be pleased. I'll send word to him." The general said, saluting. "We shall speak later."

The young warlord nodded.

The Uruv Suurt signaled his legionaries, who quickly fell into ranks and followed their commander off.

Atolgus looked to one of his own followers. "All the dead must be stripped. The bodies are to be dragged to the caves east."

The other ogre grunted, "All will be done, warlord."

As the warrior departed, Atolgus looked around the area for anything amiss. When he was satisfied that his followers had all in hand, the young warlord urged his mount away. A few of his guards attempted to follow, but a look from Atolgus made them pull up on the reins. The great warlord was riding away to commune with the spirit warriors who guided him. It was forbidden to be anywhere near him at such times The punishment was death.

Atolgus rode between two hills, and over a low ridge. He squinted as dust rose from a sudden wind. Rather than turn from that wind, the warlord forced his animal to race into it.

Pulling up near an arching formation resembling a vulture's beak, Atolgus found a smaller outcropping to which he could bind his horse's reins, and left the creature to climb over the rocky soil beneath the beak.

In the shadows just beyond the outcropping, the warlord suddenly drew his sword and planted the point in the ground. He went down on one knee, his hands still gripping the sword's hilt.

"You have done exceedingly well, darling Atolgus."

Atolgus looked up with a gaze akin to an adoring child or pup. He remained kneeling, although clearly he would have preferred to leap to his feet and rush to the beauteous goddess appearing before him.

Morgada smiled. Even her sharp, menacing teeth did nothing to lessen Atolgus's adoration. "You have pleased him, and so you please me."

She reached out and touched the ogre warrior on the forehead with one finger. There was a brief flash of blue energy.

Atolgus grunted. Morgada let her hand slide to his chin. She turned his head so that he was looking straight at her.

"He should be rewarded," the Titaness murmured in the tongue of her kind.

"Would you like to play with him for awhile? Is that it, Morgada?" came Safrag's voice. "Perhaps . . . When he's done."

She stepped back. Atolgus's gaze continued to remain on her, and it was clear that he loved and worshipped her. The female Titan had placed him under a spell.

"He's proven a good student thus far, master," Morgada replied. "Easily swayed into slaying his mate and betraying his clan, taking up arms against his commander, and those other comrades . . . A very good student, indeed."

The Titan leader stepped up to Atolgus. "Yes," he said, the talons on his hand coming within an inch of the former chieftain's unflinching countenance. "A good student. Weak enough to be malleable, but with the potential to become a finely crafted weapon. Certainly clever enough to make fools of the Uruv Suurt, who think they make him their puppet."

Safrag gestured. With his eyes still on Morgada, Atolgus rose.

"False trails, false friends, false glories," Safrag continued. "All for the benefit of a false ruler. The mongrel thinks that he controls the hunt, that he pursues traitors and the trail of the Fire Rose as he sees fit. All the while his false empire is eaten away on all sides." The lead Titan smiled like a cat. "Ah, if only Dauroth could have been seen it!"

Morgada draped an arm over his shoulder. "But he surely looks with pride on what you've achieved, master. And surely his blessing is upon us and upon the hunt for the artifact."

The lead Titan smiled. He held forth his hand, and in it appeared a tiny vial.

Atolgus's gaze at last turned from Morgada. He eyed the vial with avarice.

"One drop, one word," Safrag sang. "One promise . . ."

With two nails, he removed the stopper. There was an almost living sigh, and a small tendril of wispy smoke emerged.

The warlord leaned his head back. Safrag drew a three-sided pattern over Atolgus: a gaunt triangle with the sun on one side and stars on the other two. The pattern flared to life as he completed the spell, and it descended. As it reached Atolgus's forehead, the pattern shrank, growing small enough to fit there.

There was a slight searing sound, as if the ogre's flesh were burning. Safrag tipped the vial over just enough to let one drop of its crimson contents fall down.

As the drop struck the center of the pattern, the latter shone bright before fading away.

"So precious," Morgada whispered, referring to the vial's contents.

"For the glory of the Titan cause, the sacrifice is necessary. A drop of elixir here, a drop there, to ensure that our warlord is the able champion we desire. The spell enhances the qualities that will draw others to his cause."

"But how will that help us to find the Fire Rose?"

Safrag replaced the vial. "Because when the half-breed finds the walls of his citadel crumbling all around him, he will have no recourse but to seek that which we seek, and to find it fast." The lead Titan shrugged. "But do not fear! Golgren will not survive the finding of the Fire Rose."

He gestured for Atolgus to rise. The puppet warlord silently obeyed. There were subtle changes from the Atolgus of before. He looked slightly taller and broader, and what scars he had received from the battle were all but faded. There was also a slight, golden tint to his eyes.

"Go, my champion! Let the blood of the mongrel's followers quench the dry lands."

Atolgus saluted Safrag and Morgada with his weapon and rushed to his mount. The two Titans watched with satisfaction as he rode away.

"An interesting choice, my master," Morgada cooed.

"Not nearly as interesting as the *ji-baraki* among the Grand Khan's own trusted circle. It shall be a pleasure to see how that piece plays in the game. Very much a pleasure, indeed."

Safrag gestured. Black flames enveloped the pair.

The Titans vanished.

VI

ABOMINATION

Golgren's departure was delayed by news that was dire but hardly unexpected. Neraka had begun pushing across the border in northern Golthuu. The dark knights had moved in earnest and had easily overwhelmed the lone hand there. The force the Grand Khan intended to lead to the Vale of Vipers had originally been set to strengthen the warriors located by the overrun border.

Coincidence is the blind's defiance of truth, Sarth had once intoned to a much younger Golgren, albeit in a more crude, ogre fashion. That was before an older Grand Lord had discovered the shaman knew the Common tongue better than him.

Golgren did not believe in coincidence. The Black Shells would not happen to push into northern Golthuu at the same time as rumors placed the Uruv Suurt in the south, *and* while elements of his new army were suddenly disappearing. Indeed, for Neraka to intrude upon the former Kern meant someone had gone out of their way to devise that strategy. Old Blöde was a much easier target, lying just south of the black knights' base of operations.

The Grand Khan had no choice but to follow the trail leading to the Vale of Vipers. But his realm could not be left to fend for itself. Golthuu was at a fragile juncture. If Golgren did not maintain a show of strength and keep the borders secure, his domain would quickly return to two splintered lands, scraps of which loose alliances would fight over while the other races moved in to take what spoils they desired.

Armored and ready to march, he summoned Khleeg and Wargroch.

"Khleeg, you were supposed to guard Garantha. That is no longer necessary."

Golgren's second in command looked concerned. "My lord?"

"Neraka must be challenged. Take the new hand to join with Khemu's hand. Khemu and you and your hand will march to the settlement of Angthuul. Another hand will meet you there. That will give you three hands. You know Angthuul?"

"Aye, my lord. A day south of Styx. I have been to it." Khleeg frowned. "And Garantha?"

As ranks of ogres marched past in preparation for their imminent departure, the Grand Khan put his hand on Wargroch's shoulder. "The brother of Nagroch and Belgroch must bear the responsibility of watching Garantha. But I will always be near."

The proclamation caught the other by surprise, not only because of the responsibility being placed on the younger officer's shoulders, but because Golgren had said that somehow he would be close by to assist him. Khleeg nodded his acceptance, but asked, "The Grand Khan will need more messenger birds?"

In reply, Golgren drew from a pouch a tiny, round crystal that was light silver in color. He handed it to Wargroch, who handled it gingerly, for he and Khleeg both understood it possessed magic.

Even as the pair studied the mysterious bauble, the Grand Khan removed a second crystal from the pouch. "And Khleeg will also have the voice of Golgren to guide him."

"My lord . . ." the senior warrior responded. As he turned his crystal over to inspect it, he asked, "Great one . . . They are Titan magic?"

Wargroch looked pained, as though the crystal in his palm had suddenly turned into a festering wound.

Golgren eased their concerns. "No, the magic owes nothing to the Titans."

Indeed, he had only an hour past twisted them out of the hands of Tyranos. *A wizard as wily as the leonine one surely knows how to arrange some manner of communication for Golgren to keep in close touch with his most trusted warriors.* That was how the Grand Khan had phrased the suggestion to the human, appealing both to Tyranos's pride and the wizard's own stake in the ogre's success.

Tyranos had protested, slamming the end of his staff into the marble floor of Golgren's bed chamber. Yet in the end, the human provided had him with the three crystals—one each for Golgren, Wargroch, and Khleeg.

Hold the stone before your left eye and picture which of them you wish to speak with, the spellcaster had instructed. When Golgren had wondered at such simplistic instructions, Tyranos had shrugged and, in typical manner, asked the ogre if he *wanted* them to be made more complex and confusing.

The Grand Khan did not speak of Tyranos to either warrior, but he did repeat the instructions. Wargroch nodded, while Khleeg peered at the stone as if still wary that it would turn into something nasty.

Finally seeming to accept the necessity of the communication stone, Khleeg growled, "My lord, you must not ride alone—"

"I will ride with you as far as Ben-ihm, there to lead the hand of Barech to the Vale."

His second in command grunted in satisfaction. "Barech is very loyal. Good."

Wargroch was suddenly disconcerted. "Grand Khan!

Let Barech guard Garantha! Let Wargroch ride with you to the Vale!"

"Your Grand Khan has chosen you, and you will guard my Garantha. Yes, Wargroch?"

"Yes, Grand Khan!"

A mastark trumpeted. Golgren looked past the pair. The first ranks of warriors were nearly at the main gates of the city.

"Come!" he commanded.

A crowd had gathered near where the new hand had formed for inspection. Barking cheers rose as the Grand Khan rode up. Golgren waved to all of them, looking every bit the confident conqueror. As he neared the gates, he looked up at the carved head of a huge griffon that had only recently been installed as a symbol of the city's patron spirit. Its high, fierce head could be seen from a great distance away and also made for the proper backdrop to the ceremony about to take place.

A roar that sounded as if an eagle had swallowed a snarling cat cut through the cheers. Chained on a five-sided, wooden platform was the very creature for whom Garantha had been named. The griffon was a male, a powerful beast almost as large as a meredrake. Its torso was akin to one of the great cats: long, lean, obviously swift. However, instead of a sinewy, whip of a tail, the griffon had the plumage of a magnificent bird. The golden brown beast also had taloned feet as opposed to clawed paws. Already it had done its best to shred the platform.

The griffon had an avian head—a fearsome raptor's profile, a sharp, hooked beak—but its eyes also had a feline cast that gave it a wise and perhaps distrustful look. The beast roared again, its unique cry silencing many in the crowd.

It flapped its mighty wings, but rose no more than an inch off the platform. Its wings had been clipped, an arduous ordeal for one of its kind. The male was a recent capture, and one that had originally been intended to dwell in a temple situated near the center of the capital, the *Garan i Seraith*—The Nest of the Griffon. But Golgren needed the creature in order that all should understand the situation.

The chain that held the griffon by the throat was twice as thick as the ones generally used. Golgren had ordered that security measure after the disaster at the Nest, when his enemies had sabotaged those keeping the two in the temple at bay.

At his nod, a trumpeter at the opposite end from the griffon blew the call announcing Golgren's readiness. Flanked by Khleeg, Wargroch, and his guards, the Grand Khan stepped before the front of the platform and faced the throng.

He drew his sword. Khleeg and Wargroch imitated him. *"Iskar'ai!"* Golgren shouted. "Victory!" he repeated in Common.

There were scattered cries of both words from the crowd and the warriors of the new hand. The ogre term faded as more and more picked up the second, Common version. All were aware of the decree that Common be the tongue to speak, and all wanted to prove they were eager followers of their ruler's commands.

As one, Golgren and his two officers turned to face the griffon. The winged behemoth lunged at them, but the chain did not permit it to come anywhere near them—at least as yet. Undaunted by its savage beak or huge, slashing talons, the trio stepped up onto the platform.

As they did, Khleeg and Wargroch moved away from Golgren, flanking him from behind. They held their swords at the ready, but did not advance toward the griffon.

Holding his blade before him, the Grand Khan confidently approached the angry beast snapping its beak. Just out of striking reach, Golgren saluted the great creature.

"Let the spirit of the winged hunter fly ever above the warriors of Golthuu," he intoned loudly. "Let them strike with its swiftness, cut with the sharpness of its talons, and rip out the hearts of the enemy with the power of its bite!"

The griffon roared.

Golgren lunged. The beast's talons tore at the air just above his head, and its beak scored the shoulder of his maimed arm. The ogre leader aimed for the creature's chest, which was covered in both feathers and fur.

His blade made a nick there. A thin stream of blood dribbled out.

Golgren withdrew. He studied the tip of his weapon, which was all but clean.

The Grand Khan stared at the furious, squawking beast. He observed the grabbing talons and judged the distance between him and its snapping beak.

And again, he lunged.

One talon cut across his cheek, but Golgren avoided having his entire face torn off by rolling underneath the attack. The griffon twisted. The chain not only slowed its movements however, but made the creature stumble.

Golgren's blade came up. Its tip cut more deeply into the beast's chest. Golgren could have shoved the sword in deep, but instead he quickly withdrew the blade and threw himself to the side.

The griffon pursued, but before it could reach its tiny assailant, the Grand Khan had moved beyond the chain's length.

The crowd and the assembled warriors cheered.

Golgren raised his sword for all to see. Its top was red, and a thin streak of blood ran down to the hilt.

"The spirit of Garantha gives victory to its people!" he shouted.

Khleeg and Wargroch came to their lord's side. The two officers raised their swords so that the tips of their weapons touched Golgren's. Streaks of blood spread to their swords.

In the background, the griffon roared and roared. Its wound was a superficial one, exactly as intended. Had Golgren killed the creature during the ceremony, it would have meant that the spirits would forecast misfortune for any battle to come. On the other hand, had the griffon maimed or slain him by some chance, it would have meant that the patron spirits had decided a new ruler was needed for the sake of the ogre race.

Instead, by proving his courage, cunning, and skill, the Grand Khan had shown that those spirits still proclaimed him true master of his people and victor against all foes.

Golgren let his two officers share a bit more blood from his sword. By doing so, he symbolically extended the griffon's protection to those he most trusted. The warriors who followed Khleeg would see him as an extension of the Grand Khan, just as those under Wargroch's authority in Garantha would understand that he spoke with the voice, the wisdom, of their leader.

The horn sounded again. Golgren brandished his sword toward the warriors, and the onlookers. Finally, without cleaning his weapon, he sheathed it and returned to his steed.

As he and the pair mounted, the assembled ogres continued their barking cheers. The griffon's handlers moved in to calm and control the wounded winged hunter.

Golgren beat his fist on his breastplate. Wargroch and Khleeg returned the salute. The younger officer started to separate himself from the other two, but Khleeg chose that moment to whisper, "My lord, but how will Wargroch handle the Titans?"

Wargroch did not look pleased with the clear questioning of his abilities. Golgren stilled Wargroch with a dark look and answered, "The Titans will do nothing but obey me."

He said it with such certainty they had no trouble believing him, although it was obvious they were curious as to the reasons for his confidence. Golgren did not elaborate, however.

The younger officer saluted. "Grand Khan, my life is yours."

"Yes." Golgren dismissed Wargroch. The younger ogre rode

to where the city guard awaited. As Wargroch neared, they snapped to attention as if he were Golgren himself.

The Grand Khan looked to Khleeg. "Give the signal to depart."

Khleeg gestured to the trumpeter, who sounded the march. The hand methodically turned in the direction of Ben-ihm, some two days north. Golgren and his second took up the lead.

A blinding glint of light from the direction of the city caused Golgren to glance back. The sun did not lie that way, but with so many armored warriors on the high walls, or standing among the rest of the populace, he assumed it was some kind of momentary reflection.

But it was not the sun that glinted off of the new, shining breastplates of his proud warriors.

It was a faceless, golden figure, his bright, unsettling form reflected strong in hundreds of pieces of armor. Yet when Golgren sought out the source, he could not find the true watcher anywhere in the skies above.

And when Golgren glanced back at the hundreds of breastplates, he was not at all surprised to find that the reflections of the faceless figure had vanished there, as well.

⚬⚬⟨⚭⟩⚬⚬

Wargroch reentered the palace with a swagger that made it appear as if he, not Golgren, ruled. He grinned at the guards, who banged their fists on their chests in acknowledgment of his supremacy.

But the ogre had little true interest in the guards at the moment. Another, more delightful distraction stood hidden by the doors to the Grand Khan's chambers. Since his arrival in Garantha, the Blödian had secretly become enchanted with Idaria. It had started simply enough: her exotic looks and the fact that she was Golgren's favored had attracted his attention. Wargroch had considered her unapproachable until circumstances had worked to separate her from her master. The sudden rush of knowing that he was master of the capital—however temporary—proved too much for his buried lusts. Wargroch thought that the exotic elf slave might prove susceptible to the one who, for all practical purposes, acted as the Grand Khan.

The guards at the door saluted him and did not argue when Wargroch signaled the pair to depart. For all they knew, his authority required him to enter. Most ogres, Wargroch had often thought, were not nearly as clever as him. Not even Khleeg.

Not even his long-dead brothers.

With growing anticipation, Wargroch pushed his way inside. Immediately, he smelled the elf scents that he associated more with the exotic Idaria than her master.

"*Ga ni ifalkuni dura duri,*" he rumbled as he surveyed the chamber. The bed was huge and lush, and like nothing Wargroch had ever seen. On one side, the soft outline of a shape could be seen.

"*Ga ni ifalkuni dura duri.* Come play with me, dryad," Wargroch called.

When she did not appear, he grew impatient and began searching for her. Where could she have gone? After all, the chambers were high above the ground, and elves did not fly.

But a thorough search left Wargroch empty-handed. The Blödian officer went from room to room within the Grand Khan's personal quarters, and Idaria was nowhere to be found. Yet the presence of the guards had indicated that she had been within, and the bed had verified that she had been sleeping there not long before.

Wargroch growled. There had to be a secret passage somewhere in the Grand Khan's quarters, and the slave had slipped out. His desire began to fade as he considered what might have happened between them had she actually been in the quarters. Golgren *could* return without notice; the Grand Khan was unpredictable. Besides, Wargroch had to measure up to his new duties. Garantha was an imposing responsibility.

He glanced ruefully at the bed one last time, where the loose impression of a smaller, feminine form was still visible. Wargroch grunted and the next moment fled the chambers.

But even after several minutes had passed since his departure, Golgren's personal quarters remained empty.

⚭⚬⚭⚬⚭

Safrag entered what had once been a part of his master Dauroth's personal libraries, but had since been made very much Safrag's own domain. The rounded chamber had walls lined with bookshelves made of silver that had been built into the stone, helping secure the magic of the scrolls and other items in the chamber.

Glancing back at the door, Safrag belatedly sealed the entrance. He wanted no one to intrude at that precious moment.

Standing next to the wide, rectangular table, he summoned a glowing sphere of a similarly colored light and sent it adrift above him. The glow revealed inlaid silver in the walls that also had to do with the tomes and other papers lining the shelves.

Surely, it would not do any harm to test the Fire Rose again. Unlike Dauroth, Safrag was not afraid to wield the fragment under cautious conditions. As for the legend that each use of the Fire Rose made the desire to use it again and again more irresistible, Safrag knew well the strength of his will. He would not fall prey to such paltry fears.

At the center set of shelves, Safrag reached toward the middle one and gently touched a red stone inlaid there.

The stone shimmered, and the entire wall rippled as though suddenly formed of water.

"Falstoch, Falstoch! I would have a word with you, Abomination."

From behind the rippling wall, there came a mournful sound like nothing uttered by a mortal soul. It seemed but a wail. Yet if one listened close, words could be heard.

IIIIII cooooooommmmmmme...

IIIIII cooooooommmmmmmmeee...

Slowly, a dreadful sloshing noise became evident, as if something that was not quite flesh, not quite liquid, approached from whatever dank realm existed behind the wall. There was an agonized hint to each shudder, and the same two words repeated over and over. The voice was reminiscent of someone drowning.

A vague shape appeared behind the shelves, a shape sometimes seeming almost ogreish in form, sometimes almost that of a Titan. And most often, something macabre.

A hand suddenly thrust out of the wall. It bore four digits, five, three, and five again. Its flesh dripped to the floor, sizzled, and vanished, yet the hand looked no less whole. A thumb melted into the hand, only to thrust out at a different angle.

With the greatest of strain, the dripping hand stretched forward. Behind it came a thick limb that also dripped. Pustules formed, swelled, and popped. Dwarf limbs, some even with hands, briefly sprouted, and melted back into the main arm.

Safrag casually stepped back, remaining out of reach of the grotesque apparition. In an almost clinical manner, he studied the monstrous changes constantly assailing the one he called Falstoch.

A face thrust through the wall, a face that made even the deformities of a Titan without elixir seem beautiful by comparison.

The Abomination—Dauroth's name for the accursed thing—had no eyes, one, and three . . . and none of them exactly where eyes should be. A mouth formed, but sideways. It melted into the waxy, dripping flesh, and was replaced near the forehead by another mouth that lasted only a single breath before vanishing. The same constant transformations occurred for every other aspect of the body, be it the ears, the nose, or growths that had no identifiable function. Coarse black hair sprouted in random patches, shriveled, and fell off. Like all else that peeled away from the constantly melting form, the hair sizzled on contact with the stone floor before fading away.

The rest of Falstoch shoved its way through. If there were legs, they were lost in the bloated shape that moved like a snail and left a trail of slime worse than any such creature. Other arms and perhaps what were feet and legs continued to erupt from random areas. Nothing ever lasted long, and nothing— not even the head—was permanent. One head sank into the bubbling mass, and rose again from the right side. What eyes it had stared at the Titan from a very crooked angle.

Sssssaaffffragggggg . . . it intoned, its voice coming from all around the chamber. *Haaasssss Daaauroth forrrgivvvven ussssssss?*

"Dauroth is dead. I am master of the Black Talon and all other Titans."

His words caused an ever-so-brief hesitation in the horrific shifting of the Abomination's shape. Falstoch and those like him were Titans who had transgressed against Dauroth, and for their "crimes" had been condemned by the late master to this sad fate. They were abject lessons to the rest.

Deeeeeeadddd . . . There was a hint of grim pleasure in the ghoulish voice, perhaps the only pleasure that Falstoch had experienced since Dauroth had transformed him. Falstoch's crime had been to experiment on a possible elixir that would have freed him from relying on Dauroth's good will. The experiment had not gone far, but since it had not been sanctioned by the Titans' creator—and since Dauroth wanted no one else to have the secret—Falstoch had paid the ultimate price.

The other Abominations had been condemned for similar transgressions, all seeking to circumvent Dauroth's will.

Safrag extended his palm toward Falstoch. The tiny

fragment of the Fire Rose materialized in it.

The Abomination's reaction was immediate. *Leeeeggeendd! Rrrrrroooosssssseeee!*

"Speak truly, Falstoch. Did Dauroth use it when he cast you into your hellish state?"

Nooooooo!

That surprised the former apprentice. He had spent many hours of many days perusing Dauroth's secrets, determined that none would be lost to him. Yet he had failed in that particular one. Even in death, Dauroth could still surprise his treacherous servant.

None of that truly mattered given that Safrag had the fragment. He knew that of all the Abominations, Falstoch had always had the most knowledge of the artifact's legends.

However, speaking with such a disgusting blob did not suit Safrag.

"Sera issura alayva etoi," the Titan sang in words that were as close to that of the ancient High Ogre language as anything else Dauroth had created. As he uttered the spell, Safrag also drew a triangular pattern over the piece.

The tiny fragment of the Fire Rose blazed crimson and orange. Tendrils of fiery smoke wafted up from the fragment. Yet Safrag felt only a very comforting warmth on his palm.

The tendrils twisted around one another. As the lead Titan continued to sing, they began to create a shape that made Safrag's eyebrow arch in surprise. It was a dancing shape with arms and legs. The moment it formed, it moved with excited abandon.

And before Safrag's eyes, it leapt into Falstoch.

A shuddering cry erupted from more than a dozen spontaneously created mouths. As they sank into the body, a dozen more formed, joining the cry. After them came only one, but that actually formed where a mouth should be.

Indeed, above the mouth was a nose not that different from Safrag's. Above that nose and to each side of it, eyes of gold emerged from flesh that had taken on a slight azure hue.

Falstoch's cry altered. It was no longer agonized, but full of primal pleasure. In great globs, the putrid flesh fell away and burned to nothingness. Behind was left a more defined and growing shape, one as tall as the observing Titan. Two distinct legs suddenly appeared, followed swiftly by a pair of sleek, muscular arms that developed sharp hooks at the elbows, and hands with long, tapering fingers ending in deadly, black nails.

Falstoch's ecstatic cry echoed throughout the library, although Safrag's magic had assured that it would not be heard. A satisfied smile revealing both rows of sharp teeth grazed the Titan leader's face as the last vestiges of Falstoch's torture faded away and a handsome Titan stood with arms outstretched to the ceiling.

"I am whole again!" Falstoch roared, flexing his fingers. He was naked, but in wonder at the transformation. "I am whole again . . ." He fell down on one knee before Safrag. Falstoch had a distinctive arch to his nose and his chin was narrower, but otherwise his face could have been the other sorcerer's twin.

"Safrag! My life is yours! Command me, and I obey!" he sang.

Safrag's smile did not fade, but in cold tones, he replied, "I would not be of such great cheer, Falstoch. It seems as if your redemption is to be short-lived. Observe your right hand."

Falstoch glanced down at his hand. Where before there had been perfect, blue skin, a small area of deathly white had began to spread. "No!"

"Be not so disturbed by the briefness of it," Safrag went on, as Falstoch discovered the same blemish stretching over the back of his other hand and on his chest. "It shows that the potential is there. Dauroth's spell was incredible and likely the work of the High Ogres—"

"Safrag! I beg of you—do something!" Falstoch's fine mane of hair—only recently sprouted—began to fall off. His form was bloating.

"You know the Fire Rose as well as Dauroth did. Quickly! Did you ever come across a reference to the Vale of Vipers?"

The other Titan's body began to quiver as if ready to explode. One leg began to tremble, as if the bones within had turned to jelly.

"Vale . . . Vale . . . Yesss!"

The last traces of Falstoch the Titan dwindled away, replaced by the nightmarish thing that had first emerged from the wall.

Safrag eyed the Abomination without pity. "Thank you, Falstoch. What would you do for the chance to be whole again? For that, the Fire Rose itself must be mine."

Aaannnnything. The voice that came from all around pleaded.

"And your fellow sufferers? Them too?"

Yyyyessss.

The Titan smiled, displaying his teeth. "Let us speak with them. I will tell all of you what you must do to redeem yourselves."

VII

THE DARKENED VALE

The hand reached Ben-ihm without interruption. The settlement had been an important way station during the height of the High Ogre civilization, but had since been virtually abandoned. Only when Golgren had become Grand Lord had the territory been repopulated at his command and resumed some importance.

Ben-ihm was surrounded by a gray stone wall built by the first of those sent by the Grand Lord to settle the region. Mountains to the west protected it from the worst of the winds, but the river that had flowed centuries ago had long ago dried up. Water had to come from the mountains, originally an arduous daily job until Golgren had borrowed from the engineering ingenuity of the minotaurs to bring water to the faraway settlement. Channels dug over the years—first by ogres, slaves, and later by ogres again—enabled the water that gathered in the cold heights to run down to where one stream would meet with another and another, until they formed a river that met another river, until all rushed along one of the greater channels that finally reached Ben-ihm.

The diversion of the valuable water supply from the mountaintops was one of the Grand Khan's most under-appreciated successes. True, the inhabitants of Ben-ihm knew they could not live as well as they did without those channels, but the rest of the ogre realm considered such engineering feats as nothing compared to victories over a strong enemy.

Even Khleeg shifted impatiently atop his mount as his lord halted the column for a moment to admire the handiwork that had taken so much effort and more than a few lives to accomplish. Even his ancestors, Golgren felt, would have appreciated that kind of victory—at least more than those around him did.

Barech met them on the outskirts of the settlement, a stalwart contingent from his force peeling away to form an honor guard for the Grand Khan. Ben-ihm was not a vast place, and no building rose higher than four stories, but all the warriors and locals had turned out for what was for them an extremely momentous event.

"Grand Khan honors us," Barech declared, proud of both the occasion and the excuse to show off his grasp of Common. Like many ogres of Kern descent, he had even tried to emulate Golgren's appearance. Not only were his tusks filed down, but he had had his thick, brown hair oiled so that it bore a reasonable similarity to his lord's own well-groomed locks. Unfortunately, Barech had a very ogre countenance, with a thick brow and so flat a nose that he almost looked as if he had none. His jaw was wider than average and thrust out as well.

Golgren acknowledged the fanfare. Right at the moment when they reached the rounded, clay-topped buildings that housed the warriors of the hand, he asked Barech, "Your fighters. They will be able to march tomorrow?"

The officer grunted in surprise. "March?"

"Word was sent," interjected Khleeg with some frustration. "The *Skolax G'Ran* enter Golthuu!" Although Solamnians and Nerakans were often described by the color of their "shells" or armor, ogres had other names for them. The Knights of Solamnia were called the *Shok G'Ran,* or "the shelled ones who bite like lions" (with *shok* being the ancient word for the king of beasts). The Knights of Neraka, on the other hand, were known by the other term because the ogres considered them no better than *skolax*—an insidious, tiny scorpion with two tails, which often hunted in packs to bring down prey much larger than one could have. Ogres burned their nests whenever they came across them.

Barech grinned, eager for battle. But Golgren corrected the other ogre's assumption. "Khleeg rides to meet Khemu. Khemu and Khleeg will ride to Angthuul. Barech, your hand rides to the Vale of Vipers."

"Vale? *Skolax G'Ran* near Vale too?"

"No. Your Grand Khan goes to the Vale."

He needed to say no more. Barech saluted. "My Grand Khan rides. I ride with my Grand Khan!"

In the past, the arrival of a Grand Khan would have meant trying to put on the best spectacle that even a poor settlement could manage. But Golgren desired no spectacle. He retired to the quarters normally used by Barech. Khleeg set guards at the door; the Blödian insisted that only warriors who were thoroughly trusted keep watch over the Grand Khan. Khleeg left his lord to find the place beyond the walls where the rest of his force slept.

Inside, the furs were heavily matted and clearly infested. Discarding them, the half-breed ruler stretched on the rock floor. He had slumbered on far worse over the course of his violent life.

But Golgren did not quickly fall asleep. Almost as soon as he was alone, he had a sense that eyes were upon him, eyes that saw not only what he did, but what he thought as well. Suspecting the Titans, Golgren kept his sword close, but no enemy suddenly assailed him. Gradually, the half-breed drifted off.

Even in sleep, there was no escape from the sense of being watched. The uneasiness entered his dreams. Sinister orbs watched him. Some were the eyes of ogres, others of men, and still others were the pupilless golden orbs of the Titans.

THE FIRE ROSE

A bright light, brighter even than the sun, burned away the darkness of the dream. Golgren found himself standing alone in a beautiful golden land. The lush trees, the rolling hills, *all* gleamed. In the distance rose an amazing city whose walls and barely seen towers were also gold.

And when Golgren happened to glance down at himself, he saw that even he was not immune from the brilliant hue, which spilled over and through him and colored him.

But his glance was cursory, for the city beckoned to him as if it were a beauteous female. Golgren took a step toward the city and suddenly flew into the air. The landscape below raced past him. The walls grew tall, the towers taller. The Grand Khan could see the turrets on the towers and the glittering stones encrusting everything. He instinctively knew the glitter was of diamonds and marveled at the wealth of the builders.

There were winged creatures fluttering above the city in great numbers, sleek avians who seemed to take little notice of his approach. Golgren paid them no further mind, as he was only interested in flying over the wall and discovering what secrets lay within the mysterious place.

As he drew closer, he suddenly felt an inexplicable desire to halt. It was almost as if some invisible guardian stood nearby, whispering in his ear that he had no right to enter. The Grand Khan peered around, seeking the cause of such an odd sensation, but he found nothing suspicious. Golgren started once more toward the gleaming walls—

The massive flock suddenly turned toward him. As it did, the sleek avians grew larger and thicker. Arms sprouted, and feathers became leathery hides.

A vast swarm of gargoyles plunged eagerly toward Golgren. Their beaklike muzzles opened, revealing long, sharp teeth. Razor claws snatched at the air. They converged on the floating figure—

An astounding warmth suddenly filled Golgren, a warmth that readily burned away any anxiousness he might have concerning his attackers. With a wave of his hand, he sent the entire horde spiraling out of control. With another gesture, Golgren transformed each and every gargoyle into tiny raindrops that pelted the city.

The Grand Khan pointed at the trees below. The trees became warriors of gold, all displaying his face and wielding swords nearly as long as their arms. He turned the gold trees toward the city with the intention of having them storm it, and realized that no wall could stand against his might. He gestured at the city—

The walls, the towers—*everything*—burst into flames.

But that was *not* what Golgren had intended. He immediately dismissed the rising flames. Or at least he tried to. Not only did the fire refuse to extinguish itself, but his attempts to put out the flames had a contrary effect. The flames rose higher and stronger, engulfing all before him.

Without warning, his golden warriors raised their swords and charged headlong into the fire. Golgren moved to stop them, but they no longer obeyed. As the flames engulfed them, each *melted* into a puddle of liquid that pooled together with the many puddles around them. A great burning river formed and poured out into the gleaming countryside.

There was nothing around Golgren save fire. The warmth he had felt previously turned into a heat that seared his flesh. Fire burst from his fingertips. He tried to brush it away, but his actions only seemed to fan the flames.

Golgren suddenly sensed another presence nearby. He looked up to see someone stepping through the all-consuming fire as though it were nothing.

The faceless golden figure.

Golgren woke at last from his fiery dream. He lay on the floor, covered in sweat. There was a pressure on his chest. Immediately, he tugged on a thick chain around his neck, one that he had only removed once as of late—before he had stripped to fight the legionary whose death was used to bless the blades given to Khleeg's warriors.

The mummified hand came free. It was the same hand he had lost to the current emperor of the Uruv Suurt, when the latter had been an escaped slave. All knew that Golgren wore his own mummified hand to remind himself of his one failure; and the simple fact that he carried it put superstitious ideas into the heads of many of his rivals—just as the Grand Khan intended.

But there was more to the macabre prize. Golgren caught sight of the faint, fading glow. He twisted the yellowed appendage around to better view that which was worn on one of its sharply curled fingers.

It was a signet, a ring of magic created by the High Ogres. The circular signet bore at its center a rune that resembled a double-bladed sword turned upside down. Over the odd weapon arced a half circle, while below the sword had been set a symbol that resembled a wavy line. The last might have represented water, but Golgren suspected it symbolized the opposite: *fire.*

He had been given the signet by Idaria just as he had launched the assault against the army of undead, but she had admitted that it had been given to her by Tyranos. The wizard had never said where he had gotten the valuable signet from, but he had been eager to take it back after the struggle.

But Golgren had refused to part with the treasure that had helped him survive the *f'hanos,* as well as Dauroth. Tyranos did not try to force the ogre leader to give it to him, and thereafter, the Titans had avoided trying to strike at Golgren again.

But it was possible that returning the ring might have been the better choice. It was not the first such dream Golgren had experienced, although it was the first that was so vivid.

More to the point, Golgren had only begun to see the golden figure after possessing the ring. First among the ruins of Dauroth's mad quake, and afterward within Garantha.

Golgren had lived through the dark magic that had surrounded the Lady Nephera, his shadowy ally among the Uruv Suurt after the fall of Chot the Terrible. Emperor Hotak's mate had been the high priestess of a cult that had spread across the empire. Golgren had shed no tears when death finally claimed her.

It was with some effort that he removed the signet from the finger. His lost hand seemed to cling to the artifact as though it were alive. Golgren returned the mummified appendage to its hiding place and considered just what he might need to do with the signet. The temptation to hurl it away grew strong, and he rose with the intention of doing just that—

But as he clutched the artifact tightly, there suddenly appeared before him a vision.

Eight tall and glorious figures clad in rich, blue and green robes stood with their hands raised high. Their golden skin and perfect faces identified them as High Ogres. They seemed to be situated in a place that was both built of stone and carved from rock. High, fluted columns rose behind each figure. The eight were evenly divided between male and female, with the sexes alternating positions. They were also obviously spellcasters, spellcasters who appeared to be busy summoning something.

And what they were summoning materialized in their midst. Curious despite himself, Golgren leaned closer to see what it was—

But the figures in the vision suddenly turned as one to their left. Their faces grew horrified at whatever they spied there.

A black shadow crossed over them—and the vision ended.

Golgren eyed the signet, but he was no longer tempted to toss it away. Something about the signet had warned him that he had better continue to hold onto it, at least for the moment.

Movement in the darkest corner of the room caught his eye. Although for the moment he wasn't certain whether it might just be another dream or vision, the half-breed was taking no chances. He reached for his sword while at the same time instinctively stretching forth the hand that held the signet.

And from the object in his hand emerged a crimson glow that filled the room with just enough illumination to reveal what awaited him in the corner. A slight widening of his almond-shaped eyes was the only sign of Golgren's reaction to what he had just done. But that was his same reaction to the one *who* stood there.

Idaria.

Tyranos materialized in the vale in the dark of night, the glow of his staff muted. He would have chosen another time to enter the region, but matters were getting more and more out of hand—his hand, at least. Some of that—much of that, he corrected himself—could be laid at the feet of the Titans, whose new leader had taken an avid interest in the item the wizards most coveted.

The Fire Rose.

Too late, the lion-maned spellcaster had discovered that the signet would have been a perfect method by which to track the location of the artifact. It had only been after he had passed it on to Golgren—in most part to frustrate and confuse the Titans—that Tyranos had managed to find a translation for the symbols on the signet.

And only at that point had he realized that he had utterly outwitted himself.

But there were clues enough arising of late that had made him determined to come to that place. The Vale of Vipers was a forlorn place, a valley without green or any redeeming quality. All tales of it that Tyranos had heard spoke only of it as somewhere that creatures of all races tended to avoid, although nowhere could he find a pressing reason other than a lack of natural resources. Yet, minotaurs, humans, dwarves, and even ogres mined in far more desolate places, and the wizard was of the opinion that a knowledgeable prospector would find *something* of value.

The name alone likely kept some away. *Vale of Vipers* was a properly ominous title for the place. But Tyranos feared no serpent, and certainly that alone should not have been enough to keep some ordinary souls from journeying there.

The lack of other intruders worked for him and, indeed, encouraged the wizard in some ways. He was of the opinion that what kept the vale so desolate had to do with the High Ogres and the Fire Rose. Tyranos was annoyed with himself, for he ought to have considered that fact much, much sooner. He would not have needed Golgren, not needed *anyone*.

The burly spellcaster mulled over that last thought as he slowly wended his way along the darkened valley. When he had first sought the Fire Rose—the key to erasing the foul mistake he had made back home—the Titans had more or less commanded both Kern and Blöde with impunity. As stealthy as Tyranos could be for one of his size, constantly dodging the fifteen-feet-tall sorcerers had been a very tricky situation.

And Golgren had come—the bane of their existence. He had stepped into the role of Grand Lord just after Tyranos had initially discovered the legend. The wizard had thought nothing of the half-breed, certain that sooner or later Golgren would overstep his bounds and be either executed by his master or turned into a puddle of something grotesque by the powerful Titan leader.

And, not for the first time of late, Tyranos had realized how wrong he could be. Somewhere along the way, Golgren had made a very decisive pact with the powers that had swept over the empire. He had developed a special relationship with Nephera, the high priestess and empress of the minotaurs. She had given him power over Dauroth, enough power to keep all the Titans at bay, at least for the time being. And the wizard had accidentally granted Golgren the means to continue to keep the sorcerers from destroying him. Good luck seemed to smile on Golgren—

Tyranos frowned. If it *was* luck and not something more.

The wizard shook away such disturbing thoughts. Concentrating on the hunt, he pointed his staff ahead. The crystal flared slightly, a sign of arcane energies swirling somewhere deeper in the vale. With a grin, the hooded figure pushed on. Perhaps, just perhaps, he would not need to concern himself about Golgren for very much longer.

That made him chuckle about something else he had done. Tyranos wondered if the Grand Khan would appreciate the gift he had left for him, a gift that would serve the wizard as much as the ogre.

At first, the only sound that he could hear penetrating the vale was the incessant wind, sometimes soft, more often shrieking like a banshee. Tyranos sniffed the air, vaguely picking up a musky smell, almost as if a herd of goats had gone and died together somewhere deeper in the valley. Perhaps they had come across the mythic vipers, he thought with a smirk.

His staff hinted at more and more arcane energies lying in the same direction. Tyranos wondered how any spellcaster of sufficient ability—a Titan, for example—could have failed to notice. He did not doubt that his own skills were better than most of his calling, though there were also many who were more adept. Certainly Dauroth had been superior, and even if he had never gone hunting for the artifact, the wizard knew all too well that his successor Safrag *had*.

He hesitated for a moment, uncertain if what he sensed lying ahead was tied too closely to the Titans. That could not be. No. What he pursued was definitely far, far older and therefore more akin to something tied to the High Ogres.

And in the Vale of Vipers, what could that possibly be but the Fire Rose?

Although aware that he had a tendency to make great

assumptions when it came to hunting for the artifact, Tyranos nonetheless felt he was finally on the right track. As he climbed over a small ridge and descended into the belly of the vale, his staff's crystal grew brighter yet. Yes, he was very, very near.

As the thought went through his mind, the wind came rushing again. With it came an overpowering stench, the musky odor multiplied several times over.

For the first time, Tyranos thought he recognized the scent from somewhere.

From the high peaks above, some small rocks suddenly rolled down toward him. The wizard immediately gestured in that direction. A flash of light momentary illuminated the upper area.

There was nothing there, however. Tyranos cursed his anxiety. After a pause to collect himself, the spellcaster moved on.

The wind swirled around him. The musky scent continued to grow until it was nearly unbearable. Yet with the mountains all around him, it was impossible to guess exactly from which direction it emanated. It seemed to drift from all around.

But if the odor was the worst thing he had to face, his task would be a simple one, he thought. With more impatient strides, the powerfully built figure crossed into another part of the valley.

The crystal brightened more than before, and so suddenly that Tyranos let out a curse of surprise and covered his eyes with his free arm until his vision could adjust to the glare.

And when he uncovered his eyes, he sensed that he was far, far from alone.

There was nothing to see in the light cast by the staff, for despite the harsh brightness, Tyranos noticed that the light did not spread to cover more than a few feet around him.

Gritting his teeth, the wizard muttered, *"Tivak."*

The air suddenly filled with crackling strands of silver energy that danced in every direction.

That was when he noticed the massive flock of huge,

winged beasts perched on the rocks above and around him, their baleful gazes intent on the intruder in their midst.

Gargoyles. More gargoyles than even Tyranos, who knew much about their race, could have imagined clustered in one place.

And there was something else, something barely noticeable at first. There was a gray and black, hooded shadow, with its face bound tightly in a golden cloth that covered all but its eyes. A pair of long, oval eyes, as white as ice.

Tyranos had less than a heartbeat to register the macabre form, which vanished quicker than it had appeared. The wizard could not help but think that those eyes showed a dark amusement with him and his plight.

One of the winged watchers suddenly screeched. The others joined in, their combined cries deafening. At the same time, the silver strands of energy radiating from the staff dissipated.

The wizard muttered another word. The crystal glowed brighter, before returning to a dimmer state almost immediately.

"By the Kraken!" he growled. The command word should have enabled the staff to transport him away from the benighted place.

The gargoyle who had first called out fluttered up off its perch.

Tyranos turned and ran.

In scores, the other winged terrors leaped into the sky. The wizard did not have to look back to know they were pursuing him.

"Saariit!" he shouted, once again calling upon the staff to carry him to safety. Again it failed to do so.

The flapping of hundreds of wings vied with the eager screeches of the flyers, both sounds echoing over and over through the vale. Tyranos did not wonder at the racket. After all, there was no one around to hear, except him and their master.

He sensed rather than heard the first of the gargoyles creep up behind him. Scowling, Tyranos acted uncharacteristically for a wizard: he spun around in mid-step and, gripping his staff with both hands, struck the oncoming beast soundly across the jaw with its crystal head.

There was a flash and the sudden stench of burning flesh, but the force of the swing was as much the reason for the gargoyle tumbling backward as any magic in the attack. Tyranos's warriorlike appearance was no simple façade. The strength his body hinted at was as real as could be.

A second gargoyle suffered the same fate as the first. A third managed to dodge his swings, but Tyranos, releasing one hand, seized hold of the creature's thick throat and squeezed.

The winged one's windpipe caved in with a satisfying snap. Tyranos let the writhing body fall, swinging at another pair of the beasts who had angled around for their own attack.

Although for the moment he was keeping them at bay, the wizard did not go unharmed. There were shredded areas all over his garments and more than a few cuts along his arms and face. Worse, the gargoyles were slowly but surely backing him into a corner.

He batted away another attacker, but when the next drew near, Tyranos freed one hand again and grabbed the winged fiend by the arm.

The gargoyle instinctively flew up. Its vast, leathery wings were so powerful that, with some strain, the creature pulled the wizard up into the air with it.

Tyranos waved the staff to keep another gargoyle at a safe distance as the one that struggled with him continued its haphazard ascent. The towering spellcaster continued to be lifted up as if he were a feather. More gargoyles swarmed around him.

"Let's try and even the odds," Tyranos snarled. He beat the gargoyle clutching him hard on the leg with his staff. The creature screeched and flew higher. Tyranos peered around, trying to find some shelter in which he might drop and hide.

More and more gargoyles reached him. They rent his cloak and robe, scoring his legs as well as his arms and chest. The strain of holding tight with one hand was telling on him.

Tyranos had no choice but to force the gargoyle to descend again. Any higher than he was at the moment, and he was sure to lose his grip and die. Tyranos began striking furiously at the shoulder of the winged fury, trying to drive it groundward.

A thundering roar cut through the vale, a roar that could have come from only one leviathan of a creature.

A dragon.

The roar had an astounding effect on the gargoyles. Almost as one, they scattered back the way they had come. Their fear was so strong that the wizard could taste it. His own gargoyle fought to fly off even with him still clinging to it.

As for Tyranos, he had no desire to face a dragon of any sort or size. Whatever color or metal, the thing sounded hungry.

The frantic gargoyle began clawing and scratching at his hand as never before. Tyranos, already weary, could not fend off every scratch.

His grip faltered.

He slipped and plunged.

The ground was not so far away as he had feared, but far enough that when he struck it, every bone in his body seemed to vibrate. Pain coursed through every nerve. None of his limbs would obey his commands, and Tyranos did not know which direction was up. He bounced once and rolled helplessly for several yards before colliding with a rocky outcropping.

He was fair game for even a savage rodent at that point, and Tyranos prepared himself to be the dragon's meal. Yet several tense moments passed, and only silence filled the vicinity.

At last, the wizard heard movement behind him. For a dragon, the newcomer was soft of foot. Tyranos struggled to rise, or at least push himself onto his back so that he could face his death as his people preferred, but his body continued to betray him. He waited, steeling himself for the first awful bite.

"Not the one for whom I'm waiting," murmured a cultured voice. "But at least it is one I've been expecting."

A pair of strong hands carefully turned the injured wizard over. Through bleary eyes, Tyranos beheld a shadowed, very human face half-hidden by a dense, dark beard.

"Healing is the special skill of those of Mishakal," the man went on, reaching for something dangling over his chest. His *armored* chest. "But my patron might help nonetheless."

The thing that dangled over the breastplate suddenly glinted with light despite there being no earthly source for it. The wizard beheld what he recognized as a variation of a familiar symbol.

"I know you! You are"—his usually booming voice came out as a croak—"a cleric of *Emperor* . . . of Kiri-Jolith!"

"My name is Stefan," the other replied, nodding. "And I know you too, outcast."

VIII

Deadly Warning

Golgren had no doubt as to the reason for the elf's sudden appearance far from Garantha, and that reason was Tyranos.

Idaria's expression radiated momentary surprise, followed by a return of the calm expression she generally wore. Golgren was certain she had not intended the magical journey. It smelled of the sort of trick of which the wizard was fond. Golgren had purposely left Idaria behind, there being no place for her where he was going. A slave would only get in the way and impede him, at least that had been what he had told Khleeg.

Idaria stared at the signet, seeming to be almost mesmerized by its light. Golgren passed his hand over the artifact, and the light vanished. Aware that she could see better in the dark than he could, he pointed to where he knew an oil lamp was hanging by the door. Idaria went over to the lamp wordlessly and lit it with some tools nearby.

The elf approached him. "Grand Khan," she murmured, falling to her knees. "Forgive me. I am not—"

"Responsible. Yes. Tyranos is. We both know that, my Idaria."

"Tyranos." The elf repeated the name with torn emotions that matched those Golgren experienced each time the wizard intruded in his life. Not all were good; not all were bad.

One could never trust the leonine spellcaster's motives.

"I will return to Garantha," the slave offered. "The Grand Khan ordered me to remain there, and I will oblige—"

"No. You are in Ben-ihm. You will remain with me."

"My lord?"

He grinned without humor. "The wizard, he likes to play games. But his games are never for play."

She nodded at his wisdom. "As you command."

Reaching down, the Grand Khan cupped her chin in his hand and slowly raised her to a standing position. "My Idaria, do you believe me when I say your people will still be free?"

There was no hesitation. "Yes."

Golgren cocked his head. "That is one reason Tyranos sends you to me." He considered for a moment longer, before saying, "The discussion is ended. It is time to sleep. Tomorrow, we ride with the hand of Barech to the vale."

"Yes, my lord." Idaria started to turn back to the lamp with the intention of dousing it.

"No. Leave it lit."

"My lord?"

His gaze shifted to the shadowed corners. "Leave it."

～○※○～

Khleeg gaped at the sight of Idaria, but held his questions. His Grand Khan would tell him whatever he needed to be told.

However, there was another whom Golgren needed to tell of the elf's presence. Ignoring Khleeg and Idaria, he pulled forth the stone.

"Wargroch," he called, staring into the crystal. "Wargroch, your Grand Khan summons you."

There was a hesitation, and the muddiness transformed into a tiny vision of the younger officer's toadlike countenance. Wargroch wore a startled look, as that was the first time he had experienced the stone in action. The one contacted first heard the voice of the summoner in their head. At the same time, the stone in their possession grew noticeably warm. Khleeg and Wargroch had been ordered to keep the crystals on their persons day and night, just as their ruler did.

"My lord," the tiny face finally blurted. "The slave, Idaria . . . She is gone!"

"Idaria is with her master."

Wargroch again started. "Great lord, she is . . . She is—"

"I have sent for her. She has come." Unseen by Wargroch, Khleeg grinned at his counterpart's astonishment. The Grand Khan's second in command was no less surprised of course, as Golgren had told him only that Idaria had been brought by means familiar to the ogre leader. But that was all the explanation the loyal Khleeg needed.

"The Grand Khan is wise in all things," Wargroch finally responded.

"Garantha is secure?" Golgren asked, changing the subject.

"Wargroch stands against any enemies of his Grand Khan!" the officer declared. "My life is yours—"

"Yes, Wargroch is very loyal. We ride from Ben-ihm with the coming of the Burning." The Burning was an ogre phrase which meant the daytime. "We will speak when night falls."

As Wargroch nodded, Golgren cut off any further conversation by simply putting the crystal away. To the other officer, he said, "Tell Barech. One hour, his hand marches."

"My lord."

Barech did not fail Golgren. His column was standing ready an hour later as the Grand Khan and Idaria mounted. Idaria's horse was a gift to the ogre ruler from the local leader. That it was to carry a slave didn't matter, not when that slave was clearly a favorite of the Grand Khan, and somewhat of a miraculous sight herself, no one having witnessed her arrival.

Khleeg, his misgivings evident in his expression, saluted his lord. "It is not right. I should ride with."

"Khleeg must defend Golthuu. That is what is right."

"Yes, my lord."

The horn sounded. Barech signaled his warriors forward. As they marched, their comrades in Khleeg's hand barked their support for the other column's mission. Barech's warriors returned the cheers and salutes, aware that Khleeg's force would be heading to meet a hated foe. Humans were spindly creatures to look at, but their fighters were often skilled adversaries.

Golgren and Idaria rode close to Barech. With the reins bound around his maimed limb, the Grand Khan waved imperiously to his warriors and other followers. Even among the denizens of Ben-ihm, the ogres appeared different since Golgren had taken over. Yes, Golgren thought, looking around at the crowd cheering, ogres had always been muscular giants, but now they were muscular giants who were well fed and better dressed. The Uruv Suurt would learn to fear a healthy, mighty ogre race.

As they headed out of the settlement, the rounded buildings gave way to the pens where amaloks and goats were kept. It had taken some effort for Golgren to convince his warriors that herding animals was not children's work. The sturdy state of the pens and the healthy appearance of its occupants showed that even outside Garantha, Golgren's dictates had taken hold.

The goats bleated and pushed to the opposite side from where the ogres marched. The amaloks, ever more defiant, pressed to the front and barked at the cheering warriors. A few made vicious snaps at the air. Most were females; males were hard to keep together in numbers. The striped beasts were notorious for their combative nature and durability under the worst conditions, which was why ogres imitated their call when cheering.

An older ogre warrior stood next to the pen, the wooden rod with which he kept the animals under control clutched in his right hand. Like Golgren, his other hand was missing. In fact, his arm up to his elbow had been severed—likely in battle—and cauterized. Even so, such a warrior would have had little hope for a future in the old days. But the Grand Khan's ability to convince his people that they could not survive just on what they found, hunted, or stole had enabled the rehabilitation of that maimed fighter. His life still had meaning.

The ogre slapped his ruined limb against the side of his chest, the best he could do under the circumstances. Golgren lifted his own maimed arm and, even with the reins, saluted back. He made certain as many as possible observed his action.

Beyond the outskirts of Ben-ihm, they came across a number of ogres clad only in kilts gouging out a vast gap in the hard, harsh ground. The workers toiled with a number of tools: pick axes and flat-ended shovels, to be sure, but also a huge, iron wedge weighted at the back of its base that required four warriors to guide it and another atop a mastark to drag it forward. Under the handler's guidance, the huge beast—a leather harness around its shoulders and iron chains stretching back from the harness to the sides of the wedge—would strain forward for several steps. That, with the help of those guiding the wedge, would be enough to tear up a good-sized section of rock and baked earth. Others would come in with shovels and axes to break up and carry the debris away.

The gap was already over four feet deep, indicating that the mastark team had made more than one pass over the area. The full gap ran over fifty yards and would stretch a great distance when completed. It would provide an extension of the water system on the other side of the settlement, enabling

Ben-ihm itself to expand. The trench would be deep enough that the mastark—or another, if that one perished—would be up to its considerable shoulders when finished.

Seeing the great work made the Grand Khan think of Stefan Rennert and wish the knight could observe such progress and report back to his superiors. Ben-ihm's rebirth would surely have shown the Solamnians how *civilized* Golthuu was becoming.

He caught sight of Idaria studying the scene.

"No slaves," the Grand Khan murmured to her. "Is that what pleases you?"

"They are working so hard," she returned. "Working and not warring."

Golgren nodded. "But they will fight when they must. And they must."

The last of Ben-ihm dwindled behind them. Barech's force marched directly toward the eastern mountains. Ahead lay a path that the commander swore would take them to the Vale of Vipers, without too much struggle or detour along the way. Barech posted advance scouts to check the path for any signs of danger.

But the incessant heat was the enemy that day. *iSirriti Siroth*—Sirrion's Burning—was doing its best against the hardened ogres, but it was failing. Golgren watched with grim satisfaction as not one of the warriors flagged, much less fell to the side. Unlike past rulers of both Kern and Blöde, Golgren had made certain those who were willing to die in his name thrived under his rule until their time came.

There was no tent for the Grand Khan and his slave; Golgren preferred the night air on the journey. Barech assembled a trusted guard unit to maintain a watch around his lord's camp. The commander took more precautions than one might have expected that deep in the ogre homeland, but with the odd vanishing of more than one force, complacency was a danger in itself.

"The mountains we will reach in two days," the officer informed Golgren before taking his leave for the night. "I think the vale may be reached four after."

It was what Golgren expected to hear. "The sooner, all the better."

The outdoors suited the half-breed far more than Barech's quarters would have. In contrast to the night before, he quickly fell asleep on his bedroll on the hard ground.

And to his surprise, he awoke the next day feeling refreshed. Not once during the night had he experienced any of the thousand nightmares and memories that usually assailed him in his sleep. Idaria's eyes, staring at him, showed that she understood, for she was well familiar with his oft turbulent nights. Golgren would sometimes go from absolutely still to suddenly shaking violently or muttering in his sleep. The slave was used to awakening him at the most violent of times. It was a command that he had given her the very first night she had become his servant, and one that she had never failed to obey.

Much rested, Golgren pushed Barech to gather the warriors with the utmost haste. Golgren allowed them to eat and drink, but little else. Barech's hand moved on even before the sun's first light rose over the horizon. Their discipline was impressive.

The mountains loomed ahead like the jagged tusks of hundreds of gargantuan ogres. An outsider might have wondered why Golgren went north to send Khleeg to deal with the Nerakans and to bring himself to the vale, which lay far southeast of Garantha. Attempting to traverse the mountains by any other route than that which he had chosen would have taken *weeks* for a force so great. The same held true for where Khleeg was going. Unfortunately, the very mountains that helped protect Garantha could also hinder its Grand Khan at times.

"No one do I have who knows the vale itself," Barech informed Golgren along the way. "But there are those of Ben-ihm who have heard tales. Vipers, *f'hanos,* winged shadows—"

"Winged shadows?" Golgren interrupted, his eyes attentive.

Barech shrugged. "Winged shadows, dragons, mastarks that eat flesh. Many tales, many fools."

Golgren said nothing.

Night arrived before they could reach the edge of the mountain chain. Golgren considered continuing on for several hours, but he knew the folly of entering mountains in the dark. Whether or not there were dragons or flesh-devouring mastarks, there were certainly treacherous passes and likely meredrakes. Even the rare but deadly hageed-araki could lurk around. And they were not the mountains of the vale yet.

The column halted enticingly close to the mountains, so much so that the Grand Khan did not retire immediately but stared at the peaks, contemplating their ancient might. Making certain he was not observed, he removed the signet from its macabre hiding place and touched the symbols on top.

Nothing happened.

Not certain what he had expected in the first place, Golgren put the signet back.

From within the encampment there came several shouts. The Grand Khan whirled.

Every campfire was blazing two, three times the height of an ogre and at least twice that in width. More than one warrior was rolling on the ground seeking to extinguish themselves. Some ran to aid them while others stood transfixed and confused.

A tendril of flame whipped out of one fire. Writhing, it scorched the ground and withdrew. From another campfire, a second tendril burst forth. The rest of the campfires quickly did the same, and although no one was very endangered by the tendrils, they nonetheless pushed some superstitious ogres to the edge of panic. Their own fires appeared to be attacking them.

Golgren felt a warmth on his chest. He pulled out the

mummified hand and snatched the ring again. As he had expected, the symbols glowed a crimson-orange.

Thrusting the severed appendage away, the Grand Khan put the signet on, holding it toward the closest of the campfires gone wild.

The writhing tendrils shriveled to smoke. Suddenly from each fire stepped a figure of flame. They gathered together as they converged on the half-breed. Each stood as tall as a Titan, and each wore a crown of spiking tongues of fire.

"No!" Unexpectedly, a delicate hand covered over the signet. Golgren felt the artifact instantly cool.

The army of flame vanished in mid-step. The campfires shrank to normal.

With a snarl, Golgren struck Idaria on the jaw with the bound end of his maimed arm. The elf went tumbling back. She dropped to the ground, stunned.

Golgren found himself dropping down on one knee to seize Idaria. He looked to her injury. With a slight moan, the slave opened her eyes. She showed no fear of Golgren despite what he had done. It was the first time he had ever struck her.

"The signet," she breathed. "The signet was drawing . . . was drawing you and those flame creatures together . . . You would have been devoured."

"Devoured" was an odd choice of word, the half-breed thought, but he ignored it, more interested in something else. "And you know that *how*, my Idaria?"

"Tyranos."

A sharp intake of breath escaped Golgren as he drew her to her feet. "Yes, Tyranos. He spoke of just that happening? He spoke to you, did he?"

"No, he spoke of the signet bringing your death." She glanced at the campfires, where hardened warriors were only just daring to step close again, curious about what the two were saying but edging back, keeping a respectful, wary distance. "When I saw them, I was certain that it was what he meant."

"But the wizard did not say exactly that."

"No."

At that moment, Barech rushed up. "My lord! You are safe!"

"Yes, commander."

"Your guards will be whipped! The fires, they—"

Golgren shook his head. "No whipping."

The officer grunted. "The Grand Khan commands. I obey."

Something near one of the campfires made Golgren forget Barech's presence. Three warriors stood peering and pointing at one of the scorched areas. The trio seemed to be arguing among themselves about something they spotted in the burned patch.

Striding past the hand's commander, Golgren confronted the three. The warriors quickly struck their fists against their breastplates and retreated several steps so that the Grand Khan could have an unhindered view of what had so interested them.

There was writing in the burnt area. To be precise, it was clear that the tendril had *drawn* a symbol in the ground. It was a curved line with two tiny dots on the right side of it.

His brow furrowed, Golgren moved to one of the other campfires. As he came around to the scorched area there, he saw that, as with the first fire, there was a symbol carved in the earth.

But not the same symbol. That one was either a triangle missing one side, or perhaps a symbol representing a mountain, such as those looming nearby. In the gap where the missing side of a triangle would have been, an arched pattern that reminded Golgren of a wing had been artfully sketched.

"They are all different," whispered Idaria, suddenly at his side again. "It is a message, I think."

He saw immediately what she meant.

Golgren hurried over to the first campfire to have emitted

a tendril. There, yet another drawn symbol awaited him. The Grand Khan went to the second campfire, where, from the angle of that drawing, he had a fair idea where to find the next symbol.

In all, there were twelve of them, each distinct. They had been etched very clearly and in an obvious sequence, so there would be no mistaking their meaning. There was only one trouble.

It was no language that Golgren could read.

He looked to Idaria, who had followed in his steps. On her face there was a look as unreadable as the symbols.

"What does it say?" he quietly asked. "Do you know?"

The elf frowned. "I do not know what it says. It is an older language than mine."

"An older language?"

"Yes." Not at all to his surprise, she added, "I think . . . I think it is a variation of High Ogre."

A message. A message in High Ogre surely meant for him. But Golgren had no idea how to read it. He bared his teeth in a humorless grin and turned to one of the nearby warriors.

"Bury it. Bury all of them."

The warrior grunted. He and several others began covering over the symbols.

"My lord," began Idaria. "Should you do that?"

"I cannot read that message. I will not leave it for my enemies." He did not mention those enemies by name, but she surely knew that chief among them were the Titans, who likely *could* read the symbols.

Idaria said nothing. Golgren's decision was always final. As Barech joined them, the Grand Khan hid the signet in his fist.

"My lord, I—"

A fierce, steaming wind rose up, tearing through the encampment near where the Grand Khan and his companions stood. There was no question in Golgren's mind that the gale was as unnatural as what had happened with the flames.

With that in mind, he suddenly glanced back at the camp-fires. There, where most of the symbols had been covered over with dirt and, in some cases, heavy stones, the wind struck hardest. The dirt was flung into the air, blinding several ogres.

A moment later, the rocks went flying too. Two warriors were struck hard, one in the head. That ogre fell to his knees. The rest fled.

Golgren stepped into the furious wind. His eyes slitted, his mane whipping back, he went to the nearest campfire.

Swept perfectly clean, the symbol there pulsated like a red-hot coal. Golgren looked to the next one and saw that it was clear and burning bright too.

Whoever or whatever had sent the message wanted it to be seen, regardless whether the one for whom it had been meant could even understand it. And regardless whether leaving it visible might prove even more dangerous for him.

The half-breed's eyes narrowed again. Unless the *last* was exactly what the message intended.

IX

BETRAYAL

As Golgren marched in one direction, Khleeg marched in another. Despite his trepidation at being far from the lord that he had sworn to protect, the ogre officer was also eager to reach the area where the Nerakans were said to have crossed the border. There would be much fighting, much bloodshed, but he was very confident in the combined might of the ogre hands that would stand against the humans. The Black Shells would be crushed, their females wailing their deaths for years.

Behind him, the hand marched with all the precision of a Solamnic army. Khleeg beamed, for the Grand Khan had presented him with the finest warriors yet trained. He could only imagine that they were as fine, indeed, as the armies of the High Ogres.

It was three days before he would reach his counterpart, Khemu. From there it would take another three, maybe four days to Angthuul. Fortunately, the Nerakans had chosen a place not all that far from Garantha, perhaps because they had the misguided notion they would be able to easily conquer the capital without the ogres rallying to prevent them.

Already, Khleeg could see the crushed and bloody corpses

of *Skolax G'Ran* littering the battlefield. It would be a glorious ogre victory, one that would, in many ways, bring honor to his master. Khleeg was aware of Golgren's background, of the slaughter by the Nerakans of the village where the half-breed had been born. And the death of his mother. Each Nerakan the officer managed himself to slay he would dedicate to the Grand Khan.

One of the subcommanders rode up beside him. The other ogre was not quite as adept with Common as Khleeg, but he spoke it well enough to exclaim, "Dust! Many riders approaching!"

Straightening in the saddle, Khleeg looked around, but could not swear to what he saw. A heavy force was indeed moving at a rapid pace toward his. He frowned, wondering if somehow the Nerakans had managed to bypass Khemu and the others.

A horn sounded from the oncoming dust cloud, and its notes were familiar ones. Some of Khleeg's concern evaporated. As he squinted, the figures began to define themselves into exactly what he knew them to be: ogres.

"Khemu's hand," he announced to the other officers. "Why here?"

"Neraka?" suggested one unhelpfully.

Grunting, Khleeg continued to eye the approaching force. He could clearly make out the banner of the Grand Khan, the severed hand clutching the blood dagger. However, of Khemu, there was no sight. Instead, as the riders approached, Khleeg noticed another ogre leading the hand, one he recognized.

"Rauth." A subcommander. Had something happened to Khemu?

Something else worried Khleeg. There seemed fewer warriors than there should have been, and those that did approach appeared to have fought in some great battle only recently. Again, his fear rose that Neraka had intruded deeper into Golthuu than previously believed. Rauth would have the answer.

Khleeg made an estimation and thought that about two-thirds of the original hand marched toward him. Such a heavy loss surprised him. The Black Shells must have had a large force.

To his surprise, one warrior broke from the front ranks of the other hand. The ogre shouted at the top of his voice, and the only reason that Khleeg did not at first understand what he was saying was because the warrior was speaking Ogre, not the Common to which the officer had grown accustomed.

"Drakuth bakiin!" the lone figure cried over and over as he suddenly brandished his axe. *"Drakuth bakiin!"*

He was warning Khleeg's force that the meeting was an *ambush*.

From somewhere among Khemu's warriors a pair of arrows streaked out. With terrible efficiency the unseen archers dealt two perfect strikes to the neck of the axe-brandishing warrior.

The ogre stumbled a few steps and fell on his face, already dead.

Rauth shouted back at whoever had fired. Khleeg, meanwhile, seized his own trumpeter by the arm. "Battle!"

The trumpeter raised the curled goat horn—just as one of Khleeg's other officers thrust a dagger in the trumpeter's throat.

At the same time, a second officer attempted to similarly attack Khleeg. The only thing that saved Golgren's second in command was the sudden jerking of his horse. The assassin's blade bounced off Golgren's breastplate and left a long, wet scar across his forearm.

Before the traitorous officer could try again, Khleeg used a heavy foot to shove his assailant off his mount. The Blödian drew his sword and ran the trumpeter's killer through.

As the other ogre died, Khleeg let go of the reins and snagged the horn from the slumping trumpeter. He himself blew the warning notes—

But with mounting horror, he saw a warning was no longer needed. A goodly number of his soldiers had already turned on their own comrades. Still, many others were loyal and fought back.

Khleeg tried to rally those who stood with him. He blew the horn again before tossing it aside to defend himself against a pair of warriors converging upon him on foot. One he knew well, and that fact alone made Khleeg furious. He maneuvered his massive steed in front of the pair, reached down, and cut a river across the familiar warrior's throat. The other he dueled with for several minutes, and disarmed before doing the same as he had done to his comrade. The new warriors were well trained, but Khleeg was experienced and had learned personally under his Grand Khan, who knew not only Uruv Suurt tricks, but those of the Solamnians and the Nerakans too.

The battle was fast becoming utter chaos. No one on his side knew whom to trust; more than once Khleeg saw a warrior he was certain was loyal cut down by a sudden turncoat.

A warrior from his own hand slammed his axe into the neck of Khleeg's horse. With a shriek, the animal toppled. Khleeg was unable to leap free before the dying horse hit the ground.

The bulky corpse of the animal heavily pinned one leg. The attacker, his axe dripping, closed upon Golgren's other.

Khleeg fumbled for his dagger. As the other ogre loomed over him, the officer thrust up and under his enemy's breastplate.

His strike was perfect. The traitorous ogre stumbled back, unfortunately wrenching the dagger from Khleeg's grip. The attacker dropped his axe as he sought to yank the blade free.

The head of the weapon lay within Khleeg's reach. With his adversary distracted by his terrible wound, the Blödian stretched and pulled the axe near, before grabbing its handle.

The other ogre finally drew out Khleeg's dagger. Blood gushed from the wound. A maddened expression filled his grotesque visage.

Khleeg chopped at his foe's nearest leg. The blade struck just above the ogre's ankle and although it did not cut deep, it was enough to send the warrior stumbling to one knee.

And that brought the enemy close enough to enable Khleeg to bury the axe in the back of his neck. The blow was not powerful enough to behead the other ogre, but it came close. The body slumped next to Khleeg, who was busy struggling to free himself.

Just as he managed to drag his leg out from under the dead horse, a pair of warriors seized him by the arms. Khleeg started to fight back, until he realized the arms were coming to his aid.

Golgren's second in command saw proudly that several other loyal warriors had banded together around him and had begun to reestablish a cohesive fighting force. Such actions would have been impossible for ogres before the half-breed had instituted his methods and training. Instead, the individuals would have stood their ground as single fighters and died valiantly but foolishly.

There were more of his warriors left than Khleeg could have hoped. One who had helped him rise thrust the axe back in his hand. With a confident growl, Khleeg waved the others into a more solid line. Those foes were about to discover that those truly loyal to the Grand Khan were more than a match for traitors—

Suddenly Khleeg had a premonition that the worse was not over. He knew that his brave little band was doomed, yet not once did he think of fleeing. They would have been slain with their backs to fate, a cowardly way for any ogre to perish.

But there was one last service Khleeg could perform. He fumbled for the crystal given to him by his lord. Golgren had to be warned.

Khleeg held the stone up. Realizing he was holding the blasted thing in front of the wrong eye, he switched to the other and concentrated on the Grand Khan with all his will.

His brave warriors roared as they met their oncoming fate.

The crystal flashed—

And suddenly the world around Khleeg shifted. The battle scene vanished, replaced by rocky terrain that might have been days away or just a few yards from where he had stood.

Vertigo struck the ogre. His legs folded under him.

Khleeg blacked out.

⚬═◆═⚬

Golgren sensed the crystal calling to him as he rode just a few paces behind Barech and the scouts guiding them into the mountains. Aware that if one of the other two were trying to contact him it suggested a matter of great importance, the Grand Khan immediately located Tyranos's creation and put it to his eye.

But the crystal revealed nothing but muddiness.

Thinking of Garantha, Golgren concentrated on Wargroch. A tense moment passed before the younger officer replied.

"Grand Khan?"

"Garantha. All is well there?"

The question seemed to confuse Wargroch momentarily, but he confidently replied, "Yes, Grand Khan! All is well!"

Golgren dismissed Wargroch from the crystal without further discussion or explanation. He concentrated on Khleeg.

Regrettably, even after more than a minute, his second in command did not respond.

"What is it, my lord?" asked Idaria.

The Grand Khan thrust the crystal back into his pouch. "Nothing."

But his thoughts lingered on Khleeg. In his mind Golgren ran over the officer's intended route and found no cause for concern. The first danger should not have come until the combined hands reached the Nerakans, days away. Could the black knights have slipped so far into Golthuu as to have attacked Khleeg already? Golgren considered that highly unlikely if not impossible. Yet, there had been several incidents of late that more than verged on "impossible."

Even so, there was nothing he could do but wait and see. As with all military hands, Khleeg's would have had messenger birds at their disposal. It was possible that some note was winging its way to Garantha. Wargroch could be relied upon to alert his master of any such messages.

A mournful howl tore his attention back to the mountains. The ogre warriors tensed before they all realized the howl was nothing more than the wind coursing among the sharp, jagged peaks.

For the ogre people, the mountains had no official name, although, according to the commander, the locals called them *Isan du ihageed-araki,* the Teeth of the Burrower. They did indeed resemble teeth to Golgren, although more like those of a meredrake or dragon. At a glance, the peaks looked devoid of life, including the hardy shrubs found in southern Golthuu or even southwest of the capital. The oddly narrow mountaintops were also heavily scored, as if countless creatures over the ages had sharpened their claws on the rocky sides.

Golgren's eyes continually surveyed his surroundings. The mysterious message of the wild fires—and its lack of clear meaning—was still fresh in his wary thoughts.

The way was tight. Often, only two riders could pass through a juncture, or three to four warriors grouped on foot. The lone mastark with the hand actually had an easier time than expected, the great beast stepping on top or over most obstacles. Still, Barech voiced some concern that perhaps he had been wrong to bring the massive lumbering creature with them.

There was no choice when it came to settling down for the night. Night in the mountains fell with a great abruptness, the tall peaks casting pitch black shadows. But the one mastark had another value on the journey. The spoor of the beast was plentiful and fueled the column's fires. There was not much else to scavenge.

The fires were kept small and, for the first hours, watched from a wary distance by most. However, as the cool night air took over and the flames remained subdued, the ogres gathered in large numbers around each campfire, beginning to relax.

The wind continued to howl. Idaria stayed close to Golgren, her own gaze surreptitiously studying the vicinity as she saw to her duties.

"One could easily find freedom by fleeing into the mountains," the Grand Khan remarked as she brought him a bowl of hot broth from one of the fires. "Is that not so, my Idaria?"

She looked down as she handed the bowl to him. "One could find many things, but freedom is doubtful, my lord. Not in those mountains."

"But in Neraka, yes?"

Idaria met his gaze with one just as veiled. "Or in Golthuu as well."

Golgren nodded vaguely at her evasive reply, and began to eat. The elf knelt nearby, nibbling on some dried fruit she had brought with her. Unless she had no other choice, she didn't eat meat. Golgren's mother had learned to suffer meat; life among the ogre tribes was too difficult to survive otherwise.

They bedded down after their meals. The long trek enabled the Grand Khan to drift off fairly quickly. But once asleep, Golgren heard whispers. At first, his dreams could make no sense of the whispers, save that they sounded like a beautiful song whose words he could not understand. The whispers were neither in Common or Ogre, yet he felt that he should understand the words. Not understanding so greatly disturbed him that he suddenly awoke, finding himself covered in sweat.

Even awake, he still heard the whispers. Glancing

at Idaria's still form, the half-breed rose to investigate. The whispering seemed louder the more he moved to his right, yet at the same time, it also felt as if the whispering surrounded him.

Golgren took a few more steps to the right. He was certain the whispering grew louder, more coherent. It *was* a song, although like none that he had ever heard. Gripping his sword, he advanced a few more paces, and a few more—

A hand suddenly seized the wrist of his maimed limb. Idaria's excited voice murmured, "My lord! Why are you going so far from the camp?"

He was about to chastise her for her ridiculous statement when, staring past the elf, Golgren looked around and saw that there was no sign of the encampment. Indeed, in the dark there was hardly anything to see at all. He was in the middle of nowhere.

"Where are we?" he demanded. "How far?"

"Several minutes along the trail, my lord. I only barely saw you vanish in the distance and followed as swiftly as I could."

Golgren hissed, puzzled by how he had come so far. Yet still, he heard the whispering voices as they continued to sing the strange, unsettling song. Loud enough for him to hear plainly, the words remained as riddlesome as the message the flames had left. Did they emanate from the same source?

He glanced at Idaria. She did not appear to have heard anything.

A sudden thought sent his hand into the pouch where the crystal lay. As Golgren tore it free, the voices in his head reached a crescendo.

"No!" the Grand Khan roared. He stumbled a few steps before shouting to the slave, "Lead me!"

She did not hesitate, grabbing his maimed limb and tugging at it to guide him through the deep darkness quicker than he could have done by himself. The pair ran as fast as they could.

A rumble like thunder echoed from ahead.

The ground shook with a sudden extreme violence that brought back to Golgren memories of the confrontation with the army of *f'hanos*. He struggled to maintain his balance, but fell to one knee. As ever, the elf managed to not only keep her own graceful footing, but helped him rise and run again.

The rumble magnified, becoming deafening.

"Hurry!" Golgren commanded.

Fire flickered far ahead. The ogre leader spotted the encampment.

But getting there was an impossibility. The path ahead was blocked by stone and dirt that had fallen from the mountainsides. There was enough of a gap to see ahead, yet he couldn't attempt to climb over or around, without risking his life.

Still, Golgren did not hesitate. There was only way to stop what was happening. And that was for him to hurl himself in the midst of it all.

The avalanche was assailing the column from all sides. Great masses of mountain debris rained down upon the terrified ogre warriors. Their screams vied with the horrific rumbling.

As he fought to reach the column, the fires enabled Golgren to observe the monstrous spectacle. He saw three ogres crushed by a single rock as large as the mastark. Where much of the right flank had bedded down for the night was already a rushing mass of earth that swept over several more warriors as if it were an ocean wave. Horses darted about, but they had nowhere to go.

Of Barech, there was no sign. However, where Golgren recalled the commander had slept he saw that spot was covered by a huge chunk of earth that had dropped from high above.

Amid the chaos, the mastark recklessly charged toward Golgren. The Grand Khan leapt away from a pile of rocks and earth just as the beast reached where he'd been standing.

His decision proved life-saving. The spot where Golgren had stood suddenly collapsed, the earth there tumbling away so rapidly, while fresh rocks and debris rained from above, that Idaria also had to jump aside or die. Unfortunately for the mastark—and Golgren–the path was even more blocked than before. The battered animal trumpeted and backed up to try again.

As it did, a fresh rockslide dropped upon the leviathan, burying the struggling beast as if it were no more than an insect. The mastark let out one last desperate call before being submerged and disappearing.

Golgren pulled farther back as loose scree pelted him from all directions. Compared to the disaster that had overwhelmed Barech and his force, the danger was over for him.

The rumble gradually faded, leaving only the settling dust to echo in Golgren's ears. There was not a single sound of life within the area of the encampment, which was all but covered by the great collapse. Surely the warriors of Barech's hand were all dead. Over a thousand lives had been wiped out in perhaps no more than a few moments.

As the Grand Khan let that dread thought sink in, he realized that the warriors had perished because of *him*.

∘⚬◦⟨⬦⟩◦⚬∘

"Is that it?" sang Ulgrod, one of the newest of the Titans and among the most vocal of those who had called repeatedly for the half-breed's death. "He's to remain untouched?"

The Titans had all gathered for the magical event. Safrag had insisted that a pooling of all their power would save any individual from being too taxed with the job. Reserves of elixir were extremely low and had to be rationed.

No one in the inner circle, not even the usually outspoken Ulgrod, had dared point out that the Black Talon appeared to be far more refreshed and powerful than the rest of them.

"Of course, he is to remain untouched," Safrag responded like a soothing teacher. "The mongrel is our key to the Fire Rose. That was explained to all of you sufficiently."

131

The rest eagerly nodded; no one wished to annoy Safrag. The Black Talon and the other Titans had committed themselves to his plan. The artifact was the key to their independence and utter domination—it was the key to everything they desired. If Ulgrod wished to take chances with his life by questioning Safrag's decision, the rest were willing to let him.

They stood atop the mountains just west of where the column had met its doom, all but untouched by the wind rushing among the dire peaks. Even had it been bright daytime, neither Golgren nor any one else, not even the sharp-eyed Idaria, could have seen them. Yet the Titans could see far and with deadly accuracy, and watching their handiwork was part of the pleasure.

Destroying over a thousand lives had not been much more effort.

"But he'll surely know it was us—that is all I mean, master! We've shown our hand." Some of the other Titans cracked grins at his choice of words—considering Golgren's own physical state—but Ulgrod scowled at them. "We have marked ourselves openly as his enemies. Why should he continue on a hunt for something that he knows we also desire?"

"Because he has little choice. And because he *is* Golgren. He will assume the key to his survival is finding the Fire Rose and wielding it first, against us."

The others nodded, agreeing with the sense. Only Ulgrod dared speak again.

"And what if he does find the Fire Rose and wield it against us?"

The lead Titan only smiled more broadly. "He will not be able to do what he hopes. But we shall just let the mongrel find out that for himself, shall we not?" He raised his hands to the dark sky, a gesture immediately imitated by his gathered followers. "We shall thank him for preparing our people for our rule and finally, slowly, very painfully, put an end to him."

As the others joined him in smiling at that particular happy thought, Safrag sang out the words of a new spell.

The Titans vanished.

❧❦❧

Just as the Titans were unseen by Golgren and Idaria and the ill-fated warriors, so another figure had remained invisible to the sorcerers' gathering.

More a shadow than substance, the figure stared for a moment at the spot upon which the sorcerers had stood. Although no taller than Golgren and perhaps just a shade smaller, the figure showed no trepidation at having been so near the full might of the towering spellcasters. Indeed, its long, oval eyes of white radiated only contempt for those who had just departed. From behind the lower half of the tightly bound golden cloth that obscured all its other features, there came a brief but throaty laugh.

The gray and black, hooded figure disappeared.

X

SHADOWS AND SHADES

Tyranos awoke, momentarily uncertain as to where he was. Upon recalling, he tried to leap to his feet, only to fall back—fortunately onto a soft fur—as his head swam.

"Slowly," warned his companion. "I've had my head struck often enough to have learned the proper manner by which to rise afterward."

The wizard pushed himself up to his elbows and eyed the speaker. The Solamnian sat cross-legged to his left, as calm as if he were back among the highborn of his land and not stuck in a cave somewhere in the Vale of Vipers. Even his beard did not seem entirely out of place, for Stefan used his dagger to keep it fairly trim. There was nothing to suggest that the Knight of the Sword was concerned about *anything*.

"What happened? I remember you helping me and bringing me to the cave. But after that my mind draws a blank."

"That was about the time you fainted."

"I fainted? Never!"

Stefan put away his dagger. "I was warned you'd be full of pride. But I've had that failing too."

"You were warned? By whom?"

The Solamnian cocked his head. "You know."

The wizard sat straight up. His eyes darted back and forth as he better surveyed his surroundings. The cave entrance was several yards to his right, which meant that at a good sprint, he could reach it before the Solamnian could stop him.

But staring behind Stefan, Tyranos spotted something more valuable to him than a swift means of exit. Just beyond the Solamnian lay the wizard's precious staff.

And next to Stefan side lay the knight's sword. So unfortunately, the Solamnian could run him through before the wizard could shove him aside and grab the staff.

"Did you want it?" Stefan asked, reaching behind him and, without looking, taking up the very item his guest so coveted.

"You know I do."

Stefan tossed it to him.

The wizard was so startled that he fumbled with the magical artifact before finally getting a good grip on it. He immediately pointed the crystal at the Solamnian.

"That really isn't necessary," Stefan assured him. "He would not have brought us together if either of us meant harm to one another."

"Stop talking like that!" Tyranos managed to lurch to his feet. A calm Stefan also rose. The Solamnian did not try to reach for his sword. The spellcaster kept in mind that he still had a dagger close at hand which was good for tossing. "Mayhap *he* talks with you, but that's no concern of mine."

"He only wants to help you. You're as much a follower of his as I am."

"He, him, it! Call that one by the name he's known best! Kiri-Jolith! My path diverged from his long ago, knight—or should I say *cleric?* That's what you are claiming, isn't it?"

Stefan shrugged. "I claim nothing. I'm only doing what he asks of me."

Tyranos felt his legs buckling. Through sheer grit, he kept on his feet. "Well, he can ask all he wants of me. But I do what I desire, not what any god or cleric likes!"

"But you want to find the Fire Rose, don't you?"

Tyranos hesitated. "What do you know of that? How much do you know . . . about me?"

"What I know is between my patron and me and no one else. Not even the Grand Khan Golgren."

With a derisive snort, the wizard retorted, *"That* is a perfectly empty answer. Just like a cleric."

"I'm also a knight. And besides, I always heard that spell-casters are just as secretive."

Tyranos let slip a rueful smile. "Aye, that I'll not deny." Again his legs threatened to collapse. He quickly planted the end of the staff on the ground to help him balance on his feet. As Stefan moved to assist him, the wizard waved him off. "I will stand by myself, or not stand at all."

His comment provoked the Solamnian. "That has been your way for many years, hasn't it?"

"Will you kindly please stop trying to delve into my life?"

"As you like." Stefan sat down again. "The important question is, do you still want to find the Fire Rose?"

Teetering, Tyranos growled. "And you're going to just tell me where it is?"

"No, I can't do that, regrettably. I have an idea, because he has an idea. But where it is actually hidden is known truly by only one other, and he only gives those clues he enjoys giving."

"Bah, more empty talk. What does that mean?"

Stefan shrugged. "My patron didn't make that clear."

"A fine . . . A fine cleric"—the wizard leaned more and more on the staff—"you are . . ."

His legs gave. He fell face first to the floor.

But Stefan was somehow there before Tyranos struck the ground. The slighter man proved he was much stronger than the tall wizard, and lifted Tyranos up enough to get a better hold on him, before assisting the spellcaster to the soft fur again.

"You need some water."

"I need a good ale or some rum! Can you manage that?"

Stefan chuckled. "You'll have to make do with water."

"A fine cleric, as I said."

The Solamnian went to the innermost recesses of the shallow cave. The shadows hid exactly what he was doing, but Tyranos heard the scraping of rock. A few moments later, Stefan returned with a small sack of water.

"Did you conjure that up from the mountain?" scoffed the wizard.

"In a sense. There's a tiny spring back there. I leave something to catch some of the water and pour that into the sack."

"Truly amazing. You perform miracles."

The knight furrowed his brow. "Being a cleric is not about miracles. It's about faith. Faith finds ways."

"So does magic, thank you very much." Tyranos drank from the sack. "Better than ale, at the moment." Refreshed, he suddenly glared at his companion. "But you did heal me. From what I can recall of my injuries, that had to take more than faith."

"Did it? I had only faith and my patron."

"And do you have faith in your patron when he tells you how we can find the Fire Rose, which even he, admittedly, cannot?"

Taking the sack, Stefan confidently replied, "For that, we'll need the help of the Grand Khan Golgren."

Tyranos eyed him. "That's the least surprising thing you've said . . . Stefan. That's your name, isn't it?"

"Sir Stefan Rennert, Knight of the Sword, nephew of Sir Augustus Rennert—"

The wizard waved him to silence. "None of that, please. I've had lineages tossed at me all my life." He rubbed his broad jaw. "So, as I presumed, the half-breed is the key. Although why he of all people it should be, I'd like to know."

"That wasn't made clear to me."

"Of course not. Nothing is clear. Can you at least tell me what you want? The Fire Rose for Solamnia?"

"Not in the least," Stefan replied, his distaste evident. "I don't doubt some of those high above would prefer the artifact in their hands, but my patron has told me enough about it that I can only see catastrophe if anyone possesses it too long."

Tyranos snorted. "And yet, he wishes it in the hands of Golgren. If that isn't a contradiction, I don't know what is!"

"I only understand that I must help keep it away from the clutches of others who desire it, and leave its uses to Golgren. And also to you, to some extent, I think."

"How gracious of the gods!" the spellcaster sneered. "And did Kiri-Jolith say exactly how long I'm permitted to use the Fire Rose, or if there are any stipulations as to what I'm allowed to do with the Rose for the few moments he *permits?*"

Stefan started to reply, but suddenly he heard a sound from outside. It was a sound familiar to the wizard, judging by his reaction.

The cries of many, many gargoyles.

Tyranos clutched his staff tight, uncertain what to do.

Stefan readied his sword, but he merely used it to gesture Tyranos to caution and silence. For several tense moments the two waited, while outside the cries rose louder and nearer. The Solamnian pulled forth his triangular medallion, and Tyranos heard him speak not just with his patron, but also with several others who boasted names such as Willum and Hector.

At last, even though the wizard felt with certainty the gargoyles would have located and searched the cave, the cries faded. Within another moment, silence settled again on the area.

"They were very frustrated to find out that the dragon wasn't really a dragon," Stefan commented dryly. "I'll have to come up with another trick next time."

Memories stirred. "That roar? It was you?"

"With some faith in Kiri-Jolith and the proper ambience."

"Inspired!" Tyranos sat straight again and was pleased to discover that his head did not swim. He hoped his legs would soon follow the head's excellent example. "I think I know why

those damned things are all in the mountains. But who was
that shadow with the eyes like the Icewall?"

"Ah! You've seen it too"

"Seen it and know it played me for a fool! Set me a trap I
walked into and would've never escaped if not for your good
imitation of one of the winged behemoths!" The leonine
spellcaster growled. "By the Kraken! That shadow—I'm fairly
certain it was *he*—was able to stay among all those gargoyles
with no worries about being torn to shreds!"

That did not appear to surprise Stefan. He put aside his
sword in order to reach for some kind of meat. The wizard's
stomach was empty, so he couldn't have been more pleased.

"Why should he be worried?" the Solamnian asked as he
handed a morsel to the wizard. "From what little I saw, they
obey him as if he were one of them." Stefan shook his head.
"No, more than that . . ."

"More?"

The Solamnian tore off a piece of meat for himself.
"More. They obey him. They obey him as if he were their
very *king*."

∽∾⟨●⟩∾∽

Golgren did not sleep that night, though he rested a little.
It was something he had learned to do early in life, a tiny half-
breed like himself who was often the target of many taller
ogres. Rest restored his strength and cleared his mind.

He and Idaria sat protected from the wind between two
large outcroppings about an hour's rising from the scene of
death and destruction. Golgren had not bothered to see if there
were survivors, although the elf had recommended doing that.
He had declined because he believed all were dead, but also
because he had to keep going forward, or something else was
bound to happen.

The Titans were extremely impatient to get their taloned
hands on the Fire Rose. And so was Golgren.

With dawn, he had tried again to reach either Khleeg or Wargroch. But Tyranos's crystals did not appear to be functioning anymore. Why that was did not really matter. What did matter was that Golgren had only himself and Idaria upon whom to rely. That was a mistake his enemies would regret.

With Idaria in tow, the Grand Khan made his way among the mountains. He had no idea how far he had to travel, nor even exactly where he had to go. From his low vantage point, all Golgren could see were the tops of the mountains. He had to trust what Barech had said. The trail would lead him to the vale.

The high peaks kept the pair in shadows throughout the day, making it difficult to see much ahead. Golgren had both his sword and dagger, and could defend them against any strange animals who made the place their habitat. But they did not confront any unusual creatures, nor did they *hear* any. The wind continued to be the only sound rushing through the chain.

"No birds," the elf commented solemnly late in their trek. Her gaze had often turned skyward, where the only hint of daylight could be glimpsed. "None."

"No birds," he agreed. They both knew how peculiar that was. The mountains should have been perfect nesting areas for some of the great birds: condors, blood hawks, and the like. And there were none of the predators that stalked the winged creatures.

No birds or animals meant less chance of food. For a day or two, that would not be a great problem. Idaria did not eat much, and Golgren was used to famine. Beyond that, though . . .

Near nightfall, the slave suddenly sniffed the air. Golgren thought he also smelled something, but the elf had an even sharper nose than him when it came to certain scents.

"There is water near," she announced.

"How far?"

"Not very." Idaria nimbly stepped along the uneven ground, her fleet footsteps making the ogre leader trail awkwardly. But Golgren kept up with Idaria as best he could. Only a few minutes later, the slave paused near a small crevasse. Idaria slipped into the gap to explore, emerging a moment later.

"There is a stream. A small one, but more than enough for our needs."

The half-breed joined her inside the crevasse. The stream was as she described it, a little stream caused either by melting ice from above or a deep underground flow. The mountain chain had life after all; one merely had to be patient enough to find it.

Near the stream they found a small patch of mushrooms. Idaria plucked up one of the lumpy, gray spearheads.

"I cannot say whether it is poisonous or not—"

The half-breed quickly snatched up another and stuffed it into his mouth. After chewing and swallowing it, he said to her, "It is not poisoned."

The slave stared at him for a moment before picking a few small ones for herself. The meal of mushrooms did not put an end to their hunger, but it did lessen it considerably.

They had nothing with which to carry water; their sacks had been buried under tons of rock. Both drank as much as they could.

Just as they finished, Golgren felt a warmth on his hand. Immediately, he held up the signet.

The symbols faintly glowed.

"Look," the elf murmured, pointing.

He looked where she pointed, at where the stream gushed forth from the mountainside. There, a symbol etched in the rock also glowed faintly.

A curved line with two dots to its right.

As Golgren reached for the etching, both its glow and that of the signet faded. Despite that, he was able to trace the symbol and verify its astonishing existence.

Golgren ran his hands along the mountainside, but found

no other etchings, no hidden gaps. It was as if someone else had paused to drink and decided to leave the mysterious symbol.

"It is old," Idaria interjected. "Scratched by one of the High Ogres."

Golgren continued to trace the markings. "Yes, it would be them. Not the Titans. The sorcerers, they would have no reason for doing that."

"The vision . . ."

The Grand Khan glanced at her. "The vision?"

The slave's eyes grew veiled. "The one in Ben-ihm."

He bared his teeth slightly. "So, my Idaria was already present for the vision? You did not appear after?"

"No, my lord. I was there but a moment before you rose. I saw the vision of the casters, and the shadow that overtook them in the end."

He showed no anger at her revelation. "The High Ogres were surely dead long ago. But their magic . . ." The half-breed grinned darkly. "Their magic maybe lives."

He stroked the symbol and touched the signet to it. But if Golgren hoped for anything more to happen, he was sorely disappointed.

"We are done," he finally said to Idaria.

Departing the stream, the pair continued on through the harsh mountain pass. Without horses, the journey was certain to take much longer, but there was nothing they could do about that.

Night fell upon them and once more they found what shelter they could. The dreams and nightmares that so often haunted Golgren returned with a vengeance. He saw visions of his mother slaughtered, and her body—which he had so painstakingly carried to safety—eaten by the scavenging *ji-baraki*. Whereas in the waking world the half-breed had avenged himself on the beasts, in his nightmares they kept dragging the corpse out of reach. All the while, the unblinking eyes of his elf mother condemned him for even being born.

The other nightmares were twisted versions of important events that had marked his life. In one he led the village of his youth into battle against the Nerakans, only to watch the villagers slaughtered as the knights turned into scorpion warriors with four arms—each wielding a sword or some wickedly-barbed club—and as many tails. Worse yet, the dead stumbled to their feet to join the warriors trying to drag him down into the bowels of Golthuu's desolate landscape.

But through the nightmares there came at last a soft touch and soothing murmurs. The Grand Khan awoke to Idaria.

She said nothing more, and he did not thank her. It was her duty as his slave.

It was still dark, but Golgren had no immediate desire to return to his slumber. He rubbed his thick brow and stared at their murky surroundings. Vague rock formations took on more sinister aspects at night. Some resembled beasts, both real and mythic. There was the head of a roaring dragon. Beyond that he could see the wing and spine outline of a *V'radu Ikn,* a flying creature like a *ji-baraki* with feathered appendages. *V'radu Ikn* did not, fortunately, exist anywhere but in the imagination of ancient ogre storytellers. They were said to sneak up on a warrior the night before a significant battle in order to steal and eat his courage. Losing one's courage was the worst thing that could befall an ogre.

Yet another rock formation took the shape of a hooded figure bent over as if carrying a heavy burden. If Golgren squinted, it almost looked as if another, identical figure loomed a little behind the first, no doubt assisting with the load.

He realized that the shapes *were* moving, albeit very, very slowly.

The pair trudged along as if hardly able to stand, much less carry whatever was their shared burden. Golgren started to rise, but hesitated when he noticed two more hooded shapes behind the first pair.

From his side, Idaria quietly asked, "My lord, what is it?

Do you see something?"

That she asked the question clearly meant that the vision belonged to his eyes only. The Grand Khan suddenly looked to his hand. The warmth told him what his eyes verified a breath later—there was a faint glow emanating from the symbols.

"What do you see, my lord?" the elf inquired again.

Golgren did not answer her, and as he peered again at the figures, he saw *two more.* All moved with silence; all moved as though they carried the weight of the entire world on their backs.

The Grand Khan let out a slight hiss as he made a count of the figures. Eight in total.

There had been eight High Ogres in his vision.

Golgren slowly moved toward the figures, trying to focus better on them. Although he was able to make them out as forms, they were never very distinct. As he drew closer, he saw that they did not exactly walk, but kept jerking slightly and shifting forward, as if someone were pushing along a series of drawings.

Their poses varied. Each shift revealed slight differences from the previous manifestation. It came to Golgren's mind that he was perhaps seeing *pieces* of the past.

That he was experiencing a vision that had something to do with the artifact was obvious; perhaps the figures even carried the artifact. However, no matter the angle from which he studied the shadows, he was never able to see what it was they carried. Indeed, when Golgren tried to come around behind the figures, he discovered they had no dimension of depth. Their overall images had two sides, but not front or back—very much like drawings.

Idaria joined him, aware that something beyond her ken was taking place, yet still trying in vain to perceive what it was. She started to come around Golgren's other side, putting herself in the shadows' path without realizing it.

Golgren tried to warn her off, but it was too late. The

first shade passed directly through the slave without pause, and without any apparent effect either to her or to the shadowy figure.

Finally with some idea of what was happening, Idaria moved over behind Golgren, following him as he paced the last of the shades.

Standing, they would have been just slightly shorter than Golgren and roughly the size of an Uruv Suurt. There were faint glimpses of faces among them, but not enough to identify them.

"It is the eight," he verified to himself. "The eight casters." The Grand Khan again attempted to spot what it was that those in front carried, but all he caught were glimpses of what seemed to be a large, dark chest.

So engrossed was he in angling for a better view that he no longer paid attention to where the band was heading. It was Idaria who saved him at the last second from what might have been a hard collision with a wall of rock, the elf pulling Golgren back with a surprising display of strength. Golgren watched narrow-eyed as the final shadow entered the rock.

He thrust his hand after the last figure. Surprisingly, his fingers passed through, briefly, but they grazed the rock hard enough to warn the half-breed that the wall was no illusion.

As the final shape faded away, something new shimmered into existence. Golgren's eyes widened as he beheld the second symbol etched by the fires, scored into the rock wall.

A brief but startled sound from Idaria indicated that she saw the symbol too. Golgren studied the mark closely, trying to see if it differed in some way from the one in the encampment. As far as he could determine, they were identical.

"But what does it mean?" he murmured. *"Kya i thu den?"* Golgren repeated, momentarily slipping back into the Ogre tongue.

In a rare sign of frustration, the ogre leader banged his fist against the rock.

The signet flashed. The symbol flashed.

And a blazing gap opened up before the Grand Khan, who stumbled forward and fell through.

XI

REBELLION

There were survivors among Khleeg's hand, though not very many.

The black cloud that had descended on the struggle had materialized from nothing. One moment, there had only been the baking sun, the next it was as if darkest night had come.

One by one, followed by the dozens, the bolts had struck selectively. They fell so long as there was resistance, ending the moment that the hapless defenders finally gave in to the inevitable. More than two hundred burnt corpses gave witness to the monstrous horror. The stench of burning flesh filled the region.

Rauth's warriors and the traitors among Khleeg's hand quickly moved in to seize those left standing. The prisoners were gathered together, and those who were officers of any sort were separated from the rest.

Rauth rode up in front of the others. A narrow-eyed warrior with a crooked mouth that seemed constantly about to smile, he gestured at the officers, the first of whom was dragged forward to him.

The ogre officer leaped down. He seized the bound

prisoner by his mane and pulled his head back. The other ogre struggled, but the guards held him in place.

Keeping his axe sheathed, Rauth drew a dagger that had once been wielded by his commander, Khemu. There were stains on the blade: Khemu's blood.

"F'han!" his own followers shouted. *"F'han!"*

With a grin, the treacherous officer drew a thin red line across the captive's throat. It was not enough to slay the prisoner, but certainly put him through excruciating agony.

The guards shoved the bleeding captive down on his knees. His hands were unbound, brought around to the front, and retied tightly. He was stretched forward as far as possible.

The captive tried to pull away. Rauth sheathed the dagger and accepted a hefty axe from a comrade. He raised the weapon high over the kneeling figure.

As the axe came down, the bound officer tried to throw himself forward. But once again, the guards held him in place. They would pay the price if Rauth missed his target.

The heavy blade chopped through *both* wrists.

The kneeling ogre screamed as blood poured from his severed limbs. His arms moved about as he tried in vain to connect them somehow to the lost appendages.

Rauth's followers roared their approval, while the prisoners gave a horrified hiss. Some grew restive, but guards moved in and whipped any who looked defiant.

The maimed officer finally collapsed, the blood loss and shock too much for even an ogre to bear. The guards unceremoniously dragged his lifeless body to where the rest of the dead lay.

Rauth casually plucked up the severed hands. With blood and fragments of flesh and muscle dripping down his arms, the ogre held the appendages for the rest of the prisoners to see.

Even for an ogre, Rauth was a creature of few words. But those few words were all he needed to make his point.

"Golgren!" he roared, tossing the severed hands up in the air and letting them fall with a disconcerting thud on the blood-soaked soil.

Only the wind and the quiet, hesitant breathing of the prisoners was heard in the aftermath of the short but ghastly spectacle. Rauth grinned as he looked among them, his blood-shot gaze especially focusing on the unnerved officers.

When enough time had passed, Rauth used the axe to point at the next prisoner he wanted brought before him. Compared to the first captive, the ogre did not begin his journey to death with the slightest hint of courage. Out of his yellow-toothed mouth poured unintelligible noises of fear and terror. He twisted and turned and tried to do everything he could to keep from being dragged to the murderous traitor. There were few things that ogres outright feared, but what Rauth had done to the first victim was a mutilation they considered among the most heinous.

The officer watched with grinning amusement as the second prisoner was positioned before him like the previous victim. He drew his dagger and once more cut a thin line across the throat. The guards immediately forced the wounded warrior to his knees and brought the hands forward.

Rauth gripped the axe and raised it high over his head.

A breath later, he lowered it again. To the surprise of the prisoners, he came around to his victim's front and used the flat of the axe to raise the shivering figure's gaze to him.

"Atolgus . . ." Rauth declared, his eyes indicating the axe head. He shifted the head to a position just over the wrists. "Golgren . . ."

The captive was immediate in responding. "Atolgus! Swear to Atolgus!"

His response was not yet enough. Rauth let the axe slip closer to the wrists.

The bound ogre immediately twisted his head to the side, offering his bleeding neck to the axe. With a savage grin, Rauth touched the shallow cut with the flat of the axehead.

"Atolgus!" the prisoner roared. "I swear to Atolgus!"

From the traitors there came triumphant barks. The guards lifted the bleeding captive to his feet and untied him. He was presented with another axe.

Rauth pointed to the next enemy officer.

⋄⋆⟡⋆⋄

Nearly all the prisoners would surrender their lives to their captors, in return for becoming bound by blood oath to the traitors' dark cause. It was part of an old ogre tradition that Golgren himself had utilized at times. The cutting of the hands was a new touch designed specifically to remind the prisoners that the Grand Khan was already a thing half-condemned to a shameful afterlife, and thus hardly a ruler for whom it was worth sacrificing one's own eternal fate.

Khleeg growled under his breath at the bloody, albeit cunning strategy. To most ogres, one of the worst things that could happen to a warrior was to have his hands—which held his strength and skills—severed either before or after death. The afterlife in which most ogres believed was a place of no pity; those without hands would be forced to beg forever. A death without hands shamed the clan as well.

There was no doubt in Khleeg's mind that, had he been among the prisoners, the first maimed corpse down there would have been his. Not for a moment did he think the traitors would have granted him the chance to change his allegiance. And not for a moment would Golgren's second in command have even considered saving himself for what he felt would be a greater eternal shame.

Astounding as it seemed even to him, he lived, and he watched the foul deeds from a low ridge some distance away. He had been certain of his doom when the black cloud had suddenly arisen, for he recognized the sorcery of the Titans.

But before the cloud could strike, Khleeg had somehow been whisked away. Khleeg had only one explanation for his amazing rescue: The strange crystal that the Grand Khan had given to him had saved him. To Khleeg's straightforward mind, that was the only explanation. And yet Golgren had not informed him of any such ability on the part of the crystal. He could only assume his lord had wanted to keep that a secret for some reason.

A part of Khleeg wanted to go charging into the throng in order to smite Rauth down. However, not only would he never make it all the way to the traitorous officer, but Rauth was apparently not the true leader of the astounding insurrection.

That mantle belonged to a most unlikely choice: a young chieftain of a nomadic tribe whom Khleeg had last seen being offered an officer's rank in one of the southern hands. Khleeg recalled Atolgus well, a tall ogre eager to curry favor with the Grand Khan. It had been Atolgus who had found the knight, Stefan Rennert, and brought him to Garantha. For that, Golgren had rewarded him, and all indications had been that Atolgus was a loyal follower. Certainly Khleeg, who considered himself good at judging other warriors, had seen no guile.

The Grand Khan had let Khleeg know Atolgus had a future. That some day, once better seasoned, Atolgus would first lead a hand before joining the august circle of which the Blödian was prime disciple.

But Atolgus had proven himself as dishonorable as a hunting *ji-baraki*. That, or he was a *Jaro Gyun,* a wearer of masks, a duplicitous creature pretending to be what he had never been.

Pushing out of sight, Khleeg sought the crystal. He had tried to contact his lord before, but for some reason the crystal was dead. Khleeg hoped that it would work again.

But although he was certain that he followed the proper instructions, still the crystal did not show him his lord. Khleeg growled and nearly threw away the useless piece, but thought of the other who carried a crystal. Perhaps . . .

Holding it to his left eye, he muttered, "Wargroch."

There was a definite warmth to the stone. Encouraged, Khleeg repeated the name while picturing the younger officer.

A moment later, a startled Wargroch peered back at him. "Khleeg? Is that you?"

"Hear me!" The Blödian told all that had happened, including all he had heard about Atolgus. Wargroch made disconcerted noises, but did not interrupt the second in command's stream of explanation.

When Khleeg had finished, the other officer finally responded with a snarl of his own. He muttered something in Ogre that Khleeg could not quite make out. He rumbled in Common, "I myself will march down to southern Golthuu to find Atolgus! His head will hang from a pike at Garantha's gates!"

"No! Garantha must be protected from Rauth!" Khleeg had considered what should be done. He always sought to emulate his lord. "Warn . . . Warn hands near Sadurak!" Sadurak was deep in old Blöde, near to where the rebel leader was located. The warriors there were tried and true, one hand under a trusted commander. "Warn Jod! Jod will fight Atolgus! Jod is loyal!"

Wargroch mulled that over and replied, "Jod is loyal, yes."

"Beware Rauth! He will march to Garantha—"

Wargroch suddenly vanished. Khleeg still felt some vague link to the other officer, but for some reason, it was impossible to see or speak with Wargroch any longer.

A frustrated Khleeg again started to toss the crystal, but thought better of it and thrust it back into his pouch. He shoved himself away from the vicinity of Rauth's triumph, trying to decide what he should do next.

A sudden sound set every one of his nerves on alert. Khleeg drew his weapon as another ogre crept into sight. The disheveled warrior took one look at Khleeg and fell to one knee.

The Blödian recognized the other ogre, although not by name. Khleeg was fairly certain that the warrior was loyal.

"Rise," he ordered. "Others?"

In response, the warrior gestured behind him. Two more ogres appeared. One was wounded in the arm and carried no weapon. The other boasted a sword broken at the midpoint. If they were part of a trick to trap Golgren's second in command, they were a good one, for Khleeg found their pathetic state quite credible.

He waited to see if any more survivors would materialize, but that was apparently the entire sorry lot. Khleeg grimaced and signaled for all three to follow him. He had no idea exactly what he planned to do. The choices seemed either to head back to Garantha, or seek out Golgren.

Indeed, the ogre officer suddenly realized there was only *one* choice.

Gritting his yellowed teeth, and with his army of three trailing behind him, Khleeg picked up his pace.

꘎꘎꘎

His mind racing, Wargroch put away the crystal. Khleeg's call to him had thrown the younger officer off balance. Events were not happening as he had expected they would when he was left in command.

He summoned a subordinate. "Send word to all hand commanders in Garantha!" Wargroch decreed, trying to sound every inch as imposing and masterful as the Grand Khan in both his language and manner. "I will speak with them! Move!"

Within the hour, four hulking commanders entered the palace. To emphasize his rank, Wargroch had them meet with him in the throne chamber. Unlike Golgren, however, Wargroch filled the seat in every way. He was nearly two feet taller than the Grand Khan and, like Khleeg, was a Blödian ogre stouter in his build.

To his right, a chained meredrake dozed. The huge beast was a pet of Golgren's, who often fed him scraps of raw amalok when granting an audience. Wargroch let the giant green and brown reptile sleep. With the exception of its master, the meredrake considered anyone fooling with it as potential food.

Contrasting with when Golgren sat in Garantha, the walls were not lined with impressive, fierce-looking guards fanatically loyal to the Grand Khan. Only a pair of warriors utterly trusted by Wargroch stood near the metal doors; the only other eyewitnesses in the room were the many ghostly reliefs of the long-dead High Ogres. Blithely ignorant of current events, the latter continued their eternal festivals, hunts, and battles.

Like all hand commanders, the four had been chosen for their zealous loyalty to Golgren. Loyalty among ogres was generally of a mercurial nature, however. Grand Khans had risen and fallen in the space of months, even weeks or days, with a simple disaster or heavy loss in battle turning many against them.

There were some who maintained loyalty despite drastic turns of events. Golgren cultivated that sort as a breeder of those fighting amaloks who evinced the strongest builds, the sharpest horns, and—most of all—the fiercest tempers.

The four commanders eyed the seated Wargroch with some displeasure, as they considered Golgren the only rightful occupant of the throne. Wargroch remained seated, determined to remind them that he had been made ruler in Golgren's absence. That was important if he was to have his orders obeyed; his commands had to appear as though they issued directly from the Grand Khan himself.

"Garantha is threatened," he declared in as succinct a Common as any ogre could speak. It would have been much simpler to tell the four all they needed to know in their native tongue, but that would have looked wrong. Those warriors especially would expect to hear their orders in Common, and Common alone.

They reacted as expected, straightening and glancing at one another, before returning their narrowed gazes to him. Their forces were the primary defenses of the capital.

"The hands must march."

He received more than one surprised grunt. Wargroch did not allow the four time to think or react. He had made a decision, and he needed them to obey without question.

"They must march to meet the Black Shells."

"Neraka?" grunted one commander, his mouth twisted into an expression of hatred. "The *Skolax G'Ran*, they come?"

Wargroch nodded. "Yes, and we will meet them. We will crush the Black Shells."

He received nods and growls of approval. Mention of fighting the Nerakans was enough to whet appetites and curb any opposition. More than one of the commanders looked already eager to be off preparing his warriors.

Nor did Wargroch wish to delay them. "Varuus Sha. You march to Varuus Sha."

They knew the settlement. Varuus Sha lay near one of the more obscure parts of the western border between the ogres and the territories controlled by the Black Shells. The *Skolax G'Ran* were clever foes; they often slipped in through desolate areas.

"Varuus Sha," snarled the senior among the four. "We go!" He slapped his fist against his breastplate. The others imitated him.

With a nod, Wargroch gave them permission to leave. The commanders hurried away, grunting their eagerness. Avid as they were, they would have their forces on the march by morning.

Alone save for his pair of trusted guards, Wargroch rose. Briefly through the young officer's mind ran the images of his elder brothers, Nagroch and Belgroch.

"It is done," he muttered under his breath. "It is done."

But above the throne room, secreted in a place where he could hear all, the massive gargoyle, Chasm, let loose with a barely audible rumble. The master would be interested in all of it, of that Chasm was certain.

The gargoyle took to the air. He rose straight up and aligned himself between the sun and the ground. No ogre would see him high up there. His second eyelids slipped into place, protecting his own vision.

Chasm smelled the air, but he was not searching for any normal scent. He was linked by a magical bond to the wizard, a bond that enabled him to locate Tyranos wherever he was.

Finally the winged fury found his master, and a fresh growl escaped him. Tyranos was still in the place of the shadowed ones. They would take special pleasure in capturing Chasm and tearing him to shreds. The rivalry between his flock and theirs preceded his almost-lifelong servitude to the spellcaster.

But Chasm did not falter. If his fate was to perish under the tearing claws of his own kind, he would take many of them with him. What mattered was that he must reach his master as soon as possible.

Above all, he had no choice. Tyranos and the shadowed ones had made certain of that.

❧❀❧

In departing so rapidly, the gargoyle missed the arrival of a sweating, dust-covered rider who leaped up the steps of the ancient palace and rushed past the rearing statues of the great griffons that flanked the entrance. The gasping rider clutched in his right arm a leather pouch that was not of ogre make. Behind him, his sturdy steed gasped from exertion, the rider having pressed the animal hard even during the height of *iSirriti Siroth*. The messenger had pushed himself just as hard, sleeping little and eating less.

A sentry stopped him.

"*Wo usan i—*" The rider paused for breath. When he spoke again, it was to shout. "The Grand Khan! Must see the Grand Khan!"

His echoing cry reached Wargroch, who, accompanied by his two guards, had left the chamber of the throne with other duties in mind, but had paused to study a relief that often riveted his attention. In the picture, a beautiful female High Ogre used magic to raise from the ground a field of exotic flowers. Behind her was a hilly landscape that had, despite the centuries, remained identifiable even to that day. Wargroch easily recognized the area where his clan made their home and thus felt an affinity for that particular ghost of the past.

He heard the cries for the Grand Khan's attention. Wargroch signaled to one of his guards and, moments later, the warrior returned with the rider in tow.

"Must find the Grand Khan!" the newcomer continued to gasp. He clutched the leather pouch tightly, as Wargroch stared intently at it.

"I guard Garantha for the Grand Khan. Speak to me as you speak to him!"

The rider looked dubious. "The Grand Khan not in Garantha?"

With a growl, Wargroch signaled the guard nearest the newcomer. The guard put the edge of his sword against the rider's throat.

Grunting, the courier handed the pouch over. Wargroch nodded to the guard, who lowered his weapon.

Golgren's officer turned the pouch around in order to open it. Yet his hand momentarily froze over the leather strap sealed in thick wax, for the emblem imprinted there—the weapon, the flower, the bird—were familiar to all who knew the Grand Khan.

It was the symbol of Solamnia.

XII

LIGHT AND SHADOW

At the birth of every healthy male child—females were only considered important for breeding and domestic work, even if they did actually help fight too—there was a ceremony to mark another potential warrior to strengthen the tribe and clan. It always began at the beginning of iSirriti Siroth, for if a warrior could not face Sirrion's Burning each day of his life, he was certainly not capable of facing his tribe's enemies. Weak children perished quickly among the ogres.

Only males were allowed at the ceremony, for according to ogre thinking, a female presence would weaken the spiritual might the father wished the land to bestow upon his son. Gathered were some fifty armed males from as young as ten summers, to one lone figure known to be at least an astounding sixty summers in age. They collected at the settlement's most sacred site. Ogres always counted their age by the number of summers survived, for the Burning was most intense.

Indeed, the site itself was a place where the sun shone fiercest in that part of old Kern. The Aur nu iSirriti, Sirrion's Eye, was shaped much like a vast oval bowl scooped out by the god. It was a spot where even the hardiest ogre had to wear straps of cloth over their eyes merely to see normally, for the region was *encrusted with crystal growths that caught every aspect of the day's light and magnified it. Shamans among the local tribes claimed to observe the land's spirits, even servants of the fire god who frolicked during the height of day, although only shamans were foolish enough to peer into the* Aur nu iSirriti *at that time and without any eye protection.*

Sarth was the only one among the males who moved with ease through the bowl. Although he was spindly and much past his prime as a hunter, everyone treated him with deference. The shaman had survived far more than any of them could imagine, from the rule of dragonlords and the dread goddess known to most of the world as Takhisis, from the constant battles against the Uruv Suurt, *the* Skolax G'Ran, *and, of course, from the eternal infighting among their own kind. Sarth had survived all.*

At the edges of the bowl, four ogre warriors had set up goatskin drums nearly as large as themselves. The frames of each drum were made from the rib bones of young meredrakes; nothing was ever wasted among ogres. As Sarth entered the bowl, the four warriors began to beat a slow rhythm like that of a resting heart.

In the center of the bowl was the even more obvious reason for it being called Sirrion's Eye: a wide, onyx outgrowth that almost did resemble a staring pupil. Sarth walked alone to the outgrowth before turning in the direction from which he had come.

Among the assembled males, a towering warrior with a face savage even by ogre standards stepped forward. He carried in his meaty hands a brown cloth in which squirmed the child to be honored that day.

As the father entered the bowl, the other warriors congregated around the edge and began beating the tops of their clubs, the heads of their axes, or the tips of their swords and spears against the rocky soil, grunting in unison with the drums.

"Carn i f'dar iBraagi jusuun," *called Sarth to the father, making a sign from the sire to the infant.* "Husoch i iBraagi tu d'lach?"

The father nodded. He did not wear the face of a proud warrior who carried a son by his seed. Rather, he looked as if he wished he could hand the bundle to anyone else.

"Husoch i tu sadi d'lach." *He held up the squirming bundle, which was, to the eyes of all there, puny in comparison to what an ogre infant generally weighed at birth.* "D'lach i iGuyviri"

There were startled grunts from the other males. The drumming ceased in mid-beat. The shaman, clad only in an old, dirt covered loincloth, bared his teeth—a rare showing of consternation on the shaman's scarred and wrinkled visage.

But when he responded, Sarth spoke calm and strong. "Bya d'lach iGuyviri."

The drumming renewed. Sarth indicated for the father, Braag, to join him in the center of the bowl.

As Braag lowered the child toward the elder ogre, he revealed three jagged crimson bolts tattooed on his lower torso. They were one of the symbols marking him as chieftain of the tribe. That made the tininess of the infant even more significant, for a chief's son should be great and strong from birth. Yet there was not even a lusty cry from the child, merely writhing movement and silence.

Sarth drew the symbol of the sun in the air and gestured at a crooked gap in the onyx outgrowth.

Without preamble, Braag placed the cloth-covered infant on the jagged surface. The figure inside squirmed more, but only when Sarth gently removed the top of the cloth was the son of Braag revealed.

Premature births—generally stillborns—were all too common among ogres, who struggled day to day for survival. The infant son of Braag looked very much like the result of a premature birth, not only in size, but in the stunted features of the face and the softness of the oddly pale skin.

The eyes opened . . . eyes that were not ogre at all, but more like that of the hated elves. Almond-shaped they were, and of an emerald green reminiscent of the distant forests of Silvanost. Small wonder, since the baby's mother was an elf herself, a slave with whom the chieftain was so obsessed he had made her his mate. He even accepted the son she had birthed, a son who, by all rights, should not have been possible. No crossbreeding between the two races was known before. Neither would have wanted such a birth either. But it had come.

And a son, even one as puny and as likely to die quickly as Braag believed he would, was better than nothing at all. To the chieftain, it was a way of binding the mother to him more, a desire far greater in his heart than to see the infant live. Only for her did he treat the wriggling mass like his own blood.

"Tun i f'da oGuyviri, oGuyviri," Sarth muttered to the baby.

The eyes stared at the shaman as if understanding. Sarth grunted, and produced a rusty dagger seemingly from nowhere.

With expert precision, he drew a tiny red line across the infant's chest. The child—called Guyvir by his father—squirmed but did not otherwise react, which caused both the shaman and Braag to hesitate for a moment. Sarth finally gave the chieftain an impressed grunt, which made Braag nod approvingly. Small and pale the chieftain's son might be, but the baby handled pain better than most ogre children. That in itself was a trait in which the father might take some pride.

Sarth took the blade to Braag's chest, where, with the bloody point, he drew a similar line. Thus the tie between father and child was acknowledged. The strength of the elder would feed the younger, while the potential greatness of the younger would make immortal the elder.

Assuming the younger lived.

The sun had risen enough that the bowl was almost blinding. Even with the thin strips of cloth to protect his eyes, Braag needed to shield them with one hand. Sarth appeared to pay the increasing brightness no mind, and neither, it seemed, did the child. Guyvir did nothing but continue to stare at the elder shaman, or perhaps through him. Sarth could not help but look up over his bent shoulder. Yet there was nothing to see.

Returning the dagger to the infant, the elder ogre let the oddly soft mouth touch the blade's tip. Guyvir instinctively sought to suckle the tip, resulting in him lapping up a drop or two of the mingled blood.

The assembled males barked. The drummers doubled the beat.

Sarth set the dagger down next to the baby. The onyx outgrowth glowed with the power of the great fireball in the sky. The Burning was well underway. The shaman hurried with the ceremony. Not even a tiny child like that could be risked if there was any chance he would serve the tribe and the clan. Ogres were harsh and hardy, but not mad.

The elder ogre threw a pinch of gray powder at the staring child. Next to him, Braag let out a sound of mild surprise; the dust had seemingly come from Sarth's very fingertips. There was no pouch at his waist, no cup at his side.

Guyvir sniffed at the dust, but did not even sneeze. For a child of any age, he seemed extremely calm, patient. Sarth's brow grew more wrinkled.

"Idun tu i iGuyviri zadi tun—"

A shadow passed over Sirrion's Eye. The drummers faltered, and all looked to the sky, including the shaman.

And all were immediately blinded by the fierce fireball that was the sun.

There was an intake of breath from Sarth as he turned his gaze back to the infant. Again, it seemed as if the baby Guyvir were staring past him.

Braag suddenly seized his son, a shocking break in the ceremony. Sarth put a warning hand on the chieftain's arm, but Braag angrily shook it off.

"Gya i f'huu di iGuyviri tun jakabari ul!" Braag almost spat. His red-tinted eyes swept over his son with open loathing. Braag had taken the inexplicable shadowing of the sun as a sign his offspring was cursed.

Sarth shook his head, but Braag stalked away from the site, his warriors already gathering behind him. The shaman shook his head again; the father risked a curse if he didn't let the ceremony finish.

"Dya i f'huu di iGuyviri o iBraagi daruun," *the shaman murmured, glancing not at the retreating form of the chieftain, but rather up at the bright sky again. He nodded to himself. Turning to face empty air, he suddenly said in Common, "The fire is your destiny, Guyvir."*

❧❦❧

And, at that moment, Golgren stirred. His first impulse was to look around him, yet there were no signs of Sarth, his father, or wretched *Aur nu iSirriti.* Even so, Golgren felt as if the event which he had dreamed had only just taken place, despite the fact *he* had been the infant in the dream.

He could not, of course, recall something so far back in his life as his birth ceremony, and he had never heard anyone talk about that event in his life. And yet . . . He recalled an odd look on his father's ugly countenance whenever they had taken part in similar ceremonies, a look of *uncertainty,* as if Braag wondered if he had made some dreadful mistake.

But had that mistake been to take his child from Sirrion's Eye, or simply to let Golgren live at all?

The half-breed stood. He had no idea where he was, save that he was underground in a wide chamber that looked to have been formed by nature. A vast number of narrow, long stalactites hung over him, while in various places on the floor shorter, thicker stalagmites thrust up as if miniature mountains.

Golgren registered one very unnatural element to the chamber: He could see almost as if the sun shone down upon it. There was no discernible source of illumination, yet he could see twenty strides in every direction. In one of those directions was a gap that led away from the chamber.

The symbol carved in the rock by what he assumed was High Ogre magic had sent him here, that much was obvious.

But exactly how far he was from Idaria and his last location was impossible to know. He'd prefer to assume he was still in the mountains leading to the Vale of Vipers, but it was also possible that he was somewhere else in old Blöde, if even in old Blöde at all.

The Grand Khan glanced around again. No, there was no sign of Idaria. He did find his weapon, though, which he quickly retrieved. Whatever had conspired to cast him to the cave had evidently wanted him armed . . . unless that was just accidental.

Golgren eyed the signet. It was all innocence, a purely decorative piece of jewelry. He pointed it in every direction, but it stayed silent.

His choices seemed few. Golgren headed to the gap at the far end. Perhaps it led to a way out . . . or, better yet, to the artifact he hunted.

The dream returned to his thoughts, for the Grand Khan had no doubt it depicted events that had truly played out in his life. Golgren would have liked to question Sarth about the dream. Indeed, he would have liked to question Sarth about other matters, as well. How *old* the shaman was, for instance. Older than any ogre of whom Golgren knew. Only High Ogres and Titans lived as long, or so Golgren's assumption had always been.

A slight sound—a hint of breathing—caught his attention. Instantly the Grand Khan thought of Idaria.

His pace quickened. Golgren reached the dark gap and, without pause, entered a tunnel. It suddenly illuminated, and Golgren caught the signet doing its work. There had been a very brief glowing of the symbols just before the tunnel brightened.

But something tore his attention from the signet and the tunnel, a movement just at the end of the illuminated area. Again Golgren hurried forward, fairly certain that it must be Idaria. If it wasn't the slave, surely it was wise for him to catch up with the person nonetheless.

THE FIRE ROSE

As he reached the next darkened area, it lit up too. Golgren came to an abrupt halt as a long, rocky corridor met his wary view. There was no physical means by which anyone could have fled so fast as to escape being seen, yet the corridor was empty.

No, not entirely empty. There was something etched into the wall to the right.

It was not, however, another one of the fiery symbols from the encampment, but rather a fresh marking which he did not recognize. Two lines came together at the bottom of a symbol, with what looked like a down-turned dagger hovering over both. Golgren was certain of one thing: it was a mark of the High Ogres. The style of it was akin to what he had already seen.

The half-breed briefly bared his teeth at the mark. From behind him arose a slight, moist sound, as if a tiny pool of water had suddenly rippled.

But there had been no hint of water anywhere. Golgren turned, his sword ready.

Too late did he sense something peel off the ceiling above him.

It dropped upon the Grand Khan as if both liquid and solid, and astoundingly alive. As it covered Golgren, he felt it seize his wrist and envelop his lone hand.

He thrust the end of his maimed limb into the central portion of the mass and felt some substance. The dripping fiend twisted, giving Golgren just enough space to breathe.

Whether it was better to fight the thing in the light or the dark was debatable. Golgren grimaced as he beheld a constantly shifting mockery of a face that might have been that of an ogre, an elf, or something entirely unknown to him. Worse, the features kept melting away, growing anew. It was impossible to imagine such transformations were not painful. Surely the monster used that pain to fuel its awful strength.

Perhaps its terrible stench was useful as a weapon too, for it was all the half-breed—who had suffered many terrible odors in his time, including the decay of battlefield dead—could do to breathe. Golgren struggled to push the monster away from him, but the creature had an insatiable grip, largely on his hand. In fact, Golgren realized it took exceptional interest in his remaining hand. Or perhaps what really interested the monster was what the Grand Khan wore on one finger.

He had no intention of surrendering the signet even to that powerful, macabre creature. Golgren forced one knee under the dripping mass and did not falter even when that knee sank halfway into the deathly pale torso.

Halfway, but not *all* the way. With great satisfaction, Golgren shoved hard.

His leverage—which he, a shorter, slighter warrior among so many ungainly giants, always took into account—served him well. The slobbering menace went falling back, losing its hold on his hand.

Golgren pushed himself up and slashed deep with his sword into the attacker's chest. The sharp blade cut into the pale mass without hindrance.

But the blow appeared entirely ineffective as the cut sealed immediately. Golgren nearly lost the sword as the creature's body sealed around the tip. Only a last-second tug freed it, the point coming out with a disturbing, moist whoosh.

The thing sloshed toward him. Moving on what passed for two legs, it was much slower than Golgren, so much so that the Grand Khan felt a surge of confidence. What did he have to fear of such a shambling creature, even if his sword was apparently impotent against it? With a savage grin, he backed away from its outstretched paws.

Straight into another pair of horrific limbs that seized him from behind.

Golgren quickly gasped for air as he all but sank into the second fiend's soft, smothering body. The foul-smelling flesh enveloped his head; he had to shut his mouth tight and try to keep his nose free. He felt the insidious creature's oddly laborious breathing. Through half-obscured eyes, the Grand Khan beheld the first monster closing on him.

Mustering his will, the half-breed turned the sword toward himself. He let out a quick, savage roar and drove it upward.

The blade sank into the head of his second assailant. The monstrosity let out a sickening squealing sound. It released him and stumbled back, unfortunately taking his sword with it.

Golgren had no time to concern himself with having lost his weapon. At least it appeared he had finally found something vulnerable about the monster. However, all he had left was his fist.

That left only retreat, a tactic that Golgren never favored but understood all too well. He pressed himself against the tunnel wall, narrowly avoiding the grasping appendages. Quickly peering at the second of his attackers, the half-breed watched with some frustration as it became evident that, even though the thing was clearly in agonizing pain, the sword stuck deep in its head could not *kill* the monster. It simply stumbled around heavily as its ever-shifting fingers sought for the hilt.

Moving past the creature, Golgren growled as the shadows ahead suddenly vanished, the ring once more causing the path beyond to illuminate. It was too bad. Golgren desired darkness, but he suspected that the only way he could make that happen was to dispose of the signet.

As he registered the scene ahead, Golgren stopped short. The tunnel ended before a huge relief carved into the stone. Golgren caught glimpses of at least six robed High Ogres—more likely eight, if the vision were to make any sense.

The exact number and what the figures were doing remained a mystery, however, because two more of the horrific creatures stood there, blocking the rest of the relief from view. Yet unlike the first pair, those two were intently studying the ancient carving.

He had made too much noise, and the pair turned. One of

them pointed a melting finger at Golgren, and a disquieting voice bubbled in his head, *The mongrel!*

As they started toward him, the Grand Khan raised the signet. Nothing happened. Silently cursing the inconsistency of the artifact, Golgren looked around desperately.

To his astonishment, Idaria suddenly materialized, leaping past Golgren and moving like the wind, as though the heavy bracelets of her severed shackles did not exist. In one hand she held a dagger that the half-breed recognized as his.

As Idaria closed on the nearest monster, she plunged the blade Golgren feared was insignificant into the ever-shifting form.

The fiend let out a mournful wail. It twisted and turned, its body so fluid that surely there could be no bones within. Bits of its awful form spilled on the ground and dissipated as the creature rapidly shriveled in size. Not only did it appear to be melting, but a noxious cloud arose over its ebbing form, as though its very essence was escaping into the air.

As Idaria withdrew the dagger, she was struck hard across the jaw by the remaining monstrosity. Golgren sprang and caught the elf before her head could strike the rock floor. As he used his maimed arm to set her down as gently as possible, he seized the dagger, which the slave had somehow managed to hold in her grip.

The blade was covered not only in some thick, putrid liquid, but also traces of a more familiar sight.

Blood. Blood that Golgren guessed came from a thin stripe of a wound running along Idaria's other arm. Somehow she had turned her own life fluids into death for the horrors.

Even as he took all of it in, mulling its significance, the remaining creature loomed over them. Leaning over Idaria, Golgren drove the dagger into the beast. He hoped that enough of her blood remained on the blade to kill it and save the pair.

The howl that escaped the creature was terrible. Gobbets of flesh dropped from the area of the wound, but, unlike its predecessor, the creature did not fall back and die. It was clearly badly wounded, but whatever the elf had done to make herself poison to the other fiend was no longer as strong.

With a sudden swiftness that none of the awful figures had shown before, an oozing hand stretched out and grabbed at Golgren, enveloping his wrist and the blade he was holding.

Another howl escaped the Grand Khan's attacker. The oozing hand pulled away, ripping the dagger free. The weapon went flying to the side.

The thing shambled away from Golgren. As it did, the magical illumination began to fade.

The half-breed's narrowed eyes shot to his fingers, where the signet was gone.

He grabbed for the wounded creature, whose misshapen hand was twisted perversely, not only due to holding the blooded blade, but from what it still carried. However, even as Golgren's fingers snared the monster's hand, his adversary took on a new form, showed a new ability, becoming incorporeal.

And in the next blink of an eye, it utterly vanished.

"No!" snarled the Grand Khan, grasping at the empty air. He glanced back down the tunnel, looking for the others, but the illumination lasted just long enough for him to see them vanish also.

The half-breed ran for the dagger. He seized it up and made his way to the unconscious elf. Just as Golgren leaned over her, the last light faded around them.

Darkness returned to the ancient tunnel, a darkness that Golgren suspected might prove eternal.

XIII

Blood And Sorcery

As the griffon was the symbol of Garantha, so was the mastark the symbol of Sadurak, the city situated nearer than any other true city of the ogres to Ambeon.

The warlord ruling Sadurak in the days of the Great Chieftain Donnag's rule had been Donnag's own cousin, but had made the mistake of defending Donnag to Golgren. Since that time, a balding, one-eyed warrior named Jod had ruled with an iron fist, his authority extending all the way to the outlaw town of Pashin farther southwest. Golgren had need of outlaws only with interests akin to his, and Jod saw to it that any illegal activity there *had* to have his permission first.

Sadurak was perhaps half as large in size and population as Garantha and perhaps half as rebuilt. Jod was a loyal follower, but he didn't fully comprehend the intricacies of recreating the glories of High Ogre civilization. He therefore relied mostly on what Golgren dictated to him, not all of which he well understood. Although the formerly marble white walls surrounding Sadurak were in the process of being restored, they were being done so with whatever color and quality stone could be quarried from nearby.

With the elves no longer officially available for slave toil,

Jod needed his people to work the quarries. That meant that in addition to whatever criminals had been condemned to hard labor, his own soldiers had to spend shifts beating gigantic iron nails into the rocks with huge, flat-headed hammers.

The warriors at the task wore no breastplates, only their kilts. In most cases, they looked like a legion of corpses, for the sweat that matted their hides also collected all the dust their labors raised. It coated the ogres from top to bottom, save for where light cloth bands draped over their eyes and a larger pieces covered their nostrils and mouths. More than a few had pale, red marks upon them—wounds caused by flying stone chips.

The ogres had long lost all knowledge of quarrying as the outside world knew that job, and so had developed methods, good or ill, that suited them. As Jod—on a personal inspection—rode among the workers, he nodded in satisfaction at the latest block of marble emerging from the much-ravaged ravine. It was roughly cubic in shape, with more than three-fourths of it already dislodged and freed. Workers were busy hammering nails into what was considered the base, nails to which powerful ropes were being attached. The ropes already strained against the block, for above there were other ogres preparing for the marble's final release and lift.

A lean, young ogre male suddenly came up on the edge of the ravine and sounded three notes on his goat horn. Two workers finished hammering in a nail and rushed away, tools in hand.

Above, the ropes tightened. Eight there were in all, the ends of some ropes stretching far enough back over the top that Jod could not see their lifters. He could spy four other ogres diligently setting spikes at intervals along the top. The overseer estimated their locations and again nodded.

When the spikes were in place, the trumpeter sounded one long note. The four who had set the spikes immediately swung at them with their hammers. They struck in unison before halting.

The horn repeated the same note. The workers struck. The pattern was repeated.

After the fifth repetition, a slow groan briefly rose above the sounds of work. Jod guided his horse a bit farther back, just to be safe. The ropes strained as those at the end increased their effort. The block was nearly free.

A cloud of dust arose from the south. Jod steered his mount around, curious.

A sea of warriors coalesced from the cloud. At the head rode scores of riders, ranks of unmounted fighters behind them.

Jod was aware of all the forces under his command, and so he knew the warriors were not any who served in Sadurak. He recalled there had been some missives sent to him, questioning the absence of one force led by an eager young warrior whom Jod had met and knew was favored by the Grand Khan himself: Atolgus. Jod assumed Atolgus had marched his force into the wild and either gotten lost or been killed by a subordinate. That was how bad leaders were dealt with in the old days too.

But seeing the newcomers, the commander wondered how they had chanced upon Sadurak. Certainly, there were no other hands expected in the area; Golgren would have informed his loyal officers if any were coming. The newcomers—

Jod suddenly bared his teeth. A surprise. The veteran warrior had fought too many battles to think any surprise was a happy one. Either the warriors were fleeing from something, or they *were* something with which he should be wary.

"Varkol! Varkol!" he shouted to the figure holding the horn.

The trumpeter paid him no mind, for renewed groaning warned everyone that the block was breaking away. Jod shouted again, waving his arms to get the trumpeter's attention.

Varkol finally looked his way, but misunderstood the gesture. He blew the next series of notes, the ones that gave warning to the rope wielders that they were about to contend with tons of falling marble.

An arrow suddenly pierced Varkol's chest. The younger ogre, just finished with his sounding, toppled off the edge of the ravine.

Ogres were not known as the most proficient archers. Although the Grand Khan had worked hard to change that, such a shot as had killed the trumpeter took exceptional skill. Jod quickly peered at the direction from which the arrow had come.

There were Uruv Suurt behind the first two ranks.

Legionaries and ogres fighting side-by-side and against the Grand Khan's own troops!

The commander turned his horse about, trying to decide what would be best to do. He was an ogre leader—and no leader left his warriors behind—yet he also felt obliged to warn the city.

Jod looked back over his shoulder to where Varkol's broken body lay. He urged his mount in that direction, even though that would put him in the shadow of the precipitous block of marble.

Some of the warriors working the quarry had sensed something was wrong, while others merely looked around as though they thought perhaps replacements had come. A few of the former began racing for their weapons, which had been set with their breastplates at a nearby hut. No one had imagined a need for defense, and the only armed fighters were the guards on the perimeter.

As Jod leaped down to seize the lost horn, he wondered exactly where those guards were. Ogres did not abandon positions; indeed, they were more likely than even the most stubborn Uruv Suurt to stand their ground until slain.

Jod brought the horn to his mouth. He saw that many of his warriors were still unaware that something was amiss. The racket raised by the work in the quarry kept many from hearing the oncoming force.

Jod blew hard on the horn, sounding the notes that any warrior trained since Golgren's takeover would recognize as the call to arms. Jod repeated the signal three times, forcing all the air from his lungs each time. By the end of the third signal, the ogre was hacking from the dust he had inhaled.

But his warning appeared to have an effect. No one was working anymore. Ogres were rushing to their weapons, and the only problem the commander noticed was that many still did not realize that the threat came from the newcomers. Most in the quarry could not yet make out the horned figures approaching.

A flight of arrows shot over Jod's head just as he finished blowing the horn. The arrows flew so high that the veteran warrior, more concerned with what to do next, ignored them.

But a moment later, a terrible thundering warned him that he had made a foolish mistake.

Jod raced desperately even as the shadow swept over him. The thundering was accompanied by a familiar groaning sound, as if a giant was gasping out his last moments of life.

He grabbed for his horse's reins, but the animal was quicker than him. It sprinted away, fast outpacing both its master and the huge block of marble descending upon the ogre. The deadly flight of arrows wasn't meant for him, but for those still commanding the ropes above. There was nothing to keep the marble from falling and wreaking havoc among the defenders.

It also threatened to bury Jod beneath its massive weight.

The shadow swept ahead of him. The commander had no choice but to leap.

The ground shook as he landed. He was tossed up several feet and battered to the ground again.

A massive weight crushed his left foot. The ogre leader screamed.

Jod glanced back to see that although the main block of stone had missed him, a fragment as huge as his body had broken free and smashed his left foot to a pulp. That he was still breathing was little consolation; the gory mass that had been his appendage was bleeding profusely, and threatened his life.

He dragged himself forward, looking for something with which to bind the wound.

A second, smaller shadow fell over him. Jod gazed up to see the menacing form of an Uruv Suurt officer whose long cloak and plumed helm marked him as either a general or something close to it.

The horned legionary raised his sword.

An ogre stepped up behind the minotaur. Jod briefly took heart in the appearance of a member of his own race, until he realized the ogre seemed unconcerned over the legionary's pose.

"Jod," the ogre, a younger male, rumbled.

Through a pain-wracked eye, Jod peered at the other. *"A-Atolgus? Kyzari ut—"*

Atolgus shook his head. "You must speak Common, Jod! It is what your Grand Khan commands."

The Uruv Suurt general snorted derisively at the comment. "Golgren will command nothing but the lance upon which his head will sit and stare at the surrounding crows."

The bleeding commander snatched futilely at Atolgus's leg.

"Why do we waste time with that one?" demanded the legionary. "I must report to my emperor and assure him that all is going well, even if not quite as he might expect."

Atolgus did not answer the Uruv Suurt, but instead kneeled down to look Jod directly in the eyes. There was something different about the young chieftain that the older ogre could not put his finger on, something that compelled the attention of the overseer.

"You command Sadurak," Atolgus whispered, grabbing him, sounding more like the Uruv Suurt than an ogre who had not grown up speaking Common. Jod wanted to pull away, but could not. All he could do was stare at the dark eyes tinted with gold, gold like the sun.

"You command Sadurak," the other ogre repeated. Jod vaguely recalled the Atolgus he had first met in earlier years, not at all like the confident, overwhelming warrior. "You will speak of all of its defenses. You will tell them all to me."

Jod could no longer feel anything in his left leg. He wanted to look at his wound, but could not. Instead, words began spilling out, words in the best Common he could speak.

And when he was done, the ogre wished he could have cut out his tongue, for he had left nothing out of his description. Even if he had wanted to, he could not keep any secret from Atolgus. The eyes, more golden than ever, demanded and received all they desired.

"You have heard all?" Atolgus asked the minotaur, finally letting Jod look away.

"The defenses should be simple, even if they know that we're coming. Sadurak will be ours before the day's over!"

"Will that satisfy your emperor for the time being?"

The horned officer seemed not to notice that Atolgus's Common was even better than when they had first met. "Aye, it will. My legionaries can keep the rabble under control and solidify our holdings along the border, warlord."

Atolgus grinned. He took his own sword and, as Jod stared at him, said, *"Fya i f'han iJodi hardugh.* I give you good death, Jod."

He drove the sword into the other ogre's throat. At Atolgus's side, the Uruv Suurt grunted approval at the clean sweep of the stroke.

Withdrawing the bloody blade, the warlord gazed past the sprawled corpse. "Sadurak."

❦

Blood played a part in many Titan ceremonies and spells, blood drawn especially from the elf race. Elves were the closest race to the ancient High Ogres in terms of their innate magic, which was why their sacrifice had been required to make the elixir.

But elves were scarce those days, and Safrag was not yet ready to sacrifice those in the stockade. Besides, he had a different source in mind.

A stench filled the chamber in which the Black Talon had cast its latest spell. Residual energies drifted around the darkened room, briefly illuminating the giant sorcerers' faces in most unnatural expressions of disgust and anxiousness.

The three abominations stood clustered together in the center, with the talon symbol of the inner circle under their misshapen feet. Safrag gazed at the three, his lips pursed in mild interest.

"Three where there should be four," he sang. "Why three, Falstoch? Why?"

The lead abomination dripped forward. It was more hunched than the others, and there was a furious quivering to its constantly shifting form that the other pair did not display.

There was . . . There was the elf, Falstoch said in their minds. *The elf slave of the mongrel.*

"And what could she possibly do?"

Falstoch moaned from pain before managing to respond, *The elf slave . . . She stabbed . . . She stabbed Grahun, and he melted.*

The sorcerers muttered among themselves. Despite their unwholesome appearance, the abominations had been discovered to have some distinct advantages over their former brethren, for their constantly shifting forms made them resistant to magics which even the Titans had to be wary of. Their same shifting ability meant they could literally fit into places nothing else could. The abominations were almost truly liquid. So Safrag had used them to follow Golgren's trail into the mountains.

There was a third, very important reason why Safrag had

chosen Falstoch and the others for that momentous task, a reason not spoken of aloud but known to all. Even the monstrous beings themselves knew it. They were expendable.

But the abominations were so desperate to restore themselves to a semblance of life that they were willing to be used.

"The elf slave stabbed him, and he *melted?*" The lead Titan studied Falstoch closely. "And what of you? You are wounded also, Falstoch, but you have not melted."

The mongrel's elf cut me with her little blade. The pain is still great.

"But you did *not* perish."

No. There was blood on the blade.

"An elf . . . Blood of her race . . ." Safrag nodded in satisfaction. "Of course. What makes us glorious can also poison us. So said Dauroth, did he not, Morgada?"

"Yes, great one. The elf blood can be turned against our kind."

"No elf should know it. But she apparently does. And she even knows how it must be done." He glanced at the others, appraisingly. "Draug. You have watched the slave often of late. What is known of her that I might not recall?"

The other Titan shrugged. "She may spy for Neraka, thinking that they would help free her people. A naive notion, if she believes it. I have not been able to discover her contact there, though, for there is some magic involved—"

"The Nerakans are pawns for us, as are the Uruv Suurt," Safrag interrupted, dismissing the intelligence as of little importance to his question. "Of her past?"

"Oakborn is her family, strong among elves, but not so great as to claim ties to their leaders."

Safrag frowned. "Yet she readily guesses the weakness of something she can never have seen before, hmm. No matter! If she lives, she will give up her secrets to us." He turned back to Falstoch, who seemed to be having trouble breathing. "Tell us all else that occurred."

Falstoch did the best his labored body and mind could to relate his version of the hunt. He revealed to them the High Ogre markings and the vague comments made by the mongrel and his slave. Of more interest to Safrag, however, was the place where Golgren had used the signet to slip into the stone. From where, the Titan leader surmised, he was transported elsewhere.

"You do not know where you ended up? When you sent out the call, we brought you back. But our link was only with you. We could not sense your true location."

Do not know.

"No matter. We shall find it readily enough through the Grand Khan Golgren."

There is more. Falstoch straightened as best he could, although it was clear that his suffering far exceeded that of the duo behind him, who stayed respectfully silent. Falstoch spoke with some of the dignity of one who had once been among the august ranks of the Titans. *There is this.*

One globular hand thrust out. Although it constantly melted and reformed, what lay in its palm was visible to the sorcerers.

"The signet!" Morgada hissed.

"The mongrel's signet!" growled Draug.

"You took it from him?" Safrag angrily roared. "You took it from the half-breed?"

Safrag did not want it? the lead abomination managed to gasp, confused. *A signet of the High Ones?*

"It was the half-breed's means by which he was able to follow the trail! It responded to him as if he were born to its use!" Safrag's right hand crackled with black lightning. "I gave no order to you and your putrid ilk, Falstoch, to take the signet from him, not when the mongrel seems the only key. . ."

The other Titans sat silent as Safrag stopped. He leaned back in consideration, his golden eyes never leaving the signet.

Without warning, he reached his hand out. With a slight

wet sound, the signet flew out of Falstoch's palm and into the hand of the Titan leader.

Safrag suddenly grinned. "You have done us a great service after all, Falstoch." As the wounded monstrosity tried to bow, the handsome sorcerer added, "Go until you are needed again."

The abominations had only a moment to bemoan their protest before vanishing. The other Titans showed no curiosity as to where Safrag had sent them. *Oblivion* would have been the choice of many, but that would have been a waste of minions. Like Dauroth before him, Safrag wasted little.

"Even better," he murmured. To the air, the Titan sang, "Ulgrod, you are summoned before your master!"

Barely had he spoken than the Titan whom he had called— the last among their rank to be granted that status by the late Dauroth—appeared before Safrag and his fellows. Ulgrod's nose wrinkled, and he glanced around seeking the source of the lingering stench.

Belatedly, he looked up at Safrag. "Master, you said you'd have need of me! Are we to be done with Golgren at last? Do I bear the honor of skinning the scrawny beast alive and presenting his still living flesh to you?"

"A dramatic notion, Ulgrod, but no, not that way. With your good aid, however, I do believe that we may be done with the half-breed."

Ulgrod went down on one knee. "I'm yours to do with as you command, master."

Safrag nodded gratefully. "Your sacrifice will be remembered by all."

The other sorcerer frowned. "My—"

Safrag vanished and suddenly appeared standing next to the kneeling figure. In one hand he held the signet, and in the other he wielded a black blade made of obsidian and curved like a sickle moon.

The blade carved a slice through Ulgrod's throat. The blood that flowed from the awful wound was anything but ordinary, for it glowed with a fiery heat and radiated a magical energy that made Safrag's staring visage terrifying to behold.

None of the members of the inner circle so much as moved a finger, for they were not surprised at the shocking turn of events. They had been made aware of what Safrag intended, and although some had shown looks of horror, those had faded quickly at the promise of what the dire deed might bring them.

The Fire Rose.

Ulgrod managed no final word, not even a final sound. He slumped before Safrag, still positioned on one knee thanks to the slightest use of the other Titan's power to keep him so.

"Blood is the power, blood is the might," Safrag intoned.

The other members of the Black Talon materialized, creating a six-sided pattern within which Morgada and three others formed a square. Safrag and the late Ulgrod remained at the center.

The lead sorcerer held the blade high. "Blood is the power, blood is the might," he repeated. "Blood binds, blood guides."

Each of the other Titans drew a symbol before them, their personal mark. Dauroth had begun the tradition, and Safrag had continued it. The marks were tied to the very core of the Titans' beings. By summoning them, they opened themselves to whatever Safrag chose to do with them. By such means Dauroth had had the power to condemn Falstoch and the like to the forms they suffered. Also by such means had Safrag earlier tricked Ulgrod into giving up his life force. Ulgrod had expected to rise to the Black Talon. In a sense that was exactly what he was destined to do, for he would forever be a part of them.

The marks of each Titan glowed blue, but never the same blue as any of the others in attendance. As one, the ten knelt around Safrag, who kept the body of Ulgrod at a point beyond life but not yet true death. Were it his desire, Safrag could still save the one whom he had grievously wounded.

Instead it was Ulgrod's blood that Safrag sought to save—save and use. He had followed a clear line of thought over the past few days, and his thoughts were racing. So much magic existed in the elixir, enough to make of brutish ogres towering, flawless spellcasters like none ever seen on the face of Krynn.

Would not the very blood that flowed through *them,* the former apprentice reasoned, be capable of fantastic feats?

There had been only one way to find out and be certain, and the allure of the Fire Rose had been enough to sway the rest of the inner circle. After all, none of them would have to give up their blood.

Those who were not of the Black Talon would not learn Ulgrod's true fate, only that he had made a great sacrifice in the search for the fabled artifact. Ulgrod's death meant the meager supply of elixir would last that much longer.

The assembled sorcerers held their palms toward Safrag. They slowly thrust them forward, and as they did so, the glowing marks floated not to the lead Titan, but rather on an angle upward, toward the obsidian dagger.

As they willed it, the other Titans also began singing with one voice. There were no words to their song, only tones. The tones grew stronger the closer the magical symbols came to the blade.

And when the marks touched the bloodied tip of the blade, they seemed to be sucked within as if slipping into the middle of a vortex. The Titans groaned, and their wordless song took on a harsher, demanding tone.

Safrag murmured as the others sang. As he did, various symbols appeared around him, and faded away. Each was a tinier representation of the marks of the others, among them Ulgrod's. Like miniature stars, they flared to life, glittered, and glided over Safrag and the frozen form before dying.

Safrag lowered the blade. The other sorcerers immediately quieted.

It had been his original intention next to bleed himself

with the ensorcelled blade, mingling the power of sacrificed Titan blood with the magical essence of his own greatness. Through that technique, Safrag believed he could elevate his skills to a point where he could perhaps see beyond the ancient High Ogre wards hiding the Fire Rose in the wilderness. Were it to work, there would also be no more need of Golgren.

But Falstoch's report suggested another, safer path to his goal. The signet had proven itself bound to the resting place of the Rose. That meant he could turn the smaller artifact into a guide for the spellcasters, not the half-breed.

Bringing down the dagger, Safrag touched its point to the symbols on the signet.

A great plume of flame burst from the signet. Startled, Safrag dropped the ring.

An ear-rending hiss filled the chamber. The flames burned such a bright orange-red that even the blue-skinned Titans took on its hue.

"No one moves!" commanded Safrag.

The flames rose above the signet, spun, and whirled. As they did, limbs—golden limbs—grew from the plume.

A figure of gleaming metal formed from the fire. The flames sank within, utterly disappearing.

The golden figure had no face, no other features. It did not turn to Safrag, but rather stared off in another direction.

It was Morgada who recognized what was indicated. "He stares in the direction of the vale! I am certain of it!"

"But we know that much already!" snapped another Titan. "For all that, for Ulgrod's use, there must be more!"

"So there must." Safrag, defying the nearby presence of the golden figure, stretched down to seize the signet.

The figure reshaped, the front facing the Titan leader. Safrag paused, but the figure did not otherwise move.

With more confidence, the Titan straightened. He dared put the ring on.

"Show me!" he demanded of the gleaming figure. "Show me where to seek the Fire Rose!"

The golden figure made a sudden cutting gesture that caused the other Titans to push back in surprise. In the wake of the movement of its arm, a trail of flames briefly flared across the air toward the Titan Leader.

Both Safrag and the golden figure *vanished*.

Morgada and the others leaped to their feet. As they did, Ulgrod's body, no longer held by Safrag's magic, finished collapsing into a bloody pile. The gruesome sight was all but ignored as the sorcerers stared at the place where their leader had last stood. All that remained to mark Safrag's presence was the dagger, which Morgada finally picked up to show the others.

"It's clean of blood," she informed the others.

They all stared at it for a moment, the truth of her words obvious. The female Titan finally glanced down at Ulgrod himself, and gasped.

The others followed her gaze and repeated her exclamation.

Ulgrod's robes were lying there, not in the least stained. Of the Titan himself there was nothing but a *burnt* outline.

XIV

BLOOD AND FIRE

Golgren ran his fingers over the carving in the wall, seeking to determine its meaning. With no light by which to see the High Ogres' work, the Grand Khan tried to identify the various markings from memory of what he had seen before.

Golgren glanced into the dark behind him, whispering, "You are well, my Idaria?"

"I am, my lord. Thank you for binding the wound."

"We may have need of your precious blood again." Continuing his inspection of the wall, the Grand Khan remarked, "A fascinating idea that an elf's blood could be so poisonous. The Titans are daring indeed." Golgren did not ask Idaria how she had found the dagger. That was the least of his interests.

He sensed her step closer to him. "What may be poison to one may also give life, depending on how it is ministered."

In the dark, the slave's outline was barely discernible. "It is true that those monstrosities were of the Titans?" He had suspected that the creatures served the sorcerers, but something in what Idaria had said made him think perhaps they also had a blood relationship. "Like Donnag."

185

"Like Donnag, yes." But something in her tone lingered in the air like a question.

"And can elf blood help guide us out?" he asked Idaria.

"It cannot," Idaria replied solemnly. "When I dared cut myself, I did so only because of some knowledge I had involving the use of blood and the transformation of the creatures who do the bidding of the Titans. I took a chance that it would work."

She offered no other explanation. The Grand Khan did not care. He was concerned about getting out of that place alive.

They could have returned down the passage through which he had first traveled, but Golgren knew that he would find only another dead end. Perhaps Idaria knew a way. "How is it you were able to come to the tunnels? Did you follow me through?"

Idaria was silent for a moment before replying, "I searched for more than two hours to find a way in at the precise location where you vanished, my lord."

"Two hours? So very long? And the creatures. You recall when you first saw them?"

"Barely a minute before I dared take a chance and drew the blood."

"A curious shuffling of time," he remarked, thinking. "It is not. Perhaps . . . Ah!"

They both stepped back as a golden glow erupted from the area Golgren had just touched. The half-breed and the elf watched as the glow spread like fire throughout the entire life-sized relief.

In the growing light, Golgren glanced at his hand. There were no traces of blood upon it, as he had thought there would be. The Grand Khan had been certain that some remnant of the elf's blood was responsible for the flaring light.

If not Idaria's blood, what?

He gazed again upon the magically illuminated relief. And recognized there was something *wrong* with it.

THE FIRE ROSE

It was not the symbols and markings and the Ogres that he had glimpsed during the struggle with the monstrosities. Instead it was one vast scene with eight robed High Ogres casting a spell on what appeared to be a burning flower turned upside down. The casters themselves appeared to be surrounded by bright coronas.

Framing all that was a specific setting: mountains, great buildings with sharp, jutting towers, a river, and odd animals that looked like crosses between various, more familiar species.

"Well?" asked a voice that made Golgren bare his teeth. "You wanted to enter, and so you can."

The Grand Khan calmly turned to face *Safrag.*

"Dauroth did not understand that he entertained a viper in his midst," Golgren remarked.

"How droll," returned the Titan, striding like a god toward the two shorter figures. Safrag's head barely missed scraping the passage's ceiling. "We are in the vale, and thus I must be one of the legendary serpents."

"We are in the dread valley?" murmured Idaria. "But that was still days away."

"She is a curious slave." Safrag kept his hands behind his back as he looked from her to Golgren. "Just as you are a curious master. Is it love? Lust? Common goals? Common betrayals?"

Sneering, Golgren returned, "And is the Titan leader so interested in the souls of others? In emotions? How caring is Safrag of others!"

"Merely curious about the workings of your confused mind, oh Grand Khan. Are you ogre or are you elf?" Before Golgren could reply again, Safrag cut him off with a wave of one hand.

A hand that flaunted the signet.

Golgren's sneer became a veiled stare. Drawing the dagger, he took a step toward the sorcerer.

Flames surrounded him. The dagger became hot. He was forced to drop it and step back to the glowing panorama.

The dagger melted, becoming a puddle of metal and other bits.

"I shall make it clear in the very best Common, mongrel. There's only one reason why you still live: I have not decided if you are still of need to me given that I am on the threshold of rediscovering the most powerful artifact since the Graygem!"

"I know nothing of the Graygem," Golgren replied coldly and without fear. "And the Fire Rose will never bloom for you."

"How poetic and pathetic." Safrag gestured with the hand bearing the signet.

The rock behind Golgren rumbled. He looked at the wall and saw the relief had split in two, revealing a passage behind it.

"So close," murmured Safrag. "After so many years of biding my time, serving the ignorant and the fearful."

"Not to mention slaying your master."

The Titan looked mildly offended. "Dauroth refused to hunt for the Fire Rose, even though all we sought could have been so easily gained from it! And, besides, another betrayed Dauroth. The rest know that."

"And who betrayed the other?"

Safrag chuckled. "You still try to amuse." He gestured, and the flames died away. "But you are not amusing enough. Enter, mongrel."

Golgren stayed his ground.

The Titan was unimpressed. He extended his other hand toward Idaria.

The elf gasped. Vapors rose from her body, and her flesh started to desiccate.

The half-breed started not for her, but rather toward the new passage.

With another smile, Safrag ceased his assault on Idaria. She slipped to one knee, but the Titan immediately forced the silver-haired slave to a standing position and made her follow

Golgren. He trailed after the two smaller beings.

A slight breeze caressed the Grand Khan's face as he stepped through the cracked relief. The passage did not light up as it had when he had worn the signet. Safrag created a floating sphere of low, blue light that drifted a few feet before them, remaining constantly ahead as the trio walked.

There was also a faint golden aura around Idaria, Golgren noted, though that must have been the handiwork of the sorcerer. Curiously, no such spell covered the Grand Khan.

There was nothing inscribed on the tunnel walls, but all could sense it was no ordinary mountain passage. Safrag's breathing grew more rapid and eager as they proceeded.

But barely had they gone more than a hundred yards when the trio came to another tunnel that branched off. Safrag ordered a pause.

Holding his fist forward so that the signet faced the two choices, the blue-skinned sorcerer commanded, "Show me the proper way!"

A plume of fire burst to life before them. A figure began to coalesce within, and faded away. The flames extinguished.

Safrag looked furious.

"Something is amiss?" Golgren innocently inquired.

"It was too quick," the Titan murmured to himself. "I had no time to gather Ulgrod's blood." He focused on Idaria. "But perhaps . . ."

The elf tried to pull away, but she could not free herself of his control. Like a puppet on strings, she moved inexorably toward Safrag.

A curved dagger made of obsidian materialized in his other hand. There were stains upon it whose origins Golgren did not have to guess.

"There is a better way. A less . . . messy way," he quietly declared.

The Titan glanced at him. "And that is?"

The Grand Khan stretched out his hand. "Return the signet to me."

The towering figure roared with laughter. "You are amusing after all, mongrel! Return that powerful signet to you? And you have a reason why I should act so madly?"

"The signet will work for me. You and I both know that. There will be no need for blood, spells, questions . . ."

"And no risk to me?" Safrag bared his double rows of sharp teeth. "Wearing the signet made you safe from most Titan magic; you and I know that, oh Great Khan! Return it to you? I think not."

"I wish to find the Fire Rose. You wish the same. The signet for some reason wishes it of me also."

"Yes, it does seem to be bound to you." Dismissing the insidious dagger, the spellcaster suddenly grinned like a hungry ji-baraki about to pounce on its victim from behind. "Perhaps you can lend me a hand after all."

He gestured.

Golgren grabbed at his throat. He struggled to breathe as the chain around his neck twisted and turned.

A mound rose from his chest. It strained to be free, almost pulling the Grand Khan with it.

A grotesque missile burst away from him, slipping up over his throat and pulling with such force that it tore free of the chain, which went scattering across the passage floor.

Safrag seized the object as it came to him. He held it up, admiring the awful sight of Golgren's mummified hand.

"Exquisite work. Almost as fresh as if it had been cut off yesterday, rather than—what is it, at least *three* years?"

"Give me that." Golgren coldly whispered.

The Titan cocked his head. "It may be that I no longer need you, Grand Khan. You would do best not to test that supposition. Remain compliant and you live, at least for the moment. Oh, and I might let her live too, of course."

Golgren did not glance at Idaria. He eyed the Titan for a moment more, before retreating a step.

"That's better." Safrag turned the mummified hand toward himself, and placed the ring on one of its curled fingers with deliberation. The sorcerer summoned the obsidian blade once more, which caused the elf to start. "Rest easy, slave. Your blood is not needed yet. There looks to be enough remaining on the blade for what I need. If not, I have the signet itself."

He touched the dagger's tip to the hand. As he did, Golgren's gaze narrowed.

The hand *clenched*.

"Excellent." Safrag released it. The hand did not drop to the ground, but rather it floated as if weighing nothing. It opened and clenched again, repeating the dread sight over and over until the Titan waved his palm over it.

The disembodied hand hovered silently. The wrinkled skin smoothed, and a sheen of freshness spread over the appendage. Indeed, it appeared to have been newly severed.

And as the hand changed, the signet began to glow—faintly, but it glowed.

"Not enough." Safrag looked from Idaria to Golgren. "You will suit better. Come, mongrel."

The Grand Khan's feet thrust him forward despite all his resistance. His maimed arm rose up toward the towering spellcaster.

Safrag brought down the blade. Golgren remained emotionless as the Titan jabbed the half-breed's forearm.

"There," Safrag said mockingly. "That didn't hurt too much, did it?"

With a curt gesture, he sent Golgren back, releasing him from the spell. Safrag took the newly blooded blade and touched it not to the signet, but rather to the severed hand.

The fingers stretched. The hand looked even more alive.

More important, the signet glowed very bright.

"Lead us," commanded Safrag to the hand and the ring. "Show us."

A great plume of fire erupted from the signet and whirled to gather behind the hand. As Golgren and the others watched, the fire formed a shape very familiar to the Grand Khan . . . the golden figure.

In an astounding change from what Golgren had witnessed before, it wore *his* hand as if it were its own. As the arm of the figure fused with the appendage, Golgren's lost hand burned golden.

The gleaming figure strode forward, a blaze of flame trailing in the wake of each drifting step. It did not walk upon the ground, but rather floated a few inches above it. Indeed, it almost seemed to be gliding on the wind instead of walking.

In that manner it moved down the corridor. Golgren watched it dwindle from sight before glancing at Safrag.

"After you, oh great and glorious Grand Khan," the gigantic spellcaster declared with a slight chuckle. "After you, of course."

His countenance expressionless, the half-breed slowly followed after the shining figure. Idaria paced him, and Safrag, with a hungry smile, took up the rear.

 Twice the gargoyles had passed the cave since that first time, and twice they had failed to notice it, or the two within.

Tyranos knew something of gargoyles, especially that some breeds could sense the use of magic. Certainly, Chasm could, and he was tied close enough to the foul creatures that they should have had the ability to note strangers in their midst too.

"The abilities granted to me by my patron differ from the magic of wizards," the knight commented as he finished cooking a small lizard he had caught earlier. "They are more *subtle,* and thus beyond the senses of the creatures."

With a growl, the wizard turned on him. "Will you stop doing *that?*"

"Doing what?"

"Reading my thoughts!"

The Solamnian smiled kindly. "I can't read thoughts."

"Yet you just happen to know what I'm thinking?" Stefan touched the medallion. "My patron's given me insight into the actions of others, into their movements and, thus, I suppose, what those actions mean. You were gazing at the cave mouth with your fist clenched, and the gargoyles passed but a few minutes ago. I made a guess from that."

"You should play cards. Or is that above a cleric?"

The other chuckled. "For entertainment, no. For anything else—" Stefan suddenly stiffened. He set down their meal. Staring off, he quietly asked, "Are you fit enough to move?"

"I've been fit enough to move for the past day at least. Why?"

The knight rose. "We need to be elsewhere and quickly."

Tyranos snorted. "Did your patron tell you that?"

Stefan did not reply, instead reaching for his sword. Belting the sheath, he looked to the wizard. "Be wary. They have the chance to smell us the moment we depart from the cave."

"I may have a few tricks for that."

With the Solamnian leading the way, the duo stepped up to the mouth of the cave. Stefan paused to touch the medallion. "Thank you, lord of just cause. May you continue to guide us in what we must do—"

"Whatever that is," Tyranos added with some sarcasm.

Lowering the pendant, Stefan stepped out.

The wind immediately struck him like a slap across the face, but the knight did not flinch. The wizard joined him, brushing aside the golden brown hair that flew into his face as he surveyed the area for signs of the gargoyles.

"Looks to be clear. No sign of them, and certainly no stench."

"As they could not sense us, we might not necessarily be able to sense them until it's too late."

The spellcaster had a clever retort ready, but thought better of saying anything. It was true that when he had smelled the gathering of the winged creatures, it had turned out to be part of a trap set by their mysterious master—the "king," as the cleric had referred to him. Perhaps, as Stefan had warned, next time there would be no hint of any danger.

"So, which way?" he asked.

Stefan looked left, where the mountains stood most imposing. "That way."

"Why am I not surprised?"

The knight gave him a grim smile and moved on. The wizard glanced around, shrugged, and followed.

The howling wind accompanied them each step of the way, more than once making them think something was coming. Tyranos kept his staff ready, although whether to do battle or whisk himself away from the scene, he did not say. Nor did he know himself.

Tyranos gripped the staff tighter.

They were on the hunt for Golgren, which was as much as the wizard knew. Stefan swore he knew little more than that. Kiri-Jolith evidently was as tight-lipped a god as any of the others.

"Blasted deity," Tyranos muttered. "Blast *all* of them."

"You've little love for much in the world, don't you? Life has made you that bitter?"

"There's little to love, cleric, and that's all I'll say about it. Find the ogre, and let's be done!"

His sword drawn, Stefan kept his eyes on the rocky path ahead. "And how do you want to be done with it? The Fire Rose in your hands, and the world at your command?"

He received a derisive snort in return. "Wouldn't be the worse thing for Krynn, me calling the shots, cleric! I've lived, and I've suffered! I've been tricked! I've been led around by the nose and condemned for it! I am not my mentor, damn him!" Tyranos spat. "Would I make the worst master of the world? I think not!"

"Others have said the same before."

Tyranos suddenly walked past him, the tall wizard's strides well matched to the knight's trained ones. "If we're going to go somewhere, let us go there and quit babbling."

Stefan watched his companion from the back, smiling sadly. He picked up his own pace and regained the lead. Tyranos said nothing, but fell a step back, aware he did not truly know their path.

They wended their way deeper and deeper into the mountains, never pausing. They made good time, which Stefan attributed to his patron.

To that observation, Tyranos remarked, "It's only good time if we actually get to where we're going. Do you know where we are headed?"

"There will be a sign."

"Of course! There's always a sign! Perhaps even right around that upcoming turn—"

The spellcaster swore. For right there, visible to them on the rocky base of the nearest mountain, was an ancient symbol etched into the rock. Tyranos could not read it, but he knew the writing of the High Ogres. A sign it was, indeed.

Stefan said nothing, but merely stepped up to the marking and studied it closely.

"Aren't you going to praise your patron?" grunted Tyranos with a fierce look. "He led you straight to it, just as you thought that he would."

"But I know nothing of that particular sign," the knight murmured. He almost put his hand to the markings, a pair of arched lines like wings, with what looked like a line of mountains standing under them. "We've farther to go. I don't know what it is."

Tyranos suddenly looked around at their surroundings, noting that there were many shadows lurking in the vicinity. "I do believe you're right, Solamnian. Unfortunately . . . "

The beating of wings filled the air.

The gargoyles dropped from every direction.

Stefan slid into a battle stance, and his blade sliced cleanly through the paw of the first creature to near him. Tyranos planted his back to the knight and battered another gargoyle with the crystal head of his staff. Despite the crystal's fragile appearance, the gargoyle's bones cracked loudly. The injured creature went tumbling to the ground and crawled away.

The knight pulled free a dagger, which he waved in tandem with his sword. He slashed through the wings of another attacker, causing it to collide with another one close by. The Solamnian moved with a speed and accuracy so startling that the wizard watched him with fascination.

"By the Kraken! How can you move like that?"

"I am the vessel of my patron," Stefan quietly responded, piercing another gargoyle through the chest before its claws could scrape away his face. "My gifts are from him."

The wizard snorted. He muttered a word, and his staff grew three sharp talons of steel where the crystal and the base met. With those sharp talons, he put an end to another beast. Yet for all those he and the Solamnian had slain or injured, the numbers seeking to reach them appeared to be endless.

Through the mass of wings and gray bodies, Tyranos spotted a figure that was not a gargoyle. The gray and black, shadowy form stared back at him with its icy, white eyes. Eyes that hinted, at least to Tyranos, of amusement.

With a thundering roar, the wizard broke from Stefan. He thrust the staff forward.

"Tyranos! Come back!"

"Tivak!" called the wizard.

As they had previously, strands of silver energy shot forth from the crystal. The gargoyles in Tyranos's way scattered. He had a clear path to the sinister figure.

"No!" called Stefan. His hand seized the wizard by the cowl and, despite Tyranos's mighty size, he threw the spellcaster to the side.

A fiery light surrounded the Solamnian, a light that exploded into true hot flames. Stefan cried out.

Tyranos pushed himself to his feet. He looked quickly not at the knight, but to where he had last seen the icy-eyed figure. As with the last time the two had met, the gargoyle's master had again vanished.

"May the Maelstrom take you!" the spellcaster swore at his absent foe. He turned his attention back to the Solamnian, certain the human was dead. But Stefan was still alive. Indeed, although clearly in pain, the cleric—down on both knees—looked almost untouched by the fiery blast, even though the ground all around him was scorched black.

With a groan, the Solamnian fell face down.

The gargoyles had retreated the moment before their master's attack, but they swooped down again. Tyranos tightened his hold on the staff and opened his mouth. With a curl of his lip, he dove toward the knight's still figure. He wrapped one thick arm under Stefan's breastplate.

The gargoyles fell upon them. Tyranos beat back the first few before concentrating on the staff.

He and Stefan vanished.

❦

The moment the pair disappeared, the winged furies settled down. The vast flock perched upon the rocks, or simply alighted on the ground. They sat silent, not even beating their wings.

At the very place where Stefan had taken the brunt of the spell cast against Tyranos, the ghostly figure materialized. As one, the gargoyles lowered their heads and emitted low hisses with a respectful tone.

The icy-eyed form ignored the gargoyles, instead reaching down and thrusting out a thin, bony hand as starkly white as the orbs that gazed at the scorched area. With its index finger, the figure drew a circle around the area, a circle that momentarily burst into flames and became a band of gold light.

A slight laugh escaped the hidden mouth. As the figure straightened, the gold band faded away.

The gargoyles' lord looked to the right, the east.

To the Vale of Vipers.

XV

AT THE WALLS OF SADURAK

The horns from the quarry had been heard by sentries, who had reported them to their officers in Sadurak. Their commander had reported them to Jod's officer in charge. The officer knew of no reason why anyone would be attacking Sadurak, but he was an ogre, and an ogre must always be ready for battle.

Jod had learned the new discipline and methods well from Golgren, and he had passed on his knowledge to his subcommanders. Thus, the officer in charge not only prepared a force to go out to meet the intruders, but also set the city's defenses into motion.

When the enemy did show itself, it was not one that any of the defenders expected. The ogres were clad just as they were, and many recognized the hand to which the attackers belonged. But if there had been any question as to whether their fellows were a threat or not, that was answered by the Uruv Suurt marching among their ranks. Ogres and minotaurs did not march together unless one was the slave of the other, or both served the same taskmaster. The only time they had ever joined forces before had been due to Golgren himself, and that alliance was long dead.

But someone else had evidently forged a new one. The ogres did not march as servants of the horned ones, nor did the legionaries look at all ill at ease in the company of their former masters.

"Pikes!" growled the officer in charge, sending up ranks of warriors to the forefront. Like Jod, he had fought against and alongside the Uruv Suurt in the past. But his ogre fighters would form ranks as neat as any human knight or Uruv Suurt legionary. Behind the pike wielders formed ranks bearing swords, axes, and clubs; and behind them, archers—more archers than had ever been counted among an organized force of ogres. Jod had absorbed Golgren's teachings as if they came from the gods. Archers had slain more ogres than any other enemy tactic. Ogres, therefore, needed to train at archery. They were not as skilled as Uruv Suurt, but they were competent.

There were not only a surprising number of archers among those massing to meet the enemy, but they dotted the walls of Sadurak too. There were also catapults—a device "borrowed" from the Uruv Suurt—lined up at the walls above. Jod had spent many hours training their users until he felt they were able to fire with the utmost accuracy.

Huge forms suddenly strode over the horizon. That the enemy had brought mastarks was no surprise. The defenders had mastarks, too, at least as many, and they were as well trained as mastarks could be.

The warriors were ready. The enemy was nearly in position. But Jod's officer had no intention of leading his fighters out to confront them. Golgren had taught his followers to bide their time and let the prey come to them, just as a good predator did. The easiest victim was the one who believed there was nothing to fear. They were the ones who stepped into the jaws of the meredrake.

And the newcomers appeared to be over eager. The blood of the traitors and their Uruv Suurt allies would soon drench the parched soil.

Surprisingly, the enemy began spreading out, creating a great wide arc that thinned their ranks in such a manner that the archers' volleys would surely be less effective. However, the defenders were not yet concerned. Many would still perish, and those on the ground would deal with the rest as they battered themselves against the defenses of the city.

Among the enemy, a horn suddenly blared. The first lines started forward.

They were close enough. The senior officer raised his fist. Atop the walls, one of the trumpeters sounded the signal.

The archers aimed. A breath later, a second, longer blast sounded.

The ogre archers fired. The air filled with a shrill whistling sound as hundreds of arrows rose up and descended toward the oncoming traitors and invaders.

Suddenly there arose a burst of wind so wild and furious that it raised a dust storm blinding the defenders. The ogres on the walls coughed harshly as their lungs filled with dust.

And the coughs suddenly turned into pained cries as arrows pierced many throats, many chests. Warriors on the walls fell dead, and several in other areas perished.

They had been slain by their own arrows. The wind had been no sudden fluke. Several of the defenders growled anxiously. They knew magic and its insidious potential. The surviving officers immediately roared orders to the milling ranks, seeking to herd them together into an organized body. They beat the warriors on the heads in order to make certain that their fear of disobeying orders outweighed their fear of anything else.

Even as the defenders reorganized, a great roar was heard from the enemy, one that those protecting Sadurak readily recognized. The attackers had signaled their charge.

The officer in command gestured for another volley of arrows. He had no choice under the circumstances.

A less cohesive flight of arrows shot out among the oncoming fighters. Several of the defenders bared their teeth as the bolts neared the enemy. No wind arose. Not that time.

But with fine precision, both the ogres and Uruv Suurt raised their shields toward the flight. Arrows bounced off the rounded shields, raising a great clatter but creating little damage. A few fell earthward, but hardly any made a difference.

The enemy fired. Their arrows all but blackened the sky. The senior officer stared at his fighters, who were still trying to reorganize. "Shields!" he roared. "Shields!"

Some belatedly raised their shields, but most did not notice the danger soon enough.

The bolts decimated the front lines. There had been no need for magic; the Uruv Suurt archers were exceptional.

It was too late to order the force back into Sadurak, for the enemy was close. Worse, the defenses on the walls were disorganized and in no shape to come to their comrades' aid.

At that moment, a sound like thunder erupted from just within the city. Two of the catapults had fired, their commander evidently having managed to whip his crews into swift action.

The minotaurs were said to have a variety of missiles to cram into their catapults, but ogres used only the most basic loads. The huge boulders went soaring overhead and dropped on the enemy.

They struck the traitors and the legionaries hard, crushing several and sending many other fighters flying in the air. The massive rocks struck the ground and rolled. A third fired, and with the catapults the defenders hopes rose again.

"Ranks!" Jod's second growled. "Ranks!" The single word commands were best for his warriors, many of whom were not as well versed in Common as their leader. They understood him well enough, though, and did their best to regain some semblance of order.

And just in time.

Blades clashed against blades, and new screams arose as the attackers struck his lines hard. The lead ogre signaled the mastarks forward, deciding he had no chance to keep them in reserve. The gargantuan beasts eagerly lumbered into the struggle. They immediately lowered their helmeted heads and thrust their great, curled tusks into the advancing enemy. With but a shake of their huge heads, they each bowled over several warriors at a time.

But almost immediately, two of the mastarks were surrounded by fighters with spears who seemed as though they had been waiting for just that opportunity. One mastark was speared several times in the space of a few moments; even such a powerful beast could not suffer so many wounds without failing. The mastark stumbled and dropped to one knee, as its assailants continued to pierce it. The animal managed to knock away a few opponents with its long, serpentine trunk, but even that was speared over and over until soaked with blood.

The handler and guard atop the creature tried to keep the enemy at bay, but an arrow slew the former, leaving the guard to try to control the mastark himself. Because he was not as familiar with the animal as the chief handler, the guard's efforts only provoked further confusion in the mastark. Bleeding, uncertain as to what the one controlling it wished for it to do, the huge creature stumbled around on three legs. As it turned, it collided with the mastarks on its own side.

Those attacking the mastark took advantage of the new chaos by finishing the animal. The dying beast let out a trumpeting cry before collapsing upon several defenders unable to get out of its unpredictable path.

Even as the other mastarks were kept at bay, the traitors' beasts moved in to further harass the surviving defenders. The lead officer urged his mount toward the line of pikes.

But the pikes were already beleaguered by their own mastarks running amok behind them. Instead of ordering his pikes to take on the traitor's beasts, Jod's second-in-command had to herd his warriors together to protect themselves from their own.

The archers on the walls, and the catapults behind them, were the most effective weapons that the defenders had against the traitors and their horned allies. The commanding officer grunted with satisfaction as another boulder struck his foes. At least Sadurak had one weapon that the traitors could not neutralize.

Suddenly a cracking sound emanated from the other side of the fight, and shouts and cries came from the defenders. Several fell to the side as a huge wooden missile hurtled through their ranks. It was followed by a second, and a third.

Golgren's ogres knew of the mechanical weapons of the Uruv Suurt. Usually the ballistae were found aboard imperial warships and used to rake the decks and sails, or rip holes in hulls. The ogres had heard of their possible use on land, yet none had believed it practical.

Even if only a few fighters actually perished or were merely wounded by the fusillade, the effect of seeing the ballistae in action added yet another element of shock.

There was no choice but for the remaining defenders to pull back into Sadurak as best they could. The commanding officer managed to sound the signal for retreat; the surviving archers on the walls gave cover fire as the harassed warriors fled through the guarded gates.

As soon as the gates were barred, Jod's second in command ran up to the walls to take measure of the situation. The defenders felt much of their confidence return inside. They had tasted the traitors' magic once, but the attackers had relied on physical strength and strategy since. Against those, Sadurak could surely stand.

The commanding officer urged more and more archers to the walls, even those who were not as proficient as he would have desired. What mattered was to make any advance toward the gates costly. That would drain even the morale of the Uruv Suurt.

The walls suddenly shook as though the earth were quaking. A few of the warriors lining the top fell.

The defenders froze, aware that the tremor was no natural occurrence. Another rocked the walls. From the southern region, a warning horn sounded.

The senior officer raced to where he could see what was happening. He and others stared in amazement as two mastarks rammed their helmeted heads into the walls' stone. The veteran warrior thought the beasts' handlers mad until he recognized that particular section of wall. It was one of those most recently renovated with some of the more inferior stone from the quarries—Jod could only take what the quarries produced.

A warning horn sounded from nearer the gates. Jod's second in command leaped down to another officer. Sending him to gather warriors to defend the likely breach in the south, he readied his own force behind the cracking area by the gate, signaling the catapults to lob boulders just over the walls as best they could.

But as the crews struggled to maneuver the unwieldy weapons, another thundering crash struck near Sadurak's gates. Huge blocks of stone tumbled in, crushing two sentries and sending an archer atop the gates plummeting to his doom.

It was not a mastark that had struck the fatal blow to the wall, but another missile from the ballistae. A second blast struck home even as the defenders were recovering from the first, the huge, wooden projectile smashing into the rock right where the largest faults had spread.

The defenders' catapults were of dubious use, for the enemy was too close. The senior officer mustered his fighters as the enemies poured through. Both ogres and minotaurs rushed through the makeshift entrance, eager to be the first to claim blood inside Sadurak.

Jod's fighters met them, their desperate momentum briefly shoving the attackers back to the wall. A moment later, more than two dozen corpses lay under the struggling feet of the combatants, and the ranks of the dead doubled with each new clash.

On the walls, some of the archers turned to fire upon the intruders, but they proved as deadly a menace to their own. Jod's second in command roared for them to aim their shots outside, but his voice was drowned out by the battle and by the recurring thunder of the walls being bombarded.

A sudden surge by the attackers forced the defenders back again. Legionaries and traitors flowed into Sadurak like a river of death.

Among them came a young warrior around whom the other traitors seemed to unite.

As with Jod, the senior officer knew the face of the ogre warrior: Atolgus. He once had been considered as loyal to Golgren as Sadurak's commander, but clearly led the traitors. As was plain even to his enemies, Atolgus fought with a speed and skill astonishing for a chieftain so young.

Jod's second in command bared his teeth as he charged at the rebel leader. Atolgus would be rewarded for his betrayal with his head atop a pole.

The veteran warrior slashed his way past an eager traitor wielding an axe. The young chieftain, in the process of dispatching one of the guards, appeared oblivious to his advance. Jod's second in command lunged toward the traitor as he neared, certain that he could put a quick end to Atolgus and, if he was any judge of battles, the momentum of the attack.

Even though Atolgus had appeared to pay him no mind, the rebel leader's sword suddenly whirled around to meet the other ogre's. The startled commander stumbled back as his target beat down his weapon.

"Jod is dead! Surrender and bow to me!" Atolgus demanded with a fierce smile.

"Golgren is my master!" retorted the other. "As he was yours!"

The traitorous figure laughed. His foe flinched as Atolgus's glaring eyes shone gold at the edges and his pupils seemed to all but fade away.

"Golgren is dead," Atolgus replied. "He is *f'hanos.*"

Although certain his adversary was lying, the loyal officer could not help reacting angrily. He lunged again at Atolgus.

The younger warrior easily beat back the second attack, and thrust his blade deep into the shoulder of his adversary's sword arm. The older ogre lost his grip on his weapon.

Atolgus added a second wound to the officer's other shoulder. As the latter struggled, Atolgus set the point of his blade at his foe's throat.

"Sadurak is falling," the young ogre said, staring off as if speaking to some invisible figure. "She will be pleased that he is pleased."

Jod's second in command had a good understanding of Common, but what Atolgus had said made no sense at all to him. He also knew that the young chieftain had not spoken so crisply in the other tongue when they had last met.

With a wide grin, Atolgus repeated, "Golgren is *f'hanos.*" He raised his blade and brought it down with such swiftness that no one could have dodged the blow. "But he does not know that yet."

Jod's second in command did not reply, for his head was no longer attached to his neck. Atolgus watched with mild interest as the head rolled several feet away from the collapsing torso, before he eagerly moved on to finish the taking of the city.

❦

Another with a loyalty to Golgren and an antipathy to Atolgus angrily stalked across the unforgiving landscape of old Blöde with his tiny troop, wondering all the while if it was to be his destiny to perish so ignominiously out in the wilds.

Since escaping the betrayal of his force, Khleeg had tried to find a way back to Garantha—despite his sense of loyalty tugging him in the direction he knew Golgren had gone.

Khleeg was aware he could serve his master best by seeing that the capital remained a stronghold against the Grand Khan's enemies. He was doubtful that, for all his resourcefulness and skills, the younger Wargroch was capable of protecting Garantha from the unexpected threats that had arisen. Against warriors alone, perhaps Wargroch would have triumphed. But there was Titan magic involved, and Khleeg trusted only himself to do the best possible against the sorcerers.

The three other surviving ogre warriors kept pace behind him, their lives entirely in his hands. They would do whatever he commanded, not that he had any commands to give them except staying alive. They had been without water and food for several days, and the former was a more desperate need than the latter.

Twice, Khleeg had attempted to steer the survivors to known water sources, but Rauth had moved faster, sending bands of fighters to guard those places. Being kept far from water also meant that finding food was harder, for most plant and animals in the region generally stayed near few pools and streams.

It had been some time since Khleeg had seen any sign of the traitors, but he led the others as if Rauth both dogged his steps and rode ahead plotting ambush. It made the going slow, but the bulky ogre told himself to be patient for his vengeance.

"*Ishraali* . . ." muttered one of the warriors, forgetting his Common.

Khleeg snapped to attention. *Ishraali.* Dust.

Dust as in riders or some great force on the move.

He surveyed the distant cloud. It lay far to the south, more in the direction of Garantha. His first thought was that Wargroch had sent out another hand—but he had given the officer explicit orders to protect the capital. Sending out even one hand would dangerously impair Garantha's safety.

Another, more ominous notion occurred to him: They were other traitors moving to join Rauth. With a low growl,

Khleeg waved the others to crouching positions. The dust cloud was fast approaching. Surely there would be scouts ahead of the main force. Common sense dictated that the four act warily.

But Khleeg could not forget his duty to his Grand Khan. While he intended to be as cautious as possible, he had to know to whom the hand was loyal—or if, by some terrible magic it was even Atolgus's force. If it proved to be the missing hand from old Blöde and the young warrior was riding at its head, Khleeg would have to do something to impede his progress.

And if there was any chance of killing the traitor, even at the cost of losing his own life, Golgren's second in command was willing to take that chance as well.

With renewed purpose, Khleeg guided the others around the nearest hills. He felt certain the riders were headed to the west of his position. He would try to scout them from behind.

As he and his small party maneuvered around, he wondered at the immense size of the dust cloud. It gave every indication of being a force greater than the twelve hundred warriors of a hand. It looked worthy of at least twice that size.

He pulled out the crystal and muttered Wargroch's name. When after several moments he still did not receive an answer from the other, Khleeg repeated the call.

Still, no reply. Whatever magic had granted the crystal its amazing powers before, it appeared to have vanished.

Spitting with frustration, Khleeg put the piece away again. There would be no warning Garantha.

His wide nostrils flared. There was a slight scent in the air.

Khleeg glanced at the three warriors, all born of old Kern, not old Blöde, as he was. To his mind, those of old Kern did not have the sharp sense of smell he and their other cousins had, which might be the reason they showed no apparent concern at the moment.

"Beware—" he started to mutter.

Their attackers came at them from all sides. They caught the three warriors behind Khleeg entirely unaware. Swords at their throats forced the trio to surrender their weapons.

But the pair that thought to take Khleeg found themselves with their hands full. He had no doubt his companions would be given the chance to swear fealty oaths in the name of Atolgus, but there would be only one fate for him: death.

Worse, Rauth would no doubt take pleasure in drawing out that death with whatever tortures he thought would force secrets from Khleeg's mouth.

The two scouts from the larger force—they could be nothing less—tried to force him back against a large rock. One of their companions broke away from guarding the other prisoners to join their efforts. Slowly, they maneuvered Golgren's second in common into a precarious position.

"Surrender!" one growled in passable Common.

"Surrender?" he snarled back, gasping for breath. If not for the lack of water and food, he would not be so hard pressed. "I am Khleeg! I do not surrender!"

The one who had spoken faltered. He pulled back from the fight. "Khleeg?"

The Blödian took the opportunity to lunge at one of his remaining adversaries. He stabbed the scout in the arm, forcing the other ogre to drop his sword.

"Stop!" roared the first scout, dragging the others back. "Stop!" Once the pair had withdrawn behind him, he eyed the Grand Khan's officer. "You are—Khleeg? The Hand of the Grand Khan?"

Khleeg had heard others refer to him as such, although never within the hearing of Golgren. His weapon held before him, he retorted, "I am his hand, that will slay all enemies."

The scouts exchanged odd looks, and the speaker suddenly went down on one knee. "Great Khleeg, my neck is bare!"

The scout bent his head down so that Khleeg could easily have chopped it off. The other pair followed suit.

His mind racing, Golgren's second in command demanded, "Your commander! His name!"

"Syln."

Khleeg knew Syln well. He was a loyal follower of Golgren.

He was also one of the commanders of the forces protecting Garantha. "Why is Syln in the region? Does he hunt Rauth?"

The scouts looked up, their expressions perplexed.

"Why is Syln in the region?" Khleeg repeated impatiently.

"We are ordered. Wargroch sends us to Varuus Sha."

"Varuus Sha is not that way! You lie!"

The lead scout shook his shaggy head. "Wargroch sends us there! But Syln commands we march elsewhere. The others, they are marching to Varuus Sha, but Syln insists that way. Says we must find the Grand Khan. He must return to Garantha."

Khleeg halted his explanation. He understood Syln's dedication to Golgren, but something he heard astonished him. "Others? Syln's hand is not the only one to march from Garantha?"

Again, the scout shook his head.

"How *many?*" the officer roared, growing frustrated with having to peel each bit of information from the warrior. "Two? Three?"

"All four! All four march are ordered to Varuus Sha!"

"All—" Khleeg growled furiously. Wargroch could not be that naive! He wouldn't have gone against Khleeg's command! He could not have emptied the capital.

"Fool!" Khleeg muttered, thinking of Wargroch. The young officer had been ambitious, determined to rise to the level of respect that his brothers had earned from Golgren.

Sheathing his weapon, he roared, "You! You lead me to Syln!"

Wargroch still had the city's guard. Protected by the high walls, that guard could keep any traitorous force temporarily at bay. Khleeg had to turn Syln and his troops around, and get them back to the capital as soon as possible. Garantha would be safe again and ready for its beloved Grand Khan's return.

Assuming that Golgren still even *lived*.

XVI

BLOOD MAGIC

The Titans were without Safrag. But for the planned event their leader was not needed. He had set in motion a number of plans and left several events in the hands of his apprentice—Morgada—and various other members of the Black Talon.

No one had discussed the master's abrupt departure as anything but temporary, although some of the Black Talon secretly contemplated what *would* happen if he never returned. Some assumed that, if Safrag disappeared, Morgada would take over the reins of leadership, at least for the time being. Others—the Titans still being ogres despite their exulted status—could not see a *female* as their leader. Thus they watched for any sign of weakness on her part, any failure that could be used against her, should a struggle for power take place.

Morgada knew the hostility well, and so she kept a sharp eye on *everything* as she prepared to launch Safrag's great spell.

They gathered in the mystic forest surrounding their sanctum, for the nature of the spell demanded more room than even the most vast of the citadel's chambers could offer.

More than two score of Titans created the complex pattern that involved a star within a star, flanked by three sickle moons. The matrix of the spell involved a binding of powers rarely used by even the Titans, which was why so many had been summoned.

Some of them had not come without protest. The time was nearing when more than a few would be in dire need of the elixir. Those not of the inner circle had no idea that there was not enough remaining for all of them, or that the Black Talon would certainly make sure that *they* were the ones to imbibe first.

In the end, their need for the elixir overcame their dislike of the shadowy forest, where even in daytime it often seemed dark as night. They stood in a clearing that all knew had not been there before the ceremony, and yet looked as though it always had existed. The magic of the domain that Dauroth had created was such that the forest changed as willed—and occasionally as it seemed to desire.

The sky was shrouded by mist as the sorcerers went through a moment of meditation before beginning. Morgada guided the efforts, her form faintly glowing blue. The sorceress's eyes were shut tight, and to all appearances her chest did not even rise and fall.

At the moment she sensed all were ready, the fatally beautiful spellcaster gazed upon those surrounding her and at two members of the Black Talon in particular. She slowly raised one hand to shoulder level, and the others opened their eyes in unison with the action.

Morgada turned her palm upward, and a black vial materialized in it. Only she and the other two from the inner circle knew that the blood contained therein had been taken from the sacrificed Ulgrod. The rest assumed that it belonged to the mythic stockpile of elf blood that Safrag supposedly kept in storage for creation of the elixir.

A stopper shaped like the head of a Titan popped off the squat vial and floated in the air. Tendrils of red and silver energy rose from within, seeming to dance above the opening.

Morgada sang a magical note. The tendrils wrapped around one another like intertwining serpents, and became a scarlet mist that rose up to join that of the forest. The Titans' surroundings suddenly took on a crimson hue.

Morgada turned the vial over, letting the contents spill out. However, it did not simply form a puddle on the ground, but instead spread to every one of the sorcerers. Despite the vial's relatively slight size, the magical blood had no trouble creating the entire required pattern. Deep red lines ran from one Titan to another, and each time one segment was completed, the blood flared to brighter life. The vial's flow only ceased when the entire pattern had been recreated.

Morgada turned the bottle upright again, allowing the stopper to seal itself. She released the dread container, which vanished.

The female Titan sang another note. The others joined her, creating a sound both wondrous and terrible to hear. The treetops shivered even though there was no wind, and the mist turned more crimson as it settled down just above the spellcasters' heads.

Slowly, the wordless song lowered in volume. As it did, Morgada began drawing a certain symbol according to Dauroth's version of the High Ogre tongue. A bent tree with blazing marks was intended to represent poisoned fruit. At the base of the bent tree she drew two wavy lines that burned red.

It was the Titan symbol for the elf race as Dauroth had decided it should be drawn. The tree represented their long reign as the supposed guardians of Krynn, a guardianship that he regarded as built on the demise of the High Ogres, and the lies—hence the poisoned fruit—that the forest dwellers had spread about the ogre race's past.

And the river that flowed beneath the foul tree was the blood with which the elves would repay the ogres for the centuries of degradation.

THE FIRE ROSE

Once Morgada had finished the symbol, it drifted away, moving not to the center of the assembled Titans' pattern, but rather to an area to the east of them. As the symbol neared, the mist-enshrouded trees closest to it faded back. Wherever it flew, the symbol cleared the area of any tree or bush, the expanse growing.

When at last she was satisfied, Morgada caused the mark of the elves to hover. A glance at the two other members of the Talon verified their approval. Smiling expectantly, she altered the song again.

The change was the signal for the others to raise their hands toward her and her two companions. From the fingertips of each Titan emanated blue streams of magical energy that touched the trio, before flowing through them into the scarlet pattern. The pattern became bone white.

"Children of the lie, we see your damning hearts, we see your foul lies," Morgada sang in the Titans' musical language. "We hear your words of deceit and the whispers you make in the ears of all others. We call you by the name we know you— *Arys idu lokai!*—the Speakers of the Curse!" She clenched her hands. "We call you, *Arys idu lokai,* call you that you may speak no more your untruths and instead pay with your blood for the resurrection of the First People!"

The Titans grunted as the arcane energies flowing between them flared a hundredfold more intensely. The forest took on a new, more macabre glow.

And where the symbol Morgada had drawn hovered, there began to take shape ghostly figures. They were slim and much shorter than the gargantuan sorcerers, albeit tall enough when compared to the races of men and dwarves. Their numbers grew from a handful to dozens, scores, hundreds. The sinister forest of the Titans expanded to make room for every addition.

And as the numbers grew, the ghosts also defined themselves more distinctly. Some were shorter, like children. Many had long, flowing hair. There were males and females. The figures clustered about one another.

They were elves. Frightened, drawn elves. Their garments were in most cases tattered, and many bore visible scars.

Morgada clamped her mouth shut. The spell ceased.

The Titans turned to the fearful newcomers.

One quicker-witted elf broke from the throng. He made it to the edge of the clearing . . . only to back up in fear.

Out from the trees marched a macabre army. Only shadows at first, they resembled ogre warriors. But in the light of the sorcerers' magic, the horrific truth revealed them as skeletons, the bones of warriors who had come to serve the Titans. Dauroth had transformed them from living to dead, preferring the absolute obedience of the latter.

The lone elf stumbled, collided with the nearest skeleton, and bounced off. The unliving sentinel reached down and seized him by the throat, and raised a rusted but still usable axe.

Morgada gestured. The guardian lowered its weapon and tossed the hapless elf back among the others.

She looked to the other Titans. "The deed is done!" she sang. "You have Safrag's—and my—gratitude."

They bowed. All but the other two members of the Talon vanished.

Morgada and her counterparts glided toward the elves, who eyed them with far more anxiety than they did the surrounding ghouls. The elves recognized their value to the Titans, even if what exactly the sorcerers needed them for was mostly conjecture. The prisoners only understood that it involved blood and that those taken were never seen again.

"The mongrel cannot save you," the female Titan declared with some mockery. "Just as he cannot save himself." She waved the monstrous guards toward the prisoners. As the skeletons began herding the elves in the direction of the Titan stronghold, Morgada added, "But we can thank him for gathering you up so nicely for us, don't you think?"

The elves from the stockade in Garantha said nothing. Morgada chuckled and directed the guards on their way.

She and the remaining Titans watched as the elves were herded along.

"Why do we need them if Safrag is going to bring the Fire Rose to us?" asked one of the male sorcerers.

"You should pay more attention, Kulgrath! It may be that the proper use of the artifact might take us some weeks to understand, maybe more. We might need the blood of the elves in the meantime." She smiled. "Besides, the master wishes to experiment on many, many spells that will require their blood too! One way or another, the elf race will perish providing us with knowledge and power. Do you have any problem with that?"

He shrugged. "I merely wondered about the feeding and caring of the herd."

She laughed at his naiveté. "Feeding? Care? Why, my dear Kulgrath! How long do you think we're going to keep them alive?"

Kulgrath and the other male joined in her merriment as the dank, magical forest once more filled the clearing around them.

⚬⚬⚬✦⚬⚬⚬

The golden figure pressed on through one passage to the next, always a few paces ahead of Golgren, Safrag, and Idaria. It was questionable whether or not any of them knew where they were going. But their surroundings changed.

The first hint came as the jagged, rock walls began to smooth until finally they became utterly flat. Safrag ran a hand over the flat walls, grinning.

"Not the least imperfection! And yet so much effort was required, even with magic! Truly, the High Ogres wielded power as none other!"

"Not even *Titans?*" Golgren innocently asked.

Safrag was not rattled. "The rejuvenation of the ogre race through us has only had a generation in which to do its work, mongrel. Within several years, we shall achieve and surpass our ancestors' glory. Sooner than that, if the Fire Rose is indeed ahead!"

"And if it is not?"

"If it is not, I shall at least have the pleasure of skinning you alive layer by layer before draining your faithful slave of every ounce of her precious blood."

It was only a few moments before the smooth walls gave way to something even more fantastical. All three paused to gape. There could be no doubt that something grand lay ahead.

From the floor, and rising up the walls to the ceiling, was the most intricate relief any of them had ever witnessed. It spread ahead as far as they could see. The work was seamless, with no beginning or end, and must have been the work of a thousand dedicated artisans, so detailed was its every feature.

"It is their history." Safrag breathed. He touched the left side of the wall, where the world of Krynn seemed to hover in a mass of stars. There were symbols of each of the gods, and even depictions of the gods themselves, as represented in other High Ogre ruins. They swirled around the depicted planet, as if seeing it for the first time.

Safrag's greed meant he was reluctant to slow down, and he prevented them from studying much of the relief in detail. But certain elements stood out. There were the first dragons, the first war, the rise of the first of the High Ogres, and the granting to them of the guidance of the mortal world by the gods. The first of the great cities was built, and entire lands were tamed, as the beautiful race began to come into its own with its magic.

The first hints of other races appeared also, the elves first and foremost. Compared to the High Ogres, the elves were portrayed as pale shadows, bland as compared to beautiful. Contrary to what many modern ogres thought of the elves, the relief gave no hint as to animosity between the races.

Golgren peered above, where the acts of the gods were recounted and portrayed. The ceiling was the sky, while the left and right walls reflected different aspects of High Ogre life. On one side was the physical aspect—the striving for perfection in both appearance and society. The other side showed the growth of magic as an essential part of the race.

"They believed there were no limits to their greatness," Idaria murmured through veiled eyes, observing the depiction of a High Ogre who was busy creating a vast castle from dust.

Golgren found his gaze returning to the ceiling, to the gods. While some of them entered and exited randomly from affairs involving the race, a handful appeared to take long and definite interest in whatever the High Ogres were doing. Golgren recognized the mark of Takhisis growing more and more prevalent. She was not the only one, for there was her consort, the Uruv Suurt's main god, Sargonnas. He was perpetually confronted by the other patron of the horned ones, the bison-headed Kiri-Jolith. The head of the bison was set against that of a fierce condor, Sargonnas's emblem.

But there was another god always behind the other three, a god whose symbol kept changing but in a manner that was ever recognizable.

"Sirrion." Golgren whispered to himself.

A sudden intake of breath from Idaria, followed by an unintelligible oath from Safrag, made the half-breed look ahead.

As ever, the golden figure hovered a few paces ahead, patiently waiting. But the other travelers stood frozen, eyeing the new and horrific tableau presented to them along their path.

The walls, floor, and ceiling before them were all scorched black.

Whatever burning force had struck in the cave had done so with a thoroughness most frightening. The rock had been melted smoothly away. All traces of the relief ended abruptly.

After contemplating the sight for a moment, Safrag muttered, "Move on."

As they continued, so did their ethereal guide. Golgren rubbed his maimed wrist as he watched his animated hand, the signet thrust forward, act as part of the golden figure.

"Patience," mocked the Titan. "The two of you shall be reunited soon enough."

Golgren evinced no emotion. He was aware of the diabolical implication of Safrag's promise. The Grand Khan could imagine a hundred monstrous ways in which the sorcerer might keep his word.

The gleaming form moved on and on, revealing the passage as a black, burnt place. Golgren sniffed the air, and even though he was certain that the scorching had transpired many, many lifetimes ago, there was still a hint of fresh ash, of bitter smoke.

"We are deep, deep in the mountain," Idaria abruptly murmured to him.

The Grand Khan nodded. Someone had wanted the sanctum well hidden from *everyone.*

"Hold!" Safrag suddenly ordered. They paused, as did the golden figure.

The reason for the Titan's command was barely visible ahead. For the first time in quite a while, they saw something besides a continuation of the burnt passage. Just noticeable at the edge of the darkness was a pale rock.

"Grand Khan."

Golgren understood what Safrag wanted. The Titan was worried that the pale, green rock augured some kind of threat. Why jeopardize his own safety when there were others around to take the risk? Golgren would prove himself of value, or not.

As Golgren moved ahead of Safrag, their guide did too. What had only been glimpsed gradually revealed itself.

It was an arch. An arch carved to resemble hundreds and hundreds of fanged serpents wrapped around one another, rising up and around until they met those curling toward them from the opposite side. The entire arch was of the same faint green cast of color, although whether that had been the original hue, or if it had faded with the ages was impossible to tell.

As with the vast relief, the detail contained in the arch was phenomenal. Each serpent had individual scales, and all appeared to have closed eyes. Their sharp fangs bit into the serpent above, or their tails touched. Some were only a few inches long, others more than two feet. All were identical.

All were vipers.

"So," mused Safrag. "The Vale of Vipers perhaps reveals the source of its name."

Their guide stood just beyond the great arch, which was several feet in depth. Not bothering to wait for the Titan's command, Golgren stepped toward the guide, into the arch.

Nothing happened. He turned and gazed expectantly at Safrag.

"Go," the sorcerer ordered Idaria.

She solemnly traced Golgren's footsteps. The Grand Khan watched her closely, but like him, she passed through untouched.

Safrag smiled. As he started to follow them, he said to their waiting guide, "Proceed."

The golden figure moved on. Safrag stepped through—

A vast chorus of hisses echoed through the underworld, the sound so piercing that all three were forced to cover their ears.

The hissing was accompanied by a tremendous scraping sound. Golgren peered around, but could not detect the source.

Idaria found it. "Look there."

Golgren and the Titan followed her outthrust finger.

The top of the arch was breaking apart. No, it was *slithering* apart.

The serpents were moving.

Golgren dragged the elf toward him. Safrag moved after the pair, only to have several of the vipers fall upon him.

As they landed, their bodies shimmered a deep emerald. The Titan roared with pain.

"Come!" the Grand Khan ordered Idaria. He stared ahead, turning away from Safrag's predicament, not caring whether the sorcerer lived or perished.

The vipers coiled around the Titan's limbs, torso, and throat. With a growl, Safrag seized the one around his throat and with hands that blazed blue, tore the creature in half. As he flung the two pieces away, they reverted to the pale, green stone again and cracked in pieces when they hit the ground.

But even as the gargantuan spellcaster quickly destroyed three of his tormentors, twice that number replaced them, the vipers dropping on him from various parts of the arch. Others squirmed and slid and slithered, seeking to break free so they could add their dark power to that of their brethren.

One clamped its fangs down on Safrag's wrist. As he shrieked, another planted its fangs in his shoulder.

The Titan's cries were music to Golgren's ears, but he was looking ahead. The golden figure quietly turned its head toward the half-breed, as though beckoning him onward, but did not otherwise budge.

Golgren stretched his hand forward. The figure did the same, using the arm that ended with Golgren's severed appendage. The Grand Khan did not hesitate. Seizing the hand and the signet, he tore them free.

The faceless figure reverted to a plume of flame, and faded away. However, the symbols on the signet still glowed, and when Golgren held the signet forward, their glow magnified.

Without another word, he led Idaria on. The sounds of Safrag's struggle faded behind them, whether due to some end to the struggle or the acoustics of the passage, Golgren did not know.

As they raced along, Golgren paid little mind to the fantastic carvings and columns that lined the walls. The wonders of the High Ogres meant little to him, he who had an empire to lose. The Grand Khan had no doubt that events were taking place that threatened his reign. He needed to find the artifact and claim it for his own. At last he would have the chance to be rid of the Titans and his other foes.

At last, he could begin remaking the world as it should be.

There was no sound from behind them as they rushed through one passage after another. The great images on the walls and ceiling passed by the Grand Khan, for the most part unnoticed. Golgren paid fleeting interest to a pair of gigantic High Ogres carved in marble, because he was concerned that they, like the vipers, might prove more than merely lifelike.

The two sentinels had been carved to peer down critically at any coming in their direction. One wore an expression almost sad, while the other appeared to be mouthing a warning. The Grand Khan did not care what concerned them, as long as they did not attack him. They were a sign that, after so long, he *must* be getting close.

The signet ceased glowing.

Golgren's severed hand shriveled, again becoming the mummified relic he had for so long carried over his heart.

The Grand Khan let out an oath as the illumination around them dimmed. He tugged the ring free and thrust it on his other hand, yet that did not light up the symbols or keep the magical radiance from utterly fading away.

As darkness claimed them, Golgren also heard a short intake of breath from Idaria, who had been keeping up with him all along.

"What is it?" he hissed.

"Someone . . . There is someone ahead of us."

Feeling certain that it was either Safrag or some other Titan, Golgren thrust his lost hand into his tunic and braced himself for whatever attack was to come. He continued to hold the signet before him, as it was the only weapon he had, even if it didn't work very reliably.

Yet no sound came from ahead and certainly no flash of magic presaging his demise. Golgren sniffed the air, but sensed only an ancient mustiness.

No, there was something else: the hint of some flower, or an aromatic scent. Try as he might, the half-breed could not identify the odor.

"What do you smell, my Idaria?"

"It is a place long dead," she replied. "And I smell that."

"Do not play games. There is a scent that should be familiar to an elf's sensitive nature. What is it?"

After a moment, Idaria answered, "It is rosemary, I believe. Dried and ancient, but most likely rosemary."

"Ah, yes." He recognized the scent from its use by her and other elves who had cooked for him. Most ogres had no appreciation for such smells, being so used to blood, sweat, and decay.

But their ancestors . . . They had been more like Golgren, savoring wondrous and delicate scents.

He took a step forward, focusing his will on the signet, demanding that it do something for him as before.

The chamber suddenly illuminated, though the signet remained dull. A golden hue spread over Golgren and Idaria, and allowed them to at last see fully what the elf had only managed to glimpse.

Ahead sat a long, wide table of what appeared to be iridescent pearl, set in the center of a chamber.

Around it sat eight robed figures.

Eight High Ogres.

XVII

THE FIRE ROSE

Their once-flawless blue skin was as desiccated as the half-breed's severed hand. Their great manes of hair hung like limp strands of spider webbing. The immaculate robes were covered in dust and faded of color.

The eight had obviously been dead for many, many centuries, but their state of preservation was remarkable. Only as the pair moved closer to the bodies did such things as the lack of eyes and wrinkling of the lips show that there was little more than skin and bones left on their gargantuan bodies.

They were seated around the shining table, one at each end and three apiece on the long sides. For all practical purposes, they looked as if they had fallen asleep at different stages.

No . . . Not all of them. Golgren peered at a male seated at the far end, wearing a pendant over his robes that, ironically, bore a symbol of a griffon on it. His expression was the only one that did not look peaceful.

His expression looked enraged.

The mouth gave that effect, for even in death what remained of the lips still curled. One hand was also clenched tightly.

The High Ogre's eyes—or rather the sockets of his eyes—peered past Golgren with such an intensity that the half-breed could not help but look back to see if Safrag or some other nemesis was approaching. But the way was dark and silent.

"They were slain," Idaria reflected. "Only their leader had time to react. He was the most powerful of the eight."

Just what had killed them was a question that interested Golgren. He recalled the vision he had seen of the eight being assailed by some shadow. However, in that vision, they had been on foot, not seated at a table. Had that been representative of their deaths at the table, or did it concern them at some earlier point in time?

He and Idaria circled around the mummified figures, studying each in turn. Golgren found nothing unusual—relatively speaking, since they were all High Ogres—about the other seven. Clearly they had been powerful beings, but each appeared fairly identical to the next. None wore signets or any other personal item that might have been an artifact of power, and so Golgren quickly lost interest in the seven.

Their leader was another story. His expression told more of a tale. He was the one sure indication that it had been through violence that the High Ogres had perished, not fatigue, hunger, or disease. Golgren leaned over the leader's right shoulder, closely studying what remained of the leader's face. He had been older than the rest, likely wiser. He had probably been the one who had led them to the hidden sanctum, which in some ways looked as if it were a memorial to the entire race—

Memorial? The Grand Khan straightened as he considered all that he had seen in the caves. Yes, there was much to the ancient domain that evoked a memorial, or a tomb.

"They are from the last of their kind," he commented to the elf. "Perhaps *the* last, yes."

"My people spoke of the last few before the ogres truly fell. But those tales say little good about the last ones."

He glanced at her, his teeth just visible. "And did they speak of the Fire Rose, my Idaria? Do you know of it?"

Her face was all innocence . . . or at least she wore an exceptional mask. "No, my lord."

The corpse shifted. Golgren stepped back warily, expecting the thing to rise as a *f'hanos*.

But the High Ogre merely tilted a little, perhaps stirred by the air of words. As the mummy stilled, its pendant dangled.

With little regard for the dead, the Grand Khan tugged the artifact free. The High Ogre slumped on the shining table, his head twisting to the side.

Holding the pendant up, the half-breed studied the design of it. He could sense nothing magical about the piece, but magic was not something inherent with him. Still, it was doubtful that anything worn by a High Ogre spellcaster would be simply decorative. All that he had learned insisted otherwise.

But if it had any magical purpose, it was lost on him. Nonetheless, Golgren took the pendant and, to Idaria's surprise, placed it over her head to rest on her breast. She touched the pendant reverently, but did not question his act.

"There is more," he declared evenly. "The dead would not be in the chamber if there was not."

Yet the chamber did seem to be the very end of the trail. The walls were decorated with the fanciful designs associated with the ancestral race, but none of them, as far as Golgren could tell, gave any clue as to what had happened.

Or what they should do next.

He glanced at the corpse of the leader, and his eyes narrowed.

The body was once again seated as before. Golgren met Idaria's gaze and knew that, like him, she had not seen any movement. Yet one moment, the High Ogre had been lying with his head on the table, and in the he next breath had resumed his previous pose.

Or *nearly* his previous pose.

One skeletal finger of the dead leader was pointing past the other corpses to the nearest wall.

Golgren stepped to the wall, carefully studying the images emblazoned there. No Fire Rose, or griffon, or other intriguing design was there, only an image of the sun over a landscape in flux.

He touched the sun.

The signet suddenly flared.

The wall *melted*.

A set of golden steps led down. From wherever the steps led wafted a heat that made the ogre leader begin to sweat. Despite the heat, Golgren wasted not a moment in descending.

The walls flanking the steps glowed a bright orange-red. The heat increased as the half-breed proceeded down, but never became so stifling that he had to turn around. Still, by the time he reached the bottom of the steps, Golgren, who had faced the incessant heat of the ogre lands throughout his life, was nearly gasping for breath.

As he focused through tearing eyes on the scene before him, the Grand Khan for a moment completely forgot the heat.

Ahead lay a chamber, in the center of which stood an imposing statue of gold—a statue with no face. It was identical to the figure that had led them through the earlier passages, identical in all ways, save its tremendous size. The statue stood at least a head taller than even an imposing Titan like Safrag.

Both hands were stretched out with their palms up, as if the giant contemplated what lay in each. In the left was held a sphere that, although it had false flames rising up from it, also depicted what appeared to be landscapes.

Once more, Golgren blinked away tears as the heat stirred his eyes. He recognized a few of the areas shown on the sphere from maps. It was some sort of representation of his world, of Krynn, but as a round *ball,* not the flat plate Golgren's tribe had believed it to be.

He looked at what lay in the other palm . . . and realized that there was *nothing* in it. Golgren shook his head in disbelief; he was certain something had been there a moment before. The Grand Khan strode up closer to the statue.

As he did so, the heat surged. He was perspiring heavily. The moisture spilled into his eyes in such quantity that everything took on a murky appearance, as if he stared at the statue's palm from deep within some body of water. No matter how hard Golgren blinked, his vision did not clear. Indeed, at times thing looked as though they were changing, even as he stared—

No, what he was seeing *had* changed. And the golden figure was slowly but surely bending down toward him, its empty hand closing on the half-breed. A fiery light erupted from the seemingly empty palm. Golgren covered his eyes—

I'm so hungry . . . have you brought me something?

The voice in his head startled Golgren as little else in his life had shocked him. He uncovered his eyes and looked around. But there was not only no sign of whoever had spoken, the great statue was also *gone*.

In its place—in place of the entire chamber into which he had just stepped—was what seemed to be the interior of a temple. A curved, stone path ran from where the half-breed stood to the other end of the room. Vast reliefs of the High Ogre race spread across the near walls of the temple and across the ceiling, but just as in the one area of the passages, those farther away from him were scorched beyond recognition.

Ahead lay what was surely an altar. As Golgren stepped toward it, he saw that it was built into the rock—or had actually even been carved from it. Much of the altar consisted of a long platform of gray marble stretching across the width of the chamber. Meticulously carved into the altar—and, especially, the main ledge—were a variety of symbols that the Grand Khan assumed derived from the language of the High Ogres. Mixed with them were the symbols of the gods, dark, neutral, and light. Above the main ledge, he could see an arch with black bars running perpendicular to one another, much like those of a gate or a prison door.

And within the arch, something glowed a faint red.

He immediately started for the altar. Yet barely had he moved than his foot caught on something.

Golgren gazed down at another High Ogre corpse . . . one far more skeletal than those above. The skeleton lay sprawled headfirst toward the altar, one extended arm just touching the base of the structure.

He knew the corpse for a High Ogre, but only barely. There were too many things *wrong* with it.

The skull looked as if it had been stretched long, and the jaws—set in a scream—appeared fused to the skull, not loose as they should have been. Yet even that was not as unsettling as the rest of the body. The arm that reached for the altar was twisted at an odd angle and actually split at the elbow, from where two forearms, both ending in hands, began.

Unlike the mummified figures in the other chamber, the robes of the skeleton were in tatters, revealing a rib cage that was also oddly fused, as if instead of a series of ribs the High Ogre had only one massive rib on each side of its body. Yet despite that solid appearance, something had cause the center to *burst* open; in Golgren's mind that event was very likely what had finished off the macabre figure.

The horrific sight caused the Grand Khan to hesitate for only a moment. Whoever the other High Ogre had been in life, he had failed in his quest. Golgren, however, had no intention of doing so. Too much had led him to that moment. He was meant to succeed.

He stepped up to the altar. The glow within the small, barred alcove increased.

Golgren put a hand to the bars.

"Let the meredrake find the trail, take from the meredrake the prey. You should know that works so well."

Golgren did not even look behind him. "Good Safrag, the vipers found your poison too much for their delicate stomachs?"

A tremendous force threw the Grand Khan to the side, sending him spilling into the skeleton. Golgren rolled over the ancient corpse and came up with one of its arm bones in his grip. In one fluid movement he flung the bone at the Titan.

It came within inches of the sorcerer's handsome face, but flew off in another direction as if it had bounced off an invisible wall. The bone fell against the wall to Safrag's right with a clatter that echoed loud and long.

"You will live only long enough to witness my triumph, the *Titan* triumph, mongrel." The gargantuan spellcaster beamed toothily as he glided toward Golgren and the altar. "Would you like to know what is going on with your little realm? The foundation is cracking, oh Grand Khan. Garantha has been undermined by those you thought would give their blood to you! You are betrayed at every turn, mongrel, even by your adoring slave."

Golgren's eyes darted past Safrag, but there was indeed no sign of Idaria. Hadn't she been following him closely, as ever?

The Titan reached the altar. He extended a taloned hand to the bars.

"Be so very careful, good Safrag," Golgren mocked. "You may come away with too many hands or heads."

The spellcaster paused. He looked down at the remains of the fallen High Ogre, and glanced at Golgren. "A wonderful point, mongrel. Come, elf. I have a task for you."

At last, Golgren spotted Idaria, her face devoid of all emotion, entering the chamber at the far end. Golgren eyed her up and down, sensing no spell, no coercion. To his astonishment, she walked over to Safrag with what seemed utter willingness.

"I will open the way, elf. You'll remove that within, won't you?"

"Yes, Safrag," she replied, not looking at Golgren.

No matter how much Golgren stared, Idaria kept her eyes only on the Titan or the bars.

Safrag gestured.

The bars exploded, but the pieces did not go flying at the elf or the sorcerer. Safrag's spell made them freeze in the air and plunge harmlessly to the ground.

But the moment that the fragments fell, the original bars reformed.

The Titan chuckled. "Clever."

Again, the bars exploded. A blue glow filled the broken area and the bars remained shattered.

"Reach in, my lovely elf."

Standing on her toes, Idaria stretched her ivory hands into the glowing alcove.

The elf stiffened. Both Golgren and Safrag held their breath.

Idaria pulled forth the Fire Rose.

Dazzling red and gold light radiated from the artifact as it was brought from its long resting place, forcing the two males to shield their eyes and the elf to all but close hers. The Fire Rose was roughly a foot tall and composed of a crystal that mingled gold and red. The bottom was a thick, singular stalk with six sides that extended half way up its body. The upper half consisted of nearly a dozen projections jutted upward at various angles. The resemblance to a flower—if not necessarily a rose—was obvious.

From within the artifact could be seen the other reason for its name. Deep in its core, a turbulence was swelling, dying, and swelling again. The turbulence was darker and more vibrant than any other part of the crystalline structure, and it was the ultimate source of its glow . . . a glow like fire.

"The glory of the High Ogres!" Safrag breathed. "The culmination of their civilization."

"And the death of it?" added Golgren in mockery.

The Titan ignored him, instead reaching out for the Fire Rose. Idaria remained still as Safrag's hand touched it.

Golgren felt the signet flare. Some sense of impending danger made him look back at the entrance to the chamber.

A shadow stretched there.

And gargoyles formed from the shadow.

They flew furiously at the trio, but especially at Safrag, who turned toward them just as the first reached him. The sorcerer let out a growl, and the first gargoyle turned to white ash that scattered into the beaked faces of the others behind it.

Idaria grabbed for the artifact, but the wing of another gargoyle battered her, sending the slave tumbling to the altar's base.

Golgren seized another gargoyle from behind, using its momentum to swing him around toward Safrag. He let the beast take the brunt of the Titan's spell, which shriveled the gargoyle into something more mummified than the High Ogre dead.

Coming up on Safrag's blind side, the Grand Khan ripped the Fire Rose away. Safrag was knocked to the side by more gargoyles.

The signet glowed as bright as the Fire Rose, and with the exact same colors. The crystalline artifact took on an odd feeling, as if it were melting.

No, not melting. It was slowly disappearing.

Golgren reacted instinctively, trying to grab it with the hand that was no longer there. Coming to his senses, he did the only other thing that he could, thrusting the artifact into the crook of his maimed arm. Yet that only seemed to slow the vanishing.

He swung his hand, using the force of the action to fling the signet away. The ring struck the altar and fell atop Idaria.

Meanwhile, the Fire Rose solidified again. And the gargoyles turned toward Golgren. Worse, Safrag, who had been too besieged to at first to react to Golgren, had regained his poise and was fixing his angry gaze on the half-breed.

Golgren held the Fire Rose between them. He felt the Titan's spell strike—

The crystalline artifact grew blinding. The fiery glow enveloped both the half-breed and the three gargoyles nearest him.

The gargoyles writhed and fell to the floor. They rolled onto their stomachs, and as they did so, their wings shriveled, and their bodies twisted into something ugly and more reptilian.

Three *ji-baraki* rose in their place, immediately attacking the gargoyles nearest Golgren. The tall, sleek reptiles stood on two long legs and slashed with savage claws at the end of their paws. They snapped and bit with long rows of teeth designed to tear apart even the toughest hide. Two gargoyles fell under their attack before others began to swarm the trio.

The Fire Rose's glow decreased to its original level. The Grand Khan's brow wrinkled as he realized something. He had been thinking of the ferocity of the gargoyles and what beasts could possibly counter them . . . and the vicious *ji-baraki* had sprung to mind.

Sprung to mind and to existence, thanks, somehow, to the artifact.

He had no doubt it was capable of much more, but there was no time to consider just how he might summon its power. The reprieve the artifact had granted him was a temporary one. Only the incredible number of gargoyles standing between him and Safrag was saving the half-breed from annihilation.

The path to the steps was blocked by the sinister shadow from which the gargoyles continued to emerge. That made Golgren think of the signet. It still lay where it had fallen, near the fallen Idaria, the symbols glowing almost as bright as the Fire Rose.

As he reached for it, his eyes fixed on the elf. Clutching the ring, he grabbed for Idaria, pulling her to her feet.

"Away with you, you damned pests!" the Titan roared. There was a burst of blue light, and the gargoyles, stripped of their hard hides, suddenly lay dying at Safrag's feet.

The three *ji-baraki* were faring little better. One had already fallen to the gargoyles, and the other two were caught amid the sorcerer's attack.

Safrag's golden orbs fixed once more on the half-breed.

Aware that he could not hope for another miracle from the artifact, the Grand Khan sought some other avenue of escape. He needed to be far from Safrag, far enough to gain time to recuperate and think—

The Fire Rose burned bright.

The floor ripped up as if some giant hand had seized it in sinewy paws. Stone and earth rose between Golgren and the Titan, who recovered from his astonishment just before the two lost sight of one another. Golgren could see the sorcerer beginning to cast a spell, but by that time, there was an incredible wall cutting off the two from one another.

The half-breed's surroundings shifted and reshaped. The walls, floor, and ceiling grew as red as flame, churning as if suddenly molten. Golgren stared down, thinking that he and Idaria were about to sink down into that molten hell. Yet his footing remained solid despite everything else transforming.

No, not everything. Bursting out of the wall of molten earth and stone, the altar and the alcove were back, their presence restored. They looked exactly the same as before save that, once again, the bars were there. It was as if they wanted to keep the Fire Rose *out* rather than contain it.

The artifact continued to radiate a blinding, hot aura. Golgren forced himself to look at the blinding artifact, and realized that the signet *touched* the Fire Rose.

He released his hold on the ring.

It fell onto the shifting floor and *sank*. It was gone.

The Fire Rose's light eased. The walls began to solidify, turning a fiery crystal reminiscent of the artifact. Only the altar and alcove continued to persist in their original form.

The new chamber stretched wider, growing into a room as vast as the field of the Jaka Hwunar, the great arena located in the capital. Yet there was no sandy floor where warriors fought to the death against beasts or each other, where enemies were executed by graphic means often involving limbs torn apart or beheadings. A polished floor with wicked striations mimicking flames ended on each side with tall, flanking columns carved to resemble great plumes of fire.

The altar stood at the far end, shadowed by the imprisoning alcove, a vast sunburst etched into the gold and crimson wall above it. The heat surrounding Golgren was thick, so much so that he had trouble breathing and was forced to lay Idaria down again.

In doing so, he discovered that the Fire Rose had not left him untouched. Caught up in the chaos, the half-breed had not wondered how he had managed to do so much in his own defense.

Golgren had *two* hands again.

With the one he had never lost, he reached into his tunic and sought the severed appendage.

It was *still there.*

With a mixture of muted pleasure and heightened suspicion, Golgren turned his new hand over. It was strong and lean, and when he flexed it, he could feel the muscles tighten. It was identical to the lost one save there were no scars from years of struggle. The skin was pristine, the hair smooth. Even his fingernails were perfect, more akin to those of some elf lord before the fall of Silvanost, than those of an ogre leader.

The Fire Rose had restored him. There was no other answer. Golgren studied his fingers, turned his wrist, and clapped his hands.

Idaria stirred. The elf coughed and opened her eyes. Recalling her conspiracy with Safrag, the Grand Khan hesitated, pulling back the hand he had been about to offer her—the new one.

She saw the hand and gasped. Quickly recovering from her shock, the elf reached up to tentatively touch the new appendage.

"It *is* real," she breathed. "Did the Fire Rose give it life?" Before he could answer, the elf, studying his hand intently, suddenly shook her head. "No, it is *new.*"

"Yes, it is."

"I wonder . . . How did it happen?"

He waved off her question, instead asking his own. "You served the Titan. Explain."

She did not attempt to divert him. "He has my people. All those you gathered in the stockade for eventual release. He came upon me just as I was about to descend. Immediately, he told me the other Titans were going to use my people for their ends – unless I obeyed. He warned that you had no life, no future with which to still save my people. But he thought that I might be of some service in the future, so he promised that a *few* would join me in freedom if I followed his dictates."

"And so you betrayed me, my Idaria?" When she did not reply, he nodded. "Fair enough."

He extended the new hand to her again. The silver-haired slave paused but finally accepted it, with downcast eyes.

Golgren gripped her hand tight and brought her up. He nodded in satisfaction at the strength he felt in the hand. "Very good. Very good."

The elf surprised him by responding, "Is it?"

He started to ask her just what she meant, when the Fire Rose ominously stirred to life once more. Golgren had done nothing that should have awakened its power.

"Above the altar!" the elf warned.

The sunburst was no longer merely a carving on the wall; it had become a living, blazing thing that was swelling toward the pair. As it did so, the chamber grew so hot that the two fell to their knees oppressed. Idaria clutched Golgren by his new hand while the Grand Khan fought to keep his head from swimming.

It was nigh impossible to see. Golgren's vision was a hazy mass of shapes, worse even than during his flight with his mother's body after the savage attack on his settlement by the Nerakans. He could no longer see anything but heat blurs. The altar and all its surroundings were enveloped by the sunburst.

But in the midst of the sunburst the half-breed thought he made out a figure. Struggling to stay conscious, he peered at the murky form. At first, Golgren thought it the golden figure, for it certainly bore a similar shape But this one moved more freely, as if extremely conscious of what it was doing. Indeed, for some reason, Golgren thought that it moved as if it were *curious* about its surroundings.

Oh, I'm so very sorry! an almost amused voice suddenly bellowed in the half-breed's head. *Is it a little too hot for you? I always forget how fragile all of you are.*

As Golgren clutched at his pounding skull, the figure raised a hand. Suddenly the sunburst seemed to shrink into its palm, and the heat rapidly receded.

Slowly, Golgren and Idaria regained the ability to breathe without their lungs burning. The heat haze dissipated. They could see again. It was still very warm, but no more than any ogre—or even an elf—could tolerate.

As the Grand Khan and his slave recovered, it was to see a fantastic figure standing before them, a figure in no manner mortal. His semblance was part ogre, perhaps part elf, perhaps part human, and yet not at all like any of those. His face was long, angular, and white like the ash left by a great fire. The mane of hair framing his face was wild and unkempt, and its crimson color made it look truly afire. In fact, Golgren was not certain it wasn't on fire, for it constantly moved like dancing flames even when the tall figure stood still.

And the eyes . . .

They were long and narrow. Where the eyes of the Titans were gold, the figure's eyes were golden orange, fiery red, hot blue and even white—all the colors of flame, shifting as rapidly as any dancing fire. They were disconcerting to stare into, but Golgren could not help doing so.

It was Idaria who managed to break his gaze by tugging hard on his new hand.

He immediately returned his gaze to the strange figure, but did not look directly into its eyes. Golgren noted the orange-red robes that covered a shape thin to the point of emaciation, as if the astounding being had not eaten in years.

Indeed, its smile looked hungrier than that of any mere-drake, so hungry that the half-breed wondered if the newcomer saw the pair as its next meal. The Grand Khan shifted into a more defensive posture. In the process, he accidentally looked again into the blazing eyes, and was once more caught by them.

As before, Idaria turned his face away. "Never meet his gaze, for there is little that can fascinate any mortal creature more than what he is."

Golgren did not have to ask just whom—or what—she meant. An uneasiness filled the Grand Khan, for of all the gods that ogres paid cautious homage to, that was the one most dreaded. Even though he didn't wear Takhsis's mantle of evil, his unpredictable indifference was in many ways more deadly.

Sirrion.

XVIII

UNDER THE SHADOW OF THE MOUNTAIN

Wake up, cleric! Damn you!" Tyranos snarled. "Will you wake up?"

Stefan finally stirred. The wizard exhaled. Despite the irritation with which he regarded the knight of Solamnia, he owed him much.

The bearded cleric's eyes opened. He blinked. "Where . . . What happened?"

"You saved my life, and I got us away Although *where* I've gotten us to is a damned good question."

"What do you mean—"

Stefan stared. Tyranos said nothing, sharing the knight's astonishment.

They were still in the mountains, that much was evident, but certainly nowhere near where they had been before.

The sight before their eyes – high above their eyes, to be exact —could only have been sculpted with the aid of magic or sorcery, for even dwarves would have been reluctant to risk themselves working at such high, treacherous angles.

"A castle?" Stefan finally managed to blurt. "Or some sort of citadel?"

"Your patron doesn't tell you very much sometimes,

does he? I was hoping you'd recognize that landmark since I certainly don't."

"I know nothing of it, save that I have a feeling it must have something to do with all that is happening to us."

"A brilliant although truly useless statement." The wizard helped him up. "Perhaps instead you can tell me just how you survived what that creature threw at me. And thank you for that, by the way."

Giving the spellcaster a rueful smile, Stefan said, "If you would think before you go charging in like a bull, I wouldn't need to act as I did. And, incidentally, I had no idea I was going to survive."

"You didn't?" Tyranos was disconcerted.

"I only knew you were in danger, and I had to try and help."

"You're a fool!"

Stefan shook his head. "No. That is what you refuse to understand. I am a Knight of the Sword and the servant of Kiri-Jolith."

With a grunt of disbelief at his companion's simple manner of explaining his near-sacrifice, the wizard turned his attention to the uniquely sinister sight above them. The citadel which loomed above them had two oddly narrow towers flanking its narrow main body. All was topped by long, carved points of stone so sharp Tyranos could imagine dragons impaling themselves on them. Each tower had one black, triangular window while the main part of the citadel boasted two windows side-by-side. There seemed no entrance to the massive building, although, perched as it was on the side of a mountain, it was possible some tunnel or cave provided a hidden way inside.

The outer appearance of the structure was perhaps its oddest aspect, for whoever had created the citadel had left the walls unpolished, indeed resembling unhewn rock. There was no doubt its design helped make the place difficult to spot from a distance, as the citadel blended into the surrounding rock.

"Really, you have no idea where we are?" Stefan asked.

"I only concentrated as best I could on getting us away from the gargoyles. I didn't expect to end up wherever we are."

The cleric rubbed his chin. "I have one theory, which bodes both good and ill for us."

"What is your theory, cleric?"

"The citadel is the domain of the gargoyle's master."

Tyranos snorted. "The ill I understand, but what is the good?"

"We are still near where Golgren must be."

"Ah. Of course." Gripping his staff, the lion-maned spellcaster considered the citadel. "So you think he's up there?"

"No, I think he's far, far below."

"Below?"

Stefan started walking. "If the Fire Rose was hidden up high, the gargoyle's lord would likely have it, I'd guess."

"And he wouldn't find it as easily if it was below?"

The cleric touched his pendant. "You're the wizard. Haven't you noticed what surrounds us?"

His brow furrowed, Tyranos studied the craggy, hard, inhospitable landscape. After a moment, he closed his eyes in concentration. Barely a moment later, his eyes flashed open.

"I can't sense *anything*. No, that's not right. It's as if the entire area doesn't even exist!"

"In a sense, you're right. And something that doesn't even exist would hardly be noticed by anyone beyond that part of the valley."

Tyranos pondered long and hard as he followed the knight's train of thought. After reflecting long and hard he ended up with an idea that left a bad taste in his mouth.

"Cleric, If the citadel isn't supposed to exist to anyone who isn't granted the ability to recognize its existence, I don't like the notion that I somehow brought us right to it!"

"Yes, I've thought about that too. And it worries me also."

"It bodes ill, you mean," retorted the burly wizard.

Stefan did not respond. Tyranos paused for a moment, eyeing the Solamnian's back as he walked ahead of him on a narrow trail leading up. After a moment, he resumed following the human.

As he walked Stefan held the medallion of his order ahead of him. He continually looked left and right, as though seeking a marker.

"What're you looking for?"

"The same thing you are."

The hooded figure paused again. Holding the staff against his chest, Tyranos rumbled, "Hmm. A place where the sense of *nothing* is at its greatest."

"Exactly so. The one glaring fault in that type of deception, but only if you can tell the subtle difference. And that requires skill or, in my case, the gifts of my patron."

"Well my skills aren't having any luck. Are your *gifts* doing better?"

"Not thus far. I—"

The cleric stiffened. Tyranos almost spoke, but waited as flapping wings echoed through the mountains. The wizard silently swore. Readying the staff, he murmured, "Stand near me, cleric, and hope that I can get us out."

"I don't—"

At that very moment a gargoyle swooped down before them, a muscular beast with an eager cast to his brutish countenance. Stefan readied his sword as the creature dove upon them.

Tyranos forced the knight's arm down. At the same time, the gargoyle suddenly landed before the duo.

"Master," the creature rumbled.

"Chasm," Tyranos returned. "A pleasant surprise."

The cleric frowned, his eyes shifting between Tyranos and the waiting gargoyle. "The gargoyle serves you?"

"Since he was born. Isn't that right, Chasm?"

The gargoyle dipped his massive head. "Master is my father, and my father is master!"

"He was an orphan, his parents slain by a rival flock. I was . . . investigating a lead . . . and came upon him."

"So you raised him? And how did he find you?"

The tall mage masked his emotions from Stefan's penetrating stare. "We are tied together by many things, Solamnian. Chasm can find me no matter how far apart we are from one another."

Chasm eagerly nodded agreement. Stefan looked with fresh eyes upon the tall mage. "You are more and more surprising to me," he said to Tyranos, adding, "For one of your kind to take on—"

The staff was suddenly thrust under the Solamnian's nose. From where he squatted, Chasm gave a threatening hiss at the knight as the mage spoke between clenched teeth.

"I am my own. I do what I do. We'll speak no more of 'my kind,' right?"

"Not until you wish to speak of it, no."

With some frustration, Tyranos snapped, "I'll never wish to speak about it with you, damned cleric—" He broke off, staring past Stefan at the gargoyle. "What the devil's the matter with you?"

Chasm was shaking his head as if trying to rid it of some inner noise or pain. The winged creature snorted, leaned forward, and all but rubbed his forehead against the ground.

"Stop that!" commanded the wizard. "What's the matter with you?"

"Head hurts! Feels . . . Feels strange . . ."

Thrusting his staff forward, Tyranos studied the area just beyond and surrounding the gargoyle. A grin spread across his face. He tapped the crystal tip on Chasm's head. The gargoyle flashed bright for a moment, and the creature's face calmed.

"What is it, Tyranos?"

"As you already know, gargoyles can often sense the presence of magic. Not all flocks, but some. Trust me, I've made a very *thorough* study. Chasm is more sensitive than most. And I do believe he's found the area we've been seeking."

The cleric looked around at the nearby landscape. "So we just have to find a passage." Stefan added, "Odd that the master of so many gargoyles couldn't also find it so readily."

"As I said, Chasm is more sensitive. Unique, actually. That's why I was forced to shield his mind a little."

The Solamnian said nothing further, but continued to look around intently as the trio slowly moved along, deeper into the mysterious mountain terrain. Chasm hopped ahead, sometimes on all fours, other times just on his legs. The gargoyle sniffed the air, whether for the presence of more magic or others of his ilk, Stefan had no idea; the mage did not deign to illuminate him.

"You've been following the trail for a long time," the cleric said to the mage in a low voice, as they climbed steadily.

"I thought we'd already agreed on that. What of it?"

The knight shrugged. "I was merely curious what you hoped to do with the Fire Rose."

"And you'll remain that way: curious. Your patron chose to have you help me. As a cleric, you shouldn't need to ask more."

The answer did not aggravate Stefan, but rather made him chuckle. That, in turn, caused Tyranos to glance at his companion in irritation.

Suddenly Chasm stopped. The gargoyle hissed and began running in a circle.

Tyranos ordered him to stop, and stepped into the center of what had been his servant's circle of running. To his right began the gradual rise of another peak. To the left and ahead, a narrowing path led to a jagged gap between high rocks.

"You see or sense anything, cleric?"

"Nothing."

The wizard snorted. "By our reasoning, we should almost be on *top* of whatever is supposed to lead us to the Grand Khan and the artifact." He held the staff forward. *"Tivak!"*

The strands of silver energy crackled above them and about

the area. Tyranos quickly whirled, scanning the vicinity with the aid of his staff.

A moment later, he dismissed the magic, however. Turning to Stefan, he growled, "As you say, nothing! Absolutely—"

A golden bubble swept up out of the ground, passing through the hard earth like a phantom. It rose high, swelling in volume at the same time.

It also swallowed up Tyranos.

"No!" Stefan shouted, reaching to grab for the wizard. But the cleric had been too slow to react. As fast as the bubble materialized, it sank back down into the ground and vanished, taking the unsuspecting spellcaster wherever it went.

And leaving Stefan and Chasm.

The gargoyle immediately pounced on the spot, scrabbling desperately, trying to dig through the hard rock with his thick claws. The cleric stepped up next to him, thinking furiously.

From the direction of the shadowed castle came the sound of flapping wings. Many flapping wings.

The knight turned in that direction. He readied his sword.

Powerful paws grabbed him under his arms. Before Stefan knew what was happening, Chasm had lifted him up and was carrying the fully armored human through the air. Tyranos's winged servant veered away from the rising sound of a monstrous flock.

And as the gargoyle bore him away, all Stefan could do was stare at the ground below, where the spellcaster had disappeared.

Stare and pray to his patron.

∝∞Ο∞∝

The guards wasted no time rushing to the palace, with fear as much as duty pressing them urgently. At their head ran the captain on duty, an ogre warrior certain that he was about to lose his head, or worse.

They arrived to find an oddly contemplative Wargroch peering out over Garantha from one of the many balconies that were favored by Golgren. The bulky ogre did not even turn around when his own guards presented the four warriors to him, instead seeming to find something of interest far, far away.

The captain gestured his underlings down on their knees and waited. When Wargroch finally turned to acknowledge them, the kneeling officer banged his fist on his breastplate and waited for permission to speak.

"You I know," Wargroch muttered. "You are assigned to the stockades."

The other ogre swallowed. On the one hand, it was good for those most favored by the Grand Khan to know their subordinates. However, under the present circumstances, the stockade officer would have preferred Wargroch's complete ignorance. If the Grand Khan's chief aide knew him, that meant he had marked him—perhaps as one having potential, perhaps for another, more dubious reason. What the captain had come to tell Wargroch would almost certainly endanger his standing, as well as his life.

"I am in charge of the stockades, yes, Khan Wargroch," the captain answered in his best Common.

"I am no khan," Nagroch's brother corrected him brusquely. "Commander, yes, but no khan."

"Commander," the captain acknowledged crisply. "Great commander, there has been terrible—*Skee anoch*—magic!"

"What magic?"

"The forest dwellers gone! All gone!"

The officer described matters as best he could. Both his incomplete knowledge of Common and his confusion about the event forced him to take longer than he would have liked. He had just come on duty and had been setting the guards in place, he explained. The captives had been placid, more manageable than a herd of goats. They had been fed not all that long ago, and so the captain had not had to concern himself with that job.

Since being assigned to the great pen, the elves and their ogre guards had come to a silent understanding. The elves had realized their fates rested in the hands of the Grand Khan. No one wanted to offend Golgren. The elves were generally submissive because they preferred to nurture their faint hopes for freedom, and the ogre guards were generally tolerant, without anxiety about their captives' welfare or escape. Neither side fully understood the intentions of the Grand Khan.

So the changing of the guards was ceremonial, almost tedious, usually. The officer made certain everyone was at their post, and proceeded to prepare for the next shift.

Barely an hour had passed when there came shouts from not just one guard, but several under his command. The officer had come running up the wooden walkway to the top of the stockade to see what had alarmed his guards, the captain reported, only to discover some of them were actually shivering.

He had reached for the nearest, intending to shake the story out of him, when his gaze had drifted down into the stockade's interior.

An empty interior.

At that point, Wargroch angrily cut the captain off. "Gone? All elves are gone?"

"*Ke*—Yes! All! Much magic!" the guard officer hesitated before growling, "Titans, maybe."

Mention of the sorcerers brought a hiss from the Grand Khan's pet meredrake, which was curled up in its customary spot on one side of the chamber. Wargroch let out a similar hiss, and looked as if he were ready to strike the ogre officer giving his report. However, he finally lowered his hand, turning to the warriors behind the captain. "All true? No sign of escape?"

They shook their heads. One dared answer, "Gates bolted. Meredrakes all around." Golgren had commanded that handlers with the giant reptiles should patrol the perimeter around the wooden structure at all hours. Not so much because he thought the elves might try to escape, but to stop his own people if they were tempted to show their hatred for the forest dwellers by rushing the stockade to burn it down. "And bows above to watch all," the warrior added.

The archers were another precaution which Khleeg had suggested to the Grand Khan. More than two dozen archers stood atop the roofs of the nearest structures surrounding the stockade. Golgren had emphasized to Khleeg and Wargroch that the slaves were vital to his planned deal with the Solamnians.

Wargroch's eyes narrowed imperceptibly.

"Magic," he finally agreed with the stockade officer. "Titan magic, maybe." He waved away the captain and the others. "Go!"

Surprised, but also pleased not to have been rewarded with their heads rolling around on the floor, the captain and his staff rose to bowing positions and backed out of the chamber. As they departed, Wargroch ground his yellowed teeth in thought.

"Safrag," he finally muttered.

❧❧✦❧❧

Safrag was on the minds of the Titans too, for their leader had been absent far longer than any of them had anticipated. Morgada urged the others to be patient, aware that more than one was already measuring their future against hers.

Their long-checked attitude toward her being only female couldn't be tamped down for long. Even the pair who had assisted her with the spell transporting the elves to the sanctum acted as if she had been of little importance to the accomplishment; she had only been the conduit for Safrag's magic.

But Morgada was used to the others belittling and under-estimating her; so did Safrag himself. Safrag thought he was more clever than Dauroth, whom she had bewitched first.

True, Safrag's cunning coup over the master had caught Morgada by surprise. But the dim-witted Safrag had chosen her to be his apprentice, and all had gone as the female Titan had planned.

Morgada just needed a little time. And, if truth be told, she needed to know just what had happened to Safrag.

She entered the private quarters that her status as apprentice to the master granted her. To the unwary eye, the stone walls of the room were just that. Only she and Safrag knew where the doorway lay and how to find the entrance.

The temptress smiled. Safrag had opened the way almost as many times as she had since he had taken over as the Titans' leader, but only because she had allowed him to. There were times unbeknownst to him that, had he sought entrance, he would have been blocked without her secret acquiescence to his spell.

Morgada drew her personal mark and another secret mark just for that purpose. Safrag knew of a third mark, the one between her and him, which he thought she used to keep others from entering. Actually, without her two marks, once sealed, the door would admit *no one*. Not even Safrag, should he return suddenly.

The wall rippled. The gray, rough stone became like water, yet retained its solid appearance to all ignorant of the spell.

The female Titan stepped into the watery stone. The wall wrapped around her like honey, yet it did not cling to her as she passed through. Her hands broke through first, followed by one foot and her beautiful face.

Once inside, Morgada turned and drew the second symbol again. The wall inside her quarters solidified as normal.

With a satisfied smile, she gazed upon her pleasant chamber. It was both home and workplace. There was a squat, wooden chest in which she stored mundane matters, and a bookshelf upon which scrolls and tomes were stacked. There was no window, but a slight current of air wafted across her face anyway. Magic, of course, kept all the inner chambers in the vast citadel from becoming too stifling.

A silver platter of fruit and raw amalok meat lay on a black, wooden table to her right. Next to the black table was the open space where one might have expected a bed of some sort. However, as a Titan, Morgada did not rest as lesser ogres, elves, or humans did. Instead, on the floor of that space was a pattern of stars surrounded by a circle through which four dagger strokes had been etched. It was a pattern that could be found in each of the chambers used by the Black Talon, a pattern that served both to restrengthen and refresh their bodies and minds.

As for the female Titan, it held one more secret use.

She summoned a thick cut of the raw amalok meat from the silver platter on the black table—the fare she really preferred was not available to her. With savage gusto, Morgada tore into the morsel. Her powerful teeth ripped through the flesh, blood splattering both her face and robes. Almost like an animal, she devoured the meat, leaving not a single trace.

When she was done, the sorceress slowly licked her fingers, tasting a bit of the blood that had lingered on her lips because she had allowed it to. Running her open hand over her face and garments, Morgada magically removed all other stains.

Once again immaculate, the temptress strode over to the patterned floor. The short meal had been for more than merely sustenance. She needed extra strength, for it was not rest she intended to seek from the pattern.

Turning her back to the black table, she crossed her arms over her chest and lay back toward the floor. Her body softly tilted as if were connected to puppet strings. Midway down in its sloping angle, her feet and legs rose into the air. Morgada lay floating over the pattern, her rigid body more than two feet above the floor.

As she stilled, the pattern below her flared a blazing blue. Its radiant light shone upward to bathe her.

One hand moved over her heart, drawing an arched symbol not taught to her by any Titan. The pattern's illumination shifted, growing so dark that it looked more black than blue.

Her eyes had been open thus far, but Morgada shut them. Her perfect, full black lips parted slightly as she breathed a single word.

"Xiryn."

And in her head, a voice that gave no hint of being male or female whispered, *I hear you.*

XIX

To Possess the Rose

Is that better? asked the voice, its intensity causing Golgren's head to burn more fiercely than his flesh. He felt Idaria slump next to him and knew that she suffered the heat too.

"Ah! So tender! Forgive me again."

The voice had become a true voice, but each syllable still struck with heat and force in the Grand Khan's ears.

At least the heat was tolerable. Continuing to follow the elf's warning, Golgren looked just below the imposing figure's eyes. Sirrion—if indeed it was the god—stood just a little taller than Golgren, although clearly that was by choice, not by nature. The half-breed recalled widespread tales of Faros Es-Kalin's supposed encounter with Sargonnas, and how it was said the god had the ability to appear in more than one shape or size. Sirrion could no doubt make himself look as mighty as a giant, or tinier than a gully dwarf.

"Born of elf and ogre, an impossible mix, an improbable mix. Well, to most," Sirrion declared with some solemn humor. "And bearing the child of mine pleaded for by the High Ogres." Golgren thought he detected a chuckle.

Golgren suddenly recalled the Fire Rose. He held it reverently toward the god. "It is yours?"

"Did I speak of any desire for it?" the fiery figure suddenly roared. "If I demand it, you *will* give it to me. There is no mistake!"

Flames erupted around the god. The heat once again grew suffocating.

Golgren, who had faced down all manner of beasts, minotaurs, Nerakans, and, of course, the dread Titans, bowed low. "Forgive this humble one, oh god of fire. Never would I presume to know better than you what you desire."

"There's no need to apologize," Sirrion responded, the fury with which the deity had just spoken utterly gone, and with it the terrible flames and heat. "But that is your choice, of course!"

Golgren dipped his head again. Sirrion was very much like the incarnation of his element. Volatile.

The god peered at them, his eyes shifting from the Grand Khan to the elf. "Branchala's love. Another interesting blending! I find such change stirring!"

The flames returned, albeit in a more subdued fashion. They seemed to reflect whatever level of emotion Sirrion was feeling.

"Great is Sirrion," Idaria said of a sudden. "For without fire, there would be no civilization."

"So very true! And do you like my little flower, Grand Khan of all ogres? Does its sweet scent of possibility entice you? It did for those who begged it of me so long ago."

"The Fire Rose is . . . glorious."

Sirrion grinned. "Glorious or monstrous, the choice is yours! The choice always is all of yours."

"All of ours?"

"Oh, there are many coveting the prize, including one coming nearer by the moment! He seems very, very eager! How would he wield the Fire Rose, do you think? I'd be fascinated to watch." The god of fire had started to raise his hand toward Golgren and the Fire Rose, but lowered it again. "But that would be against what has been set in motion!"

Despite the danger of stirring Sirrion's anger, the half-breed dared ask, *"What is set in motion?"*

The deity spread his arms wide. The flames grew stronger, hotter. "So much, so much! Ah, how long I've sat back and watched, when the world constantly cried for change!" He looked at Golgren, who barely managed to keep his own gaze from being trapped again. *"You* are set in motion, child of elf and ogre! For evil and ill, for good and fortune, you and others are set in motion! Krynn has grown, and in growth some things must give way, some things must grow stronger! You and they choose that my flower blooms again, after being buried for so long."

Mention of others reminded Golgren of Safrag. The deity spoke of one who desired the Fire Rose, one who was nearing. That could only be the Titan leader.

Time was of the essence. "Oh great Sirrion, lord of fire! May this humble one ask how best to stir the Fire Rose to its glory?"

"One might well ask, where would the challenge be? Where would the reward be? The wonders of Krynn rise from the determination of its children to understand all!"

It was not the answer that the Grand Khan desired. Golgren carefully asked, "Why has the god ventured to us?"

"Why? Why?"

Idaria clutched Golgren's arm. Both Sirrion and the Fire Rose flared so bright and hot that the Grand Khan felt the artifact burn his hands. Yet despite the scorching of his hands and the rest of his suffering because of the volatile deity, Golgren stood his ground.

"Child of elf and ogre, impossible creature, I come because I do! I am fire and flame, spreading onward wherever there is a spark, creating by cleansing, birthing by burning! I am the hand of alchemy! My mere presence stirs the imagination, the dreaming. It stirs something within you that you, especially, should appreciate, Grand Khan of *all* ogres!"

The chamber rumbled, but not because of anything that Sirrion had said or done. Golgren knew that it was because Safrag had located them and was on the trail of the artifact.

"The players are in place; the time of change is upon us," the god continued, staring around at his surroundings. "The High Ogres sought change, but change sought them! They wanted a world that did not want them, and when they realized that, they begged for something with which to wipe clean the decay they saw around them. I was touched, and though my loving Shinare cautioned against it, I decided that their plea should be heard. Why not? To craft the gift is not to influence the choice! *They* made the choice, just as you and you and he and the others make it!" He suddenly thrust a finger at Golgren. "The choice is always yours, impossible child, even if the option given isn't what you expected it would be."

The chamber erupted. Golgren and Idaria were thrown to the floor. The Grand Khan clutched the searing artifact tight in his arms, but it was not completely protected. As he landed on the ground, he stared directly into the Fire Rose and saw for the first time that it was not perfect. A small piece, one of its leaves, had been broken off. It was doubtful that the break had happened by accident, for even striking the stone floor had not left a mark on the crystalline form. Indeed, the stone floor had cracked.

As dust rose around him, Golgren shoved the Fire Rose into one arm and used the other to push himself up. In doing so, he happened to glance into Sirrion's ever changing eyes.

It will be interesting, the choices all of you make, the voice, once more burning in his head, declared. *It will be interesting, the changes you demand of my flower. And the changes it demands of you and Krynn.*

Sirrion's form was rippling, just as a mirage created by the heat of the sun rippled. The god became less and less distinct, and when Golgren finally had to blink to keep his eyes from hurting, Sirrion was gone when he opened them.

With the lord of fire's departure came the return of another menace. The wall exploded inward, the fragments freezing in the air just before they would have struck the Grand Khan and his slave.

With his right hand extended palm upward, Safrag stepped into the chamber. He paused to survey his surroundings.

"Fascinating! So much to explore once everything has been put in order."

A blazing light emanated from his palm. Its hue matched that of the Fire Rose.

Golgren immediately knew the fragment in Safrag's palm was what was missing from the artifact. Safrag had used the fragment to keep on the trail of the Fire Rose.

"There is nowhere left to run, mongrel! Surrender the Fire Rose to me willingly, and perhaps I'll let you live to watch the rebirth of the ogre race!"

"Its further downfall is what you mean."

The Titan eyed him with disdain. "You will never understand exactly *what* I truly mean."

Safrag gripped the fragment, glaring at the Grand Khan.

The Fire Rose fought Golgren's hold. The half-breed clutched it tight, refusing to let it go though it shook him powerfully. Idaria grabbed hold of him from behind.

The Grand Khan was yanked into the air. Idaria lost her hold. Golgren and the Fire Rose flew toward the sorcerer.

"Surrender is inevitable, mongrel," the towering spellcaster smoothly remarked as he clamped the hand with the fragment against another part of the Fire Rose's stem. "Inevitable as my rise to master of the Titans!"

"Yes, Dauroth was blind," murmured Golgren, pulling hard. "But Safrag is blinder."

He let go with his right hand—the hand restored—and struck the Titan soundly below the spellcaster's rib cage.

Safrag let out a gasping cough and bent forward. That enabled Golgren to reach out and slug him again, under the jaw.

Tearing the artifact free, the Grand Khan turned back to Idaria. "Flee!"

But instead she rushed to him, helping Golgren to carry his burden. Golgren cradled the crystalline form as they ran from Safrag. "Would that I understood better the thing's use," he muttered.

"There may be—"

Idaria got no farther. A terrible sound wave struck them, deafening the pair and sending them tumbling. The Fire Rose slipped from Golgren's grasp and immediately flew back toward Safrag.

The half-breed managed to grab onto the stem of the crystalline artifact as it flew past. It dragged him along.

"You are as persistent as a meredrake following a blood trail," the blue-skinned sorcerer said tersely as both the artifact and Golgren sped toward him. "And when I have the Fire Rose, perhaps I'll leave you to one of those damned reptiles!"

Suddenly Golgren felt a deep hatred for Safrag and his grandiose ambitions. Suddenly he knew he would never surrender the Fire Rose to the Titan because *he* intended to use it himself. Forever and ever. If there was anyone who should wield the artifact, it was him. Only him. He had felt the touch of its power, and would give it up only upon death.

Golgren collided with Safrag, the prize pressed between them, the Titan preparing another one of his spells.

"Your *hand,*" Safrag growled, their eyes locking. "Your new hand. How astounding is the Rose, which grows all anew! Why are you so blind to what it will do for our race, mongrel? Why, it could even wash you clean of that foul elven taint! You could become a true ogre at last! Think of it!"

"If that is the best you can offer, you offer nothing."

The sorcerer sneered. "You really do take pride in your tainted existence! More than ever, you have proven yourself unfit to live among our kind, much less pretend to rule it!"

The Fire Rose burned bright all the while. Flames had

erupted around the pair. From somewhere, Idaria cried out, but Golgren did not so much as glance at her. To break from the struggle even for an instant was to lose everything to Safrag.

The ground rose, and the walls and ceiling of the chamber melted away with the heat. Safrag and Golgren were borne aloft by flames as they wrestled close for the artifact. The sky opened up above them, and a hill formed to their side.

The flames lessened. Golgren's foe laughed shrilly. "Do you see what it can do? It is said that as our race degraded, a band of High Ogre spellcasters gathered together to try to stem the fall! They spoke to all gods who might listen, but only one replied. *Sirrion,* the one they least expected! God of Fire and Alchemy, he had always remained in the background, helping those gods who came to him without judgment! Yet Sirrion heard the plea of the spellcasters looking for some way to reforge the ogre race and found that a fitting request for him!"

The Fire Rose burned hotter. The ground swirled, spinning the two combatants and their disputed prize around and around. The hill that had just formed *melted,* before becoming a small grove of fantastic trees with spiked leaves and blossoms as white-gold as the sun. Golgren and Safrag suddenly found themselves on another hill overlooking the grove. An orange-red glow covered everything, including the two opponents locked in struggle.

"But like you, the spellcasters were shortsighted! A fear arose in them as they began to use the Fire Rose! Instead of accepting it as a miracle, some of them decided to bury it forever for fear of what their own ambition would cause it to do!"

The Titan's eyes flashed with fury. Golgren felt his feet grow numb. He stared into the Fire Rose, silently commanding it to serve him and him alone. He was no spellcaster, yet for some reason, even without the signet, the artifact responded to him.

Golgren threw his willpower into the effort.

The Fire Rose stirred.

Not only did the flames rise up again, but the very ground beneath them turned into molten lava that spat and churned as if eager to devour the loser of the struggle. The Grand Khan did not for a moment think that he would be the loser, though the pain and heat and numbness spread and enveloped him.

Golgren *had* to have the Fire Rose. The desire was stronger than ever.

The numbness suddenly faded. Golgren stared up triumphantly into Safrag's dark visage. The Titan tried to shake him off, but the half-breed held tight.

Their surroundings continued to shift, with the tide of their battling minds. Hills rose and fell, lakes blossomed and dried, plants of all shapes and sizes sprouted and withered to dust. Whether they were momentary creations of the Fire Rose or would have remained permanent changes, Golgren neither knew nor cared. Such was the might of Sirrion's gift.

As the combatants were caught up in their clash, the sky darkened. Both looked up and saw the return of a common foe.

The gargoyles dove down in greater numbers than before, the winged monsters seemingly oblivious to the hot treacherous landscape beneath them. They skirted the rising flames with ease and fell upon the area where the Titan and the Grand Khan battled.

A jutting hill shot up at first, sprouting into existence with such swiftness that the gargoyles slammed against it at full speed. The crack of bone briefly overwhelmed all other sound.

Those behind the unfortunate first group immediately ascended. Yet the hill continued to grow until it reached the gargoyles, earth and stone subsuming a number of the hapless creatures.

It was impossible to say if it was by Golgren's will, Safrag's, or both in conjunction somehow. But surely the Grand Khan and the sorcerer were joined in their desire to keep the gargoyles from claiming the trophy. The pair looked around, seeking to counter the dangerous attackers.

"You'll not have it!" Safrag roared at more of the oncoming fiends. "Neither you nor your master!"

Black bolts of lightning shot not from the sky, but rather up from the ground. Each struck their target with deadly accuracy, searing the flesh of the gargoyles and leaving nothing but charred bones that clattered to the ground.

The landscape shifted anew, with Golgren and the Titan raised to soaring heights. They stood upon a towering peak, so high, and such an astounding transformation of the landscape, that it almost made the Grand Khan fumble his grip.

The gargoyles, which had been diving in relays, had to beat their wings hard and veer to extreme angles to compensate for the change. The gray beasts hissed as they swooped again, reaching with clawed paws for the Fire Rose and its wielders.

"It is between us, mongrel," Safrag said, glancing around at the gargoyles without looking at Golgren. "We've fought for the precious artifact, not sent hounds to steal it afterward!"

Golgren said nothing, though his silence was agreement enough. The pair held onto the artifact as one.

"Think of what the House of Night truly honors. Think of the *iSirriti Siroth,* the Burning of Day!"

The Grand Khan understood and followed his rival's lead.

The Fire Rose blazed brighter than ever. Both Golgren and the Titan cried out in pain, so white-hot was the artifact.

But if they found it hot, the gargoyles found it deadly. As if the sun itself had swallowed them, the aerial attackers were disintegrated to the last one by the sudden blast of heat. They barely had time to shriek their deaths. Their winged forms were suddenly outlined by the blinding light and they simply vanished. Not even a trace of ashes marked their passing.

Safrag's hand immediately came around to the Grand Khan's chest.

He gripped the obsidian dagger.

Golgren tried to twist away at the last moment, but the only way he could truly escape would have been to release the Fire Rose. Even threatened death could not make him do that.

The magical blade bore through all obstacles without hesitation, sinking between Golgren's ribs up to the hilt.

The half-breed let out a rasping cough. He squeezed tight, trying to hold his grip as he struggled to overcome the mortal wound.

Safrag pulled the blade free and struck Golgren hard under the jaw with the hilt.

Golgren's fingers slipped from the Fire Rose.

⚬⚬⚬⚬⚬

Idaria could not move. There was space around her, but only above her head and chest. Her legs and one arm were pinned. She was buried in a tiny gap under tons of rock and earth, the remains of what had once been the chamber of the altar.

She was going to die.

Elf notions of death had changed considerably since the fall of Silvanost. They were much starker, less transcendent due to all the tragedies falling upon the race. Idaria did not fear death, but neither could she peacefully embrace it.

The elf struggled to no avail. Her body was fairly intact but only served to mock her efforts with its impotence.

Her concern shifted to last minute thoughts about her people. There was no chance for them. Safrag said that the Titans had the slaves from the stockade, and she had no doubt he had spoken the truth. Whether their blood was presently being drained for the foul work of the sorcerers, or they would suffer some other heinous fate, all their deaths would be on her head.

She had erred grievously in trusting the Nerakan officer with whom she had made her pact. Idaria tried to recall either his name or face, but no longer could, such was her daze. All she could see was a vague figure in the hated ebony armor. The elf had only gone to Neraka when she had met no hope elsewhere. Indeed, the Nerakan had actually found *her* and offered the deal; information on the movements of the Grand Khan—known for his fondness for elf women—would be utilized for the advancement of Neraka. In return, the knights would free her people when they invaded the ogre lands, sending them on their way. Neraka had no use for the elves, the officer had said with enough conviction to persuade her despite her initial distrust; all the better to burden Solamnia and other neighboring areas with more refugees.

Idaria had not cared for the reasons why the Nerakan would help her, only the arrangement offered hope. The slaves were in that sorry a state. She agreed, and they had made their plans.

As she scraped at the rock above her, Idaria found herself repeatedly trying to recall other details about the Nerakan. Elves usually had exceptional memories, but although she could remember what they had said to one another, she had no luck picturing the human himself. As deadly as her predicament was, Idaria wondered why.

It grew harder to breathe. Somewhere in the back of her mind, the elf knew she was running out of air. Death was coming for her.

Sleep. Sleep and dream, her mind thought. *Sleep and dream.*

Sleep and dream. She did not have the strength to defy those two pleasant suggestions. Yet as Idaria began to drift off, a part of her protested that something wrong was happening. Something that had to do with the voice in her head.

It had not been *her* voice she had heard, not at all.

And as she finally blacked out, the last thing the elf thought was that she recognized the voice.

The voice of the very same Nerakan officer. A human whose face and name remained oddly and disturbingly vague as Idaria lost consciousness.

XX

THORNS OF THE ROSE

Dangling from Chasm's mighty grip, Stefan could not see the other gargoyles, but he knew they must be near. The knight prayed to Kiri-Jolith for guidance. He had no doubt Chasm could carry him to safety, but that did nothing for Tyranos. Nor Golgren, assuming he was alive and in the vicinity. Stefan cared little for himself, only for those he intended to aid. It was his duty to follow through on his patron's desire, and he was willing to do so even if his own life was sacrificed. But sacrifice meant nothing without victory. Failure was not an option.

His prayers were cut off by something astounding he glimpsed just beyond the mountains of the dark castle. The horizon blazed with fire, and there were more gargoyles there. They seemed obsessed with reaching one location just out of sight.

The cleric's eyes widened, and he heard Chasm grunt in surprise. For a moment it had looked as though another peak had suddenly sprouted into existence.

But that was not possible . . . Was it?

The hisses and screeches of the gargoyles behind them reminded Stefan that he had more immediate concerns.

"To the north!" he shouted, glancing up at his rescuer. Stefan pointed to his left. "Veer around the mountain!"

To Stefan's relief, the gargoyle quickly obeyed. The great wings beat hard, thrusting them forward.

They reached the peak. Chasm banked. Stefan could not tell whether what he heard was the echo of Chasm's wings, or the onrushing sound of the many attackers surely close behind them.

The gargoyle slowed, suddenly diving toward the mountain with such velocity that the human was certain they were going to die. At the last moment, Chasm turned toward the mouth of a cave, and the two dropped into it.

The moment that Chasm released his hold, Stefan rolled around and sprang up with his sword ready. He ran to the entrance and peered out.

Although he saw the gargoyles who had been trailing them, he was pleased to see they had lost track of their prey and were joining the others above in the fiery sky.

"We're safe," he said to Chasm, who grunted agreement. Stefan looked around at their surroundings. "Relatively safe. Thank you for helping me."

"Must help master," the gargoyle grunted.

"Of course I'll help Tyranos."

"Good!" Shambling on all fours, Chasm peeked out of the cave. "All gone."

"Yes, there must be something their master wants elsewhere. It might even be Golgren. Perhaps we should follow *them*."

His winged companion hissed. "Must help *master!*"

As Chasm was the only one who could fly, Stefan wasn't about to go somewhere without him. But the Solamnian felt torn. His patron had sent him on a mission that involved the ogre leader, not the wizard. As fascinating as Tyranos was—at least from what little knowledge Kiri-Jolith had granted his new cleric—the safety of the spellcaster was secondary to that of Golgren and the Fire Rose.

Clutching his pendant, the knight contemplated his options. The answer became as obvious as it was insane.

"I think I may have some idea where we can find out about Tyranos."

Chasm looked suspicious.

Undaunted, Stefan explained, "You saw the castle on the mountain. It must belong to the gargoyles' lord. The thing that took Tyranos must be his work. I saw what happened. I do not think it likely that your master is dead. He must be a prisoner. And the best way to find and free him is to search the castle. The magic may have even brought Tyranos there!"

The winged behemoth grunted and gently flapped his wings, thinking. The gargoyle glanced at the cave mouth.

"Come," he rumbled.

Sheathing his sword, Stefan joined Chasm at the entrance. He looked out and glanced at the gargoyle.

Chasm shoved him out.

Stefan fell. He opened his mouth to scream, and Chasm's thick paws seized him as they had before. The gargoyle carried him from the mountain.

The cleric recovered his breath just as the side of the mountain where the citadel stood came into view. Stefan could feel the ancient age of the place, not to mention the latent magical energies surrounding it. *No one* was supposed to find the mountain and especially not the castle.

But Stefan knew that Kiri-Jolith had intervened, partly to help his new cleric, but also because of Tyranos, who had lost the faith he had once had in that particular god.

Yes, Kiri-Jolith had intervened. That was clear. The rest was up to them, and especially to Stefan.

Chasm neared the sinister sanctum, a place that chilled the knight. Stefan had been on many dangerous missions for his homeland, but none of those missions had ever brought him to such a place. The rough-hewn walls almost reminded him of skin, as if the castle itself were a living, breathing thing.

The gargoyle let out an inquisitive grunt. Stefan understood what he wanted.

"That window there! The one in the right tower!" He had picked it mainly because it was the closest, but also because he had a hunch that it was the safest. The cleric prayed he was correct.

Banking again, Chasm flew directly for the window. The opening was large enough for either the gargoyle or the human, but not for both together at the same time. Stefan felt Chasm adjust his grip. The gargoyle intended to set him down first.

There were spells around the citadel, but thus far Stefan had not sensed anything active. Perhaps it had grown complacent.

Still. "Be wary, Chasm."

The winged creature responded with a snort. A gargoyle did not survive very long in life if he did not remain wary.

They reached the window unimpeded. Chasm held Stefan before the opening while the knight maneuvered his legs inside. Grabbing the sides, Stefan slipped through.

He immediately drew his sword and crouched. As Stefan took a step farther inside, Chasm entered behind him. The gargoyle folded his wings and followed on his hind legs and four paws.

The cleric could see nothing. He held the medallion up in front of him and muttered a prayer.

A faint light shone from the medallion. Stefan would have liked to have had more illumination, but he didn't want to alert anyone of their presence, and it was enough to light his way.

Shapes coalesced. Statues without faces, but clad in robes or armor or other garments. The style of carving varied from figure to figure, as if they had been done by a variety of artisans. Some looked older than others, even to the point where parts were cracked. All the statues lined marble walls bearing veins that Stefan associated with great age.

Chasm snuffled. Stefan had already stifled a few sneezes. There was a tremendous amount of dust in the room, as if no one had been in it for years. Peering closer at the statues, the Solamnian saw they were so covered with dust that he had not even realized they were also painted.

The other end of the chamber ended at a door that looked like iron but when cautiously opened turned out to be as light as wood. It was completely unadorned save for a handle.

With Chasm at his heels, Stefan stepped out to find himself at the top of a long flight of stairs. The dust covered stone steps wound down as far as he could see.

The knight and gargoyle descended. Chasm was especially uncomfortable during the descent, the winding steps giving him no room to spread his wings. Both showed visible relief when they reached the bottom.

A metal door identical to the previous one greeted them. Stefan took more caution opening it, but once more they were greeted by no menace.

Beyond the door, a heavy scent prompted Chasm to emit a low, warning growl. The Solamnian also knew the smell. It was a place where the great flock of gargoyles gathered.

In the limited light of the pendant, Stefan saw nothing. He looked to his companion, who sniffed the pungent air. After a moment, Chasm gave a grunt and moved forward. Stefan followed.

"Gods," the cleric murmured. Even a few steps farther into the room brought a much, much heavier wave of the stench. It was not simply a matter of how many gargoyles nested in the room, but how many *generations* of them had done so.

The vast chamber had the look of once having been a ball-room perhaps, or at least a place for a gathering of beings other than gargoyles. There was a mosaic pattern on the marble floor, but between the darkness and the disarray of the creatures living in the room, Stefan could not make out what it was.

Large patches of dried shrubs, branches, and other vege-table matter had been gathered to make countless sleeping places for the flock. Bits of food—unidentifiable meat, pieces of fur, various plants—lay scattered. There were many bones, some quite large. Stefan peered at a skull, grateful to see it was not human or some other intelligent race.

"No young," he muttered to Chasm.

"Hidden to keep alive."

"Why?"

"Males fight," the gargoyle replied with a tone that indicated Stefan should know that. "Young not quick."

"You were raised by Tyranos. How do you know—"

"All know."

"But—" The cleric hesitated. Amid the many smaller nests making up the huge one he spotted a single, dark form. The Solamnian gripped his sword tighter. Chasm, responding to his sudden tenseness, crouched in preparation for a leap.

The form remained still. Stefan closed on the nest. Unlike the gargoyles he had seen, the beast apparently had some whiteness or silver to it. He wondered if it had been dead a while.

At last, the light of the pendant washed over the unmoving figure.

The knight nearly dropped his weapon. Chasm let out a low rumble of nervousness. The gargoyle was as stunned as the human, for although they both recognized the unconscious figure, it was not anyone they had expected to find.

It was Idaria.

Setting down his sword, Stefan rushed to the elf slave's side. She looked bruised, but otherwise whole. The cleric's brow furrowed as he carefully raised her head up. The elf looked peaceful, as if she were just taking a nap.

Her eyes fluttered open. She shook her head. "Sir S-Stefan? No, you cannot be." Idaria pulled away. "You—You must be *him!* You must be—"

The elf fell back, trying to swallow air. The cleric fumbled for a water sack he belatedly recalled he had lost long before.

"Lady Idaria, it *is* me! It is Stefan Rennert—"

"No!" Her eyes widening, she tried to scuttle away from him. "The Solamnian is dead. You cannot fool me with his semblance! You are no more him than you were the Nerakan!"

"Nerakan? Lady Idaria, what are you talking about?"

The elf hesitated. In a small voice she asked, "Sir Stefan, is it you? Is it truly you?"

"I swear it."

Her eyes growing both hopeful and determined, Idaria took hold of his arm. "Sir Stefan! We must help him. The Titan fights with him. But worse, there is the—"

She stopped in mid-breath, suddenly staring with cold eyes past him. At the same time, Chasm let out a warning cry.

Stefan whirled around to discover several shadowed forms converging on the trio. He had not even heard or sensed them, yet they were so near that Chasm had to leap back to avoid being grabbed. The gargoyle took to the air—

—and was tackled by a bony form. Two others quickly joined the tangle, the three monstrous creatures bringing Chasm down as quickly as he had risen.

They were gargoyles, but gargoyles long, long dead. Only scraps of hide still clung to their skeletal forms.

Stefan had his own predicament, for other figures surrounded Idaria and him. In the pale light of Kiri-Jolith's medallion, their aspects were awful. Like the gargoyles who had just attacked Chasm, the figures were long dead. Scraps of clothing and rusting armor remained to mark what the horrors had once been.

They were all taller than Stefan, more the height of Golgren. As they stretched fleshless hands toward the knight, he noted some still wore adornments and had bits of long, flowing hair. Stefan would have taken them for elves, but they were not. They were something quite different.

Tugging Idaria behind him, the Solamnian slashed at the first corpse, severing its bony hands and chopping off its head.

He hurled the still-standing figure into the one closest to it and tried to drive two others back.

"Sir Stefan! You cannot—"

The rest of what the elf was saying was lost as Chasm let out a terrible hiss of frustration. The gargoyle's horrific counterparts had him pinned to the floor.

Chasm's fate was up to him. Stefan was already hard pressed. More and more skeletal hands grasped for him and the elf, and it was all he could do to get away. They were suddenly everywhere. The cleric struck down two more before realizing from their garments that they were the first two he had faced.

The dead were rebuilding themselves.

Uttering a prayer to Kiri-Jolith, the cleric redoubled his efforts. The undead were thrown back slightly. Stefan saw an opening.

"My lady!" he shouted. "That—"

His sword arm was seized. Two undead ripped the blade from his grip. Three more brought the Solamnian to his knees.

He heard a cry from Idaria and another desperate hiss from Chasm. Looking for the elf, Stefan forced his head up.

A bony hand wielding the knight's own sword thrust the weapon at Stefan's chest. The armor should have stopped the point, but the monstrous figure shoved the sword with inhuman strength. The blade sank through not only metal, but flesh and bone. It plunged until it reached the Solamnian's heart, though Stefan knew before that the wound was fatal.

Sir Stefan Rennert fell lifeless, his last thought only that he had failed his mission, and his companions.

꘎꘎꘎

It said much for the Fire Rose's seductive powers that even though Golgren was sorely wounded, he still managed to stretch his shaking hand forward and seize hold of its stem.

Nothing mattered more than keeping a grip on the artifact.

Safrag sought to stab him again, but the landscape went through yet another upheaval. Flames erupted around the duo, and where once the Titan had stood, a ravine formed.

The abrupt change caught Safrag so off guard he could not keep himself from falling. His hand slipped free of the artifact.

But as the sorcerer vanished from his sight, Golgren's will failed. He tumbled over and, in doing so, sent the Fire Rose flying.

Sirrion's creation went bouncing along the churning earth, fiery sparks marking each time it struck something solid. Yet its crystalline form was not marred in the least.

Golgren dragged himself after the artifact. The Fire Rose had come to rest against a fair sized rock, with the area stable once more.

His breathing ragged, the half-breed pulled himself toward the artifact one hand at time. The furious glitter of the Fire Rose ensnared his gaze much as Sirrion's eyes had done earlier. All that mattered was to reach it, hold it, possess it.

It will put everything right, a voice in the Grand Khan's head whispered enticingly. *It will heal everything.*

A shadow passed over him.

With a determined grunt, Golgren catapulted himself toward the Fire Rose. He sensed the gargoyle descending just as he grabbed the magical piece. Golgren rolled on his back, clutching the Fire Rose, and watched with disbelief as his winged attacker suddenly writhed in the air.

The gargoyle spun around, clawing at its own body. Fire burst from within it, breaking through the many cracks developing in the gray hide. The creature hissed as flames engulfed it.

But, as the last vestiges of the gargoyle became sheer fire, the fire in turn transformed into another figure.

Sirrion shook a few straggling flames away from his body and beheld the bleeding half-breed.

"I'm hungry. Do you have anything for me to eat?" the god blithely asked. When Golgren only stared, Sirrion reached down and plucked up a rock. As he held it up, the rock became an apple.

The lord of alchemy and fire did not bring the apple to his mouth, however. Instead, Sirrion ignited the apple in his palm, burning it away in a matter of two or three breaths.

"A small tidbit, but it'll have to do," Sirrion commented drily. He cocked his head as he surveyed the half-breed's injuries and wounds. "You look to be dying. Why do you mortals always look to be dying? I barely speak to one of you, and you die. They were the same, you know, the ones who begged for my flower. They asked for it, were given it, and they *died*."

He glided over to Golgren, a stream of fire beneath his booted feet. Golgren tried to talk, to say something, to plead, but the effort was too much for him.

"I was curious about something," the god continued. "Something I hadn't noticed before." He raised a hand over the half-breed.

Golgren felt a hotness stir within him. He expected to die as the gargoyle had, but instead, the brief fire faded.

"There it is. I wondered. Good and ill, the balance had to be there."

Steeling himself, the Grand Khan rasped, "Show me . . . Show me how it, it does *everything*."

"But you know already. And the choice is yours, not mine. I've always left it up to those who most want my flower. Yet they die so quickly!"

Sirrion's body burst into flames. He nodded to Golgren as he turned. Yet the god of fire did not even complete his turn before the flames appeared to consume him as they had the gargoyle.

By the time Golgren drew another ragged breath, Sirrion had vanished. Only a few lingering licks of extinguishing fire marked his departure.

Despite the agony coursing through him, Golgren wondered about the deity, who seemed to have returned for no reason other than to chide him. What reason could there have been for Sirrion's short and puzzling visitation? What had he meant about not noticing something earlier about the half-breed?

New, sharp pain wracked Golgren. Despite the heat of the Fire Rose, he suddenly felt cold.

The ogre leader turned on his stomach again. He dragged himself farther from the site of the struggle despite each movement sending renewed jolts of agony through his body.

You have brought it to me at last, came a chilling voice in his head. It was the same voice he had heard but moments before.

Another shadow crossed Golgren, a shadow cast by *nothing.* There was no gargoyle; nor was it Safrag.

There was only the shadow. The moving shadow.

Sirrion's Gift. Our Folly. The words ended in a deep chuckle.

And suddenly, a black and gray figure that was as much shadow as it was something more raised Golgren up effortlessly with one white, bone-thin finger. Eyes of ice studied the half-breed with far more interest than Sirrion's had.

So long a wait, but so delicious a victory! You are everything I promised myself, everything you could be.

Golgren tried to strike at the black-gray figure, but his hand came up far short. The veiled figure chuckled.

My impossibility, my enigma. You do me proud.

The finger bent. The Grand Khan suddenly fell face down on the ground.

And you are no longer needed.

As the last statement echoed in Golgren's head, gargoyles descended by the score. They let out eager hisses, and even when settled on the ground they beat their wings with anticipation.

"No," Golgren croaked, baring his teeth. "You will not . . ."

The shadowy form bent down. *But you have no choice with me. You would not even be without me.*

Golgren's body did not move of its own volition. His legs bent to kneel, and his arms stretched to do for the phantasm what even Safrag could not demand of him.

A second ghastly hand joined the first to take the Fire Rose away from him. As if recognizing a long lost master, the artifact glowed bright.

What happened next seemed a dream to the half-dead Golgren. A terrible wind arose, one that whipped through the area with a ferocity that enabled it to tear small rocks free and send them flinging into the air. The gargoyles were lifted up with the stones, their wings seeming to catch the wind despite their best efforts. They flew up and whirled away, all the while trying in vain to control their mad flight.

But it was his tormentor who was the most oddly affected. The wind literally tore through him. Still reaching for the Fire Rose, he disintegrated as though he had become air himself.

When the other gargoyles had been burned to ash by the Fire Rose, Golgren had assumed that the magic had been drawn from both Safrag and him. But he had managed by himself to do the impossible. He, who had no knowledge or mastery of magic.

The triumphant smile on his face lasted as long as it took him to collapse.

He lay there on the brink of death. The cold that had earlier filled him returned with a hundred times more intensity. Golgren shivered. His body refused his efforts.

How long he lay there, Golgren did not know. He lost consciousness, regained it, and lost it again. The sense that someone new was nearby stirred him just enough to feel the Fire Rose being tugged from his fingers. What he had struggled so much to defend was taken from him with the utmost ease.

His body suddenly shot up, rising more than a foot above the ground. Golgren tried to discern what was happening, but his eyes would not focus. What felt like ice enshrouded him, but if it was ice, it was ice with a dire blue tint. Like a fly caught in amber, the Grand Khan of all ogres stood fixed in a pose of death that surely presaged the inevitable.

Beyond his macabre prison, someone chuckled. *There is your legacy. There is your monument to nothing, mongrel.*

Safrag's chuckle echoed through Golgren's prison long after the sorcerer had left.

XXI

KHLEEG

Garantha was near. It had taken Khleeg the greatest of efforts to lead the hand back to the capital so quickly. The warriors were weary beyond belief, and they had lost a few of the animals in their haste, but the effort had been worth it.

Khleeg looked for some sign of military activity, some hint that Wargroch had set other elements of ogre strength into action. True, Wargroch commanded the city guard, but Garantha needed more of a defense than that, much more. Khleeg had commanded Syln to send messengers to the other hands ordered out by the younger officer, but he could not feel confident that they would return before Rauth's forces reached the capital. Fortunately, Atolgus and the rest of the betrayers were still far to the south, or else the situation would have been even more dire.

Still, as they came within sight of the capital, Khleeg feared for Garantha. There were hardly any guards visible on the walls. For one of the few times since swearing an oath to the Grand Khan, he questioned Golgren's decisions. Wargroch had proven himself a fine warrior and clever of mind, but he was obviously incapable of overseeing such an important part of the empire.

Syln, a Kernian ogre whose extended belly made it look as though he sought to pretend—badly—to be one of his stouter cousins from the south, echoed his concern. "Need more guards. The city of the griffon should be stronger."

"Wargroch will learn. No matter. We are home. We will make Garantha strong, eh, Syln?"

"Yes, Khleeg!" Despite his girth, Syln was a skilled fighter and a respected commander. His warriors were worth twice that of most other hands.

A horn sounded as they approached. Some of the sentries raised their weapons in salute. Khleeg relaxed, but only slightly. He would not be satisfied until he knew all that had gone on in his absence.

With a grinding sound, the gates slowly opened. Khleeg led the hand into the capital. In contrast to so many previous times when he had ridden with his lord at the head of a victorious army, the welcome he received was subdued and nearly silent. Warriors of the city guard stood at attention, and those who gathered to watch saluted with fists and weapons. All knew that the Grand Khan was not with the warriors; Khleeg's swift return without their ruler was not a sign they took well.

"Wargroch must tell them," he rumbled to Syln. "They must know the Grand Khan watches over Garantha, over all Golthuu."

The gates shut behind the last of the ranks. Khleeg looked for the younger officer. Wargroch should have met them.

What he saw instead was an ogre who could *not* have been able to be in the city. He should have been arrested and executed on the spot.

"Atolgus!" he roared, thrusting a meaty finger in the direction where he glimpsed the betrayer.

A puzzled Syln straightened, trying to see.

From somewhere, a horn blew the call to battle. Khleeg started, realizing too late what that horn meant.

The guards flanking the column let out fierce roars and lunged at Khleeg's warriors. The fighters in the ranks hesitated, confused by their own comrades attacking them in the very capital. They reacted in confusion, and several perished without even raising their weapons in defense.

"Traitors!" the hand commander shouted. *"Krehgu u athu*—defend lines! Defend!"

The warriors deeper in the column rushed to aid their embattled comrades. Khleeg surveyed the chaos. As with the earlier attack by Rauth, it was impossible to tell from his vantage point whether many in his vision were loyal or were betrayers. The actual line of struggle fluctuated madly, and as he watched, some of those caught up in the fighting broke into individual struggles that splintered off.

Khleeg hunted for a glimpse of Atolgus again. Kill the leader, and the other betrayers would lose heart. "Syln!"

The commander understood. Syln tapped two other mounted officers with the flat of his sword. "Follow him!"

They rode behind Khleeg as the Blödian forced his heavy steed through the packed fighters to where he had last observed the former chieftain. His mind still reeled at discovering Atolgus in the city. Atolgus should have been far south. It would have taken many days with the swiftest steed and the greatest of good fortune for him to ride to Garantha—longer with a column of warriors. Atolgus could not be in there!

Unless . . .

Two traitors tried to sideswipe Khleeg. He dispatched one with a bloody stroke across the throat. One of the officers who rode with him did battle with the second while Khleeg and the other continued on.

When he had first seen Atolgus, the young warrior had been standing atop a low, flat-roofed building waving his sword to signal his followers. Like magic, though, he had vanished from sight only a moment later. Yet, Khleeg was absolutely certain he had not imagined the image of the traitor.

A sharp pain tore at the calf of his right leg. Grunting,

Khleeg drove off another traitor. He glanced down at the wound and was happy to note that the cut was a superficial one.

Wargroch must be dead. Atolgus could not have set the trap into play otherwise. Wargroch's foolish dismissal of the hands protecting Garantha had signed his own death warrant.

What mattered was putting an end to the astounding uprising.

The officer with him grunted something unintelligible. Khleeg glanced his way and saw him pointing to their right.

Atolgus stood there watching the battle, the renegade's expression almost gleeful. He looked mad, but not with blood-lust. His eyes had an animal wildness to them.

Khleeg urged his mount on. Atolgus saw him coming. The former chieftain grinned in greeting.

Another ogre blocked the Blödian's path. Cursing, Khleeg swung at his new foe, trying simply to beat the other ogre back enough so he could go on after Atolgus. But the other warrior refused to give ground to the mounted Khleeg.

Golgren's second in command finally cleaved the other's skull. As he pulled the dripping blade up, he glanced toward Atolgus.

But once again, his quarry had vanished.

Another horn sounded, one from within the column. Khleeg looked over his shoulder to detect the hand commander trying to rally the loyal fighters. Meanwhile, the crowd of onlookers that had lined the way had vanished from view. Khleeg frowned. Ogres did not shy away from a fight. The populace should have chosen one side or another. And more than likely they would have chosen Khleeg's, since he was the Grand Khan's representative. Instead, though, they had, like Atolgus, disappeared.

Khleeg froze, uncertain where to go, what to do next. The hand commander was doing his best to keep his warriors together, but they couldn't hold the ground where they had been forced to take a stand. They needed a far more defensible location.

Only one place came to mind.

With a snarl, Khleeg signaled to the other officer to turn around. As they returned to the column, he roared to Syln, "To the palace! Follow!"

It was a sign of the other ogre's trust in Khleeg that the commander immediately obeyed. Under his guidance, what remained of the hand formed a square and began a slow but relentless move to the walled palace. Khleeg could not be certain the traitors were not already ensconced within, but if so, he could confront the guards at the entrance. Besides, they did not know all the hidden ways in and out of the ancient structure.

Golgren had hidden many secrets inside the palace that would help against an uprising. The Grand Khan was no fool; he had not ruled out such a dire event occurring during his reign.

The column retreated down the streets to the palace. The commander and his warriors followed Khleeg, trusting in him.

Khleeg only hoped their trust was not misplaced.

The palace walls rose in the distance. Khleeg rode up next to the officer. "Four riders with me! Your warriors fight to the gates!"

Syln slapped his fist against his breastplate and ordered four warriors to follow Khleeg. Golgren's second in command led them down a side street.

They met no resistance. Khleeg's eyes narrowed, but he saw no hidden threat. Atolgus had concentrated too much on his trap.

At a ruined structure southwest of the palace, Khleeg ordered everyone to dismount quickly. With reluctance, he slapped his horse on the flank, sending the animal racing off. The other horses chased after his steed.

The five loyal ogres silently entered the ruins. The official reason for the area still remaining in disrepair had to do with the precarious condition of the ground. The ruins had once been the villa of a valued ally of the predecessor to Golgren's own lord, Zharang. A fire had supposedly destroyed the half restored villa midway through Zharang's reign.

Only Khleeg knew the fire had been set at the Grand Lord's behest. And that the villa had never been rebuilt in order for Golgren to disguise other work being done by his minions.

Khleeg knew exactly where to look for what he was seeking. It was hidden deep in a treacherous-looking section of the half restored villa, two levels below the surface. Anyone scavenging in the building would have had little reason to notice the pile of stone cluttering the section. Khleeg, ducking under a broken column originally carved by some skilled High Ogre artisan to resemble a living tree, made his way directly to it. As his warriors watched in puzzlement, he twisted a piece of marble near the top of the stones, before tugging hard on the entire pile.

The pile shifted as one. Stepping back, Khleeg pointed at two of his companions and at the pile.

With ease, the pair pushed the shifted stone aside, revealing a hidden tunnel. Khleeg went first, the officer bending to enter. A few steps in, Khleeg stood to survey a passage whose solid stone walls surely dated back to Garantha's founding.

With growing eagerness, Golgren's second in command led the four other loyal ogres along the narrow path. They came across some minor cracks in the stone, but for the most part the tunnel was clear of obstructions. Since discovering the ancient passage and having it repaired, Golgren had ensured that it would remain in good working order, just in case a hidden route was needed.

There was no light in the tunnel, but there was only one direction in which to travel. The only mark of their progress was a faint silver line drawn across the width of one part of the tunnel. Khleeg knew it to indicate the point where the tunnel crossed under the protective wall surrounding the palace.

At the other end of the tunnel, he encountered a marble wall. With no light to guide him, Khleeg ran his hand over the left side of the wall until he located a tiny lump. He pressed it and used his weight to push against the wall.

The wall gave way, sliding like a door until there was enough of a gap for the huge ogres to squeeze through. Sword in hand, Khleeg entered first.

He emerged in one of the lower levels of the palace, a place left in disuse for generations by Grand Khans who had acted more as squatters than as true lords of the ancient edifice. Again, it had taken Golgren, inquisitive of the nature of the ogres' great ancestors, to discover the disused level.

The room was filled with dust and years of cobwebs. Khleeg cut through a dense curtain of silken threads, sending scores of thick, black spiders skittering away. Huge, shriveled rodent bodies hung in some of the webs, while on the ground lay bones of other creatures next to gnawed remains of the spiders.

Golgren had left the webs and bug creatures as another deterrent against explorers. Khleeg followed the narrow way his lord had shown him, without deviating from the recommended path. Khleeg knew there were other things in the supposedly empty chamber—things hidden from the sight of Khleeg and the others—that were far worse than rats or spiders.

With growing relief Khleeg led his small party through the rusting iron door at the far end and up a set of blocky steps to the next level. They were near their goal. Khleeg had confidence that Syln had in the meantime reached the gates.

They came through a newer heavy door, one with the sign of the severed hand of Golgren molded into it. Khleeg had one of the warriors cautiously shove it open.

One of the outer halls greeted the band. Khleeg paused, orienting himself. The faces and figures of High Ogres living their opulent lives filled his view from the opposite walls. Khleeg snorted at the lighthearted moments in some of the depictions that contrasted with his own tense emotions.

"That way," Golgren's second in command finally ordered, indicating a path to the right.

They had gone no more than a few steps when the sound of someone approaching sent Khleeg and his warriors behind the nearest column.

But to his surprise, it was Wargroch and two guards, who came rushing down the corridor to where they hid.

Khleeg leaped out. "Wargroch!"

The other officer stopped, surprised. "Khleeg?"

"Ha!" Golgren's second in command slapped Wargroch on the shoulder. The four warriors with him stepped out of their place of concealment. "The palace! It is secure?"

"Secure? Yes. How have you come?"

Khleeg quickly spoke of the secret passage. Wargroch's eyes widened.

"Enough!" Khleeg said. "Syln waits at the gate! Must open the way for him!"

"Syln expects that?" Wargroch rubbed his thick jaw. "Syln will enter, yes."

At that moment, more guards appeared. Wargroch gestured for them to lower their weapons. He started to lead Khleeg on.

"Atolgus is in Garantha, Wargroch."

"Yes. That I know."

The senior officer paused to stare at his counterpart. "You know?"

"I have seen Atolgus."

Khleeg grunted. "There must be magic at work. Atolgus cannot be in Garantha without magic. It is"—he searched for the Common word, but could not find it—"*ba'gharuc!*"

"Unarguable. The word is 'unarguable,' " Wargroch answered. "It is a hard word for ogre mouths."

"Unargu—Yes. It is Titan magic."

Wargroch gestured, continuing with leading Khleeg. Behind the duo, the guards and the four warriors followed.

"Titan magic, yes," agreed the younger officer. "They have taken the elves too."

The senior officer's eyes blazed. Matters were worse than he thought. "Atolgus must be stopped. After that, the Titans."

"No."

Khleeg stumbled. He stared at Wargroch. "No?"

"They must win." Wargroch leaned close to the other ogre, his face close to Khleeg's. "They *will* win."

Khleeg felt a sudden pain in his side. Wargroch stepped back, revealing a dagger in his hand.

Blood dripped from the point, spotting the marble floor Golgren had always ordered so meticulously polished.

There was also blood dripping from Khleeg's side, just where the front and back plates of his armor came together.

His warriors tried to rush to his aid, but Wargroch's guards suddenly turned their weapons on the four. An axe cut down one of them. The other three dropped their weapons.

With a roar partly fueled by his pain, Khleeg swung wildly at Wargroch. The other officer jumped back, drawing his own sword. He parried Khleeg's attack, but instead of counterattacking, simply stood back, keeping away from Khleeg.

Khleeg tried to carry the fight to him, only to have one of his legs give way. He fell to his knees.

His hand could no longer clutch his sword. The weapon dropped to the floor with a loud crash. Golgren's second in command grabbed for it, but his fingers would not work.

He stared at the only wound he had. It hurt, but it was not so bad a wound to have hurt him so quickly and terribly.

"Ta'ki'agrur," Wargroch rumbled, carefully sheathing the dagger. "The word in Common, it is 'vengeance.' *Vengeance.* It is a Common word that I like."

"Ta'ki'agrur?" The dazed and confused Khleeg was finding it hard to concentrate. "Vengeance?"

"The mongrel, he must pay with blood. For my brothers. For the blood of Nagroch. The blood of Belgroch. The mongrel will pay for their blood. With you. With his dream."

Struggling to rise, Khleeg rasped, "N-Nagroch . . . But he served the Grand Khan—"

"His life Golgren claimed with a dagger."

Khleeg knew the story. Nagroch had failed in a duel with the future warrior-mate of the Uruv Suurt emperor. Golgren had taken Nagroch's life when she had refused to kill him.

"It was n-n—"

"Necessary?" Wargroch snorted. "That also. Die, Khleeg. The mongrel will be with you soon enough."

Golgren's loyal officer could no longer speak. His vision was fading. He made an awkward grab at his wound.

In the process he lost his balance. Khleeg sprawled on the floor and lay still.

Wargroch bent down and turned Khleeg over. He looked closely. After a moment, he stood.

"The meredrakes are hungry. The poison will not kill them."

Two of Wargroch's guards sheathed their weapons and picked up the body. He watched as they carried Khleeg's body away. As that happened, another guard approached.

"The battle is over?" Wargroch asked before the other could speak.

The guard nodded. "Hand commander dead. Warriors surrender." He took a breath and added, "Atolgus comes."

His task done, the treacherous officer hurried to the front hall of the palace. Barely had he arrived than a large, armed party met him coming through the great outer doors .

At their head strode Atolgus. He was taller than when Wargroch had seen him last, taller and mesmerizing. Unlike most, Wargroch knew something about why Atolgus looked different, and why someone who had only been a minor chieftain and loyal follower of the half-breed would suddenly become Golgren's great nemesis. Wargroch knew Morgada, and understood her tremendous powers, both magical and otherwise.

But Wargroch himself had no need for such temptations. He had desired Golgren's blood ever since learning of his older brothers' deaths. Khleeg's death was one step of that plan.

Atolgus acknowledged him. "Khleeg?"

"The meredrakes feast."

The new warlord grinned wildly. "Good. She will be pleased."

Displaying his sword, Wargroch abruptly knelt before Atolgus. "Garantha is secure."

Atolgus accepted the great blade. "Golgren's . . ."

It had been presented early on to Wargroch as a sign of favor from the Grand Khan. "No, Atolgus's."

The warlord grinned again. He sheathed it and presented Wargroch with his own sword. "Yours."

Beating his fist on his breastplate, Wargroch stood and embraced the offering. "Great is Atolgus! Great is his power!"

But Atolgus shook his head. Still grinning, he replied, "No. Great is the power of the *Titans.*"

༺⚬✹⚬༻

Morgada and the Black Talon had observed the entire tableau from their safe sanctum far, far away. They and every other Titan were exhausted; the tasks given to them by the absent Safrag had been so monumental that more than one sorcerer was in danger of needing elixir to restore themselves. However, Morgada had refused all pleas. Safrag had ordered that *no one* be given any elixir until word came that he had been successful in his quest for the Fire Rose.

"Garantha is at last free of the mongrel, " Draug gasped. "The puppet did his job well."

"Which puppet?" jested another Titan, despite his exhaustion. "The one full of hate or Morgada's adoring pet?"

"Choose one and dispense with both! Neither are needed any longer! Garantha bows to us!"

"But Garantha is only the beginning," breathed Morgada with a smile. "Only the beginning . . ."

Kulgrath did not share in the good spirits spreading among his comrades. The Titan looked from one side to another before flatly stating, "But it's no beginning without that for which we've hunted! Safrag's not returned! For all we know the *mongrel* has the artifact! Imagine the Fire Rose in Golgren's hands!"

"Imagine that if you will," interrupted another, familiar voice. "But you would be indulging in flights of fantasy."

Safrag stood in the center of the chamber, exactly upon the symbol of the Black Talon. His once immaculate garments were torn and stained; there were bruises and cuts on his arms, torso, and face.

But his expression was triumphant. As the rest of the inner circle gaped, he stretched forth his arms and revealed the Fire Rose.

Its blazing light filled the chamber and brought a reddish orange cast to the face of each onlooker. The Titans sat speechless, until Morgada was the first to find her tongue.

"It is beautiful."

"It is the future," Safrag corrected.

"And Golgren?" gasped Kulgrath, unable to tear his eyes away from the dancing flames within the Rose. "Is he—?"

Safrag's song was glorious as he shouted, "Golgren is a monument to his folly! Golgren the mongrel is no more!"

As one, the rest of the Black Talon smiled, joining him in celebrating the Grand Khan's demise.

"The Fire Rose," one murmured. "Is it all we hope it to be? Can it truly do so much?"

"You would have a test?"

"Is that possible?" asked Draug. "Can you wield it already?"

In answer, Safrag stepped aside and gestured to the spot where he had just stood.

A terrible stench filled the air. Many of the Titans sat back in disgust as a dripping horror materialized.

Falstoch looked around. The abomination was still bent in pain from the wound he had suffered.

Safrag nodded to the monstrosity. "Shall we try again?"

Without preamble, he held the Fire Rose before Falstoch's constantly melting face. The abomination raised a deformed limb as the artifact's burning light bathed it in reddish orange. Falstoch let out a cry that shook even the hardened Titans.

Falstoch began to transform. His body straightened and solidified. The wound vanished. The melting wax that had been his flesh became sleek blue skin. Features aligned differently on his face, molding themselves into a handsome visage. A lush mane of hair thrust out of his skull and fell back.

The garments of a Titan materialized around the changing Falstoch. As he finished his transformation, the garments clad him.

The newly rejuvenated sorcerer stood trembling. "Will it . . . Will it hold?" he sang in faltering Titan speech. "Will it?"

Safrag only beamed. After a moment, Falstoch let out a dark howl of joy. He gazed at his hands, felt his face, and howled again.

And the Titans of the inner circle reveled in his joy, in their triumph. It had been the least of tests. The Fire Rose not only wielded great magic, but it could be wielded by *them*.

Safrag held it high. "The dawning of the new Golden Age is upon us!" he sang exultantly. "The dawning of the rebirth of the High Ogres."

XXII

GARGOYLES

Tyranos groaned as he awoke and immediately realized what he had done. Whoever was master of the gargoyles would have set some insidious trap for the rare intruder who might be searching for the Fire Rose. Yet Tyranos had not considered that possibility. Admittedly, he had a streak of smugness, which his earliest teachers had said would someday kill him despite his skills. It looked to be that day.

The massive spellcaster looked around and saw nothing. He was in utter darkness in a place that smelled to him like the grave. The reason for that became apparent as his eyes adjusted.

Corpses. Three. From the looks of them, they were all ancient, yet the smell of death still pervaded the dark, moist area. Tyranos guessed that was because there was nowhere for the smell to go. That boded ill as much as the dead themselves.

The three hung as he did, floating in what seemed to be midair with their arms and legs spread out. Tyranos could tell little about them save that one looked to be a gargoyle by its shape, while the others were closer to human or elf in form but taller.

The wizard squinted. *High Ogres,* perhaps. If so, the bodies had been trapped a long, long time.

He tried to turn his head, but only half succeeded with the movement. Still, he could turn enough to enable him to see that he was not floating, but rather seemed to be attached to several tiny strands that looked like nothing less than webbing.

"No damned spiders, thank you," Tyranos rasped, more to hear *anything* than because he truly believed it was the work of any arachnid. What he could make out of the corpses gave no indication they had perished from having their life fluids sucked out of them. The webbing itself had been the cause of their demises. They had been trapped and had starved to death.

The wizard struggled, but to no avail. Physical strength meant nothing, otherwise the gargoyle wouldn't be among the dead.

Tyranos looked for his staff. It was nowhere in sight.

"We can't have that," he muttered. Tyranos concentrated on the missing staff, trying to summon it.

It did not appear in his hand, but not because he wasn't trying hard enough. The spellcaster could sense the staff attempting to draw near, but some other greater force held it back.

"Damn!" Tyranos gritted his teeth. After a moment, he murmured a spell.

The strands lit up as if electrified. The wizard continued to grit his teeth as his body also suffered some from the spell. He stared into the sightless sockets of one of the High Ogre dead.

After several seconds, the electrical illumination ceased. The odor of something having been burned wafted under Tyranos's nose, although whether it was the strands or himself that was the source of the odor was a question he could not answer.

Taking a breath, he tugged as hard as he could on the strands holding his left hand.

Nothing happened.

A lengthy epithet escaped the wizard.

"So," he snarled to himself. "Only one choice, Tyranos. Only one choice damn it."

He set his chin against his chest and concentrated.

A heat arose just over his heart. Something radiated there, casting a vague, circular shape even though, had anyone looked, they would have seen no medallion, no tattoo.

To find the truth, they would have had to look much deeper into the wizard.

Tyranos let out a sudden roar of agony. The circular shape grew more evident beneath his robes, almost as if it were burning its way through to the outer world.

And as the circular shape glowed bright, the wizard's form began to alter. His mouth and nose stretched forward, becoming part of one unusual feature. His clean-shaven face sprouted dark hair, even on the forehead and around the eyes.

With a furious cry, Tyranos threw the power that he had summoned into destroying the strands. He heard them burn with a satisfying sizzle, but at the same time felt the changing of his body worsen.

"I—will—not—revert!" he shouted to the darkness. "I—am—no longer—that!"

His left arm suddenly tore free of the snare. His right arm followed suit a breath later.

Struggling hard, the wizard tumbled forward with such force that he collided with the nearest corpse. Tyranos instinctively pushed himself back for fear he would become entangled in the dead figure's trap.

His legs weakened. He collapsed on the floor. As he did, his face began to shrink again, finally returning to normalcy.

The glow over his chest faded. The wizard lay there, shivering.

His strength gradually returned enough to enable him to push himself to a sitting position. Yet Tyranos still shivered.

"Too damned close. But you knew that'd happen, didn't you?"

Neither he nor any invisible voice answered the question. The wizard shoved himself up onto his feet. He was free of the strands, yet hardly free of the trap itself.

"Where are you?" he asked the missing staff. "Close by, but how close by? Ah."

Gingerly stepping past the gargoyle corpse, Tyranos followed the sensation he felt. The staff was in some ways as bound to him as Chasm.

A faint glow emanated ahead. The muscular spellcaster grinned. "So, there you are! I've missed you."

He reached for the staff, which was also snared by strands. The wizard gave a good pull—

A tremendous hiss from above was all the warning that he received. The bone white form dropped down on him, its long, sinewy body quickly coiling around the wizard from chest to ankle.

A ghostly head snapped at him. It was huge snake—a viper—with fangs as long as Tyranos's fingers.

He used one powerful hand to grab the beast just under the jaw and thus keep it from sinking those fangs into his arm.

The snake pulled back its head. Tyranos immediately twisted the creature's head just to the side of his own.

A spray of venom shot forth, a spray that only barely grazed his cheek thanks to his swift reaction. Still, the slight touch was enough to make the area burn like the coldest ice.

At the same time, the coils tightened painfully. The spellcaster felt his rib cage being squeezed impossibly hard. The viper was also a great constrictor, a double threat.

But Tyranos squeezed back. "There are things in the sea my people have fought that are far worse than you could ever be, worm!"

The wizard crushed its throat.

The viper stiffened. The head cracked off and fell near his feet.

Twisting, Tyranos broke free of the rest of its body. Fragments of the viper went flying in different directions, some of them landing in the strands.

Studying the pieces still in his hand, the wizard saw that the creature had indeed turned to stone upon dying, much as it was said certain draconians did. Of course, draconians—the dragon men who had once served the dread goddess Takhisis—were living creatures, whereas the serpent had more likely been an animated carving brought to life by some magical trigger.

Tyranos discarded the pieces and tried to free the staff again. It worked after he had pulled as hard as he could. The wizard inspected his staff for damage, and satisfied, looked around in order to consider his next move.

The most logical one came to mind. Tyranos raised the staff and concentrated.

A moment later, he lowered the staff in disgust. "So. Not so easy to escape, eh? Let's see what else we can find." He glanced over his shoulder at the representatives of the dead, adding with a mocking tone, "You'll wait, won't you?"

Holding the staff before him, the wizard muttered. The crystal point shone, albeit not nearly so bright as times in the past. Grunting in frustration, Tyranos studied the area around him.

There *was* a passage beyond the webbed area, which surprised the wizard. Shrugging, he headed to the passage.

It was narrow, but passable. The walls were absolutely smooth, even where the stone blocks met. The builders had been craftsmen and—so Tyranos discovered as he held the staff close to one wall—masters of magic. Latent forces swirled within the walls, their purpose undecipherable, and therefore potentially deadly.

The passage veered at a sharp angle to the right. Tyranos turned the corner and confronted a wall.

He also encountered another skeleton clad in the robes he was increasingly certain represented some generation of the High Ogres.

The poor fool had been crushed to death by something. Every bone was broken, the skull in several unattractive pieces.

But the dead were already familiar and only of mild interest. The wizard stepped gingerly over the remains and used the staff to tap against the wall at the end.

It sounded very solid.

"Blasted tricks." Tyranos turned back.

There was a wall where the passage had been.

He was trapped.

A grinding noise sounded. The wall that had appeared behind him began moving in his direction.

The tall spellcaster was not amused. He stretched the staff forth and tapped the moving wall. Like the one he had just investigated, it sounded very solid. It continued toward him.

"And so I'm to be squeezed to a pulp am I?" It was an old kind of trap, Tyranos knew, a favorite of tomb builders who had some access to magic or very clever mechanics.

However, Tyranos had no desire to end up like the unfortunate under his feet or any of the many others he had come across in his searches. He gazed up at the ceiling, studying the point where the moving wall and the ceiling met a side wall.

Tyranos stabbed the staff's head into the point of convergence. *"Tivak!"*

The silver strands of energy burst forth and struck the area.

Hot stone pelted him as the area exploded. Tyranos kept his head covered by the hood of his robe.

When he dared look up again, it was to find that the ceiling and the walls had all been scorched black and badly damaged. More importantly, the wall had ceased advancing.

"And that's that done." Tyranos turned to deal with the wall at the other end.

But the wall was gone and shortly beyond where it had previously stood, Tyranos could see a chamber.

A lighted chamber.

Tyranos told himself to be patient, measuring each step as though he were trying to cross a raging river by means of a bridge consisting of a single piece of rope upon which he was balanced. After succeeding with one step, he would dare the next.

By the time he reached the chamber, his heart was pounding from anticipation. Yet still the spellcaster did not leap inside the room. Instead, he extended his staff just beyond the end of the corridor.

A gigantic pattern formed at the entrance, a complex, magical pattern filled with every color of the rainbow and every geometric design Tyranos had ever known. It blazed so brightly that he had to shield his eyes until they grew accustomed to the glare.

The pattern hovered there, utterly blocking his way. Yet it did nothing more aggressive. Tyranos studied the pattern, noting marks of the three moons, of the constellations as they had been before the ones designated for Paladine—once highest of the gods of light—and dark Takhisis had vanished from the heavens. There were also geographic marks, some of which he did not recognize, others that he did, and a few that were possibly places he knew, but with small variations.

The pattern altered. Some of the locations became other places. The constellations shifted positions. Several of the geometric designs realigned themselves and, as they did, Tyranos felt the magic of the pattern as a whole take on a new significance.

He cocked his head. There was something about the entire creation—

With his head high, Tyranos strode forward. He braced himself as he reached the shimmering pattern and breathed a deep sigh of relief when he emerged on the other side untouched.

"By the kraken!" the wizard rasped. He turned around to see the final traces of the pattern vanish. "So not so concerned about someone who's not bound to any High Ogre, eh?"

Tyranos had studied much about the ancient race since first hearing about the Fire Rose. He had learned about their ways and about rivalries between their different factions. The pattern was designed to keep out anyone of a certain group—or possibly one particular individual. It had also been created to sense anyone who in any way *served* that group or individual, a piece of complicated spellcasting that truly impressed him.

"But why so precise?" Tyranos asked the vanished pattern. "Why worry so much about one type of intruder and not so much about others? Did you think the other traps sufficient?"

Still puzzled, he turned back to face the interior of the chamber. He hesitated. There, before him, was a *wall* filled with the flowing, beautiful script of the High Ogres.

And nothing else.

"That can't be right. Let's just see if we can decipher what you're saying. 'The way to freedom' or something?"

Stepping up to the writing, he studied the text, one line after another. Tyranos mouthed it out syllable by syllable, sometimes learning a word by deciphering those around it.

Gradually, what had been written became known, and what became known made the wizard frown.

"Sirrion, you trickster," he muttered. "And I think I understand you a little better, oh master of gargoyles. A little better, definitely." Tyranos growled. "And what I understand, I do not like, no."

❧⊱⊰Ⓘ⊱⊰❧

The undead were extremely disciplined in their task, Idaria noted bitterly as she watched the body of Sir Stefan lifted up and carried away. Chasm, meanwhile, was bound up in rusting but serviceable chains. She remained unchained, but she expected that to be remedied shortly. In the meantime, two undead held her arms with viselike grips.

She mourned Stefan's loss and was concerned for both Chasm and herself, of course. But it was Golgren whose fate Idaria anguished over in her mind. The quest had been his above all. Something had not merely desired him to find the Fire Rose; it had *needed* him to do so. She had realized that too late.

And that something had not been Safrag, she also realized belatedly. Even so, the Titan leader might well be the victor, for he had seized the artifact from Golgren.

The skeletal guardians let Stefan's corpse drop unceremoniously to the dust-covered floor at the far end of the chamber. The body bounced hard on the stone floor before settling in the corner, face up. In death, the knight's expression looked resigned.

She muttered a short, elf prayer for his spirit. As slight as her whisper was, it still caused the undead to turn toward her.

There was something about the ghoulish figures that disturbed Idaria, even more than the army of skeletons that had marched on Garantha. There was something not right about them, something terribly not right.

The elf caught a tiny glimpse of light within the empty eye sockets of one of the undead. She looked at another and noted the same. There was no reason why she should have recognized it for what it was, but nevertheless she did.

The creatures were *alive*. Not in the sense that she or Chasm were alive, and not in the mocking sense of the *f'hanos* who had attacked the capital. Those had merely been animated, with no true recollection of what they had been when living. The magic had made them mimic their former lives, but they didn't live and breathe. Even the two skeletons of Stefan's comrades had not been like the things surrounding her, for those had been the spirits of the pair given brief resurrection in order to pass on the gift of a god to a worthy warrior.

No, the creatures were not truly undead; they were something worse, unimaginable. They were living creatures who, despite the decay of their bodies, had not ever actually *died*.

Some shambled toward her, while others were vanishing into the shadows again. Their hollow sockets filled her view as they came closer, intrigued by their captive. Their intense stare—made all the more eerie by the absence of eyelids to blink—intensified the feeling that they were inspecting her.

Tales of what the Titans did with their elf prisoners stirred fear in Idaria. The ghoulish forms finally turned and followed the rest away, leaving only the pair gripping her arms.

A rumbling sound originating from without filled the vast chamber. The rumbling grew louder, more insistent. Idaria peered high up, where one of the vast windows was located.

And through that window poured more gargoyles than she had could have imagined existed. The elf had witnessed many, many perish already. The vast flock looked renewed, undiminished.

They came in many shapes and sizes, some similar to Chasm. others with more pronounced beaks and slimmer bodies. Idaria could not see the colors of all their hides, but assumed most of them were gray or dusky brown like the ones she had previously encountered. Some had wings that stretched for many yards, and all fluttered with the ease of birds despite their great size.

The rumbling she had heard was the flapping of so many wings accompanied by the hisses and growls of the gargoyles. Those that entered the ancient edifice circled around twice and began to alight on any solid perch, be it a stone staircase rail, a statue, or even a cracked wall. Others filled the nesting areas. The rest took their places based not only upon what niches remained, but on which among them was strongest and fastest. Some made brief shows of dominance, the captive elf noted, but none went farther than hisses and the occasional swat.

More and more of the strange, hideous creatures poured into the citadel, filling it up to the ceiling and beyond.

Additional hisses and flapping could be heard outside the one in which she was imprisoned.

Many of the gargoyles, once they settled down, peered expectantly in the elf's direction, but not exactly at her.

At last the flow ceased. The smell of the gargoyles had grown pungent and was made worse by the slow beating of wings that seemed determined to push the stench in her direction.

The beating of wings stopped. The gargoyles grew silent. Their gazes were fixed just beyond Idaria, who suddenly felt the heat of eyes that stared at her from that direction as well.

Her monstrous guards slowly turned her that way. She beheld a high-backed chair that she was certain had not been there moments before. Made of stone, it had two jutting points at the top that were identical to the two points of the castle.

And in that chair—that throne—there emerged a shadowed figure with nearly fleshless white hands and long, oval orbs that glowed a deathly white. Those eyes were all that could be seen of the head or face; the rest was covered by a hood and bound by a tight, golden cloth over its features.

As the figure finished materializing, the gargoyles let out a long, slow hiss. They bowed their heads low and turned their necks in a recognizable act of submission.

Idaria's two guards also bowed their heads. The elf had no intention of imitating the bows, but her gaze was caught by that of the figure, and suddenly she found herself bending too.

A raspy chuckle filled her head and sent every nerve shivering.

I trust you are better, said a voice.

Somehow, she found her own voice. "Who are you?"

I am master here. The pale hands gestured at the many gargoyles. *It is my domain. Those are my subjects.* Again came the chuckle. *As you have also been.*

"I am not your slave. I do not serve you."

But you already have for so long, came the reply in a voice that, although it was still in her head, sounded exactly like the Nerakan officer whose name she could not remember. *And before that even, and just as you will continue to serve me.*

"Never," she responded coolly.

Several of the gargoyles hissed at her affront, but a single raised finger silenced them. Although there was no visible hint, the elf sensed amusement in the voice.

You will continue to serve me, as so many have served me in my desire throughout time, until it is mine. The shadowed form rose, standing at least as tall as Golgren or the wizard Tyranos. *You will all continue to serve me until the Fire Rose is finally back in my hands, and the world is set right, my Idaria.*

XXIII

THE FIRE WITHIN

A silence hung over Garantha the morning after the attack on Khleeg and his warriors. The populace was used to violent changes in leadership, for it was a part of ogre tradition. Yet the new Grand Khan had not announced himself and, in fact, had been seen by very few.

If his face was unknown, his name had already become widespread: *Atolgus*. Whispered from one ogre to the next, stories blossomed around the name that had little to do with fact, yet were hardly as fantastic as the truth. Atolgus had been a warrior raised by mountain spirits, was the unknown son of Zharang, was even the half-brother of Golgren, and so on and so on.

Atolgus's warriors had already secured all military elements of the capital and brought any suspected sympathizers of his half-breed predecessor to the cells beneath the Jaka Hwunar, so that they could be properly and publicly executed if deemed fit. The cells were packed to overflowing, with so many in each that no one could sit, much less lie down. More so than the Dragon That Is Zharang, Golgren had proved to have far more warriors willing to die rather than to swear oaths to another. That, though, did not seem to matter to the new Grand Khan. If the Jaka Hwunar had to be filled with a fresh sea of blood, it would be.

No one questioned how the coup could have been so quickly organized and undertaken. Such things were beyond most ogres. If a warlord managed to seize power, that was all that mattered.

And no one other than a few officers either imprisoned, already dead, or, as with Wargroch, willing collaborators, knew that much of it had been done with the aid of powerful magic.

Titan magic.

At the second hour past dawn, trumpeters blew a summoning call from the walls of the palace. Generations of habit brought the populace out in throngs to the open areas. The assumption was that the new Grand Khan would be presenting himself. There would be a great display at the arena some time later—for that was the normal way of such things—but the presentation of the new Grand Khan would be the opportunity to mark Atolgus as lord of the palace and thus of all else. Only Golgren had done some ceremonies differently from the past. But he had been *Golgren*.

At the third hour, with the streets filled with tall, hairy bodies already sweating from the heat, a procession of armored guards emerged from the palace. Holding swords and axes high, they marched toward the people. At the end of the procession, two helmed officers strode along bearing long wooden poles upon which fluttered the standard of the new ruler.

That was of interest to the onlookers. Heads craned as ogres by the hundreds sought their first glimpse of the new emblem of the next regime. Already, they could see that the field was a deep blue, a contrast to the plainer brown one that had surrounded the severed hand and bloody dagger of the half-breed. The chosen symbol was unclear at first though, due to the angle at which the wind twisted both standards.

At an opportune moment, the wind shifted abruptly—almost

magically—and the standard of the warlord Atolgus unveiled itself.

It was black, and from a distance could have been mistaken for yet another hand, albeit one bent at a crooked angle. But as it was carried closer, all semblance of a hand faded. It was, instead, a set of avian claws.

Talons.

Behind that standard emerged the warlord himself. Many ogres in the crowd roared or barked their obedience to the new leader. Atolgus was indeed impressive to behold. Even compared to before—when Wargroch, who followed a step behind him, had met with him—Atolgus was a little taller, a little more commanding.

A little less *ogre*.

His eyes bore a golden tint visible even from yards away. Whenever Atolgus turned those eyes on someone in the crowd, the individual felt compelled to fall to their knees in homage. None of the ogres questioned the overwhelming sensation.

The young warrior raised his hands, a sword in one and the other formed into a fist. The warriors on duty at the walls shouted out his name: *Atolgus! Atolgus!*

He made a sweeping motion with his fist.

The crowd stilled.

"The past is dead!" Atolgus shouted in perfect Common. *"Des rida f'han vos!"*

His warriors cheered. The crowd picked up the cheer, some within the throng slower to do so than others.

Atolgus demanded silence again. He slashed with the sword and cried, "The day of the severed hand is over!"

He did not repeat the words in the Ogre tongue, but most understood immediately. "Severed hand" referred to only one thing, one person.

Again, Atolgus's warriors cheered lustily. Wargroch pumped his fist in the air as he shouted out his warlord's name.

The throng also joined in, and if there were more who were hesitant than before, they were still drowned out by those aware that survival meant life, whereas loyalty meant joining those awaiting their fates in the arena.

In an act that confused the crowd, Atolgus turned to look back at the palace as if waiting for someone else to walk through its doors.

He went down on one knee, his sword held forward in presentation as if to be handed from a servant to a master.

Black flames erupted on the open marble path, flames with no discernible source. They rose high, twice and three times the height of the tallest ogre there.

As quickly as they had arisen, the flames died down, vanishing as if they had never been.

In their wake, three towering Titans appeared, surveying the crowd. Morgada stood at the fore, with Kulgrath and Draug just behind her. She smiled at the assembled ogres and bent down just enough to take the proffered sword from Atolgus. Lowering his arms, he remained in a subservient pose before the sorcerers.

Wargroch knelt to the Titans too. As he did, the warriors in the column performed an about-face so that they, like the rest, faced the trio of Titans. As one, all the guards imitated Atolgus and Wargroch.

At that point, *everyone* in the crowd knelt. Even those standing so far back that they could not truly see the Titans knelt, for anyone that could make all those in front show their deference had to be very, very powerful, indeed.

Morgada peered around. When it was clear only the Titans were standing, she spoke. Her voice projected throughout all Garantha, ensuring that no one could later claim not to have heard her momentous words.

"The Golden Age is coming!" the female Titan sang. Although she did so in the wondrous speech created by the late Dauroth, even the lowliest ogre understood her as if born to that tongue. So had been the dictates of Safrag for the historic occasion. "The Golden Age is upon us!"

And behind her, the aged palace of the Grand Khans, and

the High Ogre rulers preceding them, shook. Huge, crimson flames exploded throughout the great edifice, causing even the bravest ogres to suddenly leap up in preparation to flee before the massive conflagration that threatened to spread. In mere moments, one of the greatest surviving monuments to the ogres' vanished past was consumed. And yet the fires rose higher. They stretched to the skies, doubling in size, but still not spreading beyond the original length and breadth of the lost palace.

Atolgus did not so much as flinch in fear for his life, nor did Wargroch, nor any of the guards. Indeed, they looked more eager than anything else. The ogres thinking of fleeing fought down their fear, and they and the rest of the crowd watched in amazement as the flames finally died away to reveal something *new* standing where the palace had been rooted.

It stood like a giant, with sharp, glittering angles and five magnificent towers topped by arched roofs. It was as wide and as deep as the old palace, but twice the height. In the light of the glaring sun, it was at times nearly blinding, for instead of marble, it was made of a sleek substance that shone more than a thousand polished breastplates. Its greenish blue hue was like no color ever seen by the ogres, and more than one among the hushed crowd let escape a sound of awe.

There were six great columns at the front, each carved to resemble the same handsome Titan. Each took a different pose: a warrior with a sword, a teacher with a staff, another holding a lush basket of fruit, and more. But each with the same face, one soon to be recognized by all assembled.

Two great bronze doors marked the entrance, doors bearing the talon symbol. They were immense doors, surely needing three or four muscular guards to open each, yet they swung open by themselves.

And through them glided the leader of the Titans. His visage was quickly recognizable as the one on each of the column figures. He smiled benevolently at the vast crowd, at Morgada, at Atolgus and Wargroch. With one hand he greeted the thronged ogres, and in the other, the sorcerer held up the Fire Rose.

"The Golden Age is upon us!" he sang in the Titan language. Once again, even the most ignorant ogre understood perfectly—understood and envied the ability to speak such a perfect tongue. The Common that Golgren had insisted all learn was rough and unworthy compared to that beautiful language.

"The Golden Age is upon us!" Safrag repeated. "Not the Age of the High Ogres, though, for that is past! The dead shall remain dead; the living shall live anew!"

Atolgus let out a barking cheer. Wargroch and the others followed with their own cries of exultation. Within moments, *all* in attendance, whether they truly desired to or not, joined the cheering.

But with a voice that thundered even louder than Morgada's had, and which seemed to reverberate in the head of each ogre in Garantha, the sorcerer cut off the cheers. Holding the Fire Rose high and letting its radiance shine over everything, the blue-skinned sorcerer declared, "The Age of the High Ogres is dead, and in its place shall rise that of the ogre race transformed . . . the Age of the *Titans!*"

And as the Fire Rose burned bright, each ogre understood that the Titan leader promised them the very same power that he and the other three Titans present wielded, and that, one day, each would stand as tall and mighty as they.

The world would tremble before a race of sorcerers such as had not existed even at the height of their ancestors' glorious civilization.

The cheers grew stronger, echoing far beyond the walls of the capital.

Safrag smiled at his children.

❦

The block stood facing in the direction of Garantha, although Golgren had not known that when Safrag had sealed him into the crypt. The Titan had positioned the block as a last jest, even if he would be the only one to appreciate it.

But another came to view the sorcerer's creation, to view the body sealed within. The newcomer slowly stepped around the crystalline block, observing the still form from every angle.

He took the crooked piece of dried wood he had been using for a temporary staff and struck the block soundly on the side, near the shoulder of the figure frozen within.

A vein shot up from the place where the wood had hit. Another ran to the side, and a third whipped around to the front. As the watcher stepped back, the veins multiplied, spreading all over. Within moments, the entire block was scarred and veined.

He raised the staff and hit the first exact spot again.

The block shattered. The Grand Khan Golgren's body dropped limply to the rough ground. It bounced without mercy onto the rocks, finally rolled onto its back, and lay still.

The shaman Sarth hobbled over to the Grand Khan's body. He pressed the end of the wood against the stab wound, which immediately began to heal. He then set down his makeshift staff and removed from his kilt the dagger that had been sheathed there. Reaching into Golgren's tunic, he pulled free the half-breed's original, mummified hand. Sarth placed the relic on top of Golgren's chest and set both other hands atop the severed one.

The ancient ogre drew a pattern consisting of circles within circles over the hands. He gently moved aside the left hand and perfectly aligned the two right ones.

Sarth took up the dagger. Testing the edge, he muttered a few words of power before acting.

Golgren screamed. His eyes opened as wide as shields. He stared at his new right hand, which lay sprawled on the ground next to the mummified one.

Even as the half-breed drank in the horrific sight, Sarth

took a piece of green-stained cloth from a small pouch he had carried with him and wrapped the end of the stump with it.

Golgren slowly registered the sight of the shaman. "You! Why?"

"Have you seen the blood?" the old ogre calmly asked in Common. *"Ke?"*

"Ke. Yes . . . *No."*

The half-breed's almond-shaped eyes narrowed. Neither the stump nor the freshly cut appendage showed any signs of bleeding. Indeed, at the frayed wrist of the hand, there was flesh, sinew, and bone, but no blood, no moisture at all.

"The gifts of the gods must always be questioned, " Sarth muttered, rubbing the tip of his dagger in the dirt even though it was devoid of even the slightest drop of blood. "To see if they are gifts after all."

"My hand!" Golgren rasped. He grabbed with his left hand for the mummified one.

Sarth watched him replace the lost appendage under his tunic. "To possess is not to own."

The shaman drew a jagged pattern over the other severed hand. As Golgren watched, the hand shriveled, its fingers folding inward. The appendage continued to dry up, turning crisp.

Sarth brought a bony fist down on it. The hand shattered, the dust left by it suddenly blowing away until nothing remained.

Memories slowly returned to Golgren. He leaped to his feet, turning in search of Safrag and the gargoyles. And the Fire Rose.

"Var inu," responded the withered ogre. "All gone. Gone long."

"How long?"

The shaman shrugged. "They are gone."

Golgren gazed at the landscape, thinking of something else. "Idaria."

"Trails that must cross will cross, trails that must not will not."

Sarth's remark caused Golgren to focus on him as he never had before. "Sarth speaks much and speaks well. Sarth also comes to a place where Sarth would not be expected to be found." He leaned down, his face very close to that of the shaman's. "How is it that Sarth comes to be in the vale?"

"How does Sirrion light the sun?" asked the elder ogre casually as he rose. "How does the unborn one survive being born?"

Through glittering emerald eyes, Golgren studied his newly maimed limb. "He does because that is what he does." After a moment's more consideration, the half-breed looked back to Sarth. "He—"

The shaman was gone.

Golgren evinced no surprise. He looked around, but although there was no possible manner by which Sarth could have so quickly left his sight, the elderly ogre was gone.

Something caught Golgren's attention. There were images scratched into the ground, images that could only have been put there by Sarth.

There were three. One was a sun. Below it was a horned symbol that he at first took for an Uruv Suurt, but that he realized was some other creature.

The third could only be the Fire Rose.

The half-breed briefly bared his teeth. One foot shoved dirt over the images, though the images themselves were already burned into his mind. Golgren forgot very little; remembering helped him survive.

"I am tired of games," he muttered to the empty air. "Tired of yours, Sarth, and of the Titans'. Tired also of those of the gods, and tired of my own." Golgren bared his teeth again. "And so I shall put an end to all the games, yes. I will take the Fire Rose from Safrag, and I will use it but once more, to rid the ogre race of the sorcerers, gargoyles, and all else in my path." The Grand Khan raised his maimed limb, admiring its awful appearance. "And even with one hand, if it must be."

Something drew his attention back to the images he had covered. Golgren's brow furrowed as one registered. Somehow, its details had escaped his gaze when he had inspected the other two.

It was a tree. He recalled another image of a tree, one that was part of a beautiful, intricate tapestry that hung in the palace. The tapestry had been part of the spoils from Silvanost. Golgren recalled the name for that particular tree, even though he had only seen a real one once, long ago, when in the conquered elf realm. An oak.

"My Idaria," he murmured thoughtfully.

As he looked up from the drawing, he caught a glimpse of something within the mountains beyond: a single gargoyle descending.

With only his well-honed wits and his one hand as available weapons, the half-breed started for the mountains.

JEAN RABE

THE STONETELLERS

*"Jean Rabe is adept at weaving a web of deceit and lies, mixed with
adventure, magic, and mystery."*
—sffworld.com on *Betrayal*

Jean Rabe returns to the DRAGONLANCE® world with a tale
of slavery, rebellion, and the struggle for freedom.

VOLUME ONE
THE REBELLION

After decades of service, nature has dealt the goblins a stroke of luck.
Earthquakes strike the Dark Knights' camp and mines, crippling the
Knights and giving the goblins their best chance to escape. But their
freedom will not be easy to win.

VOLUME TWO
DEATH MARCH

The reluctant general, Direfang, leads the goblin nation on a death march
to the forests of Qualinesti, there to create a homeland in defiance of the
forces that seek to destroy them.

August 2008

VOLUME THREE
GOBLIN NATION

A goblin nation rises in the old forest, building fortresses and fighting to
hold onto their new homeland, while the sorcerers among them search
for powerful magic cradled far beneath the trees.

August 2009

Sword & sorcery adventure from the creator of the EBERRON® world!

KEITH BAKER

Thorn of Breland

A new war has already begun—a cold war, fought in the shadows by agents of every nation—and Thorn does all she can as a member of the King's Citadel. But her last mission has left her with gaps in her memory, and she'll have to work out what happened as she goes—after all, Breland won't protect itself.

Book 1
The Queen of Stone

The Dreaming Dark

A band of weary war veterans have come to Sharn, hoping to find a way to live in a world that is struggling to settle into an uneasy peace. But over the years, they have made enemies in high places—and even places far from Eberron.

Book 1
The City of Towers

Book 2
The Shattered Land

Book 3
The Gates of Night